A Turn of the Wheel

CATHERINE LABADIE

ISBN-10: 0578586401
ISBN-13: 9780578586403

This book is a work of fiction. Names, characters, places, and incidents either are products of the author's imagination or are used fictitiously. Any resemblance to actual persons, living or dead, events, or locales is entirely coincidental.

Printed in the United States of America.
First Printing 2019.

http://authorcatlabadie.wixsite.com/catherinelabadie

To those who doubt themselves, and to the past me who thought I'd never be able to do this.

1

Sweetheart's Night

"It's really quite simple," Aubria began, deftly wrapping her hands with a worn towel as she whisked the pie she'd just approved onto the table. "You have to be perfect."

"Talking to your pies again, are we?" Cerise Erdenwed remarked, pinching her cheeks for color as she gazed into the small heirloom mirror hung next to the window. Ignoring her, Aubria blew the steam off her pie and set it reverently next to its fellows on the table.

"See how handsome you turned out to be? Mama always knows." Aubria couldn't keep herself from grinning as she inspected the results of an afternoon's meticulous work. A buttery crust, prepared so it wouldn't crumble into flakes or sag into a soggy mess, cradled a sweet but not too sweet almond toffee filling made from last season's perfectly preserved almond harvest. Aubria had crushed or blended or rolled out each ingredient with precision, determined to make this particular pie her masterpiece. Let the other girls make their delicacies with the traditional apples and figs: she would be a pioneer this night for the beginning of the handfasting wheel.

"I'm a pioneer," she repeated aloud, conviction in her voice as she clutched both of her hands and the ragged towel to her bosom. Behind her, Cerise laughed and gestured to the other girl sitting in the kitchen, who stared morosely at her own wilting apple tart.

"Bad luck, Viola," she teased, winking at her friend to signal her mischief. "Merek will enjoy your tart even less once he sees the treat Lane will receive tonight."

"Oh, I think you're right!" Viola fretted, completely missing the strained giggles between Aubria and Cerise. "I'm no good at baking...do you think Merek will hold it against me?"

"As...as long as you're skilled in other matters, I don't think he'll hold the lack of baking talent against you," Aubria struggled to maintain her composure, but the giggles won out and she and Cerise collapsed against each other from laughing so much.

Viola missed the joke once more. "Like cooking?"

The other two laughed harder. Aubria accidentally bumped the pie and tart laden table with the swell of her hip, almost knocking one of the fig pies molded into a clumsy heart onto the floor. Viola caught it in time, though her face still slumped into a confused frown.

"Vi, you're a lovely cook. Merek knows that," Cerise relented, returning to the mirror and tucking an extra pin into the artful weave of dark braids decorating her head. Aubria, who wasn't fond of Merek's less than tender treatment of Viola, kept her opinion to herself.

"And I'm sure your apple tart will taste simply stunning, especially to Merek," she eventually added, her hands twitching with an urge to adjust her own hair. Her sleek locks were too contrary to hold most styles: Cerise had set them into an intricately braided crown an hour ago, and she'd be foolish to touch it and risk the whole thing tumbling down.

"But it's not as good as yours!" Viola despaired, glancing with jealousy at the golden-brown, perfectly baked almond pie; Aubria had layered pieces of extra crust cut into the shape of leaves over the top for that extra touch of elegance. "Almonds also symbolize love, and they taste much better than boring apples."

"Nothing's as good as an apple, my dear," Aubria comforted her distractedly, "and, good as mine or not, Merek won't know the difference. He's only supposed to eat *your* pie tonight."

Cerise choked on a sip of her cider and fell into giggles again, giddiness bringing out the color she'd tried to pinch into her cheeks. Catching her mistake, Aubria made a rude gesture with her fingers: this time their raucous laughter summoned the rest of the girls in from outdoors. Soon the modest kitchen had filled with fifteen girls in total, each of them either dizzy with anticipation for the evening's events…or, in Viola's case, anxious to see if their chosen lover would accept their poorly baked treat.

I can't believe it's finally here! Aubria mused internally, satisfaction and contentment stretching out along her spine as if she was resting in front of a warm fire with a cup of spiced mead. *Our handfasting wheel is about to begin, and we've all found someone to pair with. Even me.*

The satisfaction transformed into something sharp, a jab almost like a cramp that twisted in her gut. Aubria frowned; then, shoving the bout of uncertainty away like an unwanted guest, she took Cerise's and Viola's hands in hers and gestured for the rest of the girls to make a circle of linked hands around the table. As the eldest of the lot, it was Aubria's right to address her girlhood friends before the men arrived, just as it was her right to host the first evening of the handfasting wheel. Everyone had baked their treats at home and brought them to the Haight's cottage, which lay right on the border marking the farthest spot from the town of Loracre and the rest of the orchard.

As the eldest of the group at nineteen, Aubria had asked them to gather at the home she shared with her father. The younger girls, the childish future brides of sixteen and fifteen who had been chosen by the boys of the village, would meet at another house: they would go through the handfasting wheel this year, but would have to wait an extra span of seasons to actually wed.

"Sisters," Aubria began, her voice strong. "During Yule, we were chosen by our promised loves to join them in the handfasting wheel, the seasonal rites meant to bind our hearts closer to theirs. If all goes aright, we will be wed to our lovers next Yuletide."

"Can you believe it?" One of the girls sighed, her expression dreamy as she clutched the hands of her friends tighter. "It seems so far away!"

"Yes," Aubria snapped, not appreciating the interruption while she was trying to concentrate. "The seasons of the year will turn swiftly, never fear. But we are meant to enjoy them! Tonight is for us to formally accept the request of our betrothed with the fruit of our harvest: we have baked sweets for them, symbolizing our love and the sweetness of our company through life's hardships once we are wed."

"I think I hear them!" The dreamy girl who had sighed as if her heart had wings earlier broke the circle first, wrenching her hands away from her friends as she dashed to the window. Crying out with delight, the rest of the girls followed suit, jostling and shoving each other good-naturedly to peer through the kitchen window. Rolling her eyes, Aubria beckoned to Cerise, and she and Viola went to the front door.

Taking a deep, steadying breath, Aubria threw it open and looked out.

Below, on the winding road leading from the cottage, she glimpsed an approaching procession of men carrying torches. Well, half were carrying torches: the rest carried common peasant lutes, wooden pipes, or antique lyres, and all who could were singing their hearts out as they travelled the path to Aubria's doorstep. They'd begun singing the traditional song much earlier, so the parts that reached the ladies' ears were from the ending verses of the lengthy ballad.

Well, Aubria *thought* they were from the famous Sweetheart's Ballad. Obviously the lads had tipped back a few at the tavern with their fathers and the older bachelors of Loracre before setting out, and some of the drunker ones manipulated the lyrics horrendously.

"Nerves, the poor things," Viola cooed with sympathy from behind Cerise as she anxiously stretched her neck over the taller girl's shoulder to have a look. "My da said he softened his nerves with drink a few times when he was courting my mother."

"What nonsense," Cerise scoffed, smoothing her hands down her dress and wincing as the unmistakable sound of a lute string snapping reached their ears. "Nathan had better be sober when I clap eyes on him, or I'll throw his pie into the dirt for the beetles to appreciate."

Aubria, catching the tenor of nerves in her own friend's voice, slid her arm around Cerise for a sisterly hug.

"Don't worry," she soothed, "he's not going to change his mind."

Cerise cast her a grateful look, her dark skin gleaming in the ever closer torch light. Her easy laughter, always at the ready, resumed as she twirled Aubria around.

"You're still wearing your dingy old apron! Lane might change *his* mind if he sees you like this." She tugged at the knotted apron strings until the whole thing slipped free.

"Don't say such things, Cerise! Lane loves Aubria!" Viola scolded, but for once her rare sense of humor shone through for her to charm them all with her smile. She took the apron from Cerise and tossed it to one of the girls who had wandered behind them, hoping to peek out the door for a better look at the boys. The girl promptly dropped it on the floor, where it would have remained had not Viola's glare encouraged her to reluctantly pick it up and hang it on a hook on the wall.

"Lane LOVES Aubriaaa!" Cerise turned the phrase into a song, and Aubria blushed, glancing down at her second best pale green dress to make sure she hadn't dropped flour or crumbs on it.

Lane *did* love Aubria, and had chosen her over swanlike, willowy Viola and compact, slender Cerise. A tiny waist due to constant work, but wide hips and a sizeable carriage had caused the village boys to describe her as "pretty as a peach and plump for the plucking," but Lane had chosen her before any of them could. She had a long, elegant nose and a pert chin, but her eyes were only brown compared to Viola's crystalline blue, and too many freckles dotted her nose to be truly ladylike. At least she had her golden hair, which was a surprisingly rare trait in her village and the city beyond.

"What are you frowning about?" Cerise chided her, perhaps sensing her unkind introspection. "Enough of this, we have to get our pies and bring them outside! If another person tries to cram into this cottage I'm going to shove them right back out again!"

Still giddy, each girl seized her pie from the table and danced outside with the treat held carefully above her head for fear someone else would knock it out of her hands. Aubria was no exception, and she caught the woodsy, full-bodied scent of her almond pie with another burst of satisfaction.

That odd feeling of unease struck her again when she followed the others outside and saw Lane at the head of the men's procession, strumming his lute and smiling at her with his dreamy blue eyes and mop of sandy curls. He looked delighted to see her, though their separation had spanned only the course of the day, and all the promises of a proper betrothal were visible in his eyes and his crooked smile. Though she smiled back, the gesture was tentative, and she felt so anxious she couldn't feel her heart beating for a moment.

No. She was happy to see him, she insisted to herself, and she forced a genuine smile onto her lips.

The lad standing closest to Lane and lurching under the influence of the greatest quantity of ale stumbled towards Aubria. Strumming his lute roughly, he burst out with a bawdy and poorly organized improvisation as his bleary, red-rimmed eyes met hers.

"With golden hair, the lady fair, she laid down with the utmost care...oh no, said he, now if you please, I'd rather have you on your knees!"

A mortified silence fell over the whole group that had been so merry seconds before. Aubria's mouth dropped open at his gall: they'd never gotten along when they were children, and she hadn't been able to understand what Viola had seen in Merek, but he'd never been this inappropriate. Far more than the horrible, crass ditty, he'd usurped Lane's position as eldest to address the crowd first. A girl would get catty revenge for such a slight later, but men tended to duke out their disagreements on the spot. The crowd sucked in their breath in anticipation of a challenge.

"Oh, Merek!" Viola let out a peal of laughter shrill enough to set the birds fleeing the treetops of the nearby orchard. "How clever you are! But Aubria won't be fooled by your trickery! We already know Lane can't sing, and you're covering his lack!"

Heads swiveled from Viola to Merek to Lane to see what their next move would be. Merek bowed clumsily, his lute tumbling to the ground as he made a production of the movement. Looking nettled but ready to go back to a good-natured evening, Lane returned his focus to Aubria as if no interruption had taken place. Thanks to Viola's intervention, the first official night of the handfasting wheel was spared the indignity of a brawl.

But Merek's eyes remained with Aubria a moment too long, and she hurried to move the proceedings forward.

Holding her pie up with one hand underneath its base, Aubria rested her other hand on her hip and cocked it to the side just enough to enhance her figure. "Who are these lads who come to us with laughter and song?"

"We are young fools, my ladies, searching for our Sweethearts!" Lane called, merriment in his tone as he gazed upon her with undisguised admiration. "Shall we find them here?"

"Well, girls?" Aubria turned to her village sisters, her uneasiness melting away at the sight of their eager faces. "Have they found them?"

"Yes!" The girls chorused, and by unspoken agreement the men in Aubria's front yard assembled themselves into a line with much jostling and jovial wrestling so their Sweethearts could approach them with their gifts. Rank held no further place for the rest of the ceremony: the girls in their pastel dresses, many of which had been worn to the Imbolc gathering only a week before, fanned out in an array of loveliness to the partners who had chosen them during Yule.

Aubria beamed at Lane as she approached him with her almond pie, proud of its originality and its execution. She'd told Cerise and

Viola that she'd used almonds to symbolize her affection, but the truth was that Lane loved almonds and she was happy to bring him a treat made with them.

He made a great show of inspecting the pie for flaws and tapping the curled edges of the crust to see if it would crumble, making her laugh.

"Is this a pie worthy of your future husband, Lady Aubria?" he intoned balefully, imitating a conceited lordling from the city.

With mock solemnity, she pulled a pie knife from a pocket in her skirts. "You'll have to taste it and see."

He nodded, and the mimicry fell away. "I brought something for you as well."

Holding the pie plate with his left hand, his right dug in his pocket for an object she had yet to see. She held the pie up with both hands, her left trapped under Lane's steady grip while her right gripped the knife against the plate. He revealed to her a length of metal shaped into a hollow heart. With a flourish, he pressed the heart down into the center of the pie and used the knife to carefully pry it back out. His hands twitched nervously, but the rest of him exuded confidence as he gestured for Aubria to set the pie on the ground briefly so he could go about his plan.

"It's Sweetheart's Night," he began, deftly removing the now heart-shaped center of pie from the little cutter he'd made. "I thought it appropriate to share my portion with my love, as I intend us to share all things in the future."

"Lane, what—" Aubria began, but he hushed her by breaking the heart in half and offering part to her. The sweetness, the open love and admiration in those perfect blue eyes made her wish she could melt like a candle, and she accepted the portion he offered her with shaking hands. Locked in each other's gaze, shutting out the rest of the couples who ignored their own proceedings to watch the two of them, they each tasted the pie she'd made in an unspoken renewal of their handfasting promises.

Why was she so nervous? Why did part of this thing between them, this dream she'd wished for as a younger girl and nourished and pursued…why did it feel like shackles closing about her wrists? Why did it feel like a trap she was about to walk into with her eyes wide open?

"It's good," Lane said, clearly savoring the pie she'd baked him, but mischief danced in his eyes again. "But it's not *this* good."

Swooping in, he claimed her with a kiss that set their friends to wolf howls and cheering. It was not technically appropriate to kiss one's betrothed until the next event in the handfasting wheel…but Lane didn't care, and for the moment neither did Aubria.

Lane loves Aubria, she told herself as she kissed him back, lifting a hand to his cheek and closing her eyes as her heart fluttered pleasantly.

2

Aubria sighed as she indulged in the last bite of the pie she'd

baked with leftover ingredients from the night before. Her father had come home early in the morning while she was still abed recovering from the evening's excitement, and none of the girls who'd spent the night at her house—strewn about the floor in front of the fire with innumerable pillows and blankets—had seen fit to wake her before her father consumed what was left of the now legendary pie. They'd left without saying goodbye, even Cerise and Viola, departing with the rising of the sun to return home for chores and other orchard work.

Aubria didn't mind the solitude: after such an eventful night it had been a pleasure to have time to herself to drink a cup or two of tea and taste the pie she'd made more indulgently.

Last night had unsettled her. The trapped feeling pent up in Aubria's chest wouldn't relent, and though she felt wicked for doubting Lane and the wonderful future she and everyone else desired for her, the doubts stuck to her mind like tree sap all the same.

In spite of her misgivings about her future, and in spite of the un-springlike chill outside, the morning still felt like a holiday. Work and the rest of the world did not stop for hallowed rites, not even for the handfasting wheel, and it was market day in Loracre's sister village,

Eldacre. Aubria had spent much of the day before baking more than the almond pie: their larder was stacked with a cart's worth of all sorts of pies, tarts, and individually sized baked goods made with either fruits or nuts from the orchard or meat bought from the hunters. Eldacre was larger than Loracre and closer to the capital city, Oseren. Even if it *was* a solid three days ride by horseback away, the capital was large enough to lure visitors and trade from all over Lyrassan and the realms beyond.

Last night she had been someone's Sweetheart, and Sweethearts did not dress in drab clothes of brown and threadbare shawls. The sun shining on the cold but thawing earth cheered Aubria to no end after so long a winter. So she donned her apple green second best dress once more, untied her braided updo so her hair flowed freely over her shoulders and back, and chose her maroon shawl instead of her usual drab wrap. Finally, she picked up her wide-brimmed straw hat and adjusted the long ribbon wrapped around the cap so it trailed down into her hair. Lane had given her the ribbon for a Yuletide gift, sure that the spring green would match one of her dresses.

Not many of the other villagers had their own horse, but Aubria's father, the Widower Haight, was one of the wealthier landowners in the village and thus they used the steady old shire horse to go about town and beyond instead of a donkey. Aubria loaded up her pies, hitched dutiful Toby to the market cart, and bid farewell to her father in the garden before she drove off down the road.

As soon as she was out of sight of the cottage she slumped in her seat and held the reins dejectedly in her hands. The sunlight coaxing the world into the early stages of spring would make her drowsy during her morning drive, but it couldn't reach the root of her malaise.

The confidence that had bolstered her spirits and her vanity evaporated as she surrendered to her suffocating doubts. *Am I making the right decision? This is the only life I know, and Lane is nothing but sweet, but...*

But what? Her sensible, conscious mind scolded her fretful spirit like a mother disciplining children that had frolicked in a mud puddle. *You won't ever meet a kinder suitor, you ninny, and there's nothing wrong with your life. Enough of this nonsense.*

Cowed if not comforted, Aubria sat up straight and clucked to Toby, who took off on the familiar trail to the next village without a fuss. She couldn't help but notice the sight of a red toadstool ring laid out in a perfect circle a few steps from her front door. Faerykind rings brought neither good luck nor bad luck…but though she'd loved stories of the Fair Folk in her childhood, she didn't welcome proof of their existence in the orchard this particular morning. Rumors of the faerykind tending the orchard when the villagers slept abounded throughout Lyrassan. It was said that they enchanted the fruit to grow, blessed the wellspring river that split the orchard in two so no crop would wither from plague or pest, and conducted mischief every so often to remind the rest of the world of their existence. Aubria had never seen proof that this was true beyond a few faerykind rings, or complicated locks twined in the manes and beards of Loracre's livestock, but she'd never doubted that *something* magical had its eye on the orchard.

The road leading to Eldacre had been worn by constant travel, like a grandmother's lace shawl passed down to a granddaughter, but though it was market day Aubria was the sole traveler on the path. That was her privilege as a baker: not many people bought her goods at the start of the market, since they were busy haggling in loud voices and crying that any price higher than the one they had in mind was disreputable robbery. But wait an hour or two to start, her father had always said, and arrive by lunch time, and the cart would be crowded with people captivated by the scent of gooseberry tarts or succulent hand pies made with seasoned venison or fresh chicken. She'd always stuck with this plan, and it had always worked.

Today Aubria appreciated the solitude. Cerise and Viola, though her dearest friends, had kept quite close since Imbolc and the approach of Sweetheart's Night. She'd scarcely had any time to herself for a week.

Well, she'd *thought* she might appreciate the solitude. Her thoughts returned again and again to Lane, to the sight of his noonday bright smile that lit up his whole being, to the thoughtful gift he'd brought to share with her, to the delightful kiss they'd shared. Ostara, the rite celebrating the spring equinox, was almost exactly a month away, and three days after Ostara came Queen's Night. And Queen's Night was…well.

Aubria blushed from her cheeks down to her chest and back up to the roots of her hair. Then she clucked at Toby to pick up the pace.

When comparing Eldacre to her home village, Aubria found that in almost every case she preferred Loracre. It was perfect in its way: it had much of the bustle of Eldacre without any of the snobbery or the influx of travelers from Oseren to trouble it. Both villages were the centers of trade linking the orchard to the rest of the kingdom, since the rest of the numerous tiny villages scattered throughout the enchanted orchard that stretched over the western reaches of Lyrassan were populated mostly with seasonal workmen whose families lived elsewhere in the kingdom.

A few market attendees who recognized Aubria raised their hands in casual greeting, but most of the townspeople ignored her and went about their business. In Loracre, everyone who visited was greeted almost like a family member, and as long as the visitor wasn't churlish to the ladies or rude to the men, he was welcome at any table. Here in Eldacre, where they had more shops and an inn with a fancy stable and thought more highly of themselves for tending the traditional orchard crops instead of the wilder, less predictable fruits near their sister village, Aubria was rarely made to feel welcome.

No matter: Eldacre had its charms, but she was here to sell her pies, peruse a few stalls to pick up some goods for home, and then return. The sheer amount of extra people milling about this day caught her off guard, but she guessed the cause at once: Imbolc had passed, more fruits had been harvested, and many city dwellers had taken a short vacation to the country to stay at the local tavern and shop for home crafted goods to bring back to the city.

The tavern will be full tonight, Aubria thought, uneasily gripping Toby's reins a little tighter as a raucous group of young men, drunk far too early on a day where they would have been better off working or marketing like the people of Eldacre, passed her cart and leered at her with sodden gazes of admiration for her "charms." *Though I suppose the tavern must be full already.*

The next thing she noticed were the guards, at least twenty of them in sight without counting the ones passing in and out of the inn or the surrounding shops, milling about the people. She ducked her head in a gesture of respect as one of them glanced her way, and was glad that the brim of her hat concealed the grin she hid. For all their bluster, the guards had little experience with shrewd villagers: they haggled too stridently and often went away with nothing besides insults for their cheek. Aubria guessed they didn't realize their error, and the villagers saw little need to enlighten them.

"What's the reason for all these guards?" she asked her market neighbor, who had filled his cart with a pungent mix of freshly harvested onions, garlic, and cured travelling meats. Unusually taciturn, the man shrugged and tossed one of the bigger purple onions back and forth between his ham-like hands. He took a large bite of the sweet onion and chomped it for all to see.

"Some trouble in the capital leaking over our way, I expect. Prince Mardin and his disputes on the border must be carrying on poorly," he grunted; Aubria thanked the goddess that she was too far away to catch the aroma of his breath. Just in case, she devoted herself to the task of arranging her pies for show, lifting a winter fruit pie to her nose to hold its scent.

"What sort of trouble?" she pressed.

"I don't know, do I?" Her neighbor grumbled, polishing off his lunch in a few bites. "Old King Barric is due to raise taxes again. His thugs must be inspecting our wares to see how much they can get their paws on."

Aubria held her silence after that, except for calling out to passers-by to entice them with the contents of her bakery cart. Bored, she ended up with nothing better to do than study the scenery of Eldacre to occupy her thoughts. This was how she noticed that the smallest storefront in the village had finally been leased, against all rumors of ill luck haunting the building.

Some of that bad luck must have brushed off on me, Aubria thought crossly after a solid hour of selling next to none of her wares. Everyone usually loved pie regardless of which hands had made it, and few could resist such sweet smelling treats as those Aubria made for market days in either of the villages. Enough time had passed for her to nearly sell out on a normal day, but instead she'd only sold two pies to an elderly couple who had probably stopped by her cart out of pity.

At this rate I'll have to throw most of them out, she thought while she leaned against the edge of her cart and scuffed her boot against the dusty street. *Can a few guards really increase people's self-importance so much that they'll do without goods from Loracre?*

"Cheer up, lass," a slick voice spoke from her left. "The scent of that pie would cure a starving man of dying at once, I'm sure."

Aubria straightened at once, a beatific if terribly fake smile on her face as she greeted her potential customer. "If you think the scent is good, sir, why not chance a taste? These pies are worth every penny, I swear."

"You swear, do you?" It was not one man who had approached her cart, but three; Aubria's smile wavered. "She's given us her solemn word, gents. If we don't like her goods, we will be repaid."

The men sneered at her, one of whom was an Oseren soldier clad in the blue hydrangea on red livery of the city guards; she guessed he was off-duty for the day, and had evidently been drinking for most of the morning. But of all the troublesome figures swaying before her, she feared the slick one who'd addressed her first. He looked at her like a feral cat inspecting a helpless mouse, and his eyes glittered with the malice of one who views himself as superior to everyone else in creation.

So she ignored him, and pasted her vapid expression in place so none of them would sense her apprehension. "I can't promise you repayment, sirs, but you won't be sorry if you purchase a fallasfruit pie, or one of the preserved gooseberry tarts."

"You look tastier than a gooseberry yourself, lass, all pretty in green," the third man spoke at last, quite soppily. If he had been alone, Aubria wouldn't have been afraid: without his comrades this fellow wouldn't have had the stomach for the mischief his friends had in mind. But she laughed off the compliment, her eyes darting to her onion-obsessed neighbor for possible aid. He'd wandered off, though, searching for a more complete midday repast other than garlic cloves.

"I'm not on offer, sir, but my pies—" she began, taking a step back towards the comfort of her horse.

"Fine, fine, the pie. Let's see if it's as good as you say," the off-duty guard seized the topmost pie in the careful stack she'd made in her cart, which unfortunately did happen to be a gooseberry tart. He took a bite, chewed noisily, swallowed just as loudly, and then promptly tossed the rest of the small tart into the road. Aubria suspected that he could have tasted a pie laden with fruit directly from the gods' hands made with the sugar of heaven, and he still would have crushed the delicacy under his boot and demanded better.

"Utter rubbish," he proclaimed, holding her gaze with his cold slate eyes; a smidgen of gooseberry clung to his mustache. "Inedible pig slop. You should be ashamed to serve such swill to a king's guard."

Something about his gaze challenged her, and her blood roared in her ears. The pleasant, empty-headed smile disappeared, and in its place she allowed her shrewd business mask to take its place.

"Even if it was the grossest meal in the land you would still have to pay for it. That will be five copper ladies, sir, and that's a fair price for the delicious tart you squandered." The words rang out more confidently than she'd hoped.

"Oh?" The first man giggled, boyish in his malice. "How much for this, lass?"

Aubria spared a glance for the dense fig pie he'd chosen, and then returned to glaring at the guard. "Seven and a half-copper ladies, given that figs are out of season as yet."

The man clad in the black of a scholar in training took a careless bite of the small pie, and then promptly tossed it on the ground and trod it under his boot heel with a scornful grin. "My wise friend is correct. The pie is inedible. Why would you offer us such rubbish?"

Though she was afraid, Aubria refused to allow her anger to win her inner struggle. "You and your friends owe me an even twenty copper ladies for your considerable lack of taste."

"Is that so?" The guard leered, his red-rimmed eyes cold and hateful as he took a step forward. "You would swindle a city guard with rotten fruit from your miserable, backwards little village? You should be apologizing and offering recompense for your disgraceful behavior."

"I have some ideas!" The third man blurted, making a rude gesture that reminded her of a stallion mounting a mare. Aubria ignored him.

"I may be but a simple lass from Loracre, but we're not in the city now," she hissed her challenge. "We are in one of the miserable villages you so despise, one of the villages that keeps your friends in Oseren fat and happy on the goods from our orchard. Here we appreciate the goods we consume with solid coin. Pay up and be gone, for I'll waste none of my wares on such undiscerning fellows as you have proved to be."

"Is that so?" The first scholar repeated the insolent question his friend the guard had asked, right before he seized another pie from the cart and hurled it to the ground.

They're goading me so they have an excuse to punish someone, Aubria realized as frustration quickened her breathing and made a bead of sweat trickle down her spine. *So I won't give them one.*

"Now it's a silver gent and five more coppers, sirs," she spoke impassively, changing tactics and refusing to act further though tears of rage tickled the back of her throat. She held her composure, her hands curled into fists at her side as between the three of them they smashed another half dozen pies right in front of her. Aubria kept verbal tally of what they owed but would probably never pay for the destroyed food.

She was about to reach the price of ten silvers when she spotted the first man slyly reaching for Toby's bridle. Aubria paused mid-count and sprang into thoughtless action, dashing forward under the power of the adrenaline keeping her alert.

"Do *not* touch my horse, you vile cretin!" she hollered, clocking the oily villain on the jaw with her closed fist. He yowled in pain, and between wondering if she'd broken a finger or two she wanted to hit him again. Thankfully she was cognizant enough to seize hold of Toby's reins with her other hand and hold on for dear life.

She didn't have much time to think through anything else: a fist crashed into the side of her face with all the power of a tree falling to the ground. Aubria collapsed onto the pie-soaked street in a heap as her consciousness flickered and threatened to fade entirely. A throbbing center of pain burned on her cheek where the guard had struck her.

"Dress green as a gooseberry, hair the color of early wheat, and skin as ripe as a peach!" The second scholar roared with laughter, amused by the whole affair. Aubria's shoulder had scraped against the cart as she'd crashed to the ground, and a protruding nail on the side had gripped the fabric of her sleeve and torn that portion of the garment almost cleanly from the rest of her dress. Her hat had been knocked off her head with the blow, and with sadness she watched the pretty green ribbon turn gray with dirt from the street.

Though her tongue felt heavy in her mouth and her stricken cheek was swelling by the second, Aubria found a few choice words. "That'll be a hundred gold marks, good sirs."

She heard the guard grumbling, felt the rough hands hefting her upright, groping and unkind, and she struggled in her half-conscious state to break free...

...but then her ears caught something she had to strain to be sure she'd actually heard.

"A hundred gold marks for one of these pies sounds like a fair bargain."

The words were simple, though nonsensical in the moment, and she couldn't see the speaker thanks to the men blocking her way. The three thugs unceremoniously dropped her on the ground in a heap and left her there, striding back down the street as if nothing amiss had taken place at all. She heard the revolting sound of pie crust squelching under their boots as they departed.

What made them leave…?

Though one of her eyes was already swelling and shocked into near blindness by looking up into the sun, she risked looking up at the man who had saved her with one innocuous comment. He was tall, much taller than the men she usually encountered, tan from travel or work with brown hair highlighted here and there by the sun. He had no beard, though stubble covered a strong but pointed jawline, and a strange tattoo decorated his left eye in a swirling pattern she couldn't identify. His eyes…she couldn't name their color, but she knew she'd never forget that shade.

"I'm sorry, sir," Aubria warbled, using the same cart that had ripped the sleeve of her dress to haul herself upright and into hopeful respectability. "I'm afraid I'm a bit indisposed."

She made it to her feet before she collapsed in a graceless, inconvenient swoon, but she felt him catch her and lift her into his arms right before she passed into total unconsciousness.

Aubria awoke with a groan. A glance out of a nearby window revealed the afternoon sun hanging high in the sky; she assumed that not too much time had passed since she'd lost consciousness. Someone had brought her into a house and laid her down on what felt like a wide wooden bench.

Surprisingly, since the first thing she remembered once she awoke was the soldier from Oseren punching her in the face, she felt no more of the pain that should have been radiating from her cheek and jaw to the rest of her body.

"Don't touch that," the man who had rescued her spoke, not ungently gripping her wrist and lowering it back to her side when she reached up to verify how much damage had been done. "You're safe, and I've tended to your horse and cart for now. I've spread an ointment on the injury that will reduce the swelling and lessen the fantastic bruise you're about to show off."

"An ointment?" Aubria questioned, next attempting to sit up so she could view her surroundings. She couldn't quite open her eyes yet—the light shone brightly enough to blind her—but she tried anyway. Sitting up wasn't allowed, though; warm hands guided her back into a supine position.

"An ointment is a medicinal salve meant to treat wounds," her rescuer explained. Her cheek tingled with numbness as she frowned at him.

"I know what an ointment is. But I don't know you, *sir,*" she snapped, perhaps too bravely for someone who could barely open her eyes and had more or less endured a town square fight. Also, Aubria had no idea where he'd brought her. If he had diabolical motives after all she wouldn't know where to escape from or to.

He must have known that too, but he only chuckled; she heard him pouring liquid from a bottle into a glass. "No need to 'sir' me, lady. My name is Terran."

"Terran...?" she pressed for his full name, perhaps insolently. With every second that passed it grew easier to open her eyes a little more.

"Terran Caird, the new Potioner of Eldacre," he told her without inflection as he held a small, pine green glass up to the light and swirled the liquid inside it. "Who are you that your fellow villagers won't save you from a beating or worse? Drink this."

He helped her sit up and passed her the glass expectantly, waiting for her to take it. She squinted up at him, distracted momentarily by the intriguing tattoo adorning his left brow and part of his cheek. The ink appeared russet rather than straight black, and the design reminded her of the archaic text kept in the house of the Guide of Rites. The antiquated book detailed the lore of the gods and the particulars of their yearly rites, and the ornate calligraphy it contained—some in familiar language and some not—reminded her of the tattoo she saw on the Potioner's face.

Now that she could study them, she saw why his eyes had captivated her at the first. Their color captured the soul of the orchard she had grown up in, possessing both the green of summer leaves, the gold of light filtering through the trees, and hints of chestnut around the iris that reminded her of the trunks of the walnut trees or roots protruding from freshly turned soil. They were sunken a little in his face, in the way of someone who spent long hours studying or stayed up late worrying. She studied them for a few seconds too long, mesmerized and woozy from her injury, before she remembered herself and took the offered glass.

Potioner…where have I heard that title before? She was forgetting something, something important, but it wouldn't come to her. Defeated, she offered her own name.

"Aubria Haight, from Loracre. The good people of Eldacre often ignore what goes on with backwoods maids like me," she said all in a rush; glancing down at the contents of the cup, she made a face at the dank herbal smell. "What is this, exactly?"

"It's a concoction meant to ease your pain so you can make your way home," he told her. "Drink up so the medicines can begin their work."

"Are you eager to get rid of me now you know where I'm from?" she mocked him with too much bitterness in her tone, though she obliged and drank the potion he'd made for her.

"Each village is much the same once you've been to enough of them, Aubria Haight. Cities too. I don't discriminate based on the location of someone's birth or residence," he said, turning to the table by the window to pick up the polished mortar and pestle he had set aside when she'd awakened. "How are you feeling now?"

Aubria watched him mix ingredients for another mysterious potion

22

while the one she had so trustingly taken began to spread through her bloodstream. The concoction eased any pain she experienced, but it also made her feel light and disconnected. She noticed, too, that her torn sleeve had been pinned back in place so her modesty would no longer be compromised.

"How am I feeling?" she repeated his question, sensing she was about to launch on a weepy tirade inappropriate for a stranger to witness, one that would continue until the poisonous thoughts had leeched from her mind. "I've just been assaulted by some louts who thought I'd be easy prey. No one…no one who witnessed me and my friends grow up in these villages stepped in or said a word. I have to go home and explain to my father that I can't go to market alone anymore…and my betrothed might insist on coming with me. And *that's* dreadful because I'm not sure he's what I want, or if the life laid out for me like a quilt planned to the last stitch is the one I wish to have."

Aubria doubted her words make sense, especially to someone who must be powerful and respectable enough to send an intimidating guard and his lackeys packing with only his presence and a few calm words. Worse, humiliating tears began to trickle from her eyes, undoubtedly making a mess of her ointment laden face.

How terrible I must look, she mused in despair, *and how pathetic. Just the sort of sopping, silly girl he must have expected.*

But Terran held his tongue, and even offered her a sympathetic glance as he proffered a handkerchief for her to take. "Dry your tears, but mind the ointment."

"I'm sorry," she apologized, dabbing at her face. "I'm not sure why I told you any of that. It's…it's not like me to be so forward with a stranger."

Terran shrugged, unperturbed as he dumped the contents from the mixing bowl into another glass and added a measure of both water and what smelled like strong liquor. "It's a side effect of the potion I gave you. The unburdening of your secrets and fears is quite common."

Annoyed, Aubria tossed her hair back over her shoulders before remembering that any unanticipated movement might make her dizzy.

"Why didn't you tell me that ahead of time?"

"Fluctuating emotions are another side effect," Terran smirked, but she got the feeling he was sharing a joke with her rather than enjoying one at her expense. "I wouldn't worry."

"Easy for you to say," Aubria grumbled, sniffling as she carefully patted around her eyes. "You aren't the one spilling secrets like tea."

"Your secrets are safe with me," he assured her with a smile. "I will tell you a secret in return, something of equal value."

Aubria cocked her head to the side and tried to analyze him by the light of the window as he stirred the settling mixture in the glass with an extraordinarily long copper spoon. His hair, brown though it had first appeared, glimmered deep gold here and there in the sun, and the clothes he wore were well-tailored. The black fabric looked expensive, however, more than any she'd ever seen before. She had been cautioned against trusting men in general, especially by her father...but this one had saved her, and she didn't think he'd saved her for evil purposes.

"Very well. I will hear your secret," she agreed, her tone imperious as she summoned what was left of her dignity. Her left foot kicked against the leg of the tall medical bench she sat on, belying her supercilious demeanor.

"As you wish," Terran half-bowed to her in mock servility, before resuming his business with the murky glass; he held it up to the light and inspected it as he spoke. "My craft requires magic to make my cures. The king allows it, and the registered wizards try to pretend my power doesn't flummox them...but most in the kingdom still reject magic, and I was chased out of the town I resided in last year. You mustn't tell anyone."

"This is a grave secret, if it's true," Aubria said, curious in spite of herself as she played along. "Have you any proof that you can do magic as well as make potions that heal or injure based on their design?"

"What proof do you require?" he asked, smiling as if he'd invited

24

her into his confidence well and truly despite hardly knowing her at all. Aubria drew a blank, since being a lowly peasant girl meant that she knew nothing of magic save for the edicts preventing any unsanctioned practitioners from dabbling in the arts. Magic had mostly died out in the kingdom, save for the wizards in Oseren, so finding an illegal wizard or witch wasn't as common as it used to be.

Plucking at a fragment of dead skin near her fingernail, she spoke without any premeditation of her words. "Show me something that will help me decide the course of my future, if you can."

Terran stared at her, his expression chary as he paused swirling the flask of the potion in his hand. Aubria railed inside her own head, cursing her own brazen stupidity: she'd meant to ask him what potion he was working on at the moment, but instead because of one thoughtless demand he'd probably toss her out of his shop on her ear. Knowing this, she struggled to conceal her inner turmoil with an equally impassive mask, but the shards of hope that he *might* have something to help her with her stubborn doubts that, that he *might* be willing to sell that elusive remedy to her for a price she could afford helped her conceal the undignified earnestness behind her eyes.

"Now why would you think to ask me that?" he asked, his voice perilously soft as he stared at her. "That is not the sort of thing village girls usually request of me. The potions they seek mostly involve romance or physical enhancement."

"Is it really so strange that I'd like to know my options for the future, if I have any others?" Aubria challenged. "I've lived and worked in the orchard all my life, and there's no shame in that. But I wonder...sometimes I wonder about more than what I can find on those familiar paths."

The Potioner surprised her by breaking their eye contact first as he walked back to his desk and set the jar down on its cluttered surface. When finished with that, he turned to one of his modest but overflowing bookshelves and perused the worn titles with a critical eye, searching for a specific volume.

Aubria tried to wait for him to speak again, but her impatience won. "What are you looking for?"

"Are you always so inquisitive?" Terran bent to survey the bottom shelf, concealing his face from her view; after a few seconds, he grunted with satisfaction as he tugged three wide books free from their places and slid them to the side. "Don't answer that. I'd hate to know for sure."

Her interest increased tenfold as she watched him remove another, much more worn book from the back of where the other books had rested. He rose to his considerable height as he flipped through it, searching for a page that took him a few turns to discover.

"Magic is forbidden, as we discussed, and rituals that call upon the powers of the gods and their children are known to be perilous. But that doesn't mean the rituals and their magic don't exist." Terran rotated the book in her direction so she could observe the spidery, archaic writing slanting over the pages of the book. "I don't suppose you can read much of this, if any—"

"I can read well enough!" Aubria assured him, holding her hands out for the book so she could inspect it more closely. She forgot to be offended that he'd assumed she was illiterate when the weight of the book rested in her hands. It was heavier than it should've been for such a small volume, and the age yellowed pages crinkled at the edges in spite of the smoothness of the surface that she felt when she traced her fingertips over the thin words in an effort to track their meaning. An illustration attracted most of her notice at the top of the page, for instead of a simple title or chapter note, the author had concealed the name for the ritual in a thorny depiction of twisting vines and choking moss. She could only make out the one word after all, and the rest of the language proved too elaborate for her to easily make sense of.

"*Veritas?* What, exactly, is this ritual supposed to do?" she asked when the dated language stumped her. The Potioner took the book away without glancing down at it as he weighed her reaction with a grave expression. Aubria squirmed in her seat, fighting her own uncomfortable uncertainty as she reached up to gingerly feel how swollen her face was by now. This time he didn't stop her, and she imagined that he was testing her.

"*Veritas* is the name of a truth spirit, of sorts. When called upon it can reveal truths the summoner has been seeking…and, if the spirit feels charitable, a secret heart's desire."

Aubria's spine tingled as if she'd had a premonition of someone walking over her grave. She reached out for the book again to inspect it with more enthusiasm now that she knew the purpose of the lengthy writing on the page.

A ritual to discover truths and earn a heart's desire…

"Is it safe to call on such a creature? How would you know for sure if he's telling the truth, or if he has other motives? How—"

Refraining from passing the aged book back to her, he balanced it atop another table cluttered with the trappings of his craft as he answered.

"It's a spirit—or a demon, the text isn't precisely clear on what exactly the creature is—bound by its own nature. It must tell the truth if the ritual is followed obediently."

"And all someone has to do is go through the ceremony detailed in the book? That's it?" Aubria brushed her untidy hair out of her face as she leaned around the Potioner to peer at the book from afar. Terran laughed, amused by her interest.

"The ritual is dangerous, and not everyone will be able to interact with the spirit profitably. If the person performing the summoning has ill intentions or is otherwise in an unhealthy mental state…well, I wouldn't want to be there if the spirit decided to answer the call. But I'll tell you something else about my craft, since you seem interested. It's rare that anyone enters my shop without displaying their fear and trepidation as clear as day," he explained in a lecturing voice, as if he were the sort of teacher who genuinely cared whether or not his students learned from his store of knowledge. "You see the cabinets lining the walls? I've categorized my potions thus for ease of memory: green is for healing, black is for harm—"

"And blue?"

"Blue is for potions that will neither heal nor harm by nature. It is this potion that lends greater effect to the ritual listed in this book, if one follows all of the steps." He ventured to the cerulean cabinet he'd indicated and opened the twin doors, his hand pausing over this or that bottle until he found the one he sought. Unlike the varying sizes and materials of the green or black bottles, Aubria noted that each and every one of the blue vessels appeared exactly the same save for a convoluted and—to her—unreadable etching on its front.

"What does it do?" she asked, her fingers itching to hold the bottle in her own hands. Her ravening desire took her by surprise, making her heart imitate thunder in her chest, but she hoped she concealed the desire in her eyes by studying the bottle instead of Terran's face.

"The ritual can summon a truth spirit, but such spirits operate on a different plane than ours. This potion I crafted can be used for other purposes, but the...suggestive nature of the mixture allows the naked eye to see the sorts of things mortals can't hope to experience without help," he explained. "I believe it would add a certain measure of both clarity and safety to the process." Surprising her, he passed her the potion for her to inspect. The bottle was opaque ceramic compared to the other bottles forged with a variety of glass or clay materials, but when it touched her skin she gasped at the distinct sensation of *other,* of magic, trapped within the modest cylinder.

"Do all of your potions feel like they shouldn't be restricted by such fragile containers?" she asked, tightening her fingers around the bottle so the residual magic vibrated through her knuckles.

The Potioner's eyes widened as he took the bottle from her. "You can feel that?"

"Is that so strange?" she asked, clenching and unclenching her hand into a fist as she winced with the tightness of her muscles and the brief return of pain from her tussle in the market.

"No," Terran remarked softly. But he'd waited too long to answer as he tucked the potion she'd relinquished into his pocket. "I suppose not."

Shaking her head to clear the buzzing from her mind and her

bones, she attempted to gather her thoughts into a rational pile instead of letting them drain through the sieve of exhaustion. She didn't entirely succeed, but her lips thinned into a resolute line as one determination formed in her head: she had to get the ritual and potion, somehow.

"How much for both?" Aubria asked, knowing already that the price would be too high just like she knew that no matter what it was, she'd find a way to pay it. Anything to find out why her heart felt so burdened at the thought of her carefully mapped future, and anything to find a way to gain what she didn't know she wished for without hurting Lane or anyone else she loved.

Terran pierced her with his all too perceptive gaze again, letting her know without speaking that her hopes would be dashed. "I can't sell it to you. Magic is forbidden, after all. Most of my concoctions in the blue bottles remain there indefinitely, you know, unless someone with a permit from the king or one of his wizards has papers for one."

"Is it because you think I can't pay?" Aubria challenged, straightening her posture to look as unpathetic and uninjured as she could with a bruised face and a dirty, patched up dress. "Because—"

"The price would be too high for most people, even for the wealthy of Oseren. I wouldn't sell it regardless: it's a curiosity, nothing more, although the potion is viable enough in theory. But it's a valuable curiosity all the same, and a family heirloom."

Though she'd known it would be impossible, Aubria felt her spirits sink when he confirmed her fears. Somehow, though she scarcely knew the Potioner and hadn't encountered him with her mind prepared for mysteries and riddles, she'd failed whatever test he'd set for her.

All the old tales say that no one should rely upon magic to solve their problems, she mused as she forced her mind into swifter activity with the idea that if she acted quickly a solution for purchasing or earning the potion and ritual guide from its keeper hung within reach. *But the aim of the potion is to ask questions from a spirit who is able to see the truth. Is that so terrible?*

Besides…the Potioner is a man, *is he not?* Aubria flinched at the final thought, almost squinching her eyes closed against the uncomfortable notion of what might help her win over Terran Caird. Yet, due to her injury or the effects of the healing but befuddling potion he'd given her to dull her pain, her desperation won out; her mouth curled into what she hoped was a coquettish smile.

"Surely we can come to some sort of understanding? You helped me, after all, and if we both put our minds to it I'm *sure* we can find a way to work something out." Aubria cocked her head to the side just enough to reveal the curve of her neck under the curtain of her blonde hair, giving her the opportunity to tuck a portion of it behind her ear in a neat display of feigned shyness. Cerise had divulged other tricks, such as smoothing down the front of her dress so the shape of her breasts and the line of her figure became more visible, but Aubria had never had cause for such boldness and thus feared looking silly and unpracticed just when she needed to draw a man in for real. The mild attempt at allure would have to be enough.

Terran stared at her until she fidgeted from shame. His expression had transfigured into one carved of stone, one that let her know that she'd trespassed too far with her simple flirtation.

"These are worth more than you could afford, but no matter what you offer I cannot sell them. I merely thought to share intriguing knowledge with someone who showed an interest."

Aubria was both grateful for his tact in the face of her pathetic attempt to win him over, and angry for his lack of response. Lane had never failed to respond to her charms, and even before she'd earned his admiration during her growth to womanhood, she'd never had much cause to doubt her power over men in general. Cerise was a dark beauty, and Viola an autumn sunrise…but Aubria had been called a harvest queen with her particular brand of pretty looks. Though she avoided drawing excessive attention to herself, she'd never outright *failed* to charm a boy before.

"If you don't want to help me, why show me any of that at all?" Heat bloomed in her cheeks thanks to her unjustified indignation, but

Terran's arrogance and lack of response had enflamed her usually dormant temper into unusual potency. "You could have just patched me up, sent me on my way, and not humored my ramblings at all."

"I'm not sure why I told you," he answered her as he rearranged some of the potions he had on display; his tone sounded quite serious, and Aubria felt her ire unwillingly begin to dim as she wondered if sometimes even a Potioner could be as uncertain about his decisions as a village girl. Maybe in offering her help after her ordeal in the market of Eldacre he'd given more information than he'd meant to.

Then he changed his tune, smirking as he glanced at her from the corner of his eyes, and she regretted ever softening in the first place.

"Maybe I helped a damsel in distress because she was pretty, and it was in my best interests to impress her so she'd return another time."

The compliment might have flattered her if she'd met him under different circumstances, but she heard only the mockery in his explanation. If this was her punishment for failing so completely, she wished she hadn't wasted her charms on him.

"*Potioner* or not, Terran Caird, you are an *ass!*" Aubria marched towards the front door, quelling her dizziness with sheer force of will as the Potioner began to laugh, making things a hundred times worse.

His laughter, genuine and unfairly pleasant, followed her all the way out, silencing only with the slamming of the door behind her.

Still, she had gained one thing besides his scorn.

Aubria wasn't sure how it had happened, but a slender blue bottle hid in the pocket of her torn dress, bouncing against her leg as she exited the murky atmosphere of the Potioner's shop into the fading sunlight of the afternoon. It wasn't the one the Potioner had shown her and then pocketed, but she'd thieved it from a cluttered side table on her way out and been glad of the opportunity. She fully expected Terran to storm out of his shop at any moment once he discovered her theft...but he never did, and she struggled to resist the urge to pull the bottle out to study it in the light. Maybe it was the strangeness of the afternoon, or the healing potions he'd given her, but she didn't feel like herself at all: the adrenaline coursing through her veins felt exhilarating more than frightening, and in spite of her guilt for taking something that didn't belong to her, the thrill of not getting caught sang so much louder in her veins.

Terran had said that the blue bottles were for storing things other than healing, but not for hurting. Aubria sensed the magic contained in the cylinder, buzzing and vibrating as if insisting that she unstopper the bottle and down the contents here and now. In spite of her rash decision, she knew that taking an unmarked potion would be a dangerous business. Still, if she ever rallied the courage to drink the concoction, part of her guessed that the reward would be worth the risk.

Outside, she found Toby and her cart where she'd left them, untouched by anyone thanks to the Potioner's influence. The horse chuffed with relief when she came out, having been unsettled by the ruffians enough to fret when she went missing. Aubria patted his nose and stroked his coarse mane, cooing comfort without syllables as the pins holding her torn sleeve to her dress poked at her shoulder. She'd have to be careful not to move her arms too freely to keep them from jabbing her skin, but she was grateful for the extra modesty this gave her.

Eldacre had mostly emptied after the violent incident with the Oseren soldier and his cronies, but a few of the villagers lingered in the square. Their questioning glances cast judgment on her appearance and behavior as she walked around to see what was left in her cart. Most of the pies had been tampered with thanks to the ruffians, but a modest stack of untouched gooseberry pies wrapped in thin cheesecloth rested near the back of the wooden cart. The awning of one of the shops had protected the victuals from the damaging sun, and thankfully the season was cold enough to prevent the fruit treats from rotting in the open air.

What to do with them, though? Her father didn't require her surplus income and was unlikely to question her about it, regardless of whether or not she stopped taking her baked goods into the Eldacre market. As for the state of her dress...*that* he couldn't help but notice.

I suppose I can jump in some mud puddles to conceal the muck from the street and say I fell asleep in the cart on the way home and fell out the side. That would explain the bruise on my face as well. It's a high enough fall from the cart to the ground, Aubria deliberated on the best solution, hoping that her father would be distracted enough to ignore her pathetic excuse. Regardless...she didn't want to bring any pie home, and she was hoping against hope that her father would loiter in the village a little longer so she could get home and change before he noticed. She could sneak and repair her dress later, if she had to.

Deciding impulsively, Aubria smiled to herself as she picked up the stack of four fresh pies and walked back to the Potioner's shop to set them down on his doorstep.

It may not be much, but since he is so concerned with payment, I'd say these pies will serve as a good bounty once he tastes them.

"Home, Toby," she instructed as soon as she'd returned to her cart and settled herself in its driving seat. The stolen potion felt oddly warm in her pocket as the squire horse began the journey back to Loracre.

Later, she remembered what she hadn't been able to recall in the Potioner's shop when he'd told her who he was. No one called him the Potioner anymore, not precisely: they called him the Poisoner, since it was rumored that he'd killed the younger prince some years ago.

3

Queen's Night

*A*ubria endured another jab from a hairpin into her scalp. The trifling bit of agony would be worth it in the end, she knew for certain: she had crafted her headwear for Queen's Night with her own hands, and she'd been surprised by the delicate, beautiful object she'd created.

"Hold still," her father chided, speaking around the three or four hairpins clenched between his lips. "I told you your hair was too fine to hold a proper crown. In my day a veil decorated with these silly blossoms served just as well."

"That was a long time ago," Cerise spoke from where she reclined casually on Aubria's bed, brushing out her own bountiful raven curls until they crackled with static. "Veils haven't been in fashion for twenty years."

"I think they're pretty," Viola fussed with the sleeve of her own elegant dress, hers pale blue to complement her luminous eyes. She'd decided to add an extra fringe of country lace to the sleeves at the last minute, and now she was paying the price. As carefully as she stitched, the frothy ruffle hung limply from the edge of the sleeve. Seeing this, Cerise sighed and stirred herself to aid her friend.

"How does it look, Da?" Aubria asked as Darragh Haight harrumphed. He ignored her, jabbing another pin into her scalp in what she hoped was an efficient manner.

"I'm not senile yet, Cerise Erdenwed. Besides, I have yet to style yours or dear Viola's hair, so is it wise to tease me about my age?" His words sounded harsh, but they could hear the amusement beneath his voice as he maneuvered another of Aubria's locks into place.

"All right," Cerise conceded with a laugh, shaking her head as she swatted away Viola's fretful hands so she could stitch up the uncooperative sleeve. "Hurry up so we can reach the bonfire before morning."

Accustomed to their banter, Aubria tuned them out as she shifted her weight to unlock her knees. Darragh was young to be Aubria's father, given that he'd married at seventeen and fathered his only child by eighteen. Now a physically fit man of thirty-eight, the widower was known for his orchard knowledge, fairness, and his shocking unwillingness to remarry and beget more children. Well, that and his knowledge of women's fashion and hairstyles: since her mother had died early and he hadn't wished to wed again, he'd determined that he would be both mother and father to their child.

"You're finished," Darragh said, interrupting her meandering memories. He gave her shoulders a bracing squeeze as he set both brush and pins aside. "Would you like to see?"

Aubria nodded, allowing herself to be guided to her long, age-spotted mirror so she could view the finished work. Behind her, Cerise and Viola sighed appreciatively.

It was traditional for maidens on Queen's Night to wear the new dresses they often made or purchased for the spring festivals with extra accessories, but due to her father's wealth and penchant for fashion she'd been allowed to commission an additional garment from the coveted dressmaker in Eldacre. She'd dared to request a lower cut to compliment the fitted bodice, but the sight of her winter pale skin and voluptuous figure wasn't the most scandalous thing about the dress. She'd chosen an unadorned white fabric, the sort usually reserved for holy rituals and priestesses in the king's city. Brides wore Yule colors appropriate for the wedding season, but in older days maidens had worn white to their ceremonies.

In a fit of pique, Aubria had sought to bring back the pure look, and she was relieved not to be disappointed. The dress fell in attractive folds down to her ankles, and the supple deerskin slippers as white as the dress protected her feet for the dancing to come. Tonight she was a Queen, as was every other girl who had participated in Sweetheart's Night with their betrothed, and a Queen required a crown.

Her flowing sleeves trailing elegantly, Aubria lifted her hands to brush her fingers against the petals of the apple blossoms woven into her traditional woodland crown. The flowers were almost as white as her gown, but at their hearts a bold pink promised to complement any maidenly blushes. She'd followed tradition here more than with her dress, since she'd plucked the many flowers and buds woven into her crown from the branches of a Beltane apple tree, which always bloomed around Ostara and Queen's Night so the fruit would be ripe by the May holiday. The sweet scents of the flower crowns were intended to remind their wearers of their Queen's night for the rest of their lives, so most girls chose their significant flower carefully: Cerise had chosen purple crocuses to match her Ostara dress, and Viola had branched out for once and woven many stalks of lavender together with a few butter yellow blossoms added for extra color.

This night, Aubria felt lovely and blessed with her own unique merits. Her freckles didn't remind her of dirt marring the surface of milk, and her brown eyes gleamed like wildflower honey. Hesitantly, she smiled at herself in the mirror, cocking her head to the side so a swath of curls fell over her shoulder. Around her neck, she wore a long string of smooth wooden beads tied together to form a necklace. The beads were plain, especially compared to the rest of her garb, but every girl she saw tonight would be wearing the same type of necklace: after tonight, the beads would be painted red like holly berries, and lay in a drawer unworn until the wedding season during Yule.

"Lane will be wild when he sees you!" Viola sighed behind her,

37

sounding jealous. With that, the spell broke like a piece of fragile pottery crashing to the ground from a high shelf.

Lane loves Aubria.

"He should be here any minute now, shouldn't he? And will the rest of your men show up at your doors to find the Queens they crowned absent from their towers?" Darragh scolded with pretend severity, encouraging the girls into compliance so he could finish their hair quickly and banish them from his house. He would spend a quiet evening at home: the bonfire in Loracre's outskirts was only for lovers tonight, only for the young men to learn what a Queen would require from her husband through the nights of their impending marriage.

Cerise and Viola squealed in faux distress, snatching up their Queen's crowns from Aubria's night table so he could pin them in securely. Their own mothers could have pinned them in almost as well, but the three girls had wanted to see each other before their unpredictable evening. After tonight, perhaps none of them would be a maiden any longer.

Aubria shooed her father and her friends away once he'd finished with her friends, insisting that she needed a moment alone. He complied with a fond smile and an unexpected hug.

"I jest with your friends, Aubria, but moments like these do make me feel old," he said on his way out. "Though she only had a short time with you, your mother would be as proud to have you for a daughter as I am. Lane is a fool if he doesn't realize how blessed he is to have earned your heart."

Speechless, Aubria gave him a wobbly smile as he left her room and shut the door behind him. Darragh wasn't prone to sentimentality, so his words meant all the more to her. She tilted her head back to look up at the slanted ceiling of her bedroom, pinching the bridge of her nose so she wouldn't cry.

Is this what you want? Her doubts enticed her away from her plans, luring her with the promise of the unknown. *There might be no going back after tonight.*

I do want this, she squashed her qualms with vigor. *I do.*

Are you certain? Her internal voice hissed, reminding her of the potion hidden in the pocket of her dress. Weeks had passed since her theft, making it lay less heavily on her conscience, but she hadn't yet used the cryptically mark potion. The blue bottle had begun to feel like a totem, a good luck charm to reassure her that she could perhaps change her fate with just a few sips. She had no way of knowing what this potion did, but the blue color of the bottle reassured her that it wasn't poisonous. Her instincts, too, gave her an oddly concrete sense that the potion was harmless, which she shouldn't have been able to guess on her own.

Aubria thought of Terran, too, remembering him inevitably with her shameful and futile flirtation. Curiosity won out over her mortified memories: if the rumors of the Potioner's involvement in the younger prince's death were so common, how had he escaped the king's wrath?

Lane's knock politely battered the door. Her father wouldn't answer the knock: once a Queen's Sweetheart arrived, parents were banished from same vicinity. Aubria composed herself and padded out to the main room, where it might have been yesterday that she'd answered the door for Lane with the scent of almond pie wafting through the house and the bustle of the other girls surrounding her.

Lane bowed extravagantly as she opened the door for him, his serious expression layered over the excitement dancing in his eyes. He and every other man participating in the handfasting wheel were dressed in plain but clean dark clothing for Queen's Night: for one evening they were the servants of their maiden and would do whatever she commanded. Aubria swallowed as she glanced over his fit, rugged body, knowing that Lane would do his very best to make sure he served her vigorously this night.

"My Queen," he spoke, his eyes soft with admiration as he let his eyes drift over her body, over her willingly exposed figure. "I am yours this night. What would you have of me?"

"I…" Aubria winced as her voice cracked, though doubtless he would find even that to be charming; her fingers toyed nervously with her beaded necklace. "I wish to go to the bonfire, sir, and I would have you be my escort."

"I am yours tonight," Lane repeated, as was tradition. "But first, may I present you with this gift from my mother?"

This too was tradition, and Aubria accepted with a nod. Lane held out his hands, in which rested a package wrapped in a handkerchief. Inside it rested a small, perfect circle of cake decorated with a sugared violet. On Queen's Night the mother of the potential bridegroom baked his Queen a small cake customarily laced with contraceptive herbs like pennyroyal and king's lace flowers to prevent any early pregnancies that would interfere with the proper handfasting wheel.

"I thank her for this gift, and I will enjoy it in your presence so you may tell her so," Aubria said, accepting the tiny cake he offered and popping it into her mouth. Lane's mother was almost as good a baker as she was, and the pleasant flavor of additional natural contraceptives burst on her tongue with a fanfare: cinnamon, fig, apricot, and a dash of ginger. She dabbed at a spot of frosting on her upper lip, annoyed with her clumsiness, but Lane swooped in for a less traditional kiss. Something had changed already, though her Queen's Night hadn't officially begun. His tongue invaded her mouth not unpleasantly, and his calloused hands wandered over her body more freely than they usually did.

Still, she didn't have to push him away: he withdrew on his own, looking dazed. Aubria found that she hadn't really wanted him to stop. It had felt good to be touched...desired. The way he kissed her made her forget most of her earlier anxieties.

"Forgive me, my Queen. I was overcome by your beauty beyond the limits of my control," Lane joked, though he kept his face solemn. "May I escort you to the village?"

"You may, but only if you err once more," Aubria said, stepping out of her doorway and closing the way behind her so he could kiss her more thoroughly.

"I beg your forgiveness again," he began, speaking softly, "for if I wrong you further I believe I would continue doing so again until the sun rose."

Aubria blushed, her gut tightening with latent desire rising to the surface; embarrassment warred with longing. "O-Oh. Perhaps we should simply depart, then."

"Yes, we should," Lane laughed, taking her hands in his own and leading her from her doorstep down to the path that would take them into the village proper.

Conversation ordinarily flowed between them like the orchard wellspring, containing discussions of the local news or other things interesting to them both. But tonight, as the sun sank lower and lower against the horizon until night fell, she felt tongue-tied. Lane seemed nervous too, or too excited about the evening's events to talk much. Queen's Night may have been purposed to teach betrothed men how to properly please their wives, to set clumsy fumbling and awkward timing aside before marriage, but men usually enjoyed this point on the handfasting wheel just as well. That's what Aubria had heard whispered amongst her elders and the recently married, anyway.

After the way Lane had kissed her, she wondered with a dash of recklessness if they'd be able to stop and wait for seasonal events once they knew the secrets of the night with one another. No further fraternizing would be encouraged until Beltane and beyond, and it was poor taste to partake in marital joys outside of times appointed by the gods.

Loracre's bonfire was visible to their eyes once they passed through the empty village to the edge of the orchard beyond. It burned merrily, the flames sending spears of light towards the heavens as the embers crackled like instruments played by fire spirits. The usually crowded village would've been eerie in its silence, but Aubria knew that everyone not eligible for the handfasting wheel would remain safely indoors while the raucous young people ventured out to play. The men were still picking up their Queens: one fellow would stand at the door, knocking, and a giggling girl would open it and practically fall into his arms, often knocking her blossom crown askew. Aubria watched the proceedings with fond recognition of her friends.

They reached the bonfire after a short while, and Aubria watched as the shadows of couples dancing around the fire while they laughed or sang or drank honeyed mead cavorted on the ground. A few non-participating volunteers from the older residents of Loracre strummed instruments nearby so the young lovers would have music to dance to. She spotted Cerise with her Nathan, who was a full head shorter than her but swarthy and handsome nonetheless. She didn't see Viola, but she didn't have time to look for her: Lane pulled her into the dance, jumping into the rhythm as seamlessly as if they'd done this for most of their lives.

This is where you were meant to be, Aubria thought more than once as she spent the next couple of hours dancing with her betrothed. Time felt unimportant, a mortal construct, as Lane pulled her in and out of dance after dance and brought her mead between the rounds. This was different dancing than they'd done before: he'd always been respectful of her chastity, and therefore kept his hands in appropriate places while still letting her know he desired her. Tonight he took delight in exploring her, kissing her by the heat of the bonfire and holding her tightly to him as if he never wanted to let her go again.

This is the life you were meant to have, Aubria thought as she kissed him, tasting the mead he'd imbibed on his lips. He'd indulged in only one glass of mead, while she'd had three: one of the most well-known pieces of advice for a betrothed man instructed him not to drink heavily if he intended to serve to the best of his ability.

"Lane…" Aubria sighed as his hands wandered upwards for the first time, angling to caress her breasts. His touch felt good, but an unfamiliar sense of panic made her stiffen into rigid refusal. Withdrawing immediately, he searched her face with his eyes to see what troubled her.

"Is something wrong?" he asked, cupping her face in his hands. She resisted the urge to jerk away from his touch, instead opting for a weak smile.

"I feel a bit lightheaded. Could you fetch me some water?" she asked. He nodded, a look of knowing adorning his face, and left her alone at the bonfire to do as she'd asked. Suddenly suffocated by the bonfire's heat and confounded by the dancing shadows, she let her feet carry her to the edge of the dancers almost into the sheltering trees of the orchard itself.

This part of the town was bordered by plum and apple trees, some of which bloomed prettily under the stars, and the scent of the delicious fruits to come made her mouth water. She took shelter under an azure plum tree whose fruits were famous for curing digestive complaints and watched as an evening breeze carried some of the petals away on its back.

What's the matter with me? Aubria wondered, bemoaning her sudden attack of anxiety. *What would Lane think if he knew about my silly doubts?*

But why do I feel like I do? She countered internally, scuffing her toe against the ground with her new dancing slippers. *There has to be a reason none of this feels like…enough.*

A sound far to her right startled her, making her remember she didn't want anyone to spy on her dejected skulking away from her friends at the bonfire. Peering cautiously through the trees, she saw Viola and Merek kissing beneath the boughs of a tree similar to hers but with ivory blossoms instead of blue. A shaft of moonlight from the ripe full moon revealed half-concealed parts of their bodies to her sight, and she realized that they were doing more than kissing: Merek's drunken mouth was locked onto Viola's throat, leaving marks that might cause pain, and she saw one of his hands had disappeared up her skirt between her legs. They didn't see Aubria, but she saw Viola's pained, slightly sick expression as the hand she couldn't see fumbled with obvious lack of skill under the dress.

Embarrassed and vaguely worried, Aubria moved to walk away. Then she saw Merek's eyes under the moonlight, looking right at her as he paused his devouring of Viola's throat and smiled at her knowingly. Appalled, she hurried back to the edge of the bonfire and left them to their business.

He should be wooing her, making her feel special. It's too early for him to lead her away from the bonfire, she grumbled to herself. *We only get to be Queens*

Queens once. Is he really too selfish to let her enjoy her night?

But she felt selfish too when she reached the edge of the handfasting party and saw Lane waiting patiently for her to return as he laughed with Cerise and Nathan. The stifled feeling churning within her gut made her realize that she couldn't go back to be with him, especially not for the activities of Queen's Night.

Aubria turned on her heel and took off in the opposite direction, fleeing through the beckoning orchard. The trees seemed to be chastising her too, lowering their branches to swat at her face.

How could you deny him, she imagined they whispered to her as she passed, *how could you not fully return the love of so good a man as he?*

Lane must have seen her, for she heard the sounds of heavy pursuit directly behind her. She carried on running a few more paces, leading him farther from the crowded bonfire until panic welled in her chest again, cutting off her breath, and she forced herself to slow down. *It's Lane. It's only Lane.*

Turning to face him, she opened her mouth to blurt whatever explanation came to her first. But he was on her before she saw him properly, pushing her against a tree with his body and kissing her with more fervor than she'd ever seen or felt from him before. Gasping for air, she reluctantly kissed him back, resisting the urge to wrinkle her nose at the heavy aftertaste of mead from his mouth. He squeezed her hard enough to hurt, first her waist, and then lower, then back up to fondle her breasts at their most sensitive points. She flinched as he nudged her legs apart and bit the edge of her lip with savage teeth.

"N-No..." she started to protest, but the words died in her throat as he spoke.

"I knew you wanted me, Aubria. I *knew* it was me you wanted, not that smug bastard..." Merek, Viola's betrothed, murmured as he pressed Aubria against the tree so her dress scraped against the rough bark. His hand was on her thigh, wandering upwards as he spoke with strangled urgency.

"NO!" she half-shrieked as she struggled to push him away. The tips of his fingers brushed at the place not even Lane had touched before, and she surprised herself by keening like a wounded animal. "Merek, *no!*"

"I'll make it worth it to choose me...you'll be screaming my name by the end of the night, I swear." He didn't seem to hear her, didn't notice her shoving or trying to get away. Aubria yelped as his hand moved again, almost slipping inside her more painfully than she'd expected. She sprung into instinctive action as his other hand tugged at the top of her dress to free her breasts. Her foot snapped out, kicking his crotch with vicious anger. Stumbling backwards, she shoved him away as hard as she could and took off into the forest. He fell with a high-pitched yelp similar to the one she had made when he'd first grabbed her.

"Get back here!" he called behind her, sounding like he was already recovering from the injury if not from his drunkenness. "I'm nowhere near done with you!"

He was faster than her, and if she wasn't careful he would catch her. Thinking that now was as good a time as any, Aubria dove her hand into the pocket of her dress and gripped the potion tightly in her fist as she ran deeper and deeper into the trees. This time they sheltered her instead of rebuking, swishing back into place as soundlessly as if she hadn't sprinted past them at all. She didn't know where she was running to, just as she didn't know what purpose the potion she'd stolen actually served, but forward was the only direction she could imagine. She couldn't return to Lane, not when she'd have to tell him...when she'd have to tell *Viola*...

This orchard is full of magic, she thought as she ran, adrenaline lending swiftness to her feet like a doe fleeing the hunters; behind her, she heard Merek pursuing. *May the magic that makes it bear fruit aid me now.*

It would be stupid, unbelievably moronic to drink a potion whose contents were unknown to her, never mind her instincts that the potion was safe. But Merek was getting closer, and she had no choice. Praying to any god or goddess who could hear, she paused long enough to pull the stopper and chug the contents of the vial before continuing to flee.

Aubria noticed nothing at first, nothing aside from the pounding of her heart, from the thumping of her feet against the ground as she cut a wayward path through the orchard. But the potion worked its way through her blood quickly, its satisfyingly sour taste and silky feel coating her tongue and the roof of her mouth…then, before thirty seconds had passed, she realized she was running incredibly fast. Her senses heightened, tingling with awareness as her womanly fear of an unwanted male pursuing her faded into the simplicity of a hare fleeing a hunter. Her nose twitched once or twice as she zigzagged between trees; something felt like it had caught in her hair, but she had no intention of stopping to check what it was.

Merek's pursuit faded into nothing as she lost him, and with that her other concerns fell away as well. The moonlight sifting down between slats in the tree canopy captivated her, tempting her to try to catch the moonbeams in her hands. She couldn't marvel at the wonder of it consciously, because that was a human thing…and she no longer felt human. Her worrisome heart no longer pained her, and her troubled memories failed to perturb her thoughts. What did it matter that she didn't know what her heart desired, and couldn't envision any life other than this one?

Aubria was one of the forest creatures now, and she ran towards the moon like she would howl at it once she reached its resting place.

Her feet skidded to a stop as she reached a clearing empty of all growth and black here and there with scorch marks. She'd come all the way to the lightning field, the forbidden place at the farthest western end of the orchard, where nothing grew and where no one dared venture. Here was where they had burned evil sorcerers and terrible criminals long ago, when the villages hadn't been civilized by a king and his soldiers.

Aubria should have been afraid, but she was not. She was another beast captivated by the unhindered sight of the full moon hovering in the sky above her, heavy as if with child. She stared at it, her eyes dilated and unblinking, until her thoughts faded into quiet nothing.

4

*A*ubria knew something was wrong when she awoke curled up in a fetal position on the dry grass beneath the shade of a tree that hadn't yet bloomed. All of her senses were heightened to painful clarity, especially her hearing, and she lay on the ground as flat as she could in terror for several minutes before she could convince herself that all was well. Under the spell of either the mysterious potion or her own exhaustion, she had fallen asleep under the swollen moon at the edge of one of the most forbidden places in the orchard: the lightning field.

What happened? Aubria, feeling more sick than she had been the one time she'd indulged in too much strong winter cider, struggled to assemble her memories as she lurched to her feet and inspected her surroundings. *Queen's Night...I left Lane behind, and Merek attacked me in the orchard...I ran away, I drank the potion I'd stolen, and then...*

Blinking to dispel any drowsiness, Aubria rubbed her eyes as she looked around. The lightning field was always eerie. No matter what kind of weather held its reign on any given day, gray clouds ominous with the peril of a terrible storm lurked over the empty field. Local lore and peasant gossip had speculated about the nature of such an ill-omened place for many years, saying the land had been cursed by the gods or by the faerykind, or it was a meeting place for demons. The argument usually came to the same consensus: everyone should stay away from the field because the reason ash covered the ground was due to the frequent and unpredictable lightning that struck the ground more than a hundred times a day.

Aubria shivered, but felt no real fear: she had slept at the edge of the orchard, and the comforting trees as familiar to her as her own cottage would always provide shelter if she sought it. Turning her back on the sinister plain, she began the slow walk back along the same route she had run here like a wild animal. The sight of another faerykind ring, not far from where she'd gone to sleep, gave her a prickle of trepidation.

"Goddess above," she cursed as she noticed the disheveled state of her dress, pinching the skirt covered with dirt and grass stains and holding it up with distaste. The pure white would never recover from the stains, but in some ways that was just as well: she had intended all along to dye the gorgeous dress red for Beltane. Fortunately the dress hadn't suffered any tears, and she still had her beaded necklace. Her deerskin slippers had served her well in her flight and could be scrubbed lightly with a cloth.

As for her crown, Aubria knew not much could be hoped for. Blossoms tended to wilt overnight, and she'd noticed a sprinkling of browning pink and white petals on the ground from where she'd rested her head. There was no point wearing the silly thing any longer, beautiful as it had once been: she reached up to take out the pins keeping it in her hair. Then she stopped, freezing with horror as she felt something very different and quite furry on her head.

Whatever had been in the potion must have had a horrible side effect. Her normal human ears had been replaced by the long, fuzzy ears of a hare.

Her breath hitched in her chest before whooshing in and out of her lungs in panic as she traced the shape of the hare ears with the tips of her fingers. Then she explored the rest of her face, noting with increased dismay the odd shape of her nose that definitely felt like it belonged to a kingdom hare. *This can't be happening…*

It hadn't mattered to her at first, since she'd assumed the main reason she'd felt so off from her usual self had been exhaustion and the stress of the night before, but now she let herself catalogue the new sensations she'd been experiencing since she'd taken the potion. *I can smell every fruit and leaf and animal nearby, and I could conceivably scent my way home. I can hear hundreds of animals scurrying about in this odd twilight, and there's an owl hooting far away…*

Forcing herself to calm down, to breathe normally so she wouldn't faint or scream, Aubria inspected the rest of her body for any other surprises. Aside from whiskers next to her nose and a bit of downy brown fur on her shoulders, she found nothing.

She tested her balance with a few quick steps forward before she decided to run again. The only one who could help her with this predicament was the person she'd stolen the vial from: Terran Caird, the king's Potioner. She'd have to beg for assistance from the one person who had helped her weeks ago when the guard and his scholar lackeys had harassed her, even though he could have her arrested for a thief and taken into the city as a prisoner.

You have rabbit *ears and a* twitchy *rabbit* nose, *Aubria,* her thoughts reminded her annoyingly. *You don't have another option.*

She was cold and damp from the dewy ground she'd slept on for who knows how long, but her run to Eldacre warmed her considerably. Her wooden necklace smacked against her chest with the rise and fall of her stride, so she removed it and clutched it in her fist like a talisman. The only blessing she could think of was the fact that the swiftness from the potion also had yet to wear off. Eldacre was half a day's ride from her house in Loracre, but at this inhuman speed she would get there in far less time.

The exertion kept her warm, but she was far from sweating. Aubria reached the outskirts of Eldacre in good time. Upon her arrival she received an answer to the question that had troubled her all her way there. If she had slept through the night at the edge of the cursed field, and if she had spent the better part of two hours walking and running sporadically all the way to the neighboring village, where was the sun to announce the morning?

Now she realized that it wasn't morning at all: she'd slept only a couple of hours, and arrived in the town just before the sun began its daily ascent. More importantly, she'd arrived well before anyone would be awake.

I must be able to see in the dark, thanks to the potion, she mused as she crept forward in a weak attempt at stealth. *At least I won't be seen by anyone until Terran throws me out by these hare ears for the guards to arrest me.*

The silence of the town made her more anxious rather than less. She wanted to reach the well at the center of the square to wash her face and rinse her mouth so she would regain a miniscule amount of dignity before she knocked on the Potioner's door, but she barely dared walk through the empty main street without crouching in fear like the animal whose traits she'd unintentionally borrowed. When she reached the well, she almost screamed as she accidentally knocked a spare empty bucket resting on the edge into the depths, but she stifled the sound and focused on completing her task as quickly as possible.

Her poor ablutions complete, Aubria ran her fingers through the tangles of her hair and set off to the Potioner's house near the end of the village. Her adrenaline hadn't quite faded with her run, and she found herself nearly out of breath by the time she reached his narrow door.

If he is so wealthy and respected, why does he live in such a common cottage? She couldn't help but wonder. Raising her hand to knock, she inhaled and exhaled purposefully before rapping her knuckles against the sturdy oak door. Then she jumped back, startled by the speed with which the man she sought opened the door to greet her.

Terran Caird didn't comport himself like a man who was often or easily surprised, but his green eyes widened in genuine shock as he took in both her appearance, who she was, and why she was there at such an early hour. Aubria imagined what he saw: a foolish peasant girl in a grass stained dress and a crown of wilting flowers, both of which were outshone by the features of a common hare that she'd been so unfortunate as to come by. His flat expression was more condemning than she'd expected, knowing as she had the rudeness of her theft. She couldn't hold his gaze for longer than a second, and her shame muted her into silence.

"Aubria Haight. To what do I owe the pleasure?" Terran asked her at last, his brows drawn down into a disapproving frown. Yet his eyes danced, and Aubria heard the amusement underneath the contempt. She looked up at him pleadingly, begging him not to make her explain, but he held his silence until it obliged her to speak.

"I...I may have done something stupid," she confessed, her nose twitching to punctuate her mortification as she twisted the wooden beads of her necklace between her fingers. "I was hoping—"

"Yes, of course you were," Terran sighed, his stern manner dropping as he rolled his eyes and swung the door open for her to enter. "Come in. I'd hate to watch you grovel."

Aubria brushed past him after glancing around to make sure none of the Eldacre villagers had awoken to witness her disgrace. The heat of his body, feverish just above the levels of a normal man, made her glance up at him with interest, but his impatient gesture sent her hurrying forward into the main room of his dwelling. She hopped up on his medical table without hesitating, tucking her skirts around her legs.

Right after that, she realized she wasn't alone in the room with the Potioner.

Aubria startled, freezing in place as she stared at the richly dressed man staring at her from the other end of the room. Plain but apparently wealthy, the Oseren nobleman stared at her as if she was an exotic bird who had flown in from outdoors just to defecate on his shiny boots.

"H-Hello," Aubria stuttered, reaching up to cover her twitching nose as her hare ears drooped. *I even tremble like a frightened rabbit,* she realized with disgust.

"Caird, what is this wench doing here? I requested privacy as a condition of my purchase, as you very well know," the gentleman spoke in a deceptively nasal voice considering the size of his nose. Terran occupied himself with closing the door and glancing out of the window between artfully opaque curtains to make sure no one had followed his unexpected guest before he replied.

"Have no fear, Villor, the wench is my assistant," he explained, lying efficiently as he offered the middle-aged snob a nondescript green bottle with one hand and a handshake with the other. Suspicion in his narrow eyes, Villor wrinkled his mustache as he took the bottle and tucked it into a pocket while refusing the handshake.

"I wasn't aware you needed an assistant. You never had one in the city."

"I did have one in Oseren, though I didn't publicize her existence," Terran said, though this time Aubria couldn't tell if he was lying or not. "You don't think I taste all the potions I make myself, do you?"

Villor was supposed to laugh at that cue, and he did so with an air of great reluctance. He cast another apprehensive glance her way as he removed a pouch of coins made of exceedingly soft velvet and full to the brim from his pockets and set it on the table. Velvet was rare in Aubria's community, and her fingers itched to brush their tips against the soft purse to experience what the rich blue fabric would feel like.

Don't you remember the last time you had itchy fingers? Her mind shouted at her, bringing her back to the present with a sigh. *Besides, you have more important things to worry about.*

The gentlemen concluded their business while Aubria sat quietly on the examination bench, uncomfortable in her worn finery and pulling up the neckline of her dress with little success. Regardless of the lies told to conceal who she was, Villor would remember the bewitched rabbit maid who had barged in on his business deal. He looked affronted by the intrusion, though perhaps that was just his abrasive nature.

Villor slammed Caird's door behind him, rattling a few bottles in their neat shelves on the wall.

"I don't have to worry about you stealing anything else, do I?"

Terran cast a side-eye at Aubria as he weighed the pouch in his palm before hiding it away into a drawer in his desk at the other side of the small room. Blushing, Aubria shook her head in a negative when he faced her full on with an accusing expression on his face.

"I think the hare ears convinced me to refrain."

"I'll have to take your word for it," Terran said with a shrug. "More importantly, I know how to cure your...affliction, so you should be back to normal within a few minutes. But why should I help you? You *did* steal from me, and now I'm supposed to help you without hope of payment? Last time you gave me some pies from your cart."

Aubria couldn't tell if he was joking or not as he stepped much closer to her, standing in front of her with her knees brushing against his thighs.

"Um, what...?" she protested brilliantly as he cupped her face in both of his hands.

"Don't fear," he reassured her, drawing close with his eyes narrowed. "I'm examining the hare defects. Your eyes have gone funny too, you know. Definitely rounder than normal, even for you."

"What?" Aubria groaned: it took much of her willpower to resist dashing to the hand mirror resting on his desk so she could view the damage. "Can you fix it?"

"Yes. Contrary to what I told Villor, I end up tasting many of my own experimental potions myself. I have a solid cleansing potion that I use to clear up all or most of any...unexpected results." Terran tilted her head back, studying her hare's nose in humiliating detail.

"So this happens often?" Aubria questioned, then continued as other queries popped into her head. "What was the potion that I took? What purpose would it have served?"

"I still can't believe you just *drank* the potion," Terran said, no longer able to stifle his laughter as he stretched her long rabbit ears out for inspection on either side of her head. "Was your evening too dull sitting in front of the fire tending to your embroidery? Oh, pardon me, last night was the local Queen's Night, was it not? You didn't drink the potion for a tryst with your—"

"Watch yourself, sir," Aubria, though seated, straightened her spine to all the height she could muster; unpleasant images began to sift to the forefront of her mind, memories of Merek's unwanted hands. "You grow too bold."

"You stole from *me*, Aubria. I have a right to—" Terran began, and she exploded.

"Yes, it was Queen's Night. I should have been with Lane, but I wasn't because I wasn't sure if I wanted...then my friend's betrothed followed me into the orchard and he...I had to get away, I had to, or he might've..." Her disjointed explanation proved clear enough to convey the message she hadn't known she'd wanted to divulge. Terran kept quiet long enough to finish his inspection and walk to the blue cupboard hanging on the wall to select a potion from the array of bottles inside.

"The hare potion was to enhance speed and stealth. I use a drop of it here and there for my other concoctions," he explained as he unstoppered the cork from the bottle and passed it to her. "Three sips: no more, no less. It will burn, and the transformation back into your normal self might sting, but it shouldn't take longer than a few minutes."

Too tired to argue, and too embarrassed now that he knew the secrets of last night, she downed the amount he specified and passed the bottle back as she stifled a gag at the distinct metallic taste. Her whole body went rigid for half a second before the numbness transformed into a burning, tingling feeling in her extremities. Panic might have overwrought her control, but since Terran had forewarned her about the sensation she focused on overcoming it.

"Don't you deal in poison as well as potions? What was in the vial you gave Villor?" She surprised herself with the spitefulness with which she lashed out after he'd practically forced her to detail her assault for his benefit.

Terran's easy manner and his apologetic frown distorted into a glare as potent as any stiff drink. "That's none of your business."

"I'm your assistant, aren't I?" she laughed bitterly, unable to stop herself. "Did I witness the prelude of death for one of that courtier's associates?"

"*Enough.* I will not explain myself to you or to anyone who is not involved," Terran snapped. "I've seen more than you've had nightmares about in these strange, sleepy villages. My business and my associates are none of your affair."

"Fine," Aubria huffed, anger coloring her voice as her cheeks heated with embarrassment. *He never answered me…but the bottle he gave Villor was green. That's for healing, I think.*

Quiet ruled the Potioner's narrow cottage, and she expected him to disappear into one of the back rooms so he wouldn't have to interact with her while the cleansing potion restored her to rights. An urge to explore the place niggled at her mind, but the tingling potion reminded her that she should stay put.

"So, now that we've thoroughly offended one another…" he began at the same time as she tried to change the subject.

"You said you added the hare potion to others? Wouldn't that produce the same effects?"

Relief plain on his face, Terran hurried to answer her question. "You took one of my more experimental potions, and you downed the entire bottle. I use a few drops here and there, no more. It's interesting, though, now that I've seen what the whole dose can do."

"Oh," she replied for lack of anything else to say. Terran was far from stupid, and they both knew what she would've preferred to steal. She fought the urge to look for the book he'd told her about in the bookshelf, and resisted the call the blue potion cupboard sent her way.

It might be better that you don't have access to such magic at all, she told herself to soften the sting of not attaining what she wished for.

"Most of your hare features are gone already," Terran said after a few beats of an awkward silence. "May I?"

Aubria nodded, but he had already approached her again, turning her head this way and that as he had before to inspect her restored human features. His palms felt hot against her face as he tilted her head to the left, but his skin was pleasantly dry. The emotion of the past evening, temporarily cleansed in the fire of her racing adrenaline, threatened to crash over her in a wave of tears. Determined not to be weak, she inhaled and held her breath until her eyes ceased burning and the fit passed.

"Are you in pain?" Terran asked her, noting her reaction but misunderstanding the cause. "You weren't...did he hurt you before you ran away?"

Aubria tried to shake her head in a negative, but her face was still in his hands. His examination was complete, but still he held her.

"I'm sorry for stealing from you, Terran Caird, and I'm sorry for showing up on your doorstep expecting you to fix my mistakes. I told you, I'm not normally so...so..." Aubria spoke, unable to raise her voice above a near whisper and equally incapable of meeting his eyes. "I'm not just sorry because the potion was more than I could handle. You helped me when those ruffians harassed me in the market, and you didn't have to. You didn't have to help me now, since I'm sure it would've been easier to let me live with my mistake or throw me to the guards. But..."

"I've made more than my share of mistakes," Terran interrupted, finishing his second examination with far more gentleness than he had the first; the strange instant of intimacy passed with neither fanfare nor explanation. "You didn't do any permanent harm, regardless, and the only person you almost hurt was yourself."

"There's that," Aubria sighed, smoothing her hands down her almost ruined dress; she'd forgotten about the grass stains. "Is that all? Am I cured?"

"Yes, you're cured. But there is the matter of payment," Terran crossed his arms over his chest, making him look more intimidating that he had seconds ago. "I'll take your necklace. That will do nicely."

"My necklace?" Aubria asked, lifting her hands to cradle the smooth beads and hoping she didn't sound too surprised; if he knew about Queen's Night, then surely he knew about the significance of the necklace. "What could you want with it? You could carve the beads yourself, or buy another in the market."

Saying nothing, Terran raised one eyebrow as if to remind her that she wasn't in the position to refuse him any payment he requested. Huffing with displeasure and already wondering how she would explain the disappearance of her Queen's necklace, she lifted it over her head and passed it to him.

He's kind one minute, scathing the next...what can I make of that? She wondered as Terran took the necklace from her hands and walked away from her to tuck it into another desk drawer. His back was to her, as it so often was, and by the hunch of his shoulders she could tell he was undecided about something, hesitating on a decision. He had a similar build to her father, though Darragh Haight was her own height: defined bone structure, and a broad upper body that lent itself well to hard work. Terran contrasted Darragh with height he wouldn't know what to do with under low cottage ceilings.

"If I give you this," he said at last, turning around to show her what he'd picked up: it was the potion she'd meant to steal, the enigmatic blue bottle etched with the sigil of an eye. *"If* I give you this, I will demand one thing from you that you will not be able to refuse, not matter what I ask. The only thing I will promise is that I will not ask you to kill, maim, or injure yourself or anyone else."

"You'll...you would give me the potion and the ritual guide?" Aubria marveled, hopping off the examination table and padding towards him in her slippers; her eyes felt luminous, still too large as she gazed with longing at the simple potion.

Would you know your heart's desire? Would you know the truth?

"It seems you are single-minded in purpose, and you almost...well, you take risks you should pass by. You are the one person I've met who genuinely doesn't know what they want for their life, and I wouldn't like seeing that tear anyone apart," Terran explained, passing the potion from one hand to the other, his expression contemplative as he strode to his bookshelf to pull out one of the aged tomes. "Furthermore, because you know the consequences of taking risks such as these, I believe that you'll take extra care and do exactly as I advise you. I may demand payment, but I would hate to see you harmed."

"You told me I was too careless and too foolish last time," Aubria glared at him, suspicious; he ignored her as he set the book on his desk and took a knife to the page he'd been looking for, cutting it neatly from the binding. "You laughed at me when I told you I wanted the ritual and the potion."

"Oh, that," Terran chuckled again, his lips twitching with suppressed mirth. "I laughed because you tried to flirt with me to get your way."

"Fine then," Aubria's pride overtook her good sense as she crossed her arms in what she hoped was graceful disapproval. "I'll live my life without your potion just as well, you know. I don't need charity."

"Maybe not, but you forget that this isn't charity. I found a price at which I'm willing to sell you the potion and the ritual, and you have only to accept the offer." Terran simplified the details with another charming smile. He *did* glance down at her chest though, where her arms had unintentionally nudged her breasts higher; she noted this with a surprising amount of satisfaction that he'd proved he wasn't totally immune to her womanly allure.

His attention didn't linger, and he leaned over the desk, some of his hair falling over on his forehead as he dipped the tip of a ragged quill into an inkpot and jotted some notes onto the parchment he'd cut from the book. Aubria waited in silence, overcome with curiosity but too bashful to read over his shoulder. Once he finished his notes, he faced her and offered both the potion and the drying parchment to her with a flourish.

"When you're finished with the ritual, burn the paper and it will return to me."

"You won't ask me to hurt anyone? You won't...compromise my virtue?" Aubria reached out for them both, the potential of the ritual and the hypnotic potion that was supposed to reveal her own mysterious heart, but she hesitated a final time.

"You are safe with me, Aubria. You may not like what I have in mind, but it compromises neither your morals nor your virtue. I swear it."

She had no other excuse: she snatched the potion and parchment from him as if he'd rescind his offer any second. As soon as she held the items in her hand, a new peace fell like morning mist over her soul. A peace she hated because it proved she could be bought.

Soon, she thought to quell the self-loathing, *soon I'll know what I want. Everything will be better once I know.*

"But…why help me at all? I don't—" Aubria protested as she clutched the potion and the slightly crumpled parchment to her chest. Peaceful as she felt now that answers were within arm's reach, other questions demanded explanations as well.

"I think we could be friends, Aubria, I really do. I would like my stay in these villages to be…well, better than the last few places I've tarried in. I think having a friend who's not frightened of the king's wicked Potioner might help with that."

"You just want a friend?" she asked, her suspicion fading in the face of his honesty. She didn't know him well, after all, so it was better to be cautious than sorry…but she knew he was telling her the truth, and least the parts he could bear to share with her now. Pity squeezed her heart, which usually made her offer sympathy, the comfort of hearty food, and a commiserating hug, but she couldn't offer those things to him yet if ever.

"I don't *just* want a friend, which is why I added the clause of payment. I won't tell you the rest of my conditions until you need to know. But a friend wouldn't hurt another friend, I can promise you that."

Aubria forced her shyness aside so she could look right into his eyes to try to gain a true measure of his character, of him as a person. He may not have known what she was about, but he matched her stubborn gaze and held it. The hypnotic quality of his eyes, the bright greens outlined by burnished gold, wasn't lost on her; without realizing, she moved towards him half a step. *Who will be the first to look away?*

A knock on what sounded like a back door she hadn't known was there startled Aubria and Terran from the tension in the room. Rolling his eyes, Terran cursed under his breath as he guided her to the door.

"There's always another client, each more paranoid than the last. I'll see you out. One last piece of advice: wait two days before you try this ritual. You've had a shock, and you should be at your absolute best before you attempt any magic."

"What—" she started to ask, but he'd practically shoved her out the door and shut it behind her with a decisive click.

What could you possibly want from me? she asked no one as the sun rose over Eldacre to guide her way home.

5

Aubria had always known that a great deal of scandal took place both during and after Queen's Night. After abandoning Lane at the bonfire and rushing into the orchard like a madwoman—and after Merek's assault—she'd expected herself to become the main source of gossip for an excruciatingly long time...but she was spared the brunt of any gossip by her betrothed.

Lane had been the first to greet her when she finally returned home, limping and sore and no longer benefiting from borrowed speed and vigor. She'd felt victorious, triumphant and unquestionably nervous with the little blue bottle and the torn page tucked into her pocket. She'd read the instructions Terran had jotted down on her way back, and the words ran through her mind in an endlessly spinning loop.

Do not summon the truth spirit into your home. Begin the ritual in your house if you need to, but go outside to complete it. Do not drink the potion until you are absolutely sure you are alone, safe, and ready to complete the ritual. Make sure you follow the instructions on ending the ritual precisely and promptly. It is imperative that you send it on its way promptly after you have your answers.

Aubria had meant to read the ritual as well, but she'd decided against it. She would read through it when she was ready, after a couple of days' worth of strained patience. Terran had helped her, and his advice on facing the supernatural as her best self couldn't hurt.

The sight of Lane pacing back and forth in front of the door to her father's cottage set her teeth on edge, and she stood alone under a duet of blossoming lemon trees long enough to regain her composure.

"Are you all right?" Lane asked her on sight, dashing forward to pull her in for what could only be called a rib-crushing embrace. "I didn't want to worry your father, so I told him you'd had Queen's Night jitters and had stayed at Viola's after the bonfire."

Viola. She had almost forgotten about her friend, but she stifled a groan as she recalled what she had to tell her. If Viola would even believe the tale, which Aubria doubted.

"It was just that," Aubria took the out he offered, hating herself a little for the lie. "I...I had some jitters and the bonfire was so hot that I just wanted to get away. I'm sorry, Lane, I didn't think I—"

"Shhh, it's all right," Lane soothed as he rubbed her back with a gentle hand. "I understand. I'm sorry if I pressured you too much."

Lane had *not* pressured her at all, and her guilt reminded her of this fact with a malicious stab in her gut. She buried her face in his chest, allowing herself to give into her exhaustion and relax into his arms as she could with almost no one else. Lane's arms comforted her like always; once, that had felt like the only right thing in the world. People in both Loracre and Eldacre had discussed the fatefulness of Widower Haight's daughter making a good match with the finest bachelor in both villages, and until recently she'd never questioned their wisdom.

"Besides," he continued, as he obviously had been speaking for some time while her mind wandered. "There's always Beltane. I think we can make you more comfortable with the idea of us...being together by then."

"Lane—" She had more she needed to tell him, because he was a good person and she wanted so badly in that moment to just talk to her childhood friend who had always had the best advice. She couldn't tell him about her plan to do the ritual, or her mysterious bargain with Terran or about the Potioner in general, but she wanted to ask him what to do about Viola and Merek. She looked up, letting him hold her close as her lips parted to spill forth her secrets…

…but he simply kissed her, his arms tight around her in a mark of possession though his caress was as gentle as always.

"Lane, I'm sure you both are enjoying the new bond between you after last night, but I was wondering if I could have my daughter back for a few hours," Darragh's voice drawled from the doorway of her house. Blushing, Aubria pulled herself away from Lane to see her father lounging against the doorway with a not unhappy expression crinkling his eyes into a smile. At the sight of her ruined dress, however, his brows drew down into a frown.

"See, *this* is why I told you white was a *terrible* idea. I doubt I can salvage the garment from that many grass stains and all that dirt," he complained as he hurried down the steps to peer at the worst of the stains on the back of the dress. He glared at Lane, as if he were responsible for the damage…which, if Aubria's Queen's Night had gone as planned, he might have been. She blushed again.

"Weren't you going to dye the dress red for Beltane?" Lane stood up for her. Darragh rolled his eyes and seized Aubria's arm, shepherding her inside.

"We'll still have to scrub the fabric, you rascal," he replied. "Goodbye now, Lane. I'm sure Aubria will come see you soon."

Aubria waved a lackluster goodbye and allowed herself to be guided into the house, almost crumpling with exhaustion as she stumbled over the steps. Darragh was not a man who lacked perception, and he helped her to a chair so she could rest briefly.

"Did…I know it's not my right to pry, and a daughter would not like to tell her father what took place on her Queen's Night. But are you all right, Aubria? Lane's a good lad, but if anything went amiss—"

"I'm fine, Da," Aubria lied, her self-loathing returning. Lane hadn't hurt her, but telling her father about what Viola's Merek had almost done made her stomach roil with a sick wave of shame. She hadn't figured out what to do with the information herself, and knowing her father would take immediate and most likely violent action wouldn't help her. "Just…a long night, that's all."

Darragh grunted his skepticism, but didn't press her as he bustled about their kitchen making her a cup of tea and a sturdy repast of crusty bread, early vegetables slathered in a savory sauce, and a hunk of spiced cheese. Aubria devoured everything he put in front of her as he chatted about the other parts of her night—had any scandal taken place, who had been the first couple to wander away from the bonfire, who had had the best and the worst blossoms in their crown—and then finally she went to her bedroom to change into something suitable for the rest of her day. It had been mid-afternoon by the time she'd returned home, her walk slowed by her weariness and sore feet, but regardless of her fatigue there were still chores to be attended to and orchard work to be done. Darragh himself had a village meeting in town to discuss the distribution of one of the crops, but he'd waited for her return before setting out.

Leaving her door open just a crack, Aubria hurried to tuck the potion and the parchment into her underthings basket before tossing the stained dress out to her father for him to tend to. What was left of the crown followed, clattering to the ground and spilling the last of the dying and dead blossoms everywhere. She heard her father catch the slippers as she tossed those out next.

"Your necklace?" Darragh asked on his way out with her Queen's Night things. Aubria hesitated before she answered, struggling to shove her arms through the sleeves of her dress.

"Lost to the orchard."

So Aubria had not become an object of ridicule and scorn because no one had noticed her solitary disappearance from the bonfire after all. Except for Lane, of course, and he would be the last person to tell tales.

The next couple of days passed in their normal pattern. Business went on as usual, the orchard crops were cultivated and prepared for harvest, and an early crop of sweetwillow bulbs—a large citrus fruit with a green rind that tasted pleasantly bitter and eased numerous aches and pains—had a profitable harvest. Aubria, knowing her duty to her friend and in agony over keeping such an important secret, contrived for Cerise, Viola, and herself to be put in charge of nesting the best fruit into wooden crates for shipment into Oseren and beyond to the rest of the Lyrassan.

But when she was with them, with laughing Cerise who juggled the bruised and therefore less saleable fruit with surprising adeptness, and purposeful Viola who always filled her quota more efficiently than anyone, Aubria found her tongue had tied itself into a knot. At one point, when Cerise had left to answer the call of nature and left her alone with Viola, she tried to speak then...

"What is it?" Viola had replied kindly to Aubria's rushed explanation that she had something to tell her. "Goddess, you're white as a sheet. Are you all right? Do you need some water?"

...and Aubria couldn't find the words to tell her about what had happened. It would be like dumping a bagful of kittens in the river to drown, or at least it felt that way.

Besides, Viola seemed happy enough, and maybe Merek's assault had been the error of a man too deep in his cups. He visited Viola when Nathan came to visit Cerise, sober and as charming as could be. He didn't look at Aubria once, not even when Lane came along for his job of carting fruit into the great hall of the village for everyone to attend to in one place.

With all of her best friends together, Aubria couldn't help but feel blessed in some way and wicked for questioning her lot, but the monotonous labor left her mind free to wander. She held her silence and kept her head down as she worked, waiting for the time when she could perform her ritual.

Finally, it came.

"Are you sure you're all right?" Darragh Haight asked as he lingered in the doorway of their cottage. "I know you sometimes want the cottage to yourself, but you've been...different, lately. I don't have to stay with the Erdenweds tonight if you would rather I didn't."

"Go," Aubria insisted; it was a balmy spring night, unusually perfect for the early weeks of April, and part of her looked forward to completing her ritual outdoors rather than inside. "You worry too much."

He accepted her dismissal, and she tucked her trembling hands into the pockets of her tatty but clean apron as she watched him disappear down the path into the village. The sun had sunk lower into the sky in a memorable performance of dusky color and shadow, but her father would reach the Erdenwed's cottage in good time if he kept to the brisk pace he'd set out with. She wouldn't have to worry about him reading alone or smoking on the front step as was his wont.

For now, she had preparations to make.

Aubria heated a sufficient quantity of hot water and washed as much of herself as she could reach in the silent sanctuary of her kitchen. She hadn't bothered to pull the faded curtains closed, since the Haight residence rested on the wilder outskirts of Loracre. Though candles were expensive elsewhere, the two villages managed a great quantity of bees as well as their orchard, and beeswax candles of all colors weren't too precious in price. She'd chosen blue for truth, red for spiritual connection, and gray for balance for her ritual, and their light danced all over the cottage and created a play of shadows on the walls as she prepared herself.

After washing, she changed into her nightdress and unwound her customary braid so the cornsilk glory of her hair fell about her shoulders and down her back. Terran's warnings and the instructions of the ritual wheeled through her thoughts, since she'd memorized the contents of the parchment. Still, for caution's sake, she'd set the parchment and the potion on the kitchen table. A spot of blue wax dotted the corner; she scratched it off before reading the words aloud.

"If your heart is uncertain, if the truth eludes you at every turn, if your path ahead seems enshrouded by uncertainty and doubt, there are forces in the world which may help set your feet on the path of your heart. On the night you wish to divine both your heart's desire and the truth of your path, you may call for Veritas Daemonae *in your time of need. Below you will find the words you seek to summon the being of truth. So long as you follow the instructions, the creature will*

neither lie to you nor lead you astray," she read, shivering as she understood almost for the first time that playing with unseen forces could prove very dangerous indeed.

She hesitated one last time, rolling the small bottle of Terran's potion back and forth across the surface of the table as her brow furrowed in thought. In her mind's eye she saw her certain future laid out for her: she'd go from being Darragh Haight's beloved daughter to Lane's adored wife. She'd work in the orchard for the rest of her life, birth many children, and grow old in the company of her friends and loved ones as season after season passed. No one would love her like Lane, and there were worse things than living happily in a close community…

Uncapping the bottle, Aubria downed the potion in a gulp or two and quieted the racing of her heart as best she could as her toes curled in their deerskin slippers. A dribble of the tangy liquid traced a path down her chin from the corner of her mouth, and she wiped it away with a sleeve that stained the same curious shade of ocher as the potion.

Aubria marveled at the quick effects of the concoction as she jumped to her feet with graceful swiftness. Both more aware and less aware of her body thanks to the hypnotic effects of the concoction, her muscles felt firm and strong…though her skin tingled all over as if bathed in fresh snow and warmed by hearth fire at the same time. She stood still for a moment, letting her neck loll slightly as she tipped her head back, but then she remembered what she'd been about: the ritual.

Aubria picked up the blue candle in its brass holder and murmured the starting words of the ritual: *"Veritas Daemonae,* I call to you for aid. I call to you from the earth, with my human heart and my human spirit, for I seek the truth."

Holding the candle watchfully, Aubria began her slow procession through the rest of her home, speaking more of her lines from the ritual parchment as she blew out all of the candles one by one. "The truth I seek is about my path in this life. The truth I seek is about myself. The truth I seek is my heart's desire. The truth I seek lies within my human heart and within my human spirit."

The words rang true, true in the sense that she wasn't speaking just to herself or to an empty house, but to some *other* she hoped to greet before the night's end. Aubria passed through her house once so she could blow out her colorful candles, and once again when only the taper she held bore light. Finished, she paused in front of her bedroom mirror. Facing herself, she studied her pale skin, the shadows behind her, and the huge, dilated pupils of her eyes. A cheeky smile fluttered at her mouth: she had to admit that she looked a little ridiculous with the potion smeared against her face and with her hair charged with static. Then the solemn spirit of the moment recaptured her as she met her own eyes and blew out the final candle with a puff of breath.

"The truth I seek lies in you, *Veritas*, and I seek you for an answer."

Though Aubria knew her cottage well, she couldn't help but feel fear as she forced herself to walk through the rest of her home that now lay fully in darkness. No moon peeped through the windows, and it felt like hours of pent-up breath and an unsteady, thumping heart before she reached the kitchen and her front door. Setting aside her quenched candle, Aubria took up a fresh, unlit taper as white as milk and unlocked the door.

The spring night had turned cool, but not disagreeable. The breeze nipped playfully at her cheeks, but she didn't feel any chill. As she bore her candle into the part of the orchard owned by the Haight family, she murmured the words of the ritual once more. Surprisingly, her eyes could see quite well in the dark. The leafy shapes of the trees above her swayed and danced in the gentle breeze, shedding blossoms of pink or white or yellow whirling to the ground.

Aubria traced a path down through the orchard, treading lightly as the candle she clutched with both hands cast strange shadows before and behind her. Beneath her ribs slithered her rational fears that she was making a mistake by tampering with the unknown. The hypnotic potion quieted the worst of her anxieties, but even someone as mundane as she could sense the approaching presence of that which she had summoned.

The orchard boasted few clearings, but after a few minutes of walking she reached a place where the trees didn't cluster so densely together like maidens locked into a stately promenade. Aubria stood in the center of her chosen spot and ran through the words of the ritual a final time. This time, she added the rest of the speech as she knelt on the ground and burrowed into the soft dirt with her fingers so she could nestle both the candle and its holder into the ground.

"I bind you for a time, *Veritas Daemonae,* until my questions are answered. After, I will set you free. As a sign of good will, I ask humbly that you grant the boon of my heart's desire this night. If you do not, I will still free you from your bindings and all will be well between us," she intoned, her voice unsteady as goose bumps prickled over the surface of her skin.

Only waiting remained. Aubria knelt on the ground, untroubled regarding the dirt that might get on her nightdress. Her joints felt peculiar and nerveless, and she forced herself to lay flat on the ground as the ritual had suggested on the back of the parchment. She tucked her dress around her legs, struggling to look presentable in her prone position, but she didn't expect her meticulous care for her appearance to aid her in this situation.

I wonder how the spirit will appear? Aubria thought as she stretched out her arms to either side and tried to take comfort from the cool earth beneath her back. She felt vulnerable lying on the ground, almost like a sacrificial offering ready for the taking by some eldritch god the people had forgotten to include in their seasonal rites. She had to turn her head to see where she'd nested her solitary candle, and she couldn't restrain an astonished intake of air as she saw the shadowed figure of a man standing right behind the candle.

"It has been many, many years since anyone has called on me," the spirit said first. She'd half-expected his voice to sound rasping, almost guttural. Yet he spoke in the smooth, careful tones of a skilled bard, and the shape she glimpsed in the shadows was that of a man.

Regardless, Aubria didn't know what to say to his admission. In spite of her calling up on him, in spite of her sense that she'd brushed against a real spirit with her ritual, she was surprised that someone had actually showed up.

She still lay prone on the mossy ground as the parchment she'd read had instructed her. The candlestick she'd burrowed part way into the ground so it wouldn't fall over and set the orchard ablaze flung its light over snatches of images that her dilated mind fixated on: the white of her arms cast out to the side where her sleeves had slipped back, the trail of her glossy hair fanned out on the ground, and the glimpse of the spirit's eyes, which were the only feature she could make out from the shadowed form.

Yellow gold blended with the angled irises of a cat, both human and not human at the same time. The strong scent of smoke, vervain, and the sweet decay of honeysuckles after their prime wafted her way as the candle guttered once, the scent heady and almost as befuddling as the potion.

"Welcome, spirit," Aubria huffed as suddenly all the air returned to her lungs. Spirits could be a particularly touchy lot, she'd been told by superstitious villagers and Loracre's officious Guide of Rites, and forgetting her manners could have been a deadly mistake depending on whether she was talking to a plain spirit, one of the faerykind, or some sort of demon. "I thank you for your presence and the gift of truth."

She must have imagined she saw the demon roll his eyes. The formal air of ritual lingered in the air and reminded her of the seriousness of what she intended.

"What truth do you seek from me?" The demon asked, standing perfectly still behind the candle though the shadows wavered around him to conceal his other features. "You have summoned me in good faith, and I will grant both the truth you ask and one of your heart's desires in exchange for a truth you have lied about to another."

The request for an exchange was not unexpected: the parchment had told her to anticipate the demand. Aubria closed her eyes as she spoke the truth that was no less painful to give voice to though she had planned what she'd tell earlier.

"I do not think I can complete the handfasting wheel with my betrothed. I said yes at Yule, when he asked me to participate at his side. Yet...I believe I regret my choice." She kept her eyes closed for a moment longer, wincing as her throat tightened. He had demanded a truth from her, but that didn't necessarily mean he cared about her answer, only that it wasn't a lie. She wondered what would have happened had she risked deceit.

When she opened her eyes, the spirit no longer stood behind the candle. Instead, she could feel him on top of her, hovering over her body as he looked down at her. His feverish heat startled her, but the feline eyes, so much brighter from up close, held her temporarily spellbound.

"Very well. I will tell you your truth in turn and grant a desire of your heart," the demon said. The magic that surrounded him made Aubria feel like her whole body would crackle with electricity if anything touched it, and sure enough a static charge zipped through her bones as his hands—thankfully human instead of clawed or crafted from stone, though almost too warm to touch—gripped her wrists with surprising gentleness and pinned them to the ground above her head.

Is this part of the ritual? She frantically summoned the image of the parchment into her mind, running through what she'd read as the yellow eyes captivated her own; his body felt distinctly corporeal as he settled over her, but the shadows concealed all but his eyes and what she could feel of him from her perception. *Did I fail to bind him properly?*

"The truth you seek," the demon almost whispered in her ear as he dipped his head closer to hers, "is that you would rather have freedom than the life that has been chosen for you. You mourn the orchard, and you will mourn what you leave behind if you take the lesser known path, but nevertheless it is what you seek. Freedom, both to wander and to live."

"Freedom..." Aubria repeated, her thoughts wandering as the

spirit's lips touched her neck so briefly but so searingly she knew she hadn't dreamed the physical contact.

I thought he was a spirit...how can he feel so real? Oddly dreamy and grounded at the same time, she complied with the new development without struggling to free herself. His weight aroused rather than restricted, and against her better judgment she relaxed her limbs and listened to the sound of his voice with her eyes half-closed.

"You respect the lifestyle of those you have always known, and you resent anyone who mocks their choices. Yet you wish to be free to walk your own way, into the unknown."

"Mmm," Aubria conceded, unconcerned and unembarrassed regarding the state of her mind and body as the spirit left off pinning her wrists to the ground in favor of tracing the curved shape of her figure through her nightgown. Lane had touched her this way, once, but out of respect for her that was as far as he'd gone. The spirit had no such qualms, and as those warm hands traced a path up her thighs as he slid her nightdress higher on her body, she found the sense of danger and the enjoyable fire in her core addictive.

"You don't struggle, and I don't hold you in place," he continued, "Do you know why?"

Aubria shook her head, tilting her head to the side as his lips brushed against her throat so lightly she could barely feel the touch. Perhaps the potion had given her temporary insanity, because she *should* have been struggling and screaming and doing everything she could to get away from the creature she'd summoned so naively. Yet she didn't want to, not even a little bit.

"You seek freedom, but the handfasting wheel has awakened a hunger within you. You would experience a taste of what lies between a man and a woman without the necessity of a lifelong binding...and without waiting for someone to take it from you by force," Veritas explained, nudging for her thighs to part with what she assumed was his knee.

Aubria was not so clouded that she couldn't tell if he'd bewitched her or not. The hard ground against her back felt sturdy enough, his touch that awakened a new fire under her skin didn't burn hot enough to char all of her sense away, and as his fingertips brushed against the undersides of her breasts she knew that if she gave in to any impulse it would be of her own free will.

Then she understood: this really *was* something she'd desired. Merek's attack had scared her, and Lane's expectation and fervor for the intimacy promised during the handfasting wheel, though not unkind, hadn't helped. She wished to give away her first night by her own choice, in her own time, and to someone who wouldn't expect things out of her that she wasn't ready to promise away.

Still…

"I didn't think this was part of the ritual," Aubria tried to protect herself from retribution by spellwork or curses one last time. "You have shared with me the requirements I asked of you, and I will not bind you to more than you are willing to commit."

The figure swathed in darkness leaned back, pausing as he studied her face with his impossible, inhuman eyes. She didn't know how she knew, because she still couldn't see his face, but she guessed that he might be smiling. His hands found the spot where he'd nudged her ample thighs apart, and this time she didn't panic when someone's fingers touched that which she'd forbidden for anyone else.

As if in confirmation of his humor, she heard him laugh in a huskier tone as he left a trail of scorching kisses down her body from her now bare shoulders where he'd pushed her nightgown aside, down to her breasts where the nightgown left most of that part of her body exposed, and then lower to her stomach. "My kind often finds humans irresistible, Aubria Haight, and I am no different. I am bound to give you what you have requested from me, but I cannot deny that for a human you are beautiful. This is no trial for me."

Aubria struggled to catch her breath or gather her thoughts into anything coherent, though for once such chaos brought her peace rather than unease. Only she and the spirit rendezvoused in the orchard on this bewitched night with the moon absent in the sky, and the scent of honeysuckle and vervain and tantalizing smoke in the air dazzled her senses along with the caress of the being she'd summoned.

So she surrendered, following his lead and arching her hips upward as he stroked her entrance with skill enough to make her arch her back from the intensity of her arousal.

It felt like an uneven exchange, him giving her pleasure she'd never experienced before without any reciprocation, and she couldn't help but wonder if she looked or sounded foolish as an involuntary sigh escaped her. Aubria closed her eyes, turning her head to the side as something built with a mighty pressure within her, building closer to release with every stroke of his hands.

He laid an unexpectedly tender hand on her cheek, though his guidance was firm as he made her face him. For whatever reason, he wanted her to look at him as he caressed her, and she complied with only the flush of her cheeks giving away her awkwardness. She wondered, briefly, why he wouldn't show his face. Was he ugly? Was he too fearsome to look upon?

No, she reassured herself. *All the tales say both demons and faerykind are beautiful beyond the comprehension of mortal sight. And after all, I didn't ask to see him, just for the truth.*

As if he'd followed the direction of her thoughts, the demon withdrew his hand and guided her legs a little wider apart as he positioned himself over her body. She felt something hard pressing at the opening of her womanhood, and a quiver of anticipation and fear made every hair on her body stand on end. He moved slowly, so as not to cause her pain, which surprised Aubria greatly even as she bit her lip to keep from crying out at the expected but no less agonizing discomfort. It wasn't supposed to hurt, she'd been told, if the man was doing his work well, but the tension of this moment had wound her muscles tighter than she'd anticipated.

He leaned closer where he balanced on top and inside of her and murmured something in a language she couldn't hope to understand. The pain faded after a short time, and she tested the feeling by rolling her hips from side to side. Though everything was surprising this night, she wondered why a spirit—demon or faerykind—would care whether or not he caused a mortal girl pain from her first coupling.

Then she could no longer wonder or think, since her body demanded more and more of the pleasure and movement he offered. She curled her arms and legs around the concealed but substantial body of the being she'd summoned as he led her to the brink and encouraged her to leap. They moved as if they'd always meant to be joined thus, and in the high of untamed elation Aubria rolled them both so she sat astride him. Bliss washed over her like a deluge, and beneath her she thought she imagined his sigh of satisfaction as he reversed their positions once more and obtained release with a few more thrusts.

Minutes or hours or centuries might have passed, but the night had aged by the time they finished. The spirit who'd proved himself man enough to give her such a gift lay on top of her as if to recover from the energy they'd expended. Aubria herself lay beneath him, utterly spent and languorous on the cool grass.

I never knew it could be like that, she thought, barely noticing as she traced the length of his shadowed spine with her fingertips.

Then his weight disappeared from on top of her, and Aubria felt more alone than she had in months. She sat up, sore both from the hardness of the ground as well as what they'd just done, but she had one last task to complete before she could officially end the ritual.

Though she couldn't see him, she sensed his presence as she gathered her thoughts enough to recall the goodbye words from the parchment. The potion was wearing off, and she could feel a headache coming on at her temples, but her skin felt like it was made of silk, and the lightness of her body almost made her smile.

"You have answered my call faithfully, and you have done me no harm. I release you, *Veritas Daemonae.* May all be well with you forevermore," she called into nothing.

This time the candle's flickering shadows, weaker now the red wax had almost melted away to a stub, revealed nothing but the trees and the wind that fluttered their branches. Around the patch of dirt she saw the tops of scarlet toadstools peeping in a ring up through the stirred up earth.

"Thank you," she whispered, though Veritas had already vanished into what was left of the night.

6

Aubria plunged her nightgown back into the wash bucket, scrubbing the blood staining it with vigor. She hadn't noticed when she'd walked back last night, due to both the darkness and the effects of the hypnotic potion wearing off, but the trickle of blood from her night of rituals and revelations had stained the garment. The blemish had refused all efforts to make it disappear, and it taunted her now as a reminder that what had taken place had most certainly *not* been a dream.

She was sore, too, which she'd expected though it made her no less uncomfortable. She'd stumbled up the steps leading to her door due to her spellbound clumsiness, so she'd also gained a bruise the size of a ripe peach on her shin to enhance the experience. Her grumpiness simmered high enough to chase her father from the house almost as soon as he'd returned, muttering about "lady days" and their various inconveniences.

Aubria huffed a few fallen strands of hair away from her forehead as she scrubbed. Most upsetting to her tired mind was the fact that the answers she'd received last night hadn't actually solved any of her problems. Knowing the peculiar nature of magic as any good villager in the enchanted orchard should, she hadn't expected something as fastidious as a summoning ritual to solve everything at once. Whatever else had taken place, whatever else she'd decided to do with a creature whose face she hadn't even seen, she had received some resolution after all.

Aubria wanted freedom, and she wanted to know she could take another path from the one laid out for her. The world was a wide unknown stretching out into forever, but her recent days had awoken such hunger within her to see and experience *more* than her beloved orchard. Now that she knew the nature of her truth, she knew she had to end her relationship with Lane. How could she lead him on and make him go through the handfasting wheel with someone who couldn't give him the contentment in life he deserved?

She'd curled up under her bed quilt and wept when she'd realized what she had to do.

This is what I asked to know, she reminded herself as she pictured Lane's crestfallen face when she informed him that her heart had changed its course. *But knowing what I want doesn't make this any easier.*

The being she mentally referred to as simply Veritas had awoken within her a desire to share the truth. But there was one person she wanted to tell what she'd learned: Terran Caird, the stranger she'd found the courage to tell her secrets to.

With a weary sigh, she leaned back in her kitchen chair and stretched her arms over her head to work out the kinks in her spine from hunching over the scrub bucket. She wouldn't have to thank Terran, because he hadn't exactly given her a gift: Aubria was sure that he would not forget their bargain, and part of her expected him to appear at the Haight cottage any day now to demand a mysterious price that would undoubtedly be something she didn't want to do.

What would he say? She wondered. *He'd probably claim to have predicted what I wanted all along, though I wasn't ready to know that myself yet. Insufferable.*

What she'd done had been wrong because formally she was still with Lane. The fact that she'd had an otherworldly encounter couldn't excuse that, though he didn't know of it and hopefully never would.

This was information she wouldn't share with Terran or anyone else in her life. To him she was already a thief and a fool. Her cheeks heated as she imagined the scornful look he'd give her if he knew what she'd done, his frown as stark as the intricate tattoo that had captured her attention the first time they'd met.

A knock on window made her look up, and she almost kicked over the bucket of soapy water when she saw Lane wave at her from the other side.

"What are you doing here? I thought you were going with the group who was taking the crops into the city," Aubria asked him once he let himself in at her nod.

"We're not leaving until tomorrow dawn. Your father said you were under the weather, so I came to see you" Lane said, taking a seat at the kitchen table as if he belonged there. He'd said before that he loved to watch her putter about the kitchen, baking or washing vegetables from the garden or brewing a batch of lavender milk tea, and she could feel the weight of his gaze resting heavy on her back as she shoved the nightgown deeper into the bucket of sudsy water so he wouldn't see the stain.

"How kind," she chirped, her voice far too high-pitched as the empty greeting pinched free from the rest of the words she had to say like a segment of dough torn from the whole. "I'm fine though, really. Both of you worry too much."

"I'm not worried," Lane insisted, smiling as he gestured for her to come to him; when she'd mutely moved closer, he took her soap reddened hands that she'd dried on her apron in his own and kissed the tops of each. "You're strong, Aubria, and you work too hard. You've the right to enjoy a day or two of rest."

With him looking up at her, his handsome face and sky blue eyes and the sizeable nose she'd kissed the few times he'd been annoyed with her, she couldn't hold back any longer. The weight of her responsibility ached in her chest.

I'm sorry…but I just don't love you enough.

"I can't marry you!" Aubria burst out the news in one of the worst ways possible, unable to stem the tide of truth. Horrified, she tore her hands from his grip, lifting them to cover her face so she wouldn't have to see his reaction. Yet she had already seen his dazed look, as if she'd rolled a boulder down a mountain to land directly on top of him.

"What?" he asked, sounding as stunned as she'd expected.

"I...I've needed to say this for a while, though I didn't know it for sure until recently," she stuttered through the woeful beginnings of an explanation, lowering her hands from her face so she could see him. The least she could do was look him in the face as she tore his heart from his chest.

"Aubria?" Lane said her name with a poignant note of confusion. "What are you talking about?"

"I love you, Lane," she started, her voice breaking. "I love you, but not as much as you love me. I don't love you enough to commit to a life I...I'm not sure I want. I don't know what the future holds for me, and I don't even know how to find what I'm looking for, but I know—"

"It's not me you want," Lane finished for her softly. They'd been friends before they'd turned to lovers, and it had been their habit in the past to guess each other's thoughts and finish each other's sentences. "You're ending our betrothal?"

There was no going back after she answered him. "I am."

"You're ending our betrothal, after years of planning the future we were supposed to share together—" Lane cut himself off as his voice cracked; she had seen him weep only once before in her lifetime, and the sight of tears clouding his eyes now made grief clench her throat up tight. "You're leaving me because you want something more than being a landholder's wife?"

He did not dishonor either of them by asking if she had another lover or if she was leaving him for financial reasons or anything else superficial. Their relationship had meant more to both of them than that, and in many ways it still did. She couldn't explain anything else, however, since she didn't hold the key to those answers herself. So she only nodded, her own tears spilling down her cheeks as she clenched and unclenched her hands into her apron almost hard enough to tamper with her circulation.

"I can't change your mind? There's nothing I can do to...to win your heart back?" Lane asked her, rising to his feet and looking down at her.

I wish I could, she thought, *but that wouldn't be fair to either of us.*

"I'm deeply sorry, Lane. I wish I could explain better, almost as much as I wish I didn't feel this way, but..." She couldn't think of anything else to say, so she didn't. Aubria couldn't see much past her tears, but she forced her spine to remain straight so she could say in the future that their parting was honorable and with dignity intact on both sides.

Lane didn't speak for several minutes, so neither did she. They had nothing to say, and yet there was more she wished she could tell him. *I love you* and *I'm sorry* could only be voiced so many times before all meaning floated away like dandelion seeds in the wind.

"I love you. I don't understand why you're doing this to us, but...I wish you happiness, Gooseberry. I really do," he told her at last, using the nickname he'd addressed her by when they were children. "I hope you find exactly what you're looking for, however long that might take."

He approached her, scooping her smaller body into an embrace tight enough to add depth to the truth he'd spoken. She looked up at him, biting her lip to keep her weeping quiet for a few more moments, and then he kissed her. He tasted like himself, as familiar as the cottage they stood in, but she couldn't miss the new savor of regret as what could only be their tears mingled to add salt to the usual sweetness.

Lane loves Aubria. The thought she had once consoled herself with, the three words that had become her mantra and set her on top of the world when everything about being a grown-up had been new and exciting and Lane was the only thing she wanted...they mocked her now, breaking her heart for the first time as Lane turned his back on her and exited her cottage with the grace of a good man.

How can every single decision I make be the wrong one? Aubria wondered, torn apart by guilt; the sensation felt oddly physical as well as emotional, as if her ribs were snapping inwards to pierce her lungs and her heart.

She crumpled into the chair he'd vacated, leaning forward until her forehead rested on the smooth wooden surface of the kitchen table. Part of her wanted to take it all back, and this part hurt the most because she knew she could. If she hurried, she could throw her door open and race down the path until she caught up to him, throwing herself into his arms and saying it had all been a mistake…that she still loved him and wanted to be his wife forever and ever.

I'm sorry, she sent the thought his way, knowing that he wouldn't welcome the words if she spoke them aloud just like she knew she couldn't follow him back to the village. *I wish I could love you the way you deserve.*

Alone in her cottage, Aubria sobbed into her apron as she mourned the loss of what could have been, and the loss of someone who had loved her with all of his heart.

A week after Lane had departed for Oseren to delivering orchard goods, Aubria found more to distract her than she'd imagined. The villagers of Loracre awoke to the destruction of one of their finest crops. No one could remember a time when such wanton destruction had taken place, when neither storm nor war nor orchard blight had taken trees in the past and reduced them to kindling.

Aubria strolled among the wreckage with the rest of the bewildered townspeople who made their living from tending the trees. Ruin surrounded her: the harvest that had been destroyed had been a particularly promising batch of thornbells, whose properties made for an excellent antidote to the sort of diseases people living together in close quarters often came down with.

What happened here? She wondered as she stooped to pick up half of one of the deep purple, heavily thorned shells of the fallen thornbells. *It didn't storm last night, not a drop of rain.*

Likewise befuddled, most of the village wandered through the scarred trees and naked stumps in a daze. It was one thing to maliciously ruin a healthy crop, for the trees would still produce the next year and the next. But many of the trees, tall and slender like birches, had been felled by some craven axe. Or, not felled, Aubria observed with the critical eye of someone who'd been born in the orchard and had been raised to care for the land. Some trees had been felled normally, but many had been torn from the ground as if a great beast had rampaged through the peaceful grove intent on obliterating the greenery.

Along with the tragedy, however, she had other things to worry about. Cerise and Viola had finally tracked her down after her personally enforced week of solitude at home, and she'd been forced to divulge to them the details of her failed betrothal.

"How *could* you?" Viola sighed, dabbing at her tears with her pristine though faded apron after Aubria had told them releasing Lane from his commitment to her. "He loves you so much! We've all seen it. There isn't a soul in town who doesn't aspire to share the type of love you both have. And you rejected him because you don't know what your future holds?"

"Had," Cerise corrected her, studying an ashamed Aubria with her prominent brows drawn down in concentration. "The love they *had*, Viola."

"I know I can't explain it," Aubria tried to vindicate herself to her friends. "I can't talk about it yet. Believe me or don't, but this whole affair has broken my heart as well. Lane is one of the most wonderful men in the world, but he's...not the one for me. I want him to find the one he's supposed to be with, some girl who will never have the kind of reservations I've had."

"You're right, that doesn't explain," Cerise admitted, crossing her arms in the manner of scolding schoolmistress. "But now we know why you've been so moody lately."

Aubria knew her well enough to surmise that Cerise wanted to be supportive, but she also had high standards, and when people in her life disappointed her she tended to complain first and ask questions later. Then again, Aubria had more she could have told them, but she refrained from doing so. It was unlikely they could help her figure out what she wanted her life to hold, since they had chosen orchard men for themselves. Until they were calm enough to understand her, there was really no point in explaining.

"Are you all right?" Viola asked kindly, throwing herself into Aubria's arms in a whole-hearted hug. "I can't pretend to understand your motives, but that must have been difficult for you. I know you loved him once, even if you don't think you do now."

Unable to speak, Aubria held her sweet friend for a brief moment before stepping back. She couldn't bear Viola's forgiving spirit now. The matter of what Merek had almost done marked her like a bruise that refused to fade, but was this the moment to speak? Besides, Viola and Merek were still betrothed, and she seemed happy aside from the news she'd just received. Was it Aubria's place to interfere?

When summoned by the man whose piece of the orchard had included the ravaged land, everyone had assembled at the new clearing in the portion of the orchard that had taken the brunt of the mysterious attack. Discussion regarding the destroyed crop and the cost the swathe of felled trees would come to for Loracre was well underway among the landholders and their workers. Aubria's father stood among them, though he mainly listened while the others argued.

"This awful disaster," the Guide of Rites started to say, speaking as leisurely as any man his age could be expected to talk, "could be a sign of disfavor from the gods. We would do well, I think, to offer them sweet incense and the leavings of this wounded harvest. Perhaps in their wisdom they will show us what must be done to ensure their future favor."

Knowing her father as she did, Aubria craned her head around the tall matron standing in front of her to see him. He was scowling, of course, as he always did when the Guide of Rites ventured his opinion towards anything that might matter. Nothing had ever been solved by the Guide's penchant to cause drama, Darragh had said, so it would be better if he weren't allowed to address the naturally superstitious village with his nonsense during times of crisis or conflict.

This time, though, Aubria heeded the words of the nameless Guide, staring with her hands resting over her churning stomach as she remembered everything she'd said or done during the illicit ritual she'd performed.

I cannot deny that for a mortal you are beautiful, Veritas had said to her. She had thought of those words more often than she wanted to admit, and she couldn't pretend that she didn't want to indulge in the experience again. Rituals were taboo, and she had committed a sin by engaging in practices forbidden for mortals. Darragh may have mocked anyone gullible enough to take the whispers of the Guide to heart, but he didn't know what she'd done.

Lost in her thoughts, Aubria let her friends squabble as she walked farther from the heart of the devastation, their noise washing over her ears and fading into nothing like the music of summer cicadas. She lifted the corners of her apron into a makeshift basket as she set to work, combing the ground for any whole thornbells to salvage for medicine the village might need once the wheel of the year again turned to winter. She'd planned to be alone with her thoughts today, to wallow in the heartbreak she'd inflicted on Lane and herself for their greater good, but the catastrophe had waylaid those plans.

The pickings were slim compared to the size the full crop might have been. Still, her apron was almost too full to carry by the time she started to make her way back to the huddle of people beginning the long task of tending to their damaged orchard. She'd wandered farther from anyone else than she'd realized, and the shade of the vandalized trees reminded her that the security she'd counted on her whole life held more secrets than she was ready to confront. The soft spring grass cushioned her steps, and the leaves of the few trees that had remained standing swayed in an invisible breeze.

This is no trial for me, Veritas had told her before they'd come together in the darkness. She'd felt the truth of him then, and known that she'd had nothing to fear: her decisions were hers to make. The heat of his presence had been as real as the warm blood that had dripped down her thighs afterwards. Losing her maidenhead had hurt, but the intoxicating release she'd obtained in the process had been worth all of it and more.

Now she couldn't halt visions of what she'd experienced from tantalizing her into daydreams when she should've been focused on household chores or the more important task of doing penance for what she'd done to Lane.

Aubria frowned, slowing to a standstill as her skin prickled into awareness, into the sense that someone she knew intimately stood beside her ready to take her hand at the slightest urge. Feeling more than a little ridiculous, she turned around in a slow circle, her fingertips still pinching the corners apron into a suitable basket. She saw no one, but the sense that she wasn't alone refused to depart.

Leave, her good sense told her, transforming her confusion into dread. *Get back to the group.*

"Aubria."

She jumped, startled into dropping the corners of her apron so all of the thornbells she'd gathered spilled to the ground with dull thumps. Her fright vanished once her mind reminded her that she knew this voice.

"How did you do that?" she questioned, irritated as she knelt on the ground, hiding her flaming cheeks with her intent focus on regaining her scattered harvest. Had she wanted the presence to be that of the spirit, even after her transgression may have caused the destruction of one of the orchard's finest crops? *Foolish.*

"Do what?" Terran dropped to his knees besides her, scooping the thornbells into his hands to drop them into her apron. She reached out for his wrists, a warning on her lips, but it was too late: several of the sharper thorns embedded themselves into his skin in the time it took for him to sweep the nuts into a pile on the ground. He cursed under his breath with imaginative foulness.

"Why would you do that? Thornbells have their name for a *reason*," she sighed. Giving up on the tiny crop, she took Terran's injured hands in her own to inspect the scope of the injury. Sucking in a breath, he attempted to pull away. Aubria glared at him and pinched an uninjured part of his wrist to make him unclench his fists.

"Forgive me for my lack of familiarity with every crop in this bizarre orchard," he snapped, wincing as she tugged the thorns out with her fingertips. She bit her lip in sympathy as the hooks at the ends of the barbs pulled extra skin from his hands with each tug.

"You're a Potioner and you've never heard of thornbells?" Aubria scoffed, not paying heed to what she'd said. She looked up when he didn't reply, and his chagrined expression confirmed her words. Learned as he was, as skilled and ingenious as he was with crafting potions enhanced with spellwork or ingredients unknown to most, he didn't know much about the produce Lyrassan's orchard gifted to the world.

"I'm a newcomer," he responded. "There's a lot I don't know about this place."

Since she didn't want to talk about why Terran had come to see her or what he wanted, Aubria took her time plucking the thorns from his flesh. He didn't complain further, nor did he ask any questions or protest when she delicately scooped up one of the fallen nuts and plucked several barbs from its skin as well.

"This will help. These are better for tending to a lingering cough or helping clear up a nasty chill, but thornbells cleanse wounds and soothe the bite of a sting almost as well," she explained while her fingertips found the seam of the now bare nut and split it open to reveal the soft, pungent meat nestled within. Using her smallest finger she scooped a goodly portion from the shell and spread it over the tiny holes in his skin. His palms were rough from work, though what a

Potioner would have to do for manual labor she couldn't guess, and it took a bit of rubbing to work the salve into the wounds.

"That does help," Terran said softly by way of thank you as he wiggled his fingers to test the feel of the natural salve more thoroughly. "How clever."

"Knowledge of herb lore isn't cleverness," she protested not meeting his eyes as he rose from his kneeling position to his feet. She did take the hand he offered, sticky thought it was from the thornbell salve, and allowed him to pull her to her feet. His skin felt as warm as always, and she flushed as she wondered if he would feel just as warm all over. He'd pulled her to his chest before he released her, and she'd felt the lean contours of his body a little better than she'd wanted to.

When he looked down at her with those orchard green eyes, why couldn't she hold onto a single thought worth having? They weren't friends, and he certainly couldn't respect her after all of the embarrassing mistakes she'd made in his company.

You are a foolish goose, Aubria Haight, she scolded herself as she took an extra step backwards. The reprimand embedded into her memory by way of tying an incident to the idea: she stumbled over the pile of thornbells behind her instead of accomplishing the graceful withdrawal she'd been hoping for. She glared at Terran as he looked away, hiding a smile.

"Aubria, where have you gone?" Cerise's voice echoed through the trees farther off. Aubria had gone away from the main scene of the devastation, and she and Terran stood under the shelter of different trees that were in flower.

"We still need to talk," Terran reminded her as she looked away from him, her messy hair almost slipping free of its braid as she turned.

Sighing, Aubria gestured for Terran to follow her back to the main group. "It'll have to be later."

One of the children shrieked as he pointed a grubby, dirt-stained finger at the imposing figure of the Potioner once the group they'd left behind spotted them. The father scowled at the brat, whapping the child upside the head with a broad hand as punishment for the outburst. Terran cut a memorable figure: tall and able-bodied, though not broad in the same way as the bear-like orchard men, and gifted with a strong gait that reminded anyone present that technically this man served the king with magic no one else could guess at or understand.

Beyond the initial line of people, Viola and Cerise awaited Aubria with gobstruck expressions that were identical in spirit if not in reality. When surprised, Cerise frowned, and when shocked, Viola's eyes bugged out in an almost but not quite unattractive manner. For lack of any other option, Aubria guided Terran through the throng of people to introduce her friends with an air of great reluctance.

"Cerise, Viola, this is the man who rescued me from the ruffians in Eldacre after Imbolc," she began, shoving the shell of the thornbell into her apron pocket. "Girls, meet Terran Caird, the Potioner for Eldacre."

"How very nice to meet you?" Viola phrased the greeting as a question, though she politely curtsied to the newcomer regardless of her confusion.

"Charmed," Cerise frowned at Terran, forgoing the curtsy in favor of a suspicious glare between him and Aubria.

"The same," Terran focused his attention on Aubria. One arched brow—the one partially covered by the tattoo—spoke his intention nonverbally: they both knew why he'd come, and though she had begun to trust him, she dreaded what he might demand from her as payment.

"Potioner?" Darragh had stepped away from the group of arguing landholders and the long winded Guide to check on his daughter. "The king's Potioner lives in Eldacre now?"

"I do, but I'm not here on any particular business," Terran held out a hand for Aubria's father to clasp in greeting, which Darragh did without much reservation; the thornbell salve had dried quickly, and would no longer be noticeable. "Terran Caird, at your service."

Though Loracre had an official governor as well as the Guide of

Rites, Darragh Haight was the wealthiest in the county, which made him the other unofficial leader or spokesperson for the village: he greeted Terran in that capacity, combining friendliness and reserve with expert skill. "And we at yours, Terran Caird. You've chosen your time to visit our humble town poorly, I'm afraid. We've only just begun to sort through this bizarre mess."

"I wasn't aware of your predicament, but since I'm here I'll offer my help," Terran said, shocking everyone, Aubria most of all. "I'm sure you already have a great deal of work on your hands tending the rest of your crops. Since I'm here I can join whoever plans to clear this mess away to replant the trees as soon as possible. I may have something available that will…encourage the damaged trees to heal, and any new seeds or saplings you plant to grow much more quickly."

The villagers chatted amongst themselves, for the most part sounding excited by the prospect of regaining what had been destroyed. Yet the naysayers were the loudest, and Viola's father the noisiest of all.

"What will it cost us for your magic, eh?" he bellowed, approaching Terran with a belligerent scowl and a haughty lift to his steps. "City folk offer naught for free."

Sizing the robust, thick-bearded man up, Terran settled into a grin that reminded Aubria of her own market day smile. "I think you'll find my prices more than fair. For the potions I will make for your orchard, every house in Loracre will pay me three silvers. This is because I will have to make large quantities of the potion, which has some rare ingredients it will take me a bit of time to come by. My labor you may have for free since I am here anyway and planned to stay the day."

It was a fair deal, Aubria had to admit, little though she knew about potions. And it would be worth it in the end, for their thornbell crop had been particularly promising.

"But why have you come to Loracre?" Cerise's mother, Mary Erdenwed, asked the Potioner; she'd come to stand on Darragh's left. "Surely you had business here that we can attend to. It was supposed to be our market day, after all."

Terran let his eyes betray him by sliding in Aubria's direction, a sly smile decorating his face before he answered. "That's exactly why I came here, Madam. During my first month in Eldacre, I met a lovely lass selling pies at our market, and I confess I've developed an addiction to the taste of gooseberries ever since. The ladies of Eldacre, helpful though they may be, lack the skill your Aubria seems to possess for… assembling ingredients."

Unimpressed by the flattery that had the rest of the women in the village cooing, Aubria glared at Terran with her arms crossed over her chest. *Does all of Loracre have to know my business?*

"Fair enough," Darragh laughed, giving his daughter the sort of a smile an irrationally proud father gives his offspring. "We have much work to discuss before we begin to clear away the wreckage, so Aubria can take you to our home for a short repast. We can haggle over your offer when you return. Aubria?"

"Of course, Da," she had no choice but to say when her father turned his unsuspecting gaze her way.

Manipulating a mild expression onto her face, Aubria waved for Terran to follow her lead as she set off for her cottage at a breakneck pace. She saw Cerise and Viola begin to follow her along with Terran, but she cast them a look to let them know she didn't require their company. She couldn't bear for them to know everything that she'd done lately, as they'd surely find out if they tagged along.

He kept up with her easily since his legs were a great deal longer than hers. Not wishing to humiliate herself before him again, Aubria forced herself into some semblance of calm before she addressed him.

"That was unnecessary," she hissed, pounding her fist into his shoulder once they'd left earshot of the villagers; of course, her intention to speak serenely wore off as soon as the words left her mouth. "The whole village doesn't need to know about our business, Potioner. You're not so clever that they won't figure out something happened between us if you keep giving them clues."

"Oh? I don't recall that being a stipulation in our arrangement," Terran grinned down at her, his white teeth gleaming; when Aubria's face reddened in anger, he laughed at her but nodded to show he'd obey. "What are you so worried about? Most fathers wouldn't send their daughters home with a stranger, Potioner or not. You're betrothed, and nearly above reproach."

The hot blood that had gathered so promptly in her cheeks drained away, along with anything left of the fight in her as she again pictured Lane's betrayed, heartbroken expression.

"I ended our betrothal," she admitted.

Terran paused, letting her walk ahead a few steps before catching up. Instead of offering empty comfort, or waffling something along the lines of a sympathetic apology or "cheer up, you'll find someone else soon," he merely waited for her to continue, giving her the chance to talk about what she'd done if she needed to. But there was nothing else to say, so she walked, her arms wrapped around herself as if to fight off a chill.

"Do you feel like you're more in control of your path now?" he asked, obviously referring to the ritual although he didn't mention it directly. No one else had asked her these questions, even her father, who'd expressed his disappointment and dismay when she'd told him about her dissolution of the betrothal.

She met the Potioner's eyes, his green so striking to her common brown. "It was the right decision. I have...regrets, but—"

"If the alternative to the decision is worse, a few regrets are a small price to pay," Terran cut her off, his voice as soft as the first time he'd reassured her, back when she'd been a crying, bruised mess on his examination table right after they'd met. "You'll be just fine, Aubria Haight."

Suddenly it didn't seem so awful that she was taking the Potioner to her cottage to share a slice of gooseberry pie.

7

Aubria nudged Toby forward, coaxing him around a fallen branch as thick as a small tree. All the animals of Loracre had displayed skittish, on edge behavior since the destruction of the thornbell crop. Hamish, their goat, had snapped at her this morning after she'd tugged the corner of her dress out of his teeth.

Since Toby knew the way into Eldacre, she allowed the reins to drop into her lap once they reached the path without the hindrance of fallen branches. Adjusting the basil green ribbon holding her new hat steady atop her unbraided hair, she brushed a few wispy tendrils of loose hair away from her forehead. Ordinarily for horseback riding she would have worn the leggings most orchard girls wore for rough work; no father wanted the young men peering up his daughter's skirts when everyone was supposed to be working, after all.

Terran had instructed her on her task in a few short sentences, though as always he kept most of the crucial information to himself and remained cryptic. She was to come to him two days after he'd shown up in Loracre's ruined orchard, dressed well and prepared to charm. No matter how she asked him, he wouldn't tell her anything else until she arrived on his doorstep at the appointed time.

Upon his demand to dress well, she'd donned her third best dress out of the five suitable garments she owned. The under dress was made of tan cloth that tapered at her waist to give emphasis to her figure without making the garment too tight for work. Over her shoulders and chest down to her waist lay the straps of a deep russet apron that covered the skirt of the garment in a double layer of fabric. It had been gathered and sewn into place here and there to add volume to the skirt as well as to display the lighter dress beneath the overskirt.

Aubria fretted over her appearance and the possibility of what Terran Caird would require of her once she arrived in his dwelling. She trusted his word that he wouldn't hurt or compromise her virtue—what was left of it—but further than that she had no idea what he was capable of. Her anxious fingers twisted Toby's reins into a knot and back again over and over until she reached the engraved wooden sign announcing that she'd arrived in Eldacre.

They say, she remembered the nasty rumor she'd heard the villagers mutter anew after letting it rest for years, *that the Potioner helped hasten the younger prince to his deathbed. They say that the Potioner's old title was the king's Poisoner. He could be living in luxury in the great keep, or in his tower in Oseren…why would he be here, scratching out a living among peasants, if he hadn't been exiled for his part in the younger prince's demise?*

She couldn't know if any part of the rumor was true, let alone the whole. Terran had his moods, she knew, usually triggered by questions about his past that he didn't wish to share. Aubria most of all had used up all of her daring by asking such questions, and the Potioner would not divulge his secrets to a village girl who had proved herself unwise on more than one occasion.

Only, for a few short moments, Terran had almost seemed like a friend. His reclusive personality fascinated her, especially since he knew how to charm just as well as she could on occasion. Over full plates of gooseberry pie they'd discussed other upcoming crops, since he'd shown interest in Loracre's bounty due to the effectiveness of the thornbell balm on his injured hands. He'd kept her distracted from her grief over what she'd had to do to Lane, if only for a few minutes, and that had been a gift she appreciated.

After tying Toby's reins to the helpful fence bordering the village to avoid the fee for the local stable, Aubria dismounted and gave him a few pats on his wide nose before striding into the village as if she'd lived there all of her life. Though the Potioner's house was a block or two away, she hoped she appeared more confident than she felt as she traversed the village with her hands resting lightly in her pockets. In her childhood days before city folk had begun bleeding into the orchard village they called "quaint," Eldacre villagers would have greeted her with a halloo or a smile, going so far as to offer her spare eggs or a small bag of ribbon and fabric scraps. The old tanner had even given her a packet of fine tobacco to take back to her father in years past. Now she passed the dwellings and shops and streets leading to the Potioner's door without a single glance her way, except from Eldacre girls her age who liked to scoff at her clothes as if they didn't wear much the same styles themselves.

Terran opened the door almost before she'd knocked, gesturing her inside. She hesitated before entering, doubts filling her mind, but she stepped over the threshold anyway. He ignored her as soon as she was inside, marching through the room to continue mixing something on his desk. A pungent scent filled the area, wafting around her and smelling of clary sage, sweetflag, and a sour odor that made her nose wrinkle.

"What is *that* supposed to be?" she asked before she remembered that she probably shouldn't ask questions. Terran half-turned her way, whisking something together in a bowl that appeared to be made of red marble.

"You'll find out soon enough," he said. Then he went right back to ignoring her, focusing intently on the concoction he stirred together in the polished bowl no one in the village would have been able to afford. Aubria thought she heard him murmuring over the contents, his voice low and musical, but try as she might she couldn't make out the words. She tried to move closer, thinking to study his process from over his shoulder, but he interrupted her sneaking.

"Does anyone know you're here?" he asked; thinking better of his question when she frowned anxiously, he rephrased. "That is to say, should I expect any interruptions from your friends or relatives this afternoon?"

"Not *here*, precisely, not with you," Aubria told him, withdrawing so he wouldn't guess her motive. "I had to invent a friend in Eldacre that I intended to visit after my chores. Well, not invent, because of course I used to have friends here. I just had to pretend that I was still welcome there."

"Are you not?" Terran asked, raising an eyebrow in an unspoken question along the lines of *what did you do now?*

"Loracre denizens aren't wholly welcome in Eldacre now that so many city folk journey here to see the tame parts of the orchard these days," Aubria shrugged. "My father was the only one I had to convince, and he rarely leaves Loracre."

"Oh," Terran frowned, as if he doubted her answer. She narrowed her eyes at him, resting her hands on her hips in a posture that defined womanly indignation.

"You thought I stole something else, didn't you?"

"No, of course not!" Terran protested, lifting his hand to cover his heart as if he was about to make a solemn vow. Yet his smirk was unmistakable, and she'd come to recognize that tone.

Choosing to ignore this, Aubria sighed and smoothed down the front of her dress and performed a little turn for his benefit so her long skirts swished about her ankles. "You told me I should dress well. Do you approve?"

Terran's face remained impassive, but he nodded in approval. Then, stepping forward, he reached out for her hat and tugged a stray clump of fallen leaves from the brim.

"You look adequate," he said by way of endorsement, though his lack of a smile made her own teasing one fade.

"Are you going to tell me why you told me to dress well? Are we meeting someone else?" she pressed for more information when he offered none. Terran shook his head, holding up a hand to stave off any more queries.

"Some of my clients like to keep their business with me extremely private, so we'll be meeting at my house in the old orchard before long. I assume you travelled here on horseback?"

"Y-Yes," Aubria stammered, taken aback. She'd imagined that the Potioner lived in Eldacre proper, but now that she thought about it, it made sense that someone as wealthy as the Potioner was rumored to be would live in more than these squashed together, smoky rooms.

It was Terran's turn to squint, but he may have been doing so because he'd stopped mixing his potion to pour it into a curious bottle as round as a tomato and about the same size. "You didn't think I lived *here*, did you?"

Once he dismissed her, Aubria hurried back to where she'd left Toby. She had no fear that anyone would have stolen him, for as snobbish as the Eldacre villagers were, they would not stoop to horse thievery or let anyone else visiting get away with that sort of crime. Nevertheless, she wanted to make sure she met the Potioner where he'd indicated before going to fetch his own mount from the local stable. Once she'd hopped into Toby's saddle with all the grace she could marshal for riding side saddle, she rode through the town square to find the Potioner waiting for her astride his own horse, a gray palfrey.

Aubria let him guide her along the less worn and obviously less well tended road through the orchard land of Eldacre, taking her southeast to where his home must rest. They rode side by side in silence for several minutes, with Terran lost in his thoughts and Aubria casting side glances his way almost every other second.

Finally, perhaps unable to bear her constant if silent speculation, he addressed her.

"You may ask your questions now, if you have them. There's a few miles to go yet."

The dam of inquisitiveness broke, and Aubria's questions sprung forth in a deluge. "If your client is so secretive, why are we meeting them in broad daylight?"

"That's an easy one," Terran smiled at her as he revealed some of the mystery. "This client is only hiding a secret from his wife. It takes a few days to travel here and back each way: he could tell his wife whatever he wanted about his business or visiting a friend, and she'd be none the wiser. I assume you have better questions?"

She did, of course. It took much of her willpower to refrain from bouncing in the saddle with the buoyancy of her questions, but she managed it well enough.

"What makes a potion...well, magical?" she asked, guiding Toby to ride a little closer to him so she could hear his answer better. "And why are you allowed to practice such things? Magic performed by anyone but the Guides is forbidden throughout the kingdom, I thought, and even that had better be paltry performance tricks to please the gods."

"The king and most of his councilors, whatever else can be said about them, know that there are things in this world that can't be explained. Spellcraft and the likes of what I do are forbidden to the common folk because tampering with the energies of the world and disrespect towards the beings who dwell unseen here can be disastrous for more than just the person involved," Terran explained, his manner patient though he nudged the sides of his palfrey with his heels to encourage a bit more haste. "My bloodline has aligned with these forces for many generations, and the magic we summon behaves better and more predictably for us that with others. Many in court suspected that I was part of the faerykind...or part demon. Yet they all came to me regardless, seeking help for their ailments or potions of strength or wits or secrecy. There are other wizards in court, the tame pets of King Barric...but none of them can do what I do."

"Are you?" Aubria asked, caught up with images of fine gentleman and ladies dripping in jewels and ornaments lowering themselves in obeisance to a person they deemed as less, or more, than simply human.

"Am I what?" Terran asked, though he smiled sideways in her direction as he forced her to ask the full question. He succeeded in making her feel silly, but she straightened her spine and refused to back down.

"Would you say that you *are* part faerykind, or part demon?" Aubria smiled back, attempting to keep the friendly energy of their journey at the forefront as she lowered her eyes in what she hoped was a coquettish manner. She'd never flirted with anyone besides Lane, and she couldn't figure out why she was bothering to try with the Potioner, but her body acted almost of its own accord and she had little say in her own methods to hold his attention.

Terran answered her question with one of his own again. "Would that change your opinion of me if I was? Would you flee screaming back to Loracre with tales of the wicked Potioner and his black magic?"

Aubria rolled her eyes, impatiently shaking her head as a breeze tugged at her hair; she regretted not braiding it. "I suppose that would depend on which one you were. The faerykind are rumored to be implacable, or so I've gathered from the old faerytales my grandmother used to tell. A demon you can bargain with."

Terran's teeth gleamed in the sun as he laughed. "That's true, in a sense. Skilled with magic though I may be, you have nothing to fear from me."

Aubria loathed herself initially for her superficial attraction to the Potioner, but she decided to cut herself some slack. Aside from her wandering thoughts, she hadn't failed to notice that he had not answered her question regarding the level of his humanity.

Faerykind or demon…which one? Or is it neither and he's something else entirely? He seems…more than just a wizard. More altogether.

They rode on in silence for a while, breaking it to make casual observations regarding the agreeable weather both villages had enjoyed of late, or to take note of a certain herb growing just off their path. Finally, though she sensed that they drew close to their destination, she asked one of the riskier questions that had been burning a hole in her gut almost since she'd met him.

"Why did you leave court? If you had the people of court at your beck and call all for the price of a few potions, why leave the palace for a life on the road or in peasant villages?"

Terran didn't answer her until the house—not as large as she had expected, though still bigger than any cottage in Loracre or Eldacre and with walls of stone instead of sturdy logs—came into view. He'd waited so long to speak that she wondered if he planned to answer at all, or if he'd even heard her. Aubria chose patience over repeating her question, letting him lead the way down the path to his house. He dismounted first, hopping nimbly down from his horse and striding to her and Toby. She concealed her surprise when he offered her his hand to assist her in dismounting as well, though they both knew she didn't require his help.

He answered her when she took his hand, looking into her face so intently that she paused, her fingers cool against his eternally warm skin.

"When it became clear that they thought *I* was the one at their beck and call, I took my leave of their never-ending politics," he explained, as he clasped her work-hardened, unladylike hand in his own and gestured for her to descend. "You don't know me, but I am a proud man. Though my services as Potioner can be bought, *I* cannot be purchased."

"That is admirable, in its own way," Aubria mused aloud, her hand falling limply to her side as Terran dropped it and moved to tie up their horses. She realized her mistake at once, because how could she finish her thought without sounding rude? *If that is your reason for leaving court, why not address the rumors that you had a hand in killing our younger prince with the truth? Why let the poisonous tale spread at all?*

Terran Caird had chased off ruffians assaulting a peasant girl with only a few words spoken in a mild voice. Surely he could quash any rumor he chose, if he wanted. Unless the rumor was true, and he'd been caught and exposed.

But why wouldn't the king execute him for murder if he was guilty? Aubria wondered, not realizing that she was staring doe-eyed at the Potioner with the puzzle turning over and over in her mind. Just when she thought he was willing to answer the majority of her questions, a greater number materialized.

Terran brought her back to the present after he'd finished his task, and she noticed belatedly that she'd been holding the hand he'd grasped to her chest and glaring into the horizon, completely lost in her thoughts while he'd done her work for her.

"I can practically hear your thoughts spinning, Aubria," he sighed, waving a hand in front of her face to get her attention. Laughing in sudden good spirits when she startled back to reality, he gestured for her to follow him. "I won't promise to tell you my story at any point, but even if I did, now isn't the time. My client should arrive soon."

Stretching once his back was turned to relieve the stiffness in her muscles from riding sidesaddle, Aubria followed him once some of the soreness faded. She had expected the Potioner to live in a house unlike any she'd yet seen, but as soon as she walked through the door she knew that her assumptions hadn't been correct. Several costly windows allowed light in from all sides, adorned on either side by dusky curtains that would be drawn closed at night. Where the light fell, it showed that every flat surface had been cleaned with precision in mind, however common such things as wooden furniture and worktables had to be. Though larger than other homes she'd seen, the overall design looked similar to most cottages with not too many frills or expensive pieces, and the spring daylight filtering through the windows gave a pleasant glow rather than creating a harsh glare.

"I never knew there was a house like this in the old orchard," Aubria took the measure of the place by strolling around the perimeter. "It makes sense to use the land that we've retired from growing for places like this. It's strange that I've never heard of this place before."

Terran peered out of one of the windows down the way they'd come, searching for the arrival of his mysterious client while she browsed. "I was told that this was supposed to be the governor's house, years ago when this portion of the orchard had been first retired. It had fallen into disrepair since the governor and his son made other plans, so I took it in hand and had it repaired. I knew that after my travels through Lyrassan that I would return, at least to be within a short journey to Oseren. I wanted somewhere secluded to stay."

The stone house was nothing but charming, but the fact remained that this was the Potioner's dwelling, and some oddities caught her eye before anything else. Color-coded cabinets comparable to the ones she'd seen in Terran's shop hung in a row on the wall farthest from the door, and the skillfully crafted chairs at the dining table and in front of a massive hearth almost her own size were covered in velvet cushions instead of faded quilts and poorly stuffed pillows. Though the house had a second level, the ground floor had an open style where every room fit into one, similar to most cottages minus the bedrooms. In the substantial kitchen she found a long worktable covered in stone where two cauldrons easily the size of Loracre's massive prized pumpkins rested upon it.

"Is this the potion for our damaged crop?" she asked Terran, almost as amazed at the size of the cauldrons as she had been at the unfussy elegance of his home.

The inhabitants of Loracre had finally come to a decision on what to do about the despoilment of one of their prized crops. To her father's chagrin, the Guide had come up with the most popular idea: sacrifice many of the remaining thornbells and other fruits pleasing to the old gods, and on Beltane the community would pay extra attention to the rites and leave no stone unturned when it came to pleasing the deities. Beltane, of course, was one of the most popular events on the wheel of the year, so few if any of the villagers would have protested in showing the devoutness of their spirits on that day.

Some common sense held out after all thanks to Darragh. The men of Loracre would all take part in a rotating schedule of keeping watch over the orchard until Beltane, when it would be the easiest to communicate with the Maiden and the Green Man.

"Yes, but it's not quite finished yet," he explained as he watched her.

Aubria went to the twin cauldrons, gingerly removing the lid of one so she could inspect the contents bubbling within. This potion had developed the sharp green scent of midsummer, tinged with the pleasant rot of mulch and a bittersweet smell that reminded her of honeypommes about to fall from their branches. The liquid churned sluggishly in the pot by some magical force, a fact made more unusual since it wasn't bubbling over a hearth.

"When will these potions be done?" she asked, replacing the lid and moving away to explore other interesting parts of his house that was at least double the size of her father's cottage. As in the Potioner's shop in Eldacre, she found a bookcase neatly stuffed with volumes new and old, and she ran her fingertips across the expensive bindings with a critical eye.

"I'll be bringing them into Loracre in a week or two. Potions that require so much power often take time," he explained, stepping into another room off of the kitchen so his voice carried from afar. If he said anything more she didn't hear it, for she had become totally absorbed in reading the titles of his many books.

On Faerykind...Curses of Old...Binding Lore...

"Are you interested in magic?" Terran's voice startled her, since he stood more closely behind her than she'd anticipated. He sounded less pleased with her than he had earlier, as if she'd done something wrong by noticing his books. Aubria shook her head as she abandoned her scrutiny of the books, pretending to not feel the ravening curiosity her hungry expression might have shown. Terran held two painted and etched glass cups in his hand, each delicately crafted item as expensive as one of his mixing bowls and frosty from cold in spite of the warm spring day. Each glass contained a pale orange liquid.

"No more interested than anyone invited into the Potioner's home, I'm sure." She took the proffered glass and lifted it to her lips for a sip. Her eyes locked with his as she nonverbally questioned whether or not the liquid had been tampered with.

Terran shook his head, smiling. "It's last season's peach cider. I purchased it when I first arrived in Eldacre. As I said before, you have nothing to fear from me, Aubria."

As if to reassure her for good, he reclaimed her glass and drank heartily from it and his own in a gesture of good faith. Satisfied, she indulged in a taste of the cider that made her eyes roll in pleasure at the familiar taste. It was the coldest drink she'd had in some time: no common cellar kept cider quite this cold.

A knock on the door reminded her that Terran had summoned her here for a reason, and she took the seat he gestured to as he moved to answer the door. The client entered with a flourish of his riding cloak, breezing past the Potioner as the rapid speech he had apparently composed on his ride in from the city spewed forth.

"I can't tell you, Potioner Caird, how pleased I am that you've agreed to work with me! Your prompt reply and assurance that I could count on you had me in such high spirits, I tell you, that it almost made the three day's ride from Oseren a joy! I simply grabbed my cloak and a basket of provisions—and your proper due, of course—once I received your note and set off to meet you at once! Now I'm here—but who is this? The Potioner's lady?"

Aubria blinked, stunned both by the speech and by the portliness of the client. He stared at her now, his round brown eyes oddly hopeful as he shrugged his travel-stained cloak into Terran's waiting hands to greet her. And greet her he did, striding forward on surprisingly swift feet to bow before her and seize her hand for a courtly kiss.

"This is my professional taster, Sir Bor. She'll be working with us today, as requested," Terran explained, more to her than to Sir Bor as he met her eye over the short statured build of the portly knight. This was similar to the lie he'd fed to Villor, and one he'd obviously intended for multiple use.

"Charmed! Charming!" Sir Bor exclaimed, leaping back and gazing at Aubria with new admiration. She ignored his attention, though she forced a smile onto her face to hide the sinking feeling in her stomach. Something had happened to her each time she'd tried a potion, and if Terran's payment was that he required her to be a taster, she'd do it…but she wished she wouldn't have any witnesses.

"—it's no shadow on your skills, none at all," Sir Bor was saying as he made himself comfortable in the kitchen chair Terran gestured for him to seat himself upon. "I wish to see how this potion will affect my lady wife with my own eyes. Unfaithful as she's been, I love the little sow and I wouldn't wish her any harm."

"No offense taken, Sir Bor," Terran assured his client as his Potioner's mask concealed his true expression and hid any sense of humor at the talkative man's expense. "I am pleased to help you with your dilemma."

"You want a potion for your wife because she's unfaithful to you, but you don't want her hurt?" Aubria asked, thoroughly confused. Terran gestured for her to come and stand beside him in the kitchen, and she lost her train of thought as he pulled the round potion bottle from his pocket with a flourish. He did give her a warning look once he was sure Sir Bor was occupied with guzzling the third glass of cider Terran had brought out from his cellar for his client's benefit.

"Good observation, m'lady!" Sir Bor toasted her with his almost empty cup. "My lady wife is beautiful, though a bit too plump for most men, and an accomplished young lady ten years my junior. I can forgive her wandering eyes, because I was just so myself at that age, and it's my duty as a husband to satisfy her needs. All I wish is for her to confess to me both her wrongdoing as well as the longings of her heart, that I may fulfill them…and I wouldn't say no to a little something else in the potion that would make her look on me with more favor."

"Couldn't you do that by listening to your wife a bit more attentively, or paying attention to her needs in…in the bedroom?" Aubria asked; amazement at her own daring and the unmaidenly question shortly followed. She looked down at the potion resting on the polished tabletop, self-consciously tucking her hair behind an ear.

"How astute! How shrewd!" Sir Bor exclaimed, slamming his glass down on the table so suddenly that she startled. "I commend you for your good taste, Potioner! Dear lady, listening would require that my wife speak to me at all. She has always been shy, you see, and we are only recently married this past season. If she could give me a chance that is all I would require. So, your Potioner and I have contrived a solution that should benefit everyone involved."

"And if it does not?" Aubria questioned, bold again. "What will you do if she still chooses another?"

Sir Bor's superb mustache wilted as he sighed with genuine sadness. "I will have to let her go, I suppose, though we will have to remain married for our political stations. But I love the little tart, and I only wish she would look my way and give our marriage a chance before she casts it off. I know it's poor taste to be in love with one's wife, but I must confess that I am."

Fair enough, Aubria soothed her conscience. Sir Bor may have been a loud, middle-aged knight obviously concerned with good company and better food, but she could sense that he had a kind heart. If the potion wouldn't hurt his wife or make her unable to exert her own will, well then…what was the harm?

"All has been prepared as you requested," Terran assured his client, giving Aubria a look that could have been approving or disappointed. "All that remains is for my assistant to test the potion. Forgive her her endless questions, Sir Bor. She likes to be thorough."

Then Sir Bor and Terran stared at her expectantly, so nothing remained except for her to drink the potion. Now that she knew the purpose of the potion, she couldn't help but regard with wary concern the circular bottle, knowing as she did what it had to do with love. If the ingredients touched by Potioner magic were supposed to make her both amorous and honest, what would she say? How would she act? Would she fall upon Sir Bor like a goose of a school girl intent on the latest boy who pulled her braid to show that he liked her?

Just get it over with, she encouraged herself. Wiping her sweaty hands on her skirts, she seized the bottle from the tabletop and uncapped it, bringing it to her lips to fulfill her bargain with Terran.

"Just a sip. We only need a minute or two, and Sir Bor will require the rest of the bottle," Terran interjected before she downed this bottle as she had his other potions. She nodded to show she'd understood, and drank the amount specified in one gulp.

As soon as she swallowed, Terran turned her to face him, looking into her eyes with his hands firmly on her shoulders. She didn't know what was happening or what he was doing, but the buzz of magic trickled through her veins when he spoke, and his pupils dilated as his voice commanded her. All she could see was his eyes, sucking her in as if they would devour her whole.

"For the duration of this potion, I bind you to Terran Caird. Reveal what you must," he ordered.

No! she exclaimed in horror, though not aloud. Through her confusion, Aubria realized deep down that due to what he'd done, and what he'd concealed from her until that moment, she was about to regret the next few minutes for a long, long time.

At first, she felt nothing except revulsion for the chalky texture and the bitter savor of the clary sage in the potion. She trembled when Terran released her shoulders, leaving her to step back and almost stumbling as her vision grew fuzzy. She'd imagined herself collapsing into unconsciousness, but then the fuzzy feeling increased to the warm numbness she associated with being both drunk and exhausted, which somehow she didn't mind at all.

Her limbs relaxed, tingling all over as a dreamy expression stole across her face. Terran absorbed her whole focus, and the light streaming in through the kitchen window haloed him like he was a spirit sent by a kindly god. She laughed, reaching up a hand to trace the pattern of his strange tattoo with her fingertips. So enamored was she by his beauty that she didn't mind when he gently grabbed her wrist and lowered it from his face.

"As you can see, Sir Bor, the potion works well. If your lady wife consumes the whole amount, you should have half a day of delighted honesty from her," Terran watched Aubria smile at him, though he addressed his words to his honored guest. His professional mask held steady when she moved closer to him and danced her fingertips over the skin of his bare forearm where he'd partially rolled up his black shirtsleeves.

Underneath the effects of the magic, far below her conscious thought, Aubria squirmed with embarrassment. The fresh potion brought out her hidden attraction to the Potioner—one she'd refused to acknowledge to herself and would have chosen to conceal from him and anyone else to the end of her days—and encouraged her to act like the type of ninny she and her friends had made mockery of back when the village girls were trying to seduce partners for the handfasting wheel and the life beyond it.

"A moment, if you will, to let me observe the affects of your work!" Sir Bor held up his hand, silencing Terran from further explanation as he focused his attention on Aubria. She scarcely noticed him, since the potion and her temporary binding with Terran had ensnared all of her interest, but she did spare the knight a glance when he flapped his hand in her direction.

"What do you think of the Potioner?" he asked, as delighted as if he was a child at Yule who had received the present he'd requested.

"Terran Caird?" Aubria giggled, swaying on her feet as she cocked a hip to the side and purred with more flirtatious energy than she'd ever rallied in her life. "I find him…enthralling. I am captivated, and I wonder what it would be like if he were entranced by me. I wonder many things about the Potioner, the least of which being how it might feel to be bedded by him."

Sir Bor roared with laughter and slapped his knee. Deep down, she felt sickness rising up from her core, the sickness of abject mortification along with the very real physical sensation that she was about to vomit. Behind her coy mask brought on by the affects of the potion she had assumed would be benign, she cringed and cringed again and wished to disappear from the face of the earth.

Finally, she leaned over and vomited her guts out right at the Potioner's feet in his lovely house.

With that, the single sip of potion faded almost completely from her system after another turn of dizziness that almost made her lose her balance. The gentleman proved useful, for once: Terran sidestepped the sick she'd left on the floor and guided her to one of his comfortable chairs while Sir Bor fussed around her, tugging an immaculate handkerchief from his tunic and offering it to her with a courteous bow. Once they were both sure she was well, the men turned back to their business.

Humiliated, Aubria managed to hold her tongue and act as if she hadn't mortified herself by sitting in the chair Terran had offered her and acting as if she were overcome by the aftereffects of the potion. Shame rapidly transformed to wrath, and once that dam burst she doubted she'd have much control over the effects.

"I am quite satisfied, Potioner Caird!" Sir Bor praised Terran, ignoring the fact that one of the unfortunate side-effects of the potion was a spot of vomiting. "Here is your payment in full, and it couldn't be more deserved! A potion, and a few words addressed to my dear lady, and I might gain what I seek at long last! I may have to spend the rest of the day in the good tavern of Eldacre, though…"

Covering her eyes with a hand as if she were about to swoon at any moment, Aubria listened to the Potioner close the deal with his client and usher him out of the door after Sir Bor had enthusiastically shaken his hand and thanked him for the potion.

She heard the door thump closed. As soon as she was sure he'd disappeared far enough down the path, Aubria planned to miraculously recover from her "swoon" and take her leave. Sir Bor needed time to pass further down the road, though, so she continued her ruse for a solid five minutes while Terran stood watch over her and shuffled his feet as if he didn't know what to do with her.

"Aubria," he began, saying her name like a statement. She told herself she wasn't waiting for him to continue, that she wasn't pricking up her ears to hear either an apology or a confession, but she couldn't quite fool herself.

He only said her name, however. For once, smooth-talking Terran Caird had no idea what to say to her.

When he said nothing else after her name, nothing else except a gruff clearing of his throat, she gave up her pretense at weakness and leapt to her feet. She was tempted to kick over the mop bucket on her way out, since it would serve him right for making her sick in the first place, but that wouldn't serve her purpose of acting like a haughty gentlewoman as she sashayed out the door like nothing in the world mattered to one as important as she. So Aubria snatched her hat from the table and made a beeline for the door, cramming said hat onto her head so the new ribbon wouldn't trail on the floor from her carrying it.

"Aubria, wait!" Terran reached the door first, blocking her way with a burly arm. She glared up at him, her cool façade falling away as she resisted the urge to slap him across the face. The impulse surprised her, but she supposed that getting angry was better than anything else she might have felt.

"I'm sorry, I really am! I didn't know the potion would make you sick, and it was not my intention—that is, I expected the effects to make you, er, *affectionate*, but not to the degree—" he stuttered, but at the sight of her fury enflamed face he paused, the apple of his throat bobbing as he swallowed.

"You knew what the potion did, but you decided not to warn me that you would bind it to you until Sir Bor was there and I had no choice. I owed you for the ritual and the potion you gave me, true, and I couldn't have refused whatever you requested. But you knew what your potion would do, and you not telling me proved you are not...not the gentleman I had come to believe you were, Terran Caird." Aubria let her words wash over him in a torrent of hurt dignity, shoving him out of the way so she could open the door. She didn't want to look at his face anymore, not for one more second: she'd seen the pity in his eyes after the potion had forced her to admit to her attraction to him, and she never wanted to see that again.

He followed her, his long strides easily catching up with her shorter ones as she tried to flee the scene. Aubria managed to reach the tree where she'd left Toby tied up before he caught her, shocking her again by seizing her arm and wrenching her around to face him. The movement threw her off balance, and she stumbled into him as he grabbed her other arm to steady her.

"Unhand me, you—" she shouted the beginnings of a protest, but then her whole body softened as he stared down at her with confusion. His green eyes widened, and his lips parted as if he was about to speak, but had forgotten what he'd meant to say. In her limited experience with Lane, this pose felt familiar: unintentionally, Terran held her against him as a lover would hold his companion.

She almost forgot to be angry, but he spoke again and reminded her why she'd been so upset.

"I'm not in the market for a relationship, Aubria, but I do—"

"Naturally. So why don't you let me go?" She saw the pity returning, something she wanted no part of. Wrenching herself away, she turned to swing herself into Toby's saddle, her skirts be damned.

"I do like you!" he confessed, his voice too loud for how close they were. Aubria paused, half swung over the saddle, caught in the indecision of whether or not it was worth it to fully dismount and hear him out. Curiosity won out in spite of her misgivings, and she dropped back to the ground with a sigh and faced him again.

"I'm not...I'm not looking for the same things. I have my work, I travel a great deal, and that kind of life isn't what I want anyone else to endure. But I value your friendship, as strangely as it may have come about, and I'd like your help with crafting potions. I thought it would be less offensive if I bound you to me for the few moments the potion held sway over your judgment. I didn't think you'd appreciate fawning over Sir Bor."

"My help?" Aubria wondered, ignoring the rest and feeling her flabbergasted eyebrows rising almost near her hairline as she crossed her arms over her chest. "What *for?*"

"You're smart, and creative, and you know a damn sight more about this orchard than I ever could. I don't just make silly potions for men like you've seen today, and since I no longer directly serve the king I *do* require a fair amount of coin from other sources to continue my work and purchase ingredients. I want to help people, and that's where the bulk of my time and research tends to fall. Not just medically, though I fancy I'm skilled enough to help more than I hurt."

This was the first time Aubria had seen the Potioner without his usual checks and guards in place. Haughty and arrogant he might have been, as someone with his wits and gift for magic had a small right to be, she knew that her anger with him had somehow reminded him that showing a bit of humanity now wouldn't hurt him.

"You could consult almost anyone here for orchard lore. Why me?" she asked for her final question, biting her lip as she realized too late that he might misconstrue her question as another leading one meant to discover if he had other feelings for her besides the admiration he'd already professed.

Terran cocked his head to the side, as if surprised she hadn't guessed. "Eldacre is full of people too proud to help their sister village in times of need, and those in Loracre have yet to trust me. Even if I found someone else, they would react with either astonishment or fear regarding what I do, and I wouldn't be able to get a sensible word out of them for months. You and I met under...unusual circumstances. Not once have you seemed too amazed or to afraid of what I do to speak plainly. You *did* steal from me, but I've chosen to trust that that's not your typical behavior."

"That almost sounds like you respect me a little," Aubria studied him, narrowing her eyes in doubt. "But your actions today showed that you think of me as merely an object that you can exploit. If that's the kind of help you expect from me, I don't think I'll be willing to work with you."

"I won't defend my actions to someone who's been...hurt by my choices, but I must tell you that I withheld information today to see if you'd be suited for the position," Terran explained, running a hand through his hair as he exhaled. "Sir Bor asked to see the potion tested on a lady, since he wanted to assure himself that his wife would not be hurt if he slipped the potion into her drink. I chose you because you owed me a favor, a favor I demanded because I wanted an excuse to see if you'd make a good fit for an assistant. Sir Bor's request seemed like as good an opportunity as any, and I didn't know how you—no. I just didn't think it through. I acted like you were a means to an end, instead of the actual goal, and for that I am sorry."

A sincere apology from the Potioner? Aubria marveled, suppressing any quick replies so she could make him squirm by her silence. *At least you are someone he values enough to apologize to.*

Then the full meaning of his speech struck her, and her enforced quietude ended without flourish.

"You want me to be your assistant? Not just a blind taster?" Aubria clarified. "What would that entail?"

"Nothing that would take you from your own life too often. We would start by you coming to my shop before or after you would usually travel here on market day, for example. I would teach you basic potion craft, and over time once you learned the basics you could help me improve what I already have. Eventually we would experiment with new blends," Terran said.

"That's all?"

"I haven't really given it much thought beyond that," he laughed, his discomfort showing as he made a self-mocking face and shifted his weight to his other foot. "I had no idea what you'd say about the idea, and though my instincts alerted me to the fact that you'd be good at this, I don't know too much about you. I'm loath to expect more from you than what I've already said, since you have your own life. But you...you have something a lot of people don't, and until I can define what that is I don't want to dismiss it."

Something within Aubria tingled at his last words, like the call of one bluebird answering another from the same nest. It tugged at her midsection, flaring like a candle that made her surroundings gleam temporarily brighter with the halo of ethereal spring.

You know more than most people in my life, she though, flipping through her mental tally of secrets, particularly the ones only he was aware of. *So much has changed since Sweetheart's Night, and he's the only one aware of most of the story...*

...all except for one secret.

Aubria imagined what it would be like to work with the Potioner. For the first time in ages, excitement for her future built within her. She wouldn't have to undertake a quest to break free of the mundane but honorable life as an orchard caretaker's wife, or at least not yet. Training with the Potioner would give her a valuable set of skills, even if she had no magic, and who knew what she could do with those one day. A burden lifted from her shoulders as she made her mind up.

"For this to work, we would need to be friends as well as partners. You told me you wanted to be friends before, but I clearly have to teach you how to treat someone you want to call friend," she declared, coming to a decision more quickly than either of them had expected; Terran had been studying a shrub on the ground behind her, but his eyes snapped back to attention as soon as she spoke. "I'll be your assistant and a good student when it comes to potion craft, but you will never use me again. As far as love or truth potions go, you can find someone else to taste those for your clients. We won't speak on what that potion made me say today ever again. Agreed?"

Aubria held out her hand for him to shake in agreement, her brows lifted expectantly and her lips pursed to hide any expression that could make him disregard the serious intent of her words. He didn't hesitate or pretend to deliberate over her conditions before he took the hand she offered and shook it gravely. She trembled when their skin touched, though not violently enough for him to notice. She didn't regret her decision, and hoped she never would, but the pact she'd made felt like it had far more import than a Potioner taking on a glorified apprentice.

"Excellent. I will see you next week, then," he said, releasing her and bowing as courteously as Sir Bor had, which was to say, with an overblown show of masculine dignity that shattered her severe expression for good.

"Enough! Here, I'll give you a tip so you know I'm serious," she drew his attention back to the matter at hand, capturing his interest at once. "Dear though they may be for the next few years, you need to purchase some dried thornbell and sprinkle a little into the potion you just made, if you ever have cause to prepare it again. It will help with the nausea, ideally, and settle the stomach if someone is foolish enough to give the potion to someone who hasn't taken a meal yet that day."

Wishing to leave on a good note and not trusting their usually volatile interactions enough to provide one, Aubria hopped into Toby's saddle with as much poise as possible. Terran untied him from the post they'd linked him to earlier, and she set off back down the path she'd came for the ride back to Loracre.

"It will be a pleasure working with you!" Terran called after her, laughing as she turned in the saddle to make a face at him.

I really think it might be, she agreed to herself, smiling a little under the brim of her sun hat.

8

Beltane

Beltane approached alongside the breathtaking beauty of spring, and Aubria watched the people of Loracre surrender to the call of the season as the days led them onward. During the day everyone worked in the orchard the same as always, though couples young and old often shirked their duties to wander off and kiss during a few stolen moments. An expectant mist seemed to hang over the village and the orchard itself, awakening the secret dreams and tangled longings of those who lived under its spell.

Now that Aubria knew more than she should about the rites couples would commence during the fire festival, she understood and shared in the rising tension making everyone wait with bated breath for a mysterious signal from the gods to commence the feral celebrations.

She had partaken in the holiday before, twining ribbon around the children's Maypole with her friends and indulging in far too many honeycakes slathered with hawthorn jam. Though she had rejected her betrothed, she felt the siren call of sensuality burning in her blood.

Unable to endure the strain, Aubria fled Loracre as often as she could in the span of days leading up to the blessed rites. Taking tasks like spreading mulch under the far trees of the orchard usually tended to by the men got her away for work times, and visiting Terran in Eldacre for her potion lessons afforded her a less frequent escape. Exhaustion from long periods of physical labor served as a good antidote for the reckless sensitivity that made her feel languorous and sensual. Visiting the Potioner engaged her mind in other tasks that required her alertness and focus so she had no time to listen to the demands of her youthful body.

Without questioning her frequent visits, he taught her common words of power and gemstone and herb lore that she wasn't aware of while she shared helpful information on how this or that ingredient from the orchard could provide a useful or fascinating effect. More importantly, he asked her none of the questions villagers in Loracre queued up to toss at her like participants throwing rotten fruit at a knave in the stocks. *How could you break Lane's heart? Was he unfaithful to you while he was in the city? But no, that's not our Lane…were you unfaithful to him? Do you love another?*

She had no answers she was willing to share, so she said nothing. Her own village began to look on her with puzzled disfavor that revealed itself in an unwillingness to engage with her as friend or acquaintance in their own market days and beyond.

Aubria noted that Lane avoided her and associated only with two or three of his loyal friends who spared time for him when they weren't giving into the spirit of the holiday and chasing their girls around the town or working. She didn't want to think about that, so she spent most of her days working as hard as she could to bring in the spring crops of various types of pears, cherries, and the golden honeypomme whose properties could either encourage deep sleep or sexual vigor depending on the level of ripeness.

Cerise and Viola tried over and over to talk to her about her troubles, and each time she tried and failed to tell them what she so desperately wanted to tell *somebody*. Eventually her distracted smiles and empty reassurances of her well-being pushed even her father away, and he stopped engaging her in conversation while she knitted new clothes for winter by their evening fire. Along with everything else, it grew more difficult to ignore his concerned and less than furtive glances as the nights passed.

She observed, too, that Terran wasn't always a shut-in dabbling in his research or magic. He spent as much time out of doors as in: riding his horse through the countryside looking for herbs she'd told him about and other interesting things to use in his potion craft, exploring the vast reaches of the orchard, and helping Eldacre workers with day to day duties if he desired physical activity. Aubria had yet to be obliged to journey to his house to find him, since he spent the majority of his time in town. As haughty as the Eldacre villagers were, and though they partook in the same Beltane rites as Loracre, their Guide of Rites had not stipulated that this year pass any differently than years before. The tangible energy running rampant in her own village was also present in its sister town, but its pull did not exert itself so strongly on her as when she was at home.

Beltane came in spite of her dread, and the day dawned with her still abed shivering with strange cold. This one day dawn meant the early hours of twilight: Beltane festivities carried on for a full night, and most if not all of the villagers finished their work and holiday preparations early so they could sleep the day away and rest up for the coming revelry.

The dream she'd awoken from lingered like a maid reluctant to bid farewell to an ardent suitor, and its images played again in her mind as she remembered them.

I was in the honeypomme orchard, in my Queen's Night dress, and he came to me through the trees haloed by moonlight. Aubria sat up in bed, touching her cold fingertips to her lips as she traced the pattern of events in her dream in the most logical order. *I couldn't see his face no matter how brightly the moon shone down on us. When he reached out to touch me, he felt familiar, but he wasn't who I thought he was. We lay under the trees, as we had before...*

Before? Shuddering, Aubria realized that she couldn't tell if it was Terran or Veritas that she'd dreamed of. In her half-awoken state, she allowed herself a brief moment of indulgence before she intended to slam the door on such troublesome thoughts and unquenchable desires. Veritas was a creature of the spirit world that she knew nothing about, though he had been nothing but kind to her. She had been told that supernatural beings tended to lie or take advantage of those who failed to set rigorous restrictions on summonings, but the energy she had sensed had felt…benevolent. Dangerous, yes, enough to have made her tremble with only her candle for light under the new moon as she waited for the spirit to reveal his presence. But still benevolent.

Weeks had passed since her encounter with him, weeks during which she hadn't conceived a half-breed child or suffered any supernatural events. Aside from her heartache over Lane and her confusion over what to do next now that she knew she wanted to experience whatever lay outside of the orchard, life had continued as normal. Aubria frowned, turning her head to squint out of her window into the approaching dusk.

Even if you wanted to summon him again, she chided herself, rubbing the sleep from her eyes with both hands more forcefully than necessary, *you can't. The potion is gone, and you destroyed the page like Terran told you to. Let it be.*

Sighing, Aubria swung her legs over the side of the bed to rise; then she paused, staring into the corner of her room. Her festival dress lay draped over her chair, the former purity of white dyed the scarlet many of her fellow maidens would don this evening. Yet the dress wasn't exactly the same as before, nor would it be like any of the dresses the others wore tonight: an expensive silver sash made of silk had been sewn around the bodice, the ribbon a costly but beautiful addition to the garment fitting for Beltane. At the bottom of the chair lay the cleaned leather slippers she'd worn for her Queen's Night, and these had been altered as well: someone had taken the care to stitch a pattern of curling vines and hawthorn berries into the leather, making even her shoes a fitting addition to the holiday.

Right away, Aubria guessed who had taken such care for her

apparel: Darragh had proved himself a quiet but attentive father over and over. Seeing her unhappiness of late, he'd taken extra care with her holiday apparel in an attempt to cheer her up. Fond gratitude for her remaining parent welled up within her chest, threatening to spill over, but she let it pass and rose from her bed. Taking the few steps to reach the pile of festival wear, Aubria picked up the dress and held it against her body, testing the look of it against her figure.

"Do you like it?" Darragh asked from the doorway; he rapped his knuckles against her partially open door in a polite knock. "I wasn't sure if you would care to wear it, but I didn't want you to do without."

"I love it, Da." Her confession was honest, since she actually did love the alterations he'd made and guessed that the dress would look better on her now than it had before. But since she spoke thoughtfully rather than effusively, he frowned.

"There's no call for you to wear anything seasonal, you know, since...well, there's no use sweetening the situation. You are no longer betrothed, and therefore you can wear whatever you like," Darragh had determined to be whatever his daughter needed him to be, but matters of the heart had eluded him multiple times over the years.

Aubria laid the dress gently over her unmade bed, smoothing out the crimson skirt and rubbing the edge of the silver ribbon between her fingers as she set it down. "I really do love it, though I wish you hadn't spent so much money on silver ribbon! That had to cost—"

"What it cost is none of your affair, Aubria, so bite your tongue," Darragh smiled, stepping fully into the room as she nodded at him once she could tear her eyes away from the lovely dress. *Her* lovely dress.

"Very well," she began a joke, but it died in her throat as she caught sight of the two objects her father held, one in each hand. In his left he held a handful of wisteria and hawthorn blossoms that every woman tonight would weave into her braids in preparation for the symbolic unbinding of the hair she would perform for her chosen lover as a sign of devotion. In his right he held a yellow arm band, as plain as the romantic combination of purple wisteria and red tinged hawthorn blooms was enticing.

Darragh cleared his throat, striding forward to deposit both the flowers and the arm band next to her dress as if they'd burdened him far more than they should have. "As a grown woman you have the right to choose how you wish to celebrate Beltane. I wasn't sure if you wanted to participate as an observer or if you wished to take your chances as a maiden of the May Queen's court, so I commissioned your friends to find you some flowers an observer's armband for you."

"What should I do?" The question, needy as it sounded, escaped her before she could stuff it back down. She was adult enough to know that no one could make her choices for her, nor could they suffer any consequences in her stead. But as she gazed down at the physical representations of her choices with Beltane's twilight sinking over the land, she wished briefly that her father could step in and solve all of her problems with his clearheaded foresight.

But Darragh had stepped out of the room, giving her the privacy she had nonverbally but no less strictly demanded over the past weeks.

Aubria dressed herself slowly, glancing more than once out of her window towards the fading light of day. She didn't have long before she'd be expected in the town square if she wished to join her friends and family for the official beginning of the holiday, yet she couldn't coax her fingers into dressing any faster or winding the straps of her dancing slippers around her ankles and calves with greater speed. She'd bathed right before she'd collapsed into bed after a long day of preparing a shipment of fruit for Oseren, and she noted the slight dampness of her silken hair as she began to weave it together in a wide braid that would drape over her shoulder almost down to her waist.

Her eyes fell on the flowers her father had set on her bed, mourning the beauty of the delicate wisteria blossoms mixed with flowers from the hawthorn trees she'd harvested from only yesterday. A sensory memory of her dream came back to her in a flash, the skin on her wrists prickling as if someone had kissed or nibbled the vulnerable surface. The feeling travelled from there to her neck, and she tilted her head to the side with half-closed eyes as she remembered what it had felt like to be touched that way.

Aubria took advantage of her right as a maiden who would partake as a solitary in the May Queen's court by snatching the vines up to weave into her braid. Once she'd done so, she immediately felt better, less unsure as she finished her preparations and snatched a pile of fresh mint leaves from a bowl on the kitchen table to chew on the way as an extra method of cleansing her teeth and her breath while she walked to Loracre proper. Pleasant nerves instead of anguished ones jangled happily within her stomach, and if she felt twitchy instead of simply expectant, then what of it? There would be plenty of dancing around the Goodly bonfire each villager would take fire home from to quell her restless energy.

Since Darragh had set off ahead of her to give her some privacy to prepare herself as well as make the decision for how she wanted to spend the evening, Aubria enjoyed her solitude and hummed a festive tune as she walked with her thumbs tucked into the pockets of her dress. Tonight of all nights she should be able to achieve a similar clarity of thought to what she had experienced while under the hypnotic potion's spell: that is, she like everyone else would actively be thinking of nothing, and perhaps her instincts would guide her into the right choices for once.

Once her meandering stride carried her to the edge of Loracre, evening had fallen, and without consciously meaning to she was swept up into the crowd of people making their way through the town to the special clearing surrounding by blessed hawthorn trees where the night's rituals would mainly take place. For those who did not wish to participate and who didn't want their children to observe the sacred rites between man and woman, a Maypole had been erected in the center of the town. Elderly couples and involved parents, though tempted by Beltane's seductive whispers, would remain behind to watch over the children as they danced around the Maypole in a juvenile display honoring the nature gods.

*It could just be me, but this Beltane feels…*different, *somehow,* Aubria reflected, looking around her as the procession to the edge of the village grew larger as they passed each house. As she had on Queen's Night, she observed young lads picking up their maidens to the tune of laughter, delighted shrieks, and lute music. The men wore shades of juniper green and hazelnut brown, honoring the Green Man, and the girls wore red or white to honor the May Queen. Instead of flowers in their hair, the lads wore crowns of greenery taken from bush or bramble and tied together. Wild as the energy in the air tasted to them, as desperately as they wished to cavort and dance under the gibbous moon, they wouldn't be free to act as they chose until the May Queen and the Green Man they would tonight call the Oak King led them to the hawthorn grove and performed the rituals according to what the Guide of Rites indicated.

No one accompanied Aubria specifically until she had traversed a path almost over the whole town, though a man running by with his arms full of empty wooden festival chalices tossed her a cup so she'd have somewhere to pour either the community wildflower mead or potent May cider. She thought she saw Cerise and Nathan racing with breakneck speed to the front of crowd, but given the fact that most people wore the same coloring and there were plenty of people who shared the Erdenwed's dusky skin tone, she couldn't have been sure. Though she searched, she spotted neither her father nor Lane, and even Viola and Merek couldn't be found.

Finally, she reached the edge of the town where the bulk of the crowd had gathered. Aubria already itched to be dancing, to spin again and again around the blessed bonfire until she no longer remembered her own name. But first came the official rites.

According to tradition, the young men and women separated by gender, with the maidens grouping towards the right and the men towards the left. Partners would find each other later to jump over the edge of the bonfire: that was the only way Beltane made itself part of the handfasting wheel, since the holiday in general was so conducive to couples' rites that no separate event had been needed. Aubria followed her fellow maidens' lead, though she knew due to her own choices that no specific man would be waiting anxiously to rejoin with her after their walk to the hawthorn grove.

An old crone the children of Loracre had delightedly nicknamed Grammy meandered through the crowd with a basket of individual copper bells tied to a single, faded ribbon. Every maiden and lad would take one of these, so the procession into the wood in the courts of the May Queen and Oak King would be joyous and musical. Aubria tied hers to her wrist, following the example of the girl nearest her so she would lose neither cup nor bell in the dancing procession into the orchard.

Once everything had been distributed by the crone, the group turned their eyes to the orchard to await the arrival of the Queen, her King, and the Guide of Rites. Aubria wondered without particularly caring who had been honored this year; before, she had used to dream that she and Lane would be chosen for the sacred rites. Anyone could have been considered for the role regardless of whether or not they were partaking in the handfasting wheel, and those chosen were not always part of the same couple. But the Guide was known to dislike her father for his outspoken disdain of superstition that he deemed harmful to the community, so as she'd grown older she'd guessed the honor would pass her by.

Though the crowd of revelers held their bells still for the moment, Aubria heard the distinct sound of two bells ringing in time with the steps of the May Queen. The bells would have been tied to her ankles so all could hear her approach, and the Green Man would carry his bells as he cavorted through the orchard with his lads.

Everyone seemed to be holding their breath as the May Queen emerged from the wood, coming forward on the side of her maidens. She wore a white mask over the upper half of her face, a white as pure as the moon and just as pale, and atop her head rested a crown of flowers sharing the same color. She wore a red dress like the other maidens, though much finer than theirs and embroidered over its entirety with a pattern of hawthorn blossoms and leaves. To complete the look she wore a cloak as white as her mask, a symbol of purity that she would forswear by the next morning.

"Greetings, my children!" she called according to tradition, her smile merry in spite of the mask concealing the rest of her face. From this distance and from so few words Aubria couldn't tell who had been chosen as Queen, but since she didn't immediately recognize the voice she decided that she didn't care.

"Greetings, Beltane Queen!" The maidens answered back, some laughingly falling into a curtsy. But the Queen held attention only for a moment, since farther to the right the Oak King emerged from his side of the orchard to greet the men. His dress was less remarkable, looking much like the plain green and brown garb of the village men, but he wore the traditional painted mask of leaves that signified his position in the rite. This mask covered his full face, making him look more the part of an eldritch figure than the Queen, and the crown atop his head was made of branches carved to resemble tall antlers.

The men howled like wolves as the Green Man bowed low before them in regal mockery that set the whole lot of them to laughing.

The Guide stepped forward once the two had greeted their charges, and without a word he gestured for everyone to follow him through the orchard. Aubria, following the herd, paused as she felt eyes upon her.

The mask of the Green Man was staring at her, an enigma in the half-light since she couldn't see his eyes or any feature that would signal to her who was playing the part of the Oak King. Aubria looked away as swiftly as she could, unsure why her doubts churned anew in her belly under his attention.

Tonight she didn't want to think, so she forced her unease out of her mind and grabbed the girl nearest to her for an impromptu twirling dance as they followed the Queen's steps. Happy enough to dance and be danced with, the maid started up a jolly tune sung slightly off key, and after a few lines the rest of the assembly joined in.

By the end of the third traditional song, everyone had reached the hawthorn grove. The grove was mostly forbidden to everyone not working to bring in those crops, but that made it a wonderful place for lovers to meet for secret trysts between events of the handfasting wheel or before they entered the season based rites. Though the fruiting trees were many and the crop sizeable every year, much of the land in this area was kept flat and clear for Beltane specifically. Large as the orchard was, and unexplored in some parts, the area left clear for the rites could have fit several cottages on purpose so no one in the village would ever be left out. More importantly, however vigorously the bonfire burned, the flames wouldn't spread to destroy the whole orchard.

Aubria had never come here with Lane, though he'd offered to bring her twice. So she looked around with interest, seeing the slope of the branches and the friendly blossoms in the new light of evening. That was the most she could see, however, since no fire except Beltane fire would be permitted here: dusk had rapidly disappeared into true night. Sanctioned torch bearers had walked around the periphery of the villagers to make sure no one stumbled or was left behind, but upon reaching their destination they capped their torches to quench their light.

Aubria found herself at the forefront of the crowd as they pressed against the edge of the unlit pyre. On either side of the bonfire, though far enough to leave an area for dancing, she spotted the feasting tables laden with bowls of peppered green beans, platters of bannock and honeycakes, plates full of rosemary seasoned pork, and mead and cider enough to lure everyone to drunkenness for days. Both the men and the women in the community had contributed work and ingredients for this delectable feast, and though there were many festivals throughout the wheel of the year, only at Beltane and Yule was such a bounty prepared.

The scent of the food enticed her, but she didn't focus on it. The royalty of Beltane was ascending a set of makeshift steps underneath the largest hawthorn tree so the whole crowd could see them launch the evening's merriment.

The Guide was the only one who still held a torch, since he had to make sure everyone could see the beginning of the rites take place. Before it was over he too would snuff it out so only the Goodly Fire lit by the Queen and the Green Man would remain. For the time being he jabbed the torch into a divot in the ground so it illuminated the three people on the platform.

"My children," the Guide began, holding his hands out to either side of him in broad gestures to the masked May Queen and her equally concealed lover, the Green Man. "My children, let us thank our great Mother for the bounty she has bestowed upon us! As we honor spring with the gifts of our labor, let us grant due honor to our Beltane Queen!"

"We honor her as we honor Maiden, Mother, and Crone!" Aubria intoned with those who surrounded her, closing her eyes as she gripped the empty cup in her hands and lifted it slightly in a prayerful manner. When she opened them, she saw that the Guide had taken the May Queen's delicate hand in his own, holding it aloft as his arms were aloft.

"My children, let us honor the Oak King, the Lord of the forest who protects us with strength, honor, and truth! Honor him at this turn in the wheel of the year, for he will satisfy our souls and protect us as the days pass," he continued, taking up the hand of this wheel's chosen Oak King and lifting it as well.

"Blessed be the Young God of the Wood," the villagers intoned faithfully, Aubria among them. The three of them—Queen, Guide, and King—made a vivid image under the shade of the huge king of the hawthorn trees.

"For bringing life to all we honor thee, O Gods of our world! We shall light this Goodly Fire as your faerykind children did in the days of ancients: the flames shall purify us, and the smoke remind us of your power. May our ritual display the depth of our loyalty, that you may keep our animals safe and strong. That you may keep our land safe and strong. That you may keep those who would protect them safe and strong. May the light and heat of this everlasting blaze bestow life and health on your children."

The Guide completed the honorary words and joined the hands of the May Queen and her King at the final word. Aubria watched as he snuffed the torch he'd held earlier and moved to stand in front of them, bowing low as he took up a fresh torch from the edge of the unlit pyre and offered it to the couple. She didn't know if the Guide had magic of his own or not, but she couldn't hide her gasp when they took up the torch with their joined hands and set it ablaze without tinder or any other movement.

As the light glinted against the Queen's auburn hair, she realized that Viola had been chosen for the Beltane honor. Aubria frantically rifled through her memories, trying to recall exactly when Viola had told her the Guide had chosen her for the rite. Try as she might, she couldn't remember the exact moment. With a stone sinking in her gut, Aubria squeezed the small bell in her hands almost hard enough to bend it: she had to conclude that Viola hadn't told her at all.

I'm not the only one keeping secrets, she frowned, resolving to treat her friends better in the coming days. There were some things she couldn't tell them…but as a friend she could show more attentiveness to the goings on of their lives.

The identity of the Green Man remained a mystery since it clearly wasn't Merek who wore the mask: Merek was both shorter and broader than the Oak King, and the crowned man didn't lurch with too enthusiastic and unfortunately all too common drunkenness like Merek did.

"Cast the torch into the heart of our bonfire, Lord and Lady, that the Goodly Fire might warm us through this hallowed night and the year beyond," the Guide intoned, bringing Aubria back to the moment as he stepped aside, though neither a clearly nervous Viola nor the man chosen for the place of honor in this rite waited for him to finish speaking. Hopping down from their makeshift dais, they carried the torch to the center of the round clearing and tossed it into the huge stack of wood prepared for this night.

With the bonfire lit, Beltane began. The couples that had waited with bated breath for the holiday to start let out an untamed cheer that reverberated through the whole orchard. The Oak King had married his lady in a celebrated union of earth and sky, and they would make a stately circle around the hawthorn Maypole while the young couples supped on dry bannock or honeycakes. No one would cosset themselves too heavily, however, for fear of ruining themselves for the night of dancing under the moon and stars and the watchful eyes of the gods.

Aubria planned to dance, and the band of rotating volunteer musicians rushed into a raucous tune that had her slippered feet tapping against the ground in perfect time. She didn't yet know exactly *what* kind of dancing she planned to partake in this evening, if any of the young men not yet betrothed would have her after what she'd done to Lane, but the prospect of regular dancing cheered her burdened heart and she smiled at anyone who looked her way.

Cerise and Nathan found her as she waited in line for the feasting table. They'd obviously indulged in some hawthorn wine already, since Aubria was able to note both their euphoria and the glazed sheen in their eyes, but there was no harm in that.

"I'm glad you decided to attend, Aubria," Cerise began, crumbling a spare crust of bannock in her hands without regard for the waste. "You've spent too much time away from us lately, and I miss you."

"Though it's not likely we'll see you much tonight after this!" Nathan cut in hurriedly, since he doubtless had other plans in mind besides lingering with the unfortunate girl who had foolishly turned down a perfectly good betrothal.

"Viola is the May Queen? How long has she known the Guide chose her?" Aubria asked; she had to repeat her questions, since Cerise made herself busy punishing Nathan's audacity with a flirty smack on the arm.

"She's known for a week. You would have known too, but you've been quite busy moping. She didn't want to tell you."

That's not true, Aubria wanted to protest, but she had to be honest with herself. *I've been quite busy nursing my loneliness as well. But I'd like to not be that person anymore, if you'd be so good as to stop frowning at me, Cerise.*

More than ever she wanted to be a better friend to the girls she'd grown up with and come to love as sisters. So she tried to lighten the mood, turning the topic to gossip as she toyed with the end of her long braid.

"Who is the Oak King? I know it's not proper for us to guess yet, but since we already know the Queen is Viola…"

"I wouldn't know. They don't tell maidens until after the night's over, usually," Cerise sighed; then, her clarity briefly returning, she narrowed her loam colored eyes at Aubria. "Even if I knew, I'm not sure I'd tell you. It's not fitting that you only seek my company when you want information. Someone who would do that isn't being a good friend."

With that, she grabbed an open-mouthed Nathan and flounced away, pulling him into an early round of dancing.

That, Aubria realized as she stared at her friend's back, *is something I'm going to have to address after tonight.*

Their little spat, mild as it was to outsiders, had attracted a certain amount of attention. Several people stared at Aubria, some with interest, some with pity. She ignored the attention, for she saw the Green Man's hidden face turned her way again, and she didn't look away when he stared.

As honored maiden the Queen would have many suitors who she could choose from this night, as her King would have many female admirers. Though betrothed, the place of honor that required each of them to dance with every man or woman present also freed them for one night from their promises to their chosen partner of the handfasting wheel so far. Aubria did not think herself so daring as to pursue the Green Man herself, but when she sensed his eyes on her she put a little more effort into the swaying of her hips as she took a walk around the food table and indulged in nothing but a single honeycake and a full cup of wildflower mead.

After she'd finished both, she got her wish: she had dancing enough to quench her thirst for activity for days. Though she was becoming known as Loracre's pariah, she did not lack for partners who were happy enough to frolic with her around the Goodly Fire.

Tonight was for her, and after she awoke in the grove after a night of revelry her problems would await her attention the same as always. She may not have been the May Queen, she may not have a betrothed or any idea what to do for her future…but tonight in the fire and the bewitching smoke of the burning remains of the fallen thornbell trees, she felt like a young goddess on the cusp of something phenomenal. Aubria would dance until the assembly dispersed with Beltane torches clutched in their grip to bring the Goodly Fire into their homes.

Does everyone feel this? she wondered as her latest partner lifted her high in the air in the spirit of one of the liveliest dances in the Beltane repertoire. She shrieked with laughter as the man holding her brought her down and dipped her body almost to the ground, giving her a cheeky kiss before he bowed and leapt away to find a new partner.

For the first time in hours Aubria found herself alone amongst the couples rotating in country dances around the bonfire. She'd danced with so many young scions of Loracre, each friendly and attentive in the way of people who'd grown up doing the same work and living similar lives, but none had chosen to stay with her for the duration of the evening. She looked around at all the whirling couples, noting that none had yet wandered away from the pyre to perform their private celebrations of the rite. They couldn't, not yet: the King had to dance with every maiden present, as the Queen had to dance with all the men, and only when the King chose his maid could the rest begin to leave the warmth of the fire for the delicious cool of the night.

As if he'd planned to wait for her to notice that he hadn't yet danced with her, Aubria felt a tap on her shoulder that made her turn to face whoever desired her attention. Sure enough, the Green Man in his enigmatic, expressionless mask stood awaiting her attention. She stifled a giggle as he bowed low to the ground with a jester's flourish, his mask still upturned so he could watch her reaction through the slits for the eyes. He held out his hand to her in courteous invitation to dance, and she took it without hesitation. He pulled her body into his as he rose to his full height, his hands tight on her waist as he lifted her into the air for the beginning of the wildest dance of the night.

A surge of delight mingled with the wildness in Aubria's veins as the musicians of the hour started up their jovial tune, and she fell into step with the Oak King as they maneuvered around the other dancing couples in the complicated steps of the Beltane reel. Whoever he was, he was an excellent dancer, and he anticipated her movements with greater skill than she had expected. Whenever he touched her a spark ignited under her skin like the fire they gamboled around, and over the course of the dance he spun her in closer and closer until, if it wasn't for the mask, they would have brushed lips several times. The song of the lute and the strings whirled in her head as many voices lifted into the night sky in joyous celebration, and her blood pounded in time with her feet's thumps against the ground.

Right when the dance was about to end, the Green Man swung her into his arms like a bride and leapt over the edge of the fire with a shout. Aubria, already warm from her rigorous dancing, felt her core heat when he landed back on the ground. The Oak King had chosen her for his Beltane lover, proving his intent to lead her into the orchard to perform the sacred rite of lovemaking as the nature gods had done to nurture the fertility of the earth in ages past.

The music faded into the background as the Oak King set Aubria upright on the ground and offered his hand to her again, this time with more solemnity now that she could have no doubts about his intentions. In her peripheral vision, she noticed eager couples laughing as they led each other deeper into the hawthorn grove and beyond where prying eyes wouldn't witness how they decided to celebrate the sacred night. But the Green Man was waiting, his hand outstretched, and Aubria had a choice to make.

Smiling in welcome, she took the hand he offered and allowed him to lead her away from the bonfire. If there were any eyes on her, the stain they left on her skin would wash away another time. Even Viola's, since she could practically feel the May Queen's judgment weighing on her as the Green Man's surrogate led her away to be ravished.

In the darkness Aubria tugged off his mask and leaned in so she could kiss him. His mouth was soft against hers, though unyielding in its intensity as he kissed her back. Excitement pooled in her stomach, travelling lower as her body remembered the pleasure she'd experienced the first time she'd danced this dance.

They couldn't stop once they'd started, and his hands drifted all over her body with unashamed hunger as they stumbled further into the orchard out of sight of the Goodly Fire. She gave in to her impulses, slipping her hands under his tunic to trail her fingers over his muscular chest. Her partner held her close, unwilling to let more than an inch of space separate them. She tilted her head back as he moved her braid to the side and kissed her neck.

Her fingertips caught on the edge of a long scar etched onto the left side of her Beltane lover's stomach, as if he'd been injured during regular orchard work. More importantly, she recognized the scar, and the recognition sent a jolt of sobriety through her tipsy fog. Wrenching herself away from her partner, Aubria stepped back and pulled him with her until he stood under a patch of moonlight bright enough to reveal his identity.

Lane loves Aubria.

Aubria put her doubts about her decision to rest as she realized that she'd been hoping another man had worn the Green Man's mask. The eyes shining under the light of the gibbous moon were unmistakably sky blue, and she wondered if she'd known all along that Lane had worn the rite's mask. If she had, she'd certainly buried the realization—perhaps along with the familiarity of his hands or his mouth—deep enough to render this recognition a genuine surprise.

She hated her disappointment, almost wishing there was some way she could punish herself for her stupidity.

Lane sighed as she kept her distance from him, running a hand through his hair. He still wore the crown of greenery and antlers, but he removed it and tossed it away as soon as his hands came in contact with it. Anyone else would have looked foolish, but somehow the magic of the night helped him maintain most of his dignity.

"I didn't know, Lane," Aubria declared, softening her voice for fear of hurting him further than she had already. "If I'd known—"

"You wouldn't have come away with me, I know. I just wanted…well, Merek abandoned Viola, and the Guide came to me and asked me to play the part of the Oak King. I spoke to her about it to make sure she agreed to the idea, and she suggested that you might look on me with more favor and remember why you once loved me if I won you back while wearing the mask."

He was rambling, and they both knew it, but Aubria hoped the shadows from the trees above concealed her pity for him in this moment. In her current state, her confusion mingled with disappointed desire, his words regarding Viola somehow stuck.

Merek abandoned Viola? Why? She remembered another night not too long ago when Viola's betrothed had had her pinned against a tree, when he'd chased Aubria through the orchard intent on doing her harm. Aubria hoped Viola hadn't suffered anything remotely similar to that experience.

"I'm sorry for the deception, Aubria. It was beneath me, but I'm grateful that it gave me the opportunity to speak to you again," Lane said.

Aubria didn't know what to say, or how to react. She should have been angry that both Lane and Viola had diligently worked to deceive her, but she couldn't summon anything other than regret. They had always had her best interests at heart, and Viola had always been friends enough with Lane to wish him the same amount of happiness she wished for Aubria and Cerise.

She couldn't think. Reaching up to rub her temples to dispel an oncoming headache, she endeavored to come up with any words that could act as a salve for this painful situation.

"I *am* sorry, Lane, though it might not seem like I am now. I just…" There was nothing she could say that would help her explain her secrets and the desires of her heart to him, not without causing him more pain than she already had. He had been the one to lure her to him again with the help of the Oak King's mask, true, but she found that she couldn't be angry with him for the deception. Nothing worse would have happened without her realizing his identity along the way. Part of her wished she hadn't noticed at all, that his scar from falling from a ladder onto a pruned pile of thorny branches wouldn't have given him away, but she ignored that portion of her heart in favor of doing the mature thing for once.

"I know, Aubria," Lane said, taking up for her as soon as she trailed off. "You don't have to explain it again. Believe it or not, this feels like…closure."

"Closure?" Tired of standing in the dark, she took a step forward, joining him in the light of the moon. "How so?"

Lane settled his gaze on her face, almost like he was drinking her in as a parched traveler would look upon a pitcher of fresh water from the wellspring river. Then his eyes shuttered, almost like he was trying to hide his longing for her.

"I could tell for a while that you were…struggling. I didn't want to believe it, and then I wanted to fix it, but some things aren't meant to be. I will fight harder for us if you want me to, Aubria, but I know that you don't. I have to learn to be all right with that, no matter how much I wish—"

"Stop!" Aubria hushed him, wrapping her hands in her skirts to keep from rushing forward to comfort him as his voice cracked. "*Do not* blame yourself for this! I was the one—"

"It's all right, Aubria," Lane looked like he wanted to close the distance between them, but he too kept his hands firmly at his sides and let the chasm between them grow wider as their conversation drew to its conclusion. "Sometimes people change. I can't say I'm happy to let you be lost to change, but I would hate to get in your way. I'm a proud man at heart. I wanted to know for sure whether or not we could repair what's been broken, and now I do."

The next words she spoke struck her as some of the most heartfelt she'd ever uttered. "I wish I felt differently, Lane. I wish this orchard and you were everything I wanted."

The smile he granted her held blessing rather than condemnation. And this farewell *did* feel different from when she'd first told him she couldn't hold to the promises they'd made to each other at Yule, at the start of the handfasting wheel. She'd broken her heart and his twice now, yet this pain felt like the start of a healing bruise, like it wouldn't last forever. When he said the words she knew had been coming, it felt like a different kind of release than what she had wandered away from the festivities expecting.

"Goodbye, Aubria."

Lane left to return to the bonfire, which undoubtedly would be less populated than when he'd led her away from it. Aubria could either return at a respectable distance to find someone else, or she could make her way home and collapse into bed with nothing for company but her own regrets.

She couldn't do that. She just couldn't.

Aubria turned on her heel and fled the scene, picturing in her head the Green Man's mask that had fallen, wondering if it would remain where they'd dropped it for seasons unnumbered. The mask had been lost in the dark, and she felt a strange kinship with the fallen finery. She knew she didn't want to stay in the orchard forever as Lane's wife, as Widower Haight's only daughter. She knew she wanted someone to share this carnal night with...and part of her had hoped that, beyond all logic, the masked man she'd danced with had been Terran Caird. Yet beyond that she couldn't be sure *what* kind of life exactly she wanted, and she ran as swiftly as if fleeing the orchard would take her to a new world altogether.

Though she'd tried with all her might to not think about it, tried to the point of almost making a massive mistake, the fact was as clear to her on Beltane as it had been when the Potioner had made her taste the love potion he'd concocted for a client: Terran was who she wanted, and she wished he was here with her on this sacred night.

Eldacre has their own rites this night, she fretted, her urgency refusing to fade away as she stumbled through the trees much more slowly though with no less exigency than she had on her Queen's Night. *He must be taking part of the rituals there. There are plenty of pretty girls there to capture a man's eye.*

She tried not to remember the pitying look Terran had cast her way when she'd tasted the potion he'd prepared for Sir Bor, but it invaded her mind as if intent on accusing her of dreadful stupidity. *See? He doesn't want you! No matter what you do, you're only a goose and a fool!*

Tipsy on the atmosphere of the night and wildflower mead, Aubria stumbled and leaned against the trunk of a tree that at this moment she couldn't identify. The smell of flowers stung her nose, poisonously sweet due to her unhappiness, yet no less alluring as she breathed it in. She had long left the light of the bonfire, yet under the moon she could see the delicate silver petals drifting down to the ground like snow. The scene was so beautiful, and she was astonished that such a classically beautiful view could move her so deeply: silver moonlight illuminated drifting petals and a carpet of grass so green she could catch its earthy scent without kneeling down to bury her fingers in the strands of it.

Strange clarity descended upon her like a gift from the moon as she let her heartbeat and her breath catch up with her. She couldn't name the reasons why exactly she desired the Potioner. She knew her attraction was more than physical, for she possessed enough self-knowledge to realize that she couldn't want something more than she had anything else in her life without her heart being involved.

But it was Beltane, and her body's needs called louder than her heart's. Her lips parted to speak one word, one name, and she leaned back against an accommodating tree trunk as she called for what her flesh desired with a whisper.

"Veritas."

She had not followed any rituals, and she hadn't consumed any potions that would help her mind facilitate the supernatural mingling with her reality, but this night was a sacred night. The forces of nature circled close to earthly fire on nights like this. She wondered…she hoped…

"Aubria."

How could he have answered her so quickly? Aubria looked around for the speaker she had called, but her moon blinded eyes saw nothing except the beautiful scene she had mourned being unable to share.

Then his touch, as gentle yet as enflaming as she remembered, awakened her. Aubria had felt his hand brush against her cheek before she saw him, but his now familiar form coalesced into shadows before her eyes as she stood as still as if she was part of the tree she leaned against. She couldn't speak, but even if she'd been able to she couldn't think of anything else to say.

The mystical golden eyes glared at her, full of a rage so profound it took her breath away. She cringed back against the tree, tempted to look away and dismiss this foolish dream by fleeing towards the safety of the hawthorn grove. Yet the spirit's eyes held her captive, and she watched as the anger transfigured into something no less scorching.

When he touched her, seizing her by her waist and crushing her body against his, she sensed the fury simmering under the shadows of his surface as he yanked her head back by tangling his fingers in the base of her braid. This would not be the tender maiden's night she had experienced with him before, and part of her reveled in the forceful shove of his knee between her legs.

She felt like she should say something to perhaps cool the anger she could feel radiating from Veritas in waves. Perhaps he was angry that she sought this from him again?

"I do not seek to bind you, spirit, only—"

"Hush, maid." Veritas spoke to her in his strangely echoing voice, his other hand inching upwards under her dress. "It is Beltane, and you have called on me. Faerykind worship the gods as humans do, and far be it from me to deny the proper rites."

Aubria frowned, sensing the venom behind the words, but then she lost her concentration as he lifted her dress high enough to permit him to slip inside of her with one rough maneuver. Arching her back at the blunt pain, she gasped as she held onto Veritas for support until the pain faded. This time it hadn't hurt as much or lasted as long as the first time, which proved beneficial since he didn't wait for her to recover before he began to move.

The bark scratched against her back through her dress as he thrust inside of her again and again, but she found that she didn't care as he angled his movements to grant them both the most enjoyment. Less shy than she'd been the first time, she gripped his shoulders, firm under the shadows that masked him, and curled her body around his as pleasure gave voice to her enjoyment in soft sighs in time with his movements.

Aubria heard him, too, though he sounded as if he didn't want her to know that she gave him the same kind of delight he was sharing with her. At one point his teeth sank into her bottom lip hard enough to bruise, and she heard him stifle a groan towards the end of their coupling that brought her to the edge of completion herself.

When it was over she expected him to leave as he had before. They'd moved from their hurried joining against a tree to the ground, where she'd laid prone and let him take control. Still trembling from exertion and pleasure, Aubria curled up under the tree they'd used for balance. It would be some time before she could make her way back to the bonfire, let alone home, and the mead she had drunk and her own vigorous exercise made her almost too sleepy to stay upright.

Yet she dimly noticed when Veritas lay down beside her, still present as he curved his body at the same angle as hers in offering of himself to keep her warm. Aubria, remembering his earlier anger and sarcasm, fought back a smile as she drifted into sleep with his body keeping her from feeling the cool approach of dawn.

When she awoke from the satisfied sleep she'd drifted into with the spirit's warm presence still nearby, she felt the weight of a body on top of hers. The bleariness of sleep faded away as she focused on the face of the man pinning her down...and as soon as she recognized him she froze, unable to rationalize what she saw.

The corporeal spirit spoke to her with a familiar voice. "Did you think I would honor your disrespect?"

The knife pressed against her fragile jugular, held by hands both familiar and suddenly dangerous, felt all the sharper now that she recognized who held it. He grinned, almost feral as the shadows concealing all but its eyes and the vague shape of its form dissolved into the early morning light like the smoke drifting away from the bonfire to reveal that somehow Terran Caird and Veritas were one and the same.

9

How can this be?

The Potioner's perceptive eyes glared down at her, impossibly yellow compared to their usual green, and her instincts told her that it wasn't Terran who was with her in this moment. Terran was never anything but cool and collected, an enigma of a man who rarely shared anything of himself with others. Whoever wore this body now barely held control over his seething fury, as if would explode from him in an inferno at any moment.

"Veritas?" she questioned, hating the vulnerability in her voice. Internally, she was screaming at her past self, absolutely infuriated with her own insanity.

You called a demon to you on a sacred night and expected no consequences? Throughout the land you should be known as Aubria the Stupid, Aubria the Idiot. If anyone even finds your body when he's through with it, she thought. A scream gurgled in her throat, but the knife's edge held it at bay: would he kill her if she even imagined calling for help?

"You thought to capture me, Aubria Haight, but I tell you that I refuse to be bound by you or another human for the duration of my existence," Veritas spoke in Terran's voice, though the Potioner had never hissed at her with such loathing or such potential cruelty twisting his face into a visage she hadn't seen before.

"Capture you? I—" Aubria began, but her unwelcome explanation cut off with a yelp when the tip of the knife sank deep enough into her skin to draw a bead of blood out from under the surface.

"I am a truth spirit, girl. You cannot *lie* to one such as me," Veritas growled. The weight of his body pinned her to the ground and rendered her incapable of much movement, but the hand he used to pin her wrists above her head squeezed hard enough to grind the fragile bones together.

She cried out, words spilling forth in a flood in spite of her feeble attempts to subdue them. "The spell you—the spell the Potioner gave me was only supposed to gain your aid in helping me decide my future and learn what I truly wanted! It was never supposed to bind you! *I'm not lying!*"

The last she screamed as Veritas's eyes shimmered like an illusion and the power he summoned sent a shockwave throughout her taut muscles. She thought inexplicably about the lightning field she'd seen for the first time on her disaster of a Queen's Night, wondering if this was what it might have felt like to die on that field at the mercy of such magic.

"You are withholding information. Because you bound me after your 'simple ritual,' you knew I would come to you again when you called upon me to satisfy your carnal desires," Veritas traced the knife along her neck with agonizing slowness, leaving a thin trail of blood as a necklace against her pale skin as she whimpered; when he laughed, his voice echoed with a deeper tone in a straightforward reveal of the fact that the Potioner's body held more than one entity. "I cannot kill you, Aubria, for as I'm sure you can feel on your hip, Terran Caird would not allow me to. He has desired you from the first, you common girl with your wide hips and your golden hair and your sharp tongue. I did not lie when I called you beautiful, but it was he who hungered for you."

Aubria did indeed feel the physical proof of Veritas's words: Terran's body weighed heavily on hers, enough for all of her wriggling to perhaps excite the masculine part of him that after last night was becoming less of a mystery to her. Her mind teetered on the brink of insanity, since she hadn't yet learned to reconcile the longing she felt for Terran with the danger she was in from the being who possessed his body now. She shuddered, opening her mouth to speak, but Veritas tilted her head up with the knife to encourage her silence.

"You have bound me when I am already bound to the Potioner and his bloodline. You summoned me on a sacred night and used the old ways of binding so I will come to you when called and answer your questions and fulfill your desires," he said, his voice softening as he looked down into her eyes as if he wished to pluck them out and serve them to her on a platter. "I repaid you kindly on night you called me with the Potioner's aid. Terran already trusted you, in spite of your dubious record of mistakes. I surrendered to your charms and to my own nature, intrigued that you sought my consent rather than imperiously demanding my compliance. I should have known better than to trust another treacherous mortal."

Questions spun in Aubria's head, making her feel dizzy though she lay flat on the ground. *If Veritas is here now, where exactly is Terran? Did he know the nature of the being he encouraged me to contact beyond assuming that it was a benign truth spirit?*

It would have been difficult to concentrate under pressure of losing her life if any of her replies were unsatisfactory, but her traitorous body responded to the proximity of Terran's and the position he had her in, carrying heat through her limbs and making her feel sick with the heady blend of fear and desire.

Veritas toyed with her further and traced the tip of the knife lower down her neck, delicately enough to tickle the tops of her breasts without slicing through the skin. He held her gaze, his lips curled into a mordant grin as she noticed his pupils narrow into eerie slits.

"I can hear you, you know. Because we are bound. Whoever taught you how to bind me didn't tell you everything," Veritas derided, his humor almost as menacing as his frown; his laugh was both ominous and alluring. "Terran may have given you the potion and the ritual in an attempt to test your mettle and assure your return to his workshop, but there are many, *many* things he is unaware of. You will find that he's not aware of anything that transpired during our initial meeting."

Aubria went perfectly still and deadweight, hoping that her total lack of movement or protest would indicate her submission and her honorable intentions. *I didn't bind you, I never wished you any harm, I didn't bind you…*

"When you called me again, called me so I had no choice but to obey, I guessed what you had done. I wouldn't have guessed that you knew the old ways of binding…but you did, and though I am bound to you, perhaps you did not think that I would have free will of my own?" Veritas laughed again as he continued, basing his explanations after the pattern of her chaotic thoughts. "Terran's ancestor bound me to his line and expected much the same. Why should an ignorant peasant girl be any different?"

His eyes were so close that she saw herself reflected in them with ease: a white face illuminated by the dawn, panicked doe eyes dark under her river of blonde hair. She looked frightened and weak, and if she knew anything about spirits or demons or faerykind, she knew that they would exploit any signs of weakness simply due to the capricious nature the gods had granted them.

So she would have to not seem weak.

"I'm *not* an ignorant peasant girl, and if you would listen to me you would know I'm telling the truth!" she almost shouted, losing her own temper in a burst of recklessness she had to blame on her dire situation. "I didn't bind you to me or to anyone else, not only because I wouldn't guess at how to do that nor be so foolish as to try, but because I don't think anyone should be bound to another against their will!"

Veritas glared down at her, perhaps displeased that his monologue had been interrupted by her outburst. Yet after a pregnant pause, his tight grip on her wrists loosened, making her gasp as circulation began to return and her bones screamed in release from the pain. The knife at her throat no longer pressed so dangerously against her windpipe.

"You *are* telling the truth, somehow," he marveled, clearly taken aback. "I am still bound, and you are still the cause, but you didn't intentionally bind me."

"That's what I've been trying to say!" Aubria groused, testing his commitment to hurting her by resuming her struggle to free herself from his oppressive weight. "I don't know what happened any more than you do. Obviously I know nothing about your connection to Terran Caird except what you have told me, but I can tell you for certain that I haven't the slightest idea how to bind or control a demon or any other creature."

Veritas's eyes—*Terran's* eyes, changed though they were—bore down into hers as if he wished to burn any secrets into the light simply by the power of his focus. She forced herself to stare back without flinching, without trying to mark the differences between the man she'd known and the new creature that had taken over his body.

"How odd," he spoke via Terran's lips. "You should not have been able to bind me without foreknowledge, but you genuinely had none to base your spell on."

"I guess you were the one stupid enough to engage with a woman without protection," Aubria snapped, though the unintentional softness of her voice cushioned the barb. Her heart skipped ahead a few beats, and she hoped rather than believed he wouldn't notice.

Veritas rolled off her and leapt to his feet in one smooth movement, almost too swiftly for any mortal to accomplish. Showing a new display of courtesy, he stretched out his hand in a silent offer to help her to her feet. Aubria wouldn't have taken it, but the shock had tampered with her balance. She didn't bother, however, concealing her reluctance to accept his help.

"How are you bound to the Potioner? If you have magic of your own and can make or break spells, how can one such as you be bound to a bloodline without remedy?" Aubria was unable to stop herself from asking as she smoothed out her skirts and pressed her fingers against the shallow cuts he'd left on her neck. She burned where

Veritas had offered her his hand, her nerves tingling with the residue of foreign magic.

"I am faerykind, not a demon. We used to interact with humans more freely. The Caird ancestors were full of bloodlust and greed, hungry for power. Eventually one succeeded in binding me to their bloodline so I would be forced to lend my magic whenever they ordered," Veritas said, leaning back against the tree that had supported their connected bodies the night before. Contrary to his earlier wrath that had faded like the summer storms that blasted leaves and fruit from their branches before dissipating into mist, he seemed to be in quite a good mood. He twirled the knife in his fingers with expert skill, his eyes never leaving hers as he spoke.

"I take it that the binding didn't go as planned?" Aubria asked. Veritas's answering grin was savage.

"They bound me, but in return granted me access to the firstborn son of each line until the end of time, or until someone found a way to break the ancient binding. Faerykind have no physical form, since we lost the power to link our spirits and magic to animal or tree or our own bodies in ages past. Many of us choose to possess humans a few times in our life, though for beings now used to living as spirits it grows harder to bear the weight of a corporeal form the longer we use one. Eventually the human spirit trapped in there with us regains enough sentience to break free, and we lose everything we strove for while playing in a mortal skin."

Aubria closed her eyes in a sudden headache, wincing as the discomfort pounded against her temples.

"How can that be true? I've known neither of you long enough to tell, but there are stark differences between you and Terran. If you had just taken him over, or taken the men in his bloodline over in turn, how could he have developed his own personality and—oh."

"Oh?" Veritas questioned her pause, generously giving her time to consider whether or not it was a dangerous idea she was about to voice.

"Why are you so willing to tell me all of this?" she asked, changing tactics. Veritas's direct gaze dropped to the ground, surprising her with the vulnerability of the gesture. It only lasted a second, and when he looked up at her again any uncertainty had concealed itself in the depths of his arrogance.

"It is my opinion that we need each other to break this binding. I couldn't kill you for that reason, even if I wished to, and…and in spite of my forced binding to the Potioner, I wish him well, and Terran trusts you. For that reason I've decided to seek your help instead of manipulating you into obligation as my kind tend to do." Veritas looked as if the words pained him to admit, as if it were shameful for one of the faerykind to value their host enough to keep to themselves and let the host live a relatively normal life.

"Is that why you…share his body, rather than just taking over completely?" Aubria asked, her words trailing off at the last as she wondered if he'd take real offense at her rudeness. Veritas flipped the knife into the air, and it hung suspended in space for a moment before it slowly descended back into his hand. Then he threw his head back and barked a laugh.

"You *do* ask whatever question pops into your head first," he complained, though he looked amused rather than offended. He still rested with his back against a tree, feigning a casual mood. Due to the nature of their conversation Aubria guessed he was anything but calm. Practicing more courage than she felt, she arched her eyebrows and stared at him, a cue that she stood by her question and would say nothing more until he explained.

"Terran didn't choose to be bound anymore than I did. By nature my kind tends spite as some tend to virtue…but if it were my choice I would not have taken a host at all. As it is, since the Cairds bound me, I have taken their minds as payment for my power. Terran is the first of that bloodline to have a spirit free from greed and deceit since I was bound. I respect truth and honor in whatever form it comes." Veritas conceded with a sigh, glancing up at the canopy of leaves dewy in the leisurely rise of the early morning sun. "You have dragged more information from me than I was willing to give, Aubria Haight. What say you? Will you help undo our binding?"

She came to a decision quickly, though the adrenaline from him threatening her life and cutting her with one of the Potioner's knives still coursed through her body and had yet to be purged. Aubria had no doubt that he *would* coerce her into helping, given the chance, but given his words about honor and truth, she wondered if it wouldn't be better to work with him up front rather than risking more of his ire. He still held the knife, and his form was taut with unspent energy since a being like him probably wouldn't tire at the same rate as a mortal.

Besides, she had Terran to think of. If Terran had no knowledge of Veritas, or only partial knowledge…should she even try to save him? She'd have to test how much he knew about Veritas, to be sure.

"I don't know much about this, obviously, and one solution for this problem is me never using the binding to call on you again," she began; Veritas opened his mouth to protest, since he and anyone in their right mind would rather have the surety of freedom than an empty promise of it. Holding up her hand, she talked over the beginnings of his arguments. "But if I'm the cause of magic I didn't know I was capable of casting, I will help you undo the binding that links you to me. I'll even help you unbind yourself from the Potioner, if you wish. You have my word."

Veritas was on her in a flash, his skin glowing faintly with power he could only just contain. Aubria stumbled backwards, caught off guard by the sudden and total lack of humanity in his expression. She thought she saw the dim shapes of the Potioner's bone structure, illumined by the unearthly spark, but that couldn't be possible. *Could it?*

"Be careful who you give your word, village girl. You can't change your mind later."

Then it was over, and the glow that had lit Veritas from within faded. He even bowed to her, a mockery of gratitude that made her bristle with irritation.

"I've already said I'd be willing to work with you without your games or your threats," she snapped. "There's no need to put on a show for a simple village girl, after all. It's not like I'm smart enough to appreciate your antics anyway."

Veritas chuckled, surprising her with the authentic depth of his humor. "Never fear, Aubria, in spite of our…predicament, I admit I must be grateful to you for any help you'd be willing to offer. In return, I will offer you knowledge you do not yet have."

Still offended, Aubria crossed her arms over her chest and waited for him to share whatever knowledge he wanted to share with her. She wished she could tell him to shove his information somewhere where the sunlight would never reach it, but she held her impetuous tongue and waited for him to speak. Yet he was also waiting for her to ask, and for a full minute they stood like ancient statues in the middle of the orchard, one glaring and one adopting a pleasant expression meant to cause the most vexation.

This is childish, Aubria thought, her impatience almost getting the better of her. Then, rolling her eyes, she parted her lips to speak just as he finally broke the quiet. She suspected that he'd waited for her to submit, toying with her nerves, then took the high road before she could.

Ugh.

"Last night another of your crops was destroyed, and I know who is to blame."

"What? Which harvest?" Aubria gasped, any arguments with Veritas forgotten as she pictured in her head the ruin of the thornbell crop that had already cost Loracre a significant amount and would continue to drain resources for the next few years. Terran had made enough potion to heal any damaged trees that could be repaired and encourage new plantings to grow at greater speeds, but that help had had its price, and she doubted anyone could afford much more assistance if another crop had been lost.

Veritas shrugged. "Much of your hawthorn grove has been destroyed. The faerykind were not pleased by your outright disrespect for their wishes."

Aubria lifted her hands to her long braid, clutching it tightly as she felt the pricks of hawthorn stems and wisteria vines woven into the now unkempt locks. The petals in her hair might be the last blossoms she'd see for several years, depending on the scope of the damage, and she doubted she'd be able to follow the Beltane ritual of tossing the wilted flowers into the Goodly Fire they'd brought home from the festival to their hearth in three days.

"Disrespect? How?" she asked, beginning to pace without taking note of her own path; Veritas's eyes glittered as he watched her, but she was too distraught to pay further attention. "The faerykind have never interacted with us, not for years and years, and suddenly they begin destroying the orchard they supposedly helped us build in eons past? Why? We didn't even see any toadstool rings that would have marked their presence...how can you be sure they're to blame?"

"I sense the expense of power it takes to destroy the orchard after the deed is done. It was *their* orchard. They helped the humans cultivate it when they came to this continent in ancient days. Is it so strange that they want it back now it's thriving?"

Aubria contemplated what little she knew about the history of the people of Lyrassan interacting with the faerykind. All she knew involved the faerytales told to her when she was a little girl: the faerykind were children of the nature gods, bound by different laws than humans and gifted with immortality and an extra measure of otherworldly beauty. They could be as malicious and cruel as the gods themselves, but in the stories either the humans ended up besting them at their own games or routing them fairly in combat with the blessings of the gods.

Somehow, she doubted that interacting with any faerykind in real life would be so straightforward.

"What do they want, exactly?" she paced on the soft grass of the orchard ground until she noticed and stopped. "More precisely: how do we get rid of them?"

Veritas shrugged, though she doubted that even he could be so cavalier about the approaching possibility of a conflict with the faerykind. "You love this orchard, then, even if in your heart you seek to leave it so you won't be trapped here?"

Is this a trap? Aubria loathed these games, and hated not knowing any straight answers even more...but she couldn't deny that part of her reveled in the danger, seduced by the uncertainty.

"Yes," she answered, hoping that her hesitation didn't damn her. "Yes. I love my homeland and every root and tree in our orchard. I would mourn its loss until the end of my days."

"Then you must persuade my distant kindred to leave by offering something they desire more than their ancient lands. Failing that, if they refuse all persuasion, you must threaten them with something that will make them feel fear instead of desire for this orchard," Veritas said. He and Aubria endured another impasse as she challenged him to continue, begging him for more helpful information with her eyes since she was too proud to voice any further request. Yet he bade her humble herself again with his silence, and for the sake of the orchard she spoke first again.

"Is that all? We have nothing to offer except for the bounty of our trees! And as for making them fear us, what could we possibly do? Much of Lyrassan mocks our quietude—"

"Perhaps you should involve your king, then, since he may negotiate with the faerykind on behalf of his people," he suggested. Aubria grit her teeth together: they both knew that King Barric was a figurehead in his old age, and his remaining son, Prince Mardin, had yet to prove himself as anything other than a vain, boastful buffoon intent on disputing with the neighboring kingdoms.

"The king will be of no use, as you very well know," she hissed, wishing in spite of her apparent addiction to intrigue that she could compel him to offer her useful answers. "What am I supposed to do? How can I convince them to leave if we have nothing to trade or threaten them with?"

Veritas shrugged, straightening from his reclined position against the tree. "I have not spoken to any of my kind for a few generations. But fret not: I will keep an ear to the ground for information, now that they've made their presence known in the orchard. If we are to remove the binding on us as well as the curse linking Terran and myself, we'll have to have a safe place to work."

"Thank you?" Aubria uttered the phrase like a question, since due to Veritas's derision she hadn't expected much help from him at all. The awkwardness of her situation struck her all at once, and in spite of the danger she'd just endured at the hands of a capricious faerykind, all she could feel was her exhaustion from the mystic events of Beltane and her desire to go home. Her head was too full, and she swayed on her feet with her weariness apparent even to the truth spirit.

"Go home, Aubria. We will see each other again soon," Veritas's voice reached her as if from a great distance, and she found herself willing to obey. The concern in his voice made him sound more like Terran than Veritas, but for now she wanted to end this strange night that should have been only a dream.

Aubria stood in place as she waited for him to leave, watching with half-hooded eyes as he shrugged the stiffness from his shoulders and began the journey back to the Potioner's dwelling off of Eldacre proper. He had to have journeyed here by magic to answer her call so promptly, but apparently he didn't see the need to expend any more to return homewards. She'd have to walk home as well, but that felt more tolerable than untangling a game where faerykind had come to play...

"Wait!" Aubria called as Veritas nearly disappeared through the trees. She stumbled, her slipper not much use against the grass bedecked with the morning dew, but the idea that had just occurred to her demanded her speed, however clumsy she was. "Wait!"

Veritas paused, though he didn't turn to face her; in the early light, when she couldn't see his eyes, she could have imagined that Terran stood before her, if she wanted. This time she didn't, given what she had to ask.

"You came to me as a *man*, Veritas, in a human man's body. What if...will a child result from our tryst?" Her voice cracked on the last syllable, revealing her panic as she tried and failed to catch her breath. She pressed her hands against her flat, work-hardened stomach, wondering if before long a babe would grow in her womb. She'd always imagined herself becoming a mother, someday, some distant day that she didn't have to think about, but under these circumstances…

Suddenly Veritas was in front of her, his face inches from her own. He'd moved with such lightning speed it threw her off balance, and his arm snaked around her waist to keep her upright while his transfixing eyes, both the Potioner's and his own, hypnotized her like prey.

Once she was steady on her own feet he sank slowly to his knees, like a supplicant beseeching a monarch for succor. Aubria fought her rising nausea and a strange sense of desire as Veritas lifted her dress inch by inch until her bare stomach was exposed to the light. Her composure threatened to flee when his warm lips grazed her skin, once on the left, once on the right, and a final time low enough to send a tremor through her muscles.

When he laughed at her, she hated him for it. Aubria shoved him away as hard as she could, yanking her dress down as he fell backwards. When she glared at him reclining where he'd fallen on the grass his laughter quieted, though not for fear of her ire.

"There will be no child. I came to you in Terran's body the first time as well, though neither of you knew it. Even I had no notion of what the desire of your heart would require of me until I saw you. At the time I couldn't sense what you wanted…but faerykind can control the creation of their offspring at will."

Too angry to breathe any sigh of relief, Aubria continued to glare. Why must he toy with her so? He'd clearly resented the binding he thought she'd placed on him enough to threaten her with death…so why touch her with such disdainful tenderness?

She would have no answers to those questions that morning. When she blinked, Veritas was gone, and so Terran was too; he must have expended some magic to return to Eldacre after all. Aubria had her long walk back to her cottage to think of, and too much time to wonder how she would tell Terran what she and Veritas had done.

10

The week after Beltane passed in a haze of shock that had Aubria going through the motions of her day with the bare minimum of effort. Her mind ran over the events of that night almost to the exclusion of all else. In any scope of her imagination, she never would have dreamed that Terran Caird was the cursed vessel of the truth spirit—the truth *faerykind*—Veritas. It had been difficult for her to accept that faerykind and spirits were real enough to interact with someone like her. She'd worshipped the nature gods along with everyone in her village her whole life, though perhaps due to her father's skepticism she had been less devout in her practices.

Now someone she was coming to trust and care for was under some sort of spell that she'd agreed to break, and her home village was beset by creatures intent on destroying the orchard if the humans didn't give it back to them.

Aubria couldn't escape this new knowledge that had turned her world upside-down. As before, she and everyone else in Loracre had had to repair the damaged grove as best they could, hoping against hope that there would be enough to salvage for the purpose of rebuilding. They still had other crops to harvest and preserve and sell: sweet nespola, tart cherries in six varieties, heavy spinefruits that grew weighty enough to snap their branches off the tree trunks if they weren't plucked precisely in season, and others. There was always work to be done, and the late spring and early summer crops were times when both villages could least afford extra work.

Though she was busy with work, and her hands grew coarse and raw from clearing the orchard, plucking and cleaning the fruit, and other menial tasks, she noticed other happenings in her hometown that proved the truth of what Veritas had told her. Signs of faerykind presence were bountiful, and she wasn't the only one who detected them: Cerise's mother had complained about her milk going bad before its time, all of the cats in the village who were usually fine mousers had begun to act strange and watchful while their prey ran free, and one of the village children claimed to have spotted a faerykind ring. The child had been scolded for lying, Aubria had heard—and sympathized, for no one had ever believed her own tales about seeing evidence of the faerykind when she was young either— but one of the other villagers who had gone to inspect the ring in the hopes of finding edible early porcine mushrooms nearby had confirmed the story.

Try as she might to avoid these stories and her own experiences of faerykind mischief—she'd spent hours untangling witch knots from Toby's white mane, and her father's cat did little else but follow her around and watch her every move when she was home—there was only so much she could ignore. During one of many late nights when she toiled in her kitchen to preserve and bake the black cherries from the Haight's personal plot of the orchard, her father had come home in a bad mood thanks to the fresh blustering of the Guide of Rites.

"It's all poppycock, Aubria, but many in Loracre hearken to his words too closely for my liking," he complained before sneezing like a thunderclap; he'd come down with a seasonal cold, and it lay particularly harsh on him this spring.

"What's he saying this time?"

Darragh nodded his thanks as she passed him a cup of warm cherry cider that she'd heated over the fire for his return; the cat jumped up in his lap as he took a seat at their table, its eyes fixed on Aubria instead of its master. She stuck her tongue out at it, but neither her father nor the cat took notice.

"He's insinuating that someone in the orchard incited the wrath of the gods before or during Beltane. The reckless ruin of our orchard perpetrated by the ancient ones will continue until we find and rebuke this poor sinner with cleansing fire."

"*What?*" Aubria gasped, an uncomfortable chill unfurling in her chest though the rest of her warmed with outrage. "That's absurd! We don't live in ancient days, and we haven't had executions by fire since—"

"By fire he means the lightning field. Then he wouldn't have to get his hands dirty at all, which makes sense since he offers no help but 'healing prayer' in this time of need," Darragh said before gulping a long draught of the cider. Then he coughed, his eyes watering at the striking flavor. He sneezed ferociously a few more times as he fumbled for a clean handkerchief in his pocket, but for lack of anything better he seized one of the kitchen rags lying on the table and pressed it to his dripping nose to halt the mess.

The lightning field. Aubria remembered her encounter with that bleak place when she'd awoken at the edge of it with hare features and a pounding headache, and she had no desire to ever see it closer. But she might, if somehow the Guide learned about her forbidden dealings with the faerykind—with Veritas—and informed the rest of the village. Magic was forbidden, a genuine offense to research and practice if not sanctioned by the king, and if someone were to find out about her...

"Does the Guide have any suspicions as to who this 'poor sinner' might be?" she asked carefully as she lifted the shawl from one of the chairs and nestled it around her father's shoulders. He was not old, not by any means, but when the yearly sickness was upon him he looked pathetic indeed.

Darragh snorted. "Of course not. That would imply that there was someone to suspect in the first place, someone to divert attention to rather than fixing the problem at hand. Everyone wants someone to blame for nature's misfortunes, and that's what this is. It would be much better to blame the king's poor leadership for our trouble, or the whimsical magic of the orchard itself."

Well, they're both right...in part. The Guide was right to suspect that they'd angered the ancient ones, but the faerykind would have arrived to torment the villagers for the return of their historical lands regardless of whether or not Aubria had gone through with the ritual to summon and accidentally bind one of them to herself. But her father was right to dread the inevitability of the Guide whipping the villagers into a "holy" frenzy against whatever poor soul he chose as the scapegoat for Loracre's tribulations. Peasant communities succumbing to mob mentality with their torches and pitchforks was what had gotten magic banned for common use in the first place.

He'd mentioned the king, though she noticed a few seconds too late and almost lost her chance to ask at all. "The king? What's he got to do with it?"

"The king—and by the king, I mean his son Mardin, since the old fool is all but useless by now anyway—has seen fit to raise our taxes for year's end to fund his border disputes. The Guide blamed this on our loss of the gods' favor, but in this case most of us know better. It will be a troublesome few turnings of the wheel with the elder prince in charge of us all," Darragh explained the politics of the village and the realm to his daughter as if it wasn't unusual for a father to divulge such masculine matters to his female child. "The only highlight to our monthly meeting was Potioner Caird's arrival with the concoction he made for our thornbell clearing. He arrived in time to—"

"Terran Caird was there?" Aubria interrupted before she could think better of it; to avoid Darragh's scrutiny at the eager tone of her voice and her flushed cheeks she turned back to the bowl of cherries she'd been pitting when he'd arrived.

"Yes, to drop off the potion we paid him for...handsomely, I might add," Darragh sneezed into the kitchen rag again, groaning as the rough cloth chaffed the raw skin on his nose. "A few of our company went out to pour it over the trees with the lads still working.

He told those of us that remained that he didn't suspect that the cause of our misfortunes was due to the transgressions of any one person, and that the faerykind we were so terrified to offend were not as benevolent or devoted to the gods as we believed."

"I bet the Guide didn't like that!" Aubria tried to joke, but her thoughts were busy picturing Terran in that moment, how his quiet voice would ring through the meeting hall and command the full attention of anyone present. Her father snorted, either from derision or from his seasonal sickness, and she returned to the present long enough to finish her work and tuck him into bed with a stack of fresh handkerchiefs and a hot toddy. The cat blinked curiously at her as she closed the door, and she crossed her eyes at it again before the latch clicked into place.

Before Beltane she'd escaped some of her troubles by going to visit Terran and learn his potion craft. After...she was busy, true, occupied to the point of utter exhaustion by the time the sun set each day. Yet given what she knew and what she'd promised Veritas, she should've made time to journey to Eldacre to work out what he knew from their encounters and how she could help him break his curse.

She'd put it off as long as she could. Now it was time to face what had caused her such fear and heartsickness. If anyone could help her undo the bindings tying Veritas to her and Terran to Veritas, if anyone could help her discover what faerykind feared or desired more than the orchard itself, it would be the Potioner.

So, a week and a half after Beltane with mountains of work awaiting her at home, Aubria found herself standing outside the Potioner's door shifting her weight from foot to foot as she resisted the urge to gnaw her nails to the quick from the anxiety. She'd worn her hat again in defense against the sun, and she carried a painstakingly decorated nespola pie with both hands. As if it would help her apology when she divulged her full dealings with Veritas to Terran—since it had been his body that the truth spirit had used, though of course Aubria had had no way of knowing that at the time—she'd carved tiny leaves from the pie crust and laid them over the surface of her pie like real leaves dancing in a spring breeze.

Cerise would have mocked her. Viola would have said it was pretty. Lane would have accepted the apology pie without hesitation. But none of them were around, and given that these were her mistakes, the burden rightfully fell on her shoulders alone.

I'm sorry, Terran. I don't know what else to say other than that.

Aubria sighed as she transferred the warm dish to one arm so she could rap her knuckles against the door again. She'd been waiting for a bit too long to be plausible if the Potioner was home, and had shamefully peeped into his window on the chance that the curtain would be up and she might see him puttering around inside with another outlandish customer.

"You waiting for Potioner Caird?"

Aubria turned, her loose braid falling over her shoulder as she stepped down from the front step as if the speaker had caught her for a thief. It took her a second to recognize him, but she realized that the man shouting to her from the street was the same person she'd used to set her market cart next to.

"I am, actually," she replied, adding a lie to flavor the truth in case he or anyone else milling through Eldacre might report her whereabouts to someone in Loracre. "My father has the seasonal sickness, and I was hoping I might purchase something that would help him recover with more speed."

"The seasonal sickness! Aw, he's one of those, is he?" Her market friend—"Sir Onion-Eater" in her head—guffawed as he waved her closer so they didn't have to bellow rudely at each other across the way. "Caird's down at the stables: I saw him head there a few minutes ago myself. But where have you been, lass? I sold my onions and garlic much better after people filled up on your mess of sweet treats."

"I hadn't realized you'd missed me at market, sir," Aubria frowned at the perhaps unintentional affront, though she was a little touched that he'd missed her. "The last time I came here to sell my pies and tarts I met with a little trouble."

"Aye, I heard about that. I'd taken a break for some repast and a drink during, or those hooligans—"

"Please, sir, don't mention it. It was months ago." Aubria cut him off, having no desire to relive the traumatic memory of her fear and panic in the face of the bullying city guard and his inebriated cronies. Holding her pie in front of her as if it would shield her from further conversation, she marched past the portly and unpleasantly fragrant onion seller with purpose in her steps.

"Right, well you have your own business to be getting along with, I'm sure," he called after her. "But don't you be afraid to stop by our market again, lass! We don't hold with Oseren's folk bullying our girls in *this* town, no we don't…"

He trailed off, and Aubria frowned before she shook off the interaction with a shrug. She had more important matters to attend to than the snobbery of Eldacre, and now she had to track Terran down at the stables.

Proving that the onion merchant had spoken truly, she found the Potioner in the village stable in a stall with his sturdy yet regal gray horse. He didn't notice her at first, since she'd walked quietly inside amidst the hubbub of Eldacre's grooms tending to the beasts stabled in their charge, so she had a moment to observe him at work when he wasn't aware he was being watched. She may have experienced his body under Veritas's control, but she was glad she hadn't seen it or known it was him. Whatever innocence he possessed was visible to her now in the calm strokes he used to brush his horse and the unconscious upturn of his lips that revealed that in this span of time he was content. His hair fell down over his brow in attractive disarray, darker out of the sunlight, and she longed to brush it out of his eyes with the tender gesture of a girl who cared for a boy.

Veritas had told her that Terran had desired her from the first. She hadn't known what to do with that information at the time, and now she had even less of an idea how to move forward. Aubria was not so naïve to assume that affection always accompanied desire…but still, she wondered as she worried at her chapped lips with her teeth.

Not allowing herself further indulgence, she cleared her throat so both man and beast glanced her way.

"I would have reported you as truant, Aubria Haight, if we had agreed to such under the terms of our partnership," Terran grinned at her as he set the brush for his horse aside and dusted his hands together to remove any dirt. "I expected to see you when I came into Loracre with my scheduled potion delivery, but you were nowhere to be found. I didn't want to draw attention to you by inquiring as to your whereabouts. What have you to say for yourself?"

Dumbstruck by the easy friendship of his greeting that would have thrilled her two weeks ago, Aubria stared at him open-mouthed until she remembered to snap her jaw closed.

"What—do you not remember?" she asked, stepping around to the front of his palfrey as the beast snuffled with interest towards the pie dish in her arms. She spun away, holding it out of reach of the long nose, and the horse chuffed with disappointment and then feigned disinterest as it nosed Terran's shoulder for more brushing.

"Remember that you haven't been to see me for your potion lessons in over two weeks? I wouldn't forget that." Terran frowned at her in mock severity, crossing his arms as if he really were a schoolmaster she'd abandoned to have fun. Then, as if something else had occurred to him, his smile waned and a dash of uncertainty darkened his summer green eyes into the verdant shade of pine needles. "Was there something else?"

Do not tell him yet, Aubria, a voice echoed in Aubria's mind quite suddenly, making her feel both sick and dizzy as she staggered backwards away from the Potioner.

Veritas?

I can speak to you through your mind due to the binding we somehow engineered together. Terran's voice in her head, both more sibilant and silken than what her ears could hear, shocked her. *Do not tell him of what has transpired between us.*

Why not? She asked. *You told me he—*

Deal with the matter at hand. We will talk later.

"Well, you know, we had Beltane, and then another of our crops was destroyed..." Aubria stammered an inelegant response, half-expecting to see Veritas jump forward in Terran's eyes at the mention of the fateful night she'd discovered the truth; she added another unhelpful explanation with a high-pitched squeak. "I brought you a pie! It's nespola!"

"I can see that." He took the pie when she offered it to him, and without words she pulled a spoon out of her pocket and passed it to him. When she'd pictured the scene where she'd confessed everything and begged for his help, they'd been in the cool shelter of his familiar potion shop, and she'd given him the pie to eat while she explained. She'd figured the stables would do just as well, but now she wasn't sure what was off limits.

Terran's eyebrows quirked in confusion as she indicated that he should eat the pie, but he took a seat on the bench outside of his horse's stall and offered her the remaining seat. After removing the cloth protecting the dish, he hummed his appreciation as he dug into the corner of the pie and shoveled a bite into his mouth. When he finished chewing he passed her the spoon.

"What are the properties of this nespola?" he asked as she tentatively scooped a half moon of fruit from the pie dish. The pale orange fruit intrigued her anew as she ran through the list of uses in her head before answering.

"The fruit of the nespola is light and good for sore throats, deep coughs, and the beautification of skin afflicted by pimples and rashes. The leaves and stems, however, are poisonous, and should never be consumed."

"Interesting," Terran said, as he usually did whenever she shared information about the orchard crops with him; then he surprised her by asking her a follow-up question. "What potion would you make with such a fruit, if you could do so?"

"What potion?" Aubria traced the tip of her tongue over the edge of the spoon to prevent any sweet syrup from dripping onto her dress; Terran watched her, and she saw him swallow harshly from the corner of her eyes. "Practically, I would make a potion for the youths in our village to cleanse the worst of any pockmarks on their faces from scratching pimples. Less practically…I would make a potion that would help someone say the hard things…that would help someone find the right words to say in impossible situations."

He nodded as she passed him the utensil they were sharing. "Good. We can start on that when I get back, if you're willing."

Aubria's heart sank, and she shook her head after Terran took a bite from the pie and tried to pass the spoon back to her. "When you get back?"

"I'm going into the city for some time, I'm afraid. I have business there that can't be avoided, and I've scheduled to leave tomorrow morning."

He's leaving? Aubria's exhaustion and the stress of everything she knew and had to fix finally got the better of her, and she ducked her head to hide the tears brimming in her eyes. *"For some time…" What does that mean? How can I help him or help Veritas if he's gone?*

"That sounds…lovely!" she choked out the words, jumping to her feet and nearly overturning the pie onto the dusty, hay covered ground. Terran set it aside immediately, also rising as he stared at her with bemused concern. "Well, I won't keep you! You really should pack—"

Terran caught her by the wrist as she nearly whirled out of his reach in her haste to get away before her tears escaped. "What is happening right now?"

Aubria hadn't meant to, but before she knew it she was pouring forth some of her hurts and frustrations at his feet.

"I didn't mean to skip out on our potion lessons, and I don't particularly relish the idea of you leaving for who knows how long! I know it's silly and that I've already made myself look quite foolish in front of you a number of times, but I-I value your company and I'm loathe to lose it when you inevitably decide to stay in Oseren for good. Eldacre is hardly the most hospitable place in Lyrassan, and Loracre is strange with our rituals and obsessive caretaking of the orchard…"

Terran flushed as she sniffed and backed out of his reach as soon as he released her wrist. Aubria dabbed at her eyes with the end of her braid; they had no clean handkerchiefs in the house thanks to her father's illness, and she hadn't had the foresight to bring even a clean kitchen cloth in her pocket in case of sneezes or tears.

"I'm not leaving for good, though, and only business summons me into Oseren. You can believe me when I say that I'd rather be dead than trapped in that city for any longer than I have to be." He dipped his hand into his own pocket, still flustered, and passed her a square of dark green silk that must have cost him a fortune. A watery laugh bubbled in her throat as he handed it to her, since the affectation of expensive handkerchiefs seemed out of character for him. One of the young grooms who'd taken note of the scene, of the infamous Potioner and the Loracre girl who sold fancy pies sitting together while the lass cried, stared at them wide-eyed until his superior boxed him about the ears to remind him that the work for the day was ongoing.

"Can I start over?" Taking her laughter either for tentative agreement that he could start from the beginning or as indication that she'd lost her sanity, Terran launched into a fresh explanation as soon as they both sat down on the bench again. "I'm leaving for Oseren for a few days, that's all. I have business there that requires my actual presence, which I usually avoid. I wanted...when I ventured into Loracre a few days ago I had the idea of asking you to come with me. But since I couldn't find you and hadn't heard from you in weeks I thought you were avoiding me and that our partnership was over."

"You want me to come with you?" Aubria crinkled the handkerchief in her hand reflexively until she remembered that it was expensive and that she'd probably have to give it back once she laundered it. Terran watched her as she pinched the damp edges to smooth the wrinkles from them, appearing more anxious than she'd ever seen him before.

"Yes, and it's all right if you say no. It's probably better if you do, actually...but I'd much rather you said yes."

Aubria's breath huffed out in a frustrated exhale, because while she longed to say yes without reservation, there were other responsibilities that still demanded her time. Besides, if her father knew about this idea he would surely deny her request to accompany a man on a journey that would throw them together on the road for days without any chaperone.

She said as much to Terran, but with less of the doubt she felt bringing on a migraine. "I have things I'd need to attend to, you know. My father has the seasonal sickness: right now he needs tending. Even if he was well, I doubt he'd let me go...unless I told him that I needed time away from Loracre since my breaking my betrothal to Lane is still the talk of the town. The make-believe friend I have in Eldacre would suffice as an excuse, I suppose, though he knows I don't really care for Eldacre at all—"

The Potioner nimbly cut through her rambling with a sideways smile, which made her crumple up the handkerchief in her hands all over again. "You sound like you're planning your departure rather than making excuses not to come with me. If it helps ease the deception I can promise to be a perfect gentleman for the duration of our journey."

"That doesn't change the fact that he's ill—wait. Can you give me something for the seasonal sickness so he can move about on his own? If you help me with that, I can take care of the rest." Aubria committed to her answer wholeheartedly, the hope that during this small quest she could find the answers to every problem that troubled her kindling within her. *I can tell him about Veritas during the journey, maybe. Or after. And Oseren is said to have a huge library open to the public...the library might have books on faerykind that I can look into.*

"The seasonal sickness is common this time of year, so I've been told and so I've seen," Terran ventured as he reached into one of his other pockets and pulled out a small, wide canister made of clay that was about the size of her palm. "I've been carrying these around since so many people have come to me asking for help with their summer ailments. Give your father these and tell him to take one per day for four days. He will feel better each day until the symptoms pass."

"What do I owe you for this?" she asked as she cupped the container in her palm once he passed it to her.

"Nothing, of course. You brought me another pie, and in this case the potion craft you asked for costs me very little to make." Terran said; he laughed as she narrowed her eyes at him suspiciously, lifting his hands so the palms faced outwards in the universal gesture of surrender. "You're doing me a favor by offering me company and your talent with potions for several days. It's the least I can do to take care of your father's seasonal sensitivity and your travelling expenses."

Another thought occurred to her at the innocent mention of "company."

"What will people in Oseren think of the Potioner travelling with an unmarried lass?" she asked as she stood to leave. "They imagine us to be half-wild pagans. Surely they will notice that someone as prominent as you has brought a girl from the so-called heathens with him without a chaperone?"

"Due to the nature of my career and the...image I've labored to create of my capacity as Potioner, few people would dare question me on what I'm about. Especially lately...but no matter. No one would dare breathe a word against me, but if it troubles you I can pass you off as my cousin instead of my assistant."

Aubria glanced down at her pale blonde hair and imagined the shape and depth of her own features as she compared herself to Terran's feline sharp eyes and brown hair. "Well, we're both tan now. Maybe that will be enough to make people think we're related."

Terran laughed again; now that she thought of it, she'd never seen him quite this lighthearted. Despite what he'd told her, was it the notion of returning to the city that had put him in such good spirits? Or, her vanity wished to assure her, was he genuinely this happy that she'd agreed to go with him?

"It's settled, then. Go home, gather your things, and make your excuses to your father. I'll drive through the evening and pick you up by sunrise tomorrow morning, if you haven't changed your mind by then," he said, turning away from her to resume attending to his horse now that he considered the matter settled. Aubria started to turn away herself with a careless remark that she wouldn't change her mind, but the seriousness of what she'd committed to—lying to her father, journeying alone with a man who wasn't her betrothed or anyone she'd grown up with in the sister villages—struck her all at once along with the weight of the binding and the quest laid upon her.

She caught his attention by clearing her throat again, though she couldn't dispel any of her awkwardness once his eyes were on her. "I have something to tell you when we're on the road. If I go…you must promise to listen to me and trust that I'm telling you the truth."

Terran's jovial demeanor faded as a frown angled his mouth downwards when he faced her again from halfway inside his horse's stall. She expected him to protest, or to demand answers ahead of time, but he only nodded as she stood and tucked the handkerchief and small pot of medicine into the pockets of her dress in preparation to return to Loracre.

"Did anything happen…during Beltane?"

Terran's question, voiced with hesitant uncertainty, caught her off guard. Aubria met his searching gaze as forthrightly as she could, though internally she was squirming with guilt over her deceit.

Yes. Something did happen.

"No! Well, aside from our hawthorn grove falling to pieces, that is. Nothing happened. Why do you ask?"

Terran held her captive with his probing stare a moment longer before he exhaled and let the matter rest. "All right. You look tired, and I only wondered."

I will tell him eventually, Veritas, she voiced mentally, feeling silly for speaking to someone in her head. *I will. It's not really lying if I mean to tell him the truth as soon as I can.*

She was halfway out of the stables when she paused once more. When she turned around, she saw Terran standing there watching, as if he was sorry to see her leave.

"Why, Terran?" she asked while she had the courage. "After…well, we've not known each other long, but we've had our share of trouble and my own foolishness. Why ask me to come along at all?"

He desires your company as much as he desires you, a voice said in her head, and for a second she couldn't be sure if it was her own thoughts or Veritas's voice that she'd heard.

But the Potioner approached her, following her steps until they stood facing each other under the arch of the stable roof where they were shielded from the early afternoon sunlight. Her heart stuttered in her chest as she looked up at him, since his proximity to her now felt different from the easy camaraderie they'd shared on the bench, and she shoved her hands into her pockets to keep from twisting the end of her braid in her hands.

"You are talented in my craft, and one of the smartest women I've ever met. You still have much to learn, but you bring insight and knowledge that I have no concept of to the table. But that's not enough for me to bring you into the city, because I am a different person there...and it's dangerous for an unmarried woman to travel without keeping her wits about her," he admitted. Neither of them had moved, but Aubria imagined that she felt his piercing stare like a caress against her cheek.

"If that's not enough, then what is?" she dared ask, forcing her voice to sound light and normal...though she felt anything but.

"I don't know, Aubria. But I mean to find out."

When they parted, his words haunted her all the way back to her cottage like a musical refrain she'd never be able to banish from her mind. She realized she'd forgotten to ask: what business, exactly, had summoned him to the city after months spent in the orchard villages?

11

Aubria yelped as she almost slipped on a damp patch of grass on her way to meet the Potioner on the outskirts of Loracre. Ordinarily she had no trouble keeping her footing, since she'd had to learn how to balance skillfully on the rickety ladders the villagers used to climb the tall trees of the orchard. This time she lugged a heavy cloth satchel with her, which had caused her to stumble often enough to exacerbate her irritation. She hadn't known what to pack, which clothes or potion-making herbs and preserved fruits to bring that wouldn't make her look like an ignorant country bumpkin, so she'd brought her nicest clothes and a little bit of everything she could fit into her small wood carved medicine chest so there was less chance she'd be found wanting by the city dwellers or by Terran himself.

*Terran…*she mused, already disgusted with how delighted she was to spend so much time with him. *You have more important things to mull over on this little adventure than what it would feel like if he kissed you. Besides, how would you know if it was really Terran at all? Veritas concealed his presence from you before. He could do it again.*

That sobered some of the giddiness that had kept her fighting off a secretive smile as she gave her father the clay canister the Potioner had given her and told him of her intention to stay in Eldacre for a few days to get away from the local gossips. Darragh Haight spoiled his daughter, the villagers whispered often enough shortly after her mother had died, and this would likely bring about more of the same mutters. But Aubria wouldn't be there to hear them for a while, and she knew that her father noticed that she worked hard; taking the occasional holiday was no evil thing. Besides, if he believed she was staying in Eldacre, most likely she'd be helping her "friend" bring in the reliable crops in that village.

Straining her ears for the sounds of an approaching cart, she paused under the dewy shelter of a black walnut tree near the side of the road. Her vision had acclimated to the dark since she'd awoken early to journey to the outskirts of the village well before Terran had said he'd meet her. She'd done this mainly to avoid the prying eyes of any early risers who might see her ride off with the Potioner and gossip about it, but she had to admit to herself that a tiny part of her was afraid he'd leave her behind if she wasn't there waiting for him.

The sound she heard after a few minutes of waiting both for the sun to rise and for the Potioner to appear was not that of sturdy cart wheels rolling along the road, but the sound of eight hooves making their way in her direction. She heaved her satchel over her shoulder anew, hoping she didn't resemble a bent-backed crone seeking passage in someone's rickety apple cart as she waited by the road.

When Terran appeared, she saw no cart. The rising sun illuminated the pale coat of his gray horse along with the white and brown dappled mare he led beside his own mount. Aubria had expected a cart much like the one she hitched Toby to either for carrying baskets of fruit to and fro or for the baked treats she'd once sold in Eldacre, but he didn't have one.

"Two horses?" she observed once he reached her and dismounted in one fluid motion that reminded her that the nobility of Lyrassan often rode horses for sport most days. "What about your potion goods?"

Terran's answering smile was bright, though his eyes were heavy with sleep he'd lately shaken off. "Everything I need fits into Cloud's

174

saddlebags, and we can pick up food from the inn between us and the city. That will mean a night or two under the stars, I'm afraid, but the weather looks too fine for us to worry about a sudden downpour. Oseren has most of what I need for my potions."

"And the mare?"

"She's yours for the journey. I didn't think your father would want to spare your work horse for as long as we'll be gone, nor would the gentle beast be happy in the city," Terran answered, leading the mare to her with one coaxing whistle. "Her name's Clearwater, if you're interested. I borrowed her from a gentleman visiting Eldacre for his health who won't need her for a few weeks."

Typical, Aubria thought as she glanced down at the clean but worn skirts of her work—and now travelling—dress. *A man wouldn't think of such things.*

Still, she approached the mare with a coo of admiration. Clearwater's delicate beauty had enchanted her already, both by the sleek, well-brushed coat and the sinuous muscles that flowed under the dappled skin. Aubria had worn leggings under her dress, of course, since the mornings were damp and chilly, but she'd never ridden a horse astride in the presence of anyone other than Cerise or Lane. (Sidesaddle obviously wasn't an option for a journey of this length.)

Besides, there was the matter of her luggage…but then she saw the neat leather saddlebags hanging to either side of the mare he'd borrowed for her. It would be a simple thing to repack the items in her satchel along with the cloth carrier itself into the spacious bags.

"All right," she sighed, relenting. "Give me a moment to repack and then we can go."

Clearwater waited patiently for her to finish, and though Terran offered to help her she waved him away as she ducked behind her mare's flank to shove her more personal items into the bottom of the bag. With that taken care of, she walked around to the right side of the horse to swing herself into the saddle as best she could with her skirts somewhat hampering her progress.

"Have you eaten?" Terran asked her once she'd settled herself less than gracefully atop the long-suffering mare, who sighed with good-natured exasperation as they started off down the road.

"No, but for where we are now that's no trouble." Aubria answered, looking around her as her stomach grumbled. Then, spotting what she'd been searching for, she directed Clearwater to the side of the path to an obliging tree bedecked with spiraling green vines. After searching the vines carefully, she lifted herself up in the saddle as high as she dared to grasp the root of the vine and pull. It detached from its tree with a gratifying snap, and she let Clearwater carry her back to Cloud's side.

"This is a mendacia vine," she explained once she returned; taking the vine carefully between her two hands, she jabbed her thumbnails into the center of the vine and worked her way up until the whole green strand had been split in two. Inside the dangling vine lay row upon row of tiny black berries no bigger than the nail of her little finger, each one nearly bursting with succulence. "We call it the liar berry, since it hides so skillfully from anyone who wouldn't know to split open the vines. They're very nourishing, and once one gets past the sourness they turn sweet after a few bites."

"Interesting," Terran observed, popping a few of the berries into his mouth after she trickled a few into his open palm. "The flavor isn't unpleasant. Is there anything else they can do?"

"No, and they're not good at all unless they're fresh. That's another reason we call them the liar berry: anything so hard to find tends to be beneficial or poisonous in some way, but these silly things take a fair amount of effort for very little payoff. They're popular with Loracre children since these are a good replacement for candy."

"I asked if you were hungry because I brought you breakfast," he said. Reaching into his own saddlebags, he picked up a small, cloth wrapped bundle from the pile and leaned her way for her to take it. "It's a significant journey, and we won't have any real food until tomorrow night when we get to the inn."

Touched, Aubria picked up the pie and unwrapped the crumbling pastry. Her stomach growled again as she brought it to her mouth to take a bite, but she made a face at the bland taste as soon as it touched her tongue.

"Well, we can't all bake like me," she joked, and was rewarded with a smile from her new companion.

"It was the best I could do, really. Bachelors aren't exactly known for their cooking," he replied.

"Terran Caird. You are a *Potioner*. It's your job to combine ingredients just so. How have you kept your career for this long?"

They continued to banter back and forth for a ways until Aubria's nerves got the better of her and she lapsed into a heavy silence. The only men she'd really spent time with alone had been her father and then Lane: the one was obviously a parent and thus an easy companion, and Lane's assured devotion had given her confidence from the start of their understanding. But Terran...he was an enigma. Given that she had a complicated mess of feelings she avoided confronting, she hardly knew how to interact with him.

"What business drags you into Oseren?" Aubria asked after a short period of silence. "You seemed...reluctant to go."

It was the worst way she could have phrased her question, and she winced for fear of what he'd think she was fishing for. She still had to find a way to lead into the confession that she knew about Veritas and *knew* him in a carnal sense as well.

Relax, a voice that wasn't hers murmured in her head. *He doesn't think the worst of you whenever you speak. Your constant tension is wearying for me, however.*

Veritas! Can't you give some warning that you're spying on my thoughts before you startle me to death? She snapped at him, though relief that he was present coursed through her. She had little to no knowledge of how the Potioner and the spirit bound to him could interact, if they ever really had, but there was the small chance that Veritas would help her explain...if she begged.

That would ruin the fun, but if it troubles you too much I suppose I can behave myself. The spirit in her head laughed, a distinctly odd sensation that made her feel like she'd gone mad. She couldn't help but picture the memory of him making the same sound closer to her ear when she had been beneath him.

Shuddering, Aubria brushed the crumbs from the breakfast pie off her fingers and tried to ignore both Veritas and the memory.

"I have business, like I told you. Some of my clients are...insistent about remaining in the city or anywhere 'civilized,' and when their urgent letters stack up to a certain height I make a journey into the city to satisfy their demands and make some coin," Terran answered the question she'd almost forgotten she'd asked in the wake of Veritas's mischief, delaying for his own reasons.

"Shouldn't they come to you regardless of how uncomfortable our heathen villages make them? You gave me the impression that you're important in the city," she asked, teasing a little. Still, indignation that the city dwellers who relied on the bounty of Loracre's and Eldacre's crops and the villagers' sweat and toil had been bred into her from birth, and she allowed herself to enjoy the full scope of this as she frowned.

"Maybe. But...it's good for me to remember." Terran leaned down to brush a leaf from Cloud's mane, perhaps using the movement to avoid her interested gaze. But no, that couldn't be true, because he rarely showed any discomfort with her questions. Unless...

"Remember what?" Aubria asked, anticipating his lie.

"Remember what I left behind. *Why* I left it behind."

That didn't sound like a lie, but she felt the weight of what he didn't want to tell her resting like a broken bridge between them.

It took them most of the first half of their journey to break free of the orchard on the narrow road leading to the city from Loracre.

The road had been designed to cut the quickest path through the trees for trade purposes. Ordinarily, any soul with a hankering to wander could have lost themselves under the trees forever without finding a way free if it hadn't been for the village settlements beyond Loracre and the road itself.

It felt bizarre to travel without the shade of the trees she'd grown up under her whole life. The open sky, filled with puffy clouds drifting through the firmament like foam-crested waves in the ocean she'd heard tales about, made her feel like she was trapped under a dome and yet unbearably exposed to the universe. But all things pass, and after a few hours she grew used to the feeling and saved her wild notions for her dreams.

After a day and night of travelling, during which Aubria and Terran chatted on and off about everything and nothing—potion craft, the parts of their past they were willing to share, and so on—they reached the inn Terran had spoken of that lay between the orchard villages and the great city. When she was a child, Darragh had brought her into the city for a holiday and they'd stayed at this same inn. But that had been over a decade ago, long enough to dim her memories into the fog of forgetfulness that blanketed most childhoods, and she doubted anyone would equate the plump, sandy-haired child she had been with the young woman that stepped over the threshold in the present.

In spite of how long it had been, she still dreaded someone recognizing her and carrying their tales of where she was back to Loracre or Eldacre. Her fears proved groundless within the first few minutes of their arrival: the Potioner cut a much more intriguing figure, and she more than anyone else was dazzled by the switch in persona she witnessed. They'd talked more than they ever had before on their journey, and though she hated herself for it, Aubria wished she hadn't had to sleep alone under the stars with the thick quilt she'd artfully rolled into a log and tied tightly with twine.

Then again, Aubria had been the one to talk the most since her past held less mystery or trauma than Terran's. She realized this as he imperiously ordered the attendants at the inn around and flashed coin like it was nothing—because he didn't fear anyone stealing from him—that she really didn't know him well at all. Sobered by the insight, she was glad to leave him for her separate rented room by the time they ate and drank their fill of a country repast and mulled wine not even half the quality of what they produced in the orchard.

But that night, she dreamed of Veritas...or he dreamed of her, and they met in the middle.

Once again, she was standing in the orchard near the lightning field in the white dress that she'd dyed red for Beltane. In the dream, the dress seemed to be halfway white and halfway red, as if someone had begun to change its color and neglected to finish the job. Flowers sharing the same strange ailment of color trailed down from vines tangled into her long hair, pale enough to gleam under the hypnotic moonlight...except where they were dark red like fresh blood.

Aubria wasn't alone here, she knew from the start, and to learn anything at all or wake up from the dream, she had to move forward. So, frowning with distaste, she clenched her hands in the folds of her bizarre colored skirts and followed the unfolding path her subconscious led her along.

"He's declined to tell you why we're going into the city, I see," Veritas told her once she made her way to the edge of the lightning field to find him. She'd sensed his presence all along, somehow knowledgeable in this dreamscape, but she still loathed to approach the field.

"He *did* tell me, though I'm not stupid enough to believe that's the only reason. I don't suppose you could illuminate the truth for me?"

They both stared out at the lightning field, and when he didn't answer right away she puzzled over why he'd brought her *here* of all places, if he was indeed the one moderating this dream. Or was it her own anxiety over the risky journey she had undertaken with the Potioner? She had experienced visceral fear in the marrow of her bones the first time she had looked on this place as an adult, when she'd woken up beside it alone in the orchard. Mightn't she have associated that experience with the unsettling feeling of danger all along?

"Our kind fears this place as well, for lightning can kill us as swiftly as any mortal," Veritas interrupted her musings. "Long ago, in the primordial days of humankind, this was where many of us gathered every few centuries to dance under the blessed moon. It wasn't the lightning field then, though. It was merely the most beautiful place in the orchard...so I was told. I am mature for one of the faerykind, but not as old as most of us."

"I thought I told you not to pry into my mind," Aubria reminded him. "Yet here you are, or here *we* are, in this strange dream of a place neither of us would go to again willingly."

Veritas shrugged, the gesture different even though in this dream landscape he still wore Terran's body. Yet he didn't pass for a full mortal as Terran usually did: luminous shards of light split free from his skin with his movement, at times, and once again Aubria endured the sickening sight of seeking the framework of Terran's bones when Veritas pressed his palm against the bark of a graying tree as if it were the grave of an old friend.

"Why did you stop me from telling Terran about the ritual and our accidental binding? Then was as good a time as any other."

"I knew he wanted to invite you on this journey, and surely you can figure out why I needed to make sure you came along. You've been angry at me, but stop and think about it for a moment and you'll understand."

Grumbling under her breath as he waited expectantly for her to comply, Aubria crossed her arms and thought back to when they'd stood in Eldacre's stable days ago. She'd been too overwhelmed to think everything through, and her exhaustion from working sun up to well past sundown hadn't faded until she'd departed Loracre with her new companion.

"The library in Oseren. We might find our answers there...in fact, I doubt we'd be able to find answers anywhere else. I've been told there are books enough to address hundreds of problems like ours, with our binding and the faerykind intent on stealing the orchard back. Is that it?"

"Yes. And no."

"No?" Aubria drew a pattern in the dirt with the tip of her shoe, but when she looked down she saw something else entirely, following the usual pattern of changeable dreams. The circle she'd traced embedded itself into the earth and spiraled out to carve its own pattern, wider and wider until she and Veritas stood in a crude replica of the sacred wheel of the year. But she refused to be distracted by the machinations of her own dreams: marching forward, she seized Veritas's arm and made him turn to face her head on.

"Speak plainly, or let me leave this dream. I swore I'd help you break the binding, but I refuse to let you lead me around any longer by withholding information."

Veritas glanced down at her hand on his arm, his expression mild with one pointedly arched eyebrow, but she glared at him until he looked back at her. When he did so, she deigned to drop her hand.

"You can't hurt or threaten me in a dream. I would like some answers, please, and quickly. I'm a light sleeper, so who knows when I might wake up," she snapped, surprised at her own daring. She expected him to challenge her, or try to scare her, and she steeled herself for the fury…but it never came.

"There are things you should know about Terran—about *me*—that I am not at liberty to tell you plainly. If I am cryptic, it's because I'm trying to think of ways to work around my own nature and my enforced loyalty to the Caird bloodline. I cannot lie, as you know, but there are truths I cannot yet speak." Veritas sighed as he explained. This time she witnessed a little of what was going on under his cool exterior: he was just as frustrated as she was, and bound by far more complex rules.

Reluctant though she was to accept such an impediment, Aubria had to relent. "Is there anything you *can* tell me? I know that there is more I need to know, some…rumors I need to settle before I can help either of you. It would help to know whether or not I was on the right path."

"Which rumors?" he asked. "There are many. They say that the Potioner is a heathen god in a human body. They say that he uses the black arts to buy himself strength and eternal youth. They say that he cheats at cards, has left penniless bastards all over the country, and they say that he was the king's assassin in days past."

Aubria snorted. Terran was not personable enough to play cards with people in taverns, let alone sleep with enough women to leave bastards over all of Lyrassan. She discarded the rumors about his black magic as well, since the Potioners had always been magically inclined and people loved to gossip about those who were different from them. If he possessed great strength and vitality, it was because of his own bloodline and Veritas himself.

The assassin rumor, though...

"They say," she started to speak, but her words failed her until she could gather them to herself like making a basket for fruit with her apron. "They say that the Potioner is to blame for the younger prince's death. They say Prince Mardin hired him to remove his brother from succession in case King Barric chose him to rule instead."

"Do they now? It doesn't shock me that that tale travelled from the listening walls of the keep all the way to Loracre." Veritas smiled, congratulating her, but there was a whisper of danger behind his courtesy. "Do you believe that what you've heard is the truth or the lie?"

Aubria met his stare head on and answered his challenge with the truth she hadn't wanted to say. "I may not know the particulars or the reasons behind the choice he made, but...I want to have faith that there is a piece of the puzzle I'm missing that would justify the murder if he took part in it. Maybe that's foolish...no, of course it's foolish. I know nothing of court, or of Terran Caird the Potioner. But I would hear the truth from him, if I could. It's not my place to judge a story I only know part of."

Veritas came to a halt on the etched symbol of fire in one spoke of the wheel on the ground: the fire signified Beltane, which she doubted was a coincidence.

"There are things neither he nor I can bear to tell you yet, Aubria, and this is one tale that escapes us both. It would behoove you to investigate the threads of this tale while you are in the city. If you gather enough of the threads on your own one of us might be able to break our silence."

Or you could just tell me now! The bratty child Aubria had been once screeched its outrage, but for once she understood the hesitation and the potential for shame one or both of them must be going through, whether the story was true or not. It was why she had been glad, really, and relieved at heart when Veritas had demanded that she wait to tell Terran her secrets.

"I will do as you say," she promised, "but I want something in return."

"Oh?"

"I will need your help in the library. I might not even be able to enter on my own merit, though it's supposedly open to the public. There might be books they refuse to let me access, and I'm not too proud to admit that I'm not the strongest reader when it comes to ancient scripts. Besides, it's *our* binding we'd be working on, and *your* people that I'm attempting to overcome. I hope to—"

"Don't oversell. I'll do it. Terran can finish what he needs to in the mornings and evenings during our stay. I will meet you in the library during the afternoons that we are free." Veritas cut her off.

It still sounded strange hearing the truth spirit talk about his life with Terran in terms of "we" while still referring to himself as a separate entity. Aubria could barely wrap her head around the concept, though between faerykind mischief and the other events of her life she had developed more and more immunity to the oddities of the unseen world she'd grown up not truly believing in.

Her head tipped in an almost bow of respect for his unexpected willingness to listen to her and speak to her like an equal. After their first encounter she had expected far worse treatment, even in a dream that they shared. She began to wonder about the nature of their bindings once again, and she cocked her head to the side thoughtfully as she wondered if Veritas was always awake and active when Terran slept, since he inconvenienced the Potioner as little as possible during his waking hours.

"We are not all cruel," Veritas told her in a soft voice, and she rubbed the back of her neck with chagrin; she'd forgotten yet again that he could poke through the knotted yarn of thoughts in her head. "I have directed the corrupt bodies of the Cairds for centuries now, and if we do not break this binding then I will again. Terran is determined not to reproduce, but others have thought the same before him...regardless. It is no easy thing to wait a lifetime for the chance to use a body completely as my own, with no regard for a soul as gray and rotten as this accursed field...but I am no thief, and I respect that which is good in humankind. I can wait, and in the meantime inconvenience my host as little as possible."

How can he be both honestly good and yet a murderer of the younger prince? She wondered, but Veritas did not comment on that question as it spun through her head like chaff in the wind. Instead, he changed the subject, grimacing as if his next words pained him.

"Be careful, Aubria Haight. Those in Oseren tolerate peasant customs as long as they stay far away from them, but when those beliefs trespass into their territory they can become hostile."

Aubria didn't remember such stark contrasts, since she'd been a child riding on her father's shoulders on their last and only visit. "Is it really so bad? Our crops should keep everyone in the city well fed, and in the flatlands I hear tell of miles of golden wheat and pleasant gardens bedecked with nourishing vegetables."

Veritas ceased his pacing of the wheel she'd accidentally carved into the dreamworld earth to approach her. One minute he stood several feet away, and the next he was right in front of her and tilting her chin up with his warm hand.

"You are with the Potioner, and thus it will not go so badly for you. But you are unranked on the social ladder, and appealing enough to draw attention wherever you go. They will think you are weak and half-wild, and try to take advantage. Do not fuel their prejudice or stir their violence by speaking of your life in the orchard or any of your beliefs. Remember, most of the people in Lyrassan worship only one, ruthless god, and to speak against him is heresy regardless of how the king allows your people worship the nature gods of old."

She would have nodded, but he held her face in both of his hands now as if she were something that he feared to lose.

"I'll be careful," she promised, her voice a whisper as the yellow eyes she feared would steal her secrets held her captive with their focus.

"Good," Veritas said as he traced the pad of his thumb across her bottom lip. "You're of value yet, orchard girl."

Then he kissed her: tenderly, sweetly, as if he was saying goodbye only for a time and meant to see her again soon. Aubria hesitated, unsure of his game, but her body betrayed her when she kissed him back as she lifted her own hands to rest over his.

"Is this you, or am I out of the dream?" she asked, breathless when he withdrew.

Veritas grinned…then it was morning, and she awoke to a knock on the door.

*T*hough she had been prepared for a radical change in scenery,

Aubria was immediately overwhelmed with color and sound and scent as soon as they passed the city gates. Since Oseren was known throughout the world for its hospitality and the beauty of its ancient architecture she had expected greatness, but what greeted her was the highs and lows of a city filled with mainly the exceedingly rich or the frightfully poor. The sturdy towers with their pointed domes that had been built and mortared by the elder giants when such creatures had still existed in the world caught her attention first, but at the bottoms of those towers scrambled such a press of humanity that she almost turned on her heel and fled.

Terran didn't see the need to guide her through the crowds, but the comfort of his presence lingered as people ebbed closer and away again. Aubria was glad they had left their horses at the stable right on the edge of the city since she was sure Cloud and Clearwater would have enjoyed the press of the crowd even less than herself. Still, there was much to see and enjoy for an orchard girl who hadn't ventured out of her home town in over a decade.

"Have we arrived during market day?" she asked Terran as soon as they drew close enough to hear one another.

"No, but the city gates open straight into the bulk of the merchant's district. It makes for a rude awakening into city life, but for the most part this area of the city is harmless...aside from the cutpurses and the overzealous guardsmen. Stay close to me until we get out of the district."

Aubria agreed with her whole heart. She'd brought a few coppers and her five precious silver gents from her savings, which she'd tucked carefully into a pocket she'd sown into what could only be called her riding leggings now that she wore them without a dress bunched up around her hips. For now she was too besieged by the smell of unwashed bodies and exotic spices concealing faintly rotting cooked meat from the market stalls to wander. The sight of so many guards wandering around with their formally mustachioed faces and gleaming helmets brought back the sick remembrance of almost being at one of their number's mercy not too many months ago.

It felt freeing to walk without the weight of her skirts, plain though they were compared to the silk and velvet laden works of art donned by the noble ladies she glimpsed as they passed from the market district into that of the nobility who were not privileged enough to live in the castle alongside their king and the raucous elder prince. Yet Aubria hunched her shoulders as the pinch of hundreds of eyes watching her and Terran pass through their numbers nipped at her. Surely to their prying eyes she looked like a vagabond with her leggings and straw hat and the satchel she'd repacked from Clearwater's saddlebags and slung over her shoulder. The Potioner himself, though travel-stained, commanded attention and respect wherever people noticed him: whereas they only had shifty glances and mouths that curled in revulsion for the peasant that trailed the king's former favorite like a pet, they appeared delighted that he'd graced their city with his presence again after so long an absence.

Finally they reached the place Terran had been leading her through Oseren towards, and she almost ran into him when he stopped.

Aubria craned her head to look up at the tall building: they'd reached the fabled Potioner's tower at last. The lower bricks were stained with dirt and grime from the streets, as every establishment in Oseren bore with pride, but the smooth marble halfway up and near the top boasted regal cleanliness and majesty. They marched up a set of smooth swept stairs to reach the front door, which was made of etched stone gilded here and there with runes of protection carved either by Terran himself or one of his ancestors. She stretched out a hand and impulsively traced her fingers over the etched sigils. She could sense the magic exuding from this place like mold from a dungeon, though the tingles it sent to make her hair stand on end weren't unpleasant in the same way.

"Are these your doing?" she asked Terran.

"You can sense that?" he asked instead of answering her question as he rested his palm on the sigil that had taken the place of a doorknob; the gold gleaming through his skin reminded her of Veritas's otherworldly light, and she took a step back as the Potioner's eyes glinted silver. "How interesting."

Then the door swung inwards, Terran motioned her inside, and she had no choice but to decide whether or not to enter.

It's all right, she muttered to herself in the coaxing voice of her father when he'd found their latest cat as a kitten, curled up by their stack of firewood. *You've nothing to fear.*

When she passed through the wide foyer into the proper rooms of the house, she couldn't restrain a gasp of wonder as she looked all around at the finery. Dropping her satchel to the ground with a thump, she tossed her hat on top of it and she dashed forward without regard for propriety. All around her and under her feet flowed smooth, pale marbled ribboned with streaks of stately gray, yet this place felt neither cold nor like the dungeon she'd imagined. Patterned rugs not at all surrendered to the blight of dust crushed satisfyingly under her tread, and the various tables and places to sit looked like they'd been crafted with materials more expensive than ten of the cottages in Loracre.

"Why keep this place at all if you never visit?" she asked, turning around and around in the main room as she stared up at the domed ceiling painted to look like the heavens; it was grander than anything she'd seen in her life. "It seems so dear an expense to pay for a house and attendants you don't make use of."

"If it was just me I would brave the sordid little inns and avoid this place. But I thought you might enjoy staying here, especially compared to our other alternatives of unpleasantly crowded inns or the cold of the keep itself." He watched her for her reaction, as if she were a specimen of nature he'd captured in the wild and had only just come to understand.

But did he understand at all, or even see the nature of what he'd found? She wondered this as her amused smile faded: did he expect her to fall on her knees and thank him for this opportunity to stay in so grand of a house?

"Yes," she said as she ducked into a contemptuous curtsy, as if she were playing along with a jest. "I imagine that my fresh eyes might help you appreciate your former home as only an orchard girl might."

"Stop that," Terran insisted, his eyes beginning to narrow. "That's not what I meant and you know it."

"Do I know it? Is that not how you—"

"My lord Caird?" A new voice broke into their conversation, startling them both. A female servant clothed all in sensible brown stood in the doorway of the main room, confusion on her face as she looked between an aggravated Terran and his new guest. "We were not aware you had returned, though of course we have kept your home in readiness for—"

Terran seemed in the mood to interrupt people, for he waved away her excuses with generous authority. "Of course, Madam Herst. If you could ascertain that my rooms are prepared along with separate lodging for my cousin, I would be grateful. When you are finished, bring me the house ledgers and show Lady Aubria to her rooms."

The housekeeper's eyes darted back and forth between her two unexpected guests as she curtsied in acknowledgment of her orders; fine lines appeared around her eyes as she squinted at Aubria's travel stained man's shirt and leggings—not so out of touch for a peasant who had work to do, but definitely out of place in the world of nobles and courtiers—with suspicion.

"Will you require tea or sustenance, my lord?"

"No, that will be all." Terran smiled at his attendant as he pointed at the empty table with clawed legs next to an ostentatious settee. Aubria tried not to gape once it filled with a porcelain tray laden with a steaming tea pot and a variety of delectables that had her mouth watering from afar. She thought she caught sight of a nespola biscuit, huddled away under a trio of costly cream puffs.

Squinting at Aubria once more, the housekeeper departed with a swish of her starched skirts. Her sour face troubled Aubria less than the realization that Terran could do more, possibly *far* more, than cobble together whatever potions he dreamed up.

"But that was magic! *Real* magic!" she exclaimed as she dashed to the table of tea and treats to see if it was real and not an illusion; then she whirled on Terran, her messy braid almost coming undone at last. "I knew you were the Potioner, and a wizard too, but you never perform magic like that…"

Terran's expression didn't change under the burden of her effusions, and her captivated smile slipped a notch as he held up a hand thoughtfully. Flames the same green of his eyes wavered at his fingertips, reflecting against the gilded paint of the ceiling and the vast fireplace. After a moment of watching them flicker he extinguished them with a sigh.

"I am a Potioner: that's the majority of my work. Magic comes with a cost, even if that cost isn't clear at first…but the king, and now the prince, likes to…remind others of my abilities, whether I wish to show them off or not, to ensure that others do not forget what kind of powerful people he keeps under his command."

"Meaning?" Aubria had no head for politics. She tried to act casual by taking one of the cream puffs as well as a seat on the firm cushions of a nearby chair, but when she remembered the state of her clothes she jumped back to her feet with less grace than when she'd sat down.

"Meaning that when I am in Oseren I am expected to conduct myself as one of his prized officials. As a man who ensures the fear and respect of everyone around him. In this city you will find that often the walls seem to hear all secrets. It doesn't hurt to expend the magic I must to keep up appearances for servants who will be sure to gossip and tell tales of how fearsome and demanding I can be."

Maybe she didn't understand, maybe she was going about this all wrong and asking the wrong questions, but she couldn't hold her interest at bay now that she knew for sure the Potioner was more than he seemed. "But you have magic! Wouldn't it be a gift, the ability to do what you wish most of the time?"

Terran raised an eyebrow at her, the one covered with the intricate tattoo she hadn't yet been able to decipher. "We all have magic, Aubria. I'm beginning to realize that you have more magic as your birthright than I expected, since you wouldn't be able to sense or understand as much of my craft as you do without a touch of the gift. But magic is both a privilege and a danger. Wasting it on trivialities is not something I wish to be known for."

She didn't know what to say to that, so she muttered a bit around the bite of the cream puff she'd taken while he spoke. Besides, too many questions battled to be asked first: why did he come to the city if he hated it and loathed having to use his magic for show instead of for the craft he was passionate about? Had he brought her along as a charity case, or as a friend to help him with his work? He'd said she had traces of magic, so if she did…how could she access it?

Another worse question almost won out before she crushed it, and she paled with the implications regardless. *Is the Caird bloodline's magic from Veritas and their binding? If I were to undo the binding, what would become of Terran?*

She hoped that Veritas hadn't heard *that* particular thought.

"All has been done as you requested, my lord, and I have the ledger here for your perusal." The polished accent of the housekeeper broke into her thoughts, and she hoped that they scattered like dandelion seeds, too many for Veritas to bring together again. This time the housekeeper didn't bother to hide her glare once Terran took the heavy, leather bound ledger from her hands and turned away.

I am a creature out of my place and a girl imagining above her station to them, Aubria thought with a sick flash of mortification. *He's said I'm his cousin, but I doubt they believe it. Do they think I'm his whore? Some stupid village lass he'll take advantage of before sending her home with a fat purse?*

Pay them no mind, Veritas's voice slipped through her veil of embarrassment to offer unanticipated solace. *They are servants, and whatever else people want to say, Terran did bring you here as his assistant. That makes you above most people in this city, as in the elder days those who possessed the ability to wield true magic were above all else but the royal family.* Aubria struggled to hide the relief that dappled her anxious nerves as Terran's searching gaze landed squarely on her shoulders. It was difficult not to answer back aloud, as if Veritas could respond openly, but she managed it and took her leave with the servant who the Potioner had gestured to take her to the room she'd stay in during her time in the city.

But I'm the sort of girl who would dream to come and work in a place like this, if that was my only way to live a life outside of the orchard. I've a bit of skill with herbs and a knack for potion craft…but I don't have magic, not really. At heart I'm just a nobody, no matter how much I dream of being a somebody.

I don't think so, Veritas's voice purred against her discomfort, rubbing against it as a cat might when it conditionally sought affection.

You are very much a somebody, Aubria Haight. We will find out how much of one soon enough.

She might have smiled as she trudged up the curving staircase the housekeeper led her to, but she didn't want Terran to see.

12

The business Terran had come to the city to manage took him away from his ostentatious house in Oseren, but Aubria had other things to think about. He left her plenty of work, enough to counter her secret mission to get to the city library, and enough to remind her that this hadn't been a pleasure visit at all.

It hadn't been *meant* to be a pleasure visit. Though Aubria missed her orchard, and missed the swaying, fruit laden tree boughs that formed the canopy of her home, she found that she was having the time of her life working alongside Terran in a place so different from anything she'd ever known. For fear of seeming reluctant or getting left behind in Loracre, she hadn't precisely asked how many days they'd be staying in the city. She'd told her father that she wasn't sure when she'd be returning from Eldacre, but that she'd keep him up to date with letters or a messenger if she needed to. Of course she couldn't do this from Oseren, but she'd hoped rather than known for certain that they would only spend a few days here rather than a week.

Her anxieties over not being seen as a worthy associate for someone as well-known as the Potioner purely based on her appearance faded after a warm bath to wash the dust of the road off her hair and skin the first night. The housekeeper had led her to a marble washroom without giving her a chance to refuse, as if by washing this dirty peasant she would somehow cleanse the taint from her master's richly decorated house. Aubria hadn't minded, thanks to the final result. She'd scrubbed herself thoroughly and brushed her drying hair by light of the hearth in her bedroom until it shone like platinum gold. More importantly, from what she'd seen in the city, the few dresses she'd brought from home would not shame her here: unless Terran intended to bring her before king and court, her attire served perfectly for a Potioner's assistant who wanted to spend every spare moment in the public library.

The first morning after she'd awoken early and dressed in her sturdy, dark blue dress, a knock at the door was followed by the housekeeper herself breezing into her bedroom as if it were her own. Aubria hid a sigh of relief that she'd already cleansed her mouth with the thin wooden brush dipped in fresh, mint infused water that one of the servants had set out for her. Terran had claimed that only a few retainers had been kept on by the nature of his power in court during his absence—though he chose not to use it most of the time—but even if only the housekeeper and a few other servants kept watch over the house and its inhabitants, Aubria felt a little pampered.

The older woman peered around the wide-windowed, generous sleeping quarters with a poorly disguised sneer of distaste, and the breakfast tray laden with sugary buns, fresh bacon, and fluffy eggs wobbled as she set it down on a nearby night table.

"Thank you?" Aubria said, voicing the words as a question when the housekeeper refrained from leaving. Her nerves creaked uncomfortably, as if her knees were supposed to bend in respect to this woman instead of the other way around. As far as Madam Herst was concerned, Aubria was a relation and honored guest of her master, the king's Potioner. Yet she looked more than a little displeased with this concept.

"My master seeks your company in his workroom as soon as you finish your breakfast. I am to fetch you in a quarter hour."

I'm supposed to eat comfortably with this gargoyle guarding my door? I don't think so, Aubria concealed a frown with a puzzled look before she smiled as politely as she could.

"There's no need for that. I'll eat on the way," she said. Without giving her the chance to protest, Aubria did as she'd declared and snatched a long strip of bacon and a warm biscuit for good measure. Thinking better of the mess, she grabbed a cloth napkin folded on the edge of the tray and tucked it into the pocket of her russet apron.

Madam Herst looked like she was about to collapse into a fit of rage, especially in the face of Aubria arching her brows in unspoken challenge, but she held her tongue and restrained herself to a cold glare as she turned on her heel and led Aubria out of her room.

Yesterday she would've thought that she'd never become used to such a grand house...a house that didn't seem built and furnished according to the tastes of the Terran she knew. Grand paintings with gilded frames greeted her at every turn, their historical scenes mostly unfamiliar to her, and her sturdy boots—as clean as she could get them, since she'd scrubbed them with an old but unsoiled rag before they'd left Loracre—clunked against the smooth marble floors with the rhythm of her steps. There were few windows that looked out on the streets at the ground level of the tower, but as they passed through room after room and ascended the curving stairs she noted that more and more light brightened the area as the number of windows increased. Each was framed by dark curtains, like eyelids ready to close over a sleep heavy gaze. Whatever Terran or his ancestors had been like, they had all agreed on the necessity for privacy.

Her calves were burning only a little by the time they reached the top of the stairs, but Madam Herst was trying and failing to conceal her huffing and puffing. This must have furthered her resentment: she tapped her knuckles twice against the robust oak door barring them from the Potioner's work room and abandoned her charge there without another word.

Rolling her eyes, Aubria entered the room and closed the door behind her. Her skirt snagged on the edge, but she caught it in time and concealed her minor embarrassment with a cough. She knew, too, that she should apologize for the unwanted pique she'd inflicted on him upon their arrival yesterday, and that too put her off.

Then she forgot about all of that—along with the rudeness of Terran's housekeeper—when she saw the magnificence of the room she'd entered.

Unlike the rest of the house, this room bore none of the burden of grandiose rugs and artwork and cold marble statuary she was now certain Terran had had no hand in choosing for himself. Only the floor was smooth marble, and she noted with some interest that there were somehow six walls instead of four. Each wall held something different, either shelving or drawers from ceiling to floor. Three of the shelf walls were filled with different colored bottles in all shapes and styles, and some made of more materials than ceramic or glass alone.

Green for healing, black for hurting, and blue for...blue is for magic, she remembered later than she should have. A memory of running through the orchard with the ears and sight and part of the mind of a woodland hare made the tip of her nose tingle, and as she beheld the countless blue bottles she wondered what each one could do.

The drawers, she assumed, were full of the ingredients and tools a Potioner might require for his craft, and these too made her itch to uncover what secrets lay within them. The only wall not covered by shelving or drawers held the door she'd entered, and she looked up at long last to see that the light spilling into the enclosed room from above was from a domed sky light which angled the morning light onto two long tables that stood a little apart from the surrounding walls. The potions, some of which might have been sensitive to light or heat, weren't touched by the streaming sunlight, but she could still read any labels in sight.

Terran stood slightly hunched over one of the two opposite tables, muttering to himself as he poured a quarter of the contents of a black bottle into a blue one through a copper funnel. Not muttering...*casting,* she realized, as her ears caught the accent of words she'd never heard before. The part of her that knew nothing of the world should have been frightened, or at least shocked now that she was seeing real magic at work for the first time: the potion began to glow through the opaque container it had been poured into, which no liquid should rightly have been able to do.

Aubria had been unsettled by the changes she'd seen in him on the road and after they'd arrived in this strange tower inhabited only by themselves and a few servants, and felt like maybe she'd begun to sell her heart piecemeal to someone she didn't know in the slightest. But this...she smiled as she watched him, content that for once she was allowed to see the real Terran in his natural habitat.

Not sure what else to do since he seemed so focused, she coughed as unobtrusively as she could. It seemed right, somehow, to see him like this and to hear and watch him work. In his workshop in Eldacre he must have taken more care to make it seem like what he was doing wasn't entirely magical and more scientific, but the process she watched him perform now looked as natural as watching a blacksmith hammering steel into a sword. The unexpected butterflies in her stomach made her feel like she'd come home for the first time, or recognized something about herself that she hadn't before.

"Oh," Terran said when he saw her, as if she'd surprised him even though he'd been the one to summon her. "Are we back to dresses, then?"

Aubria looked down at her skirts, which were more practical than voluminous compared other gowns she'd seen in the city. "Leggings aren't proper outside of the orchard during workdays. I mainly wore them so I could go astride on Clearwater during our journey."

"Hm," he remarked, his eyes already glazing over and making her assume that he was thinking about something else as he tapped the bottom of a glass potion bottle against the table to settle its swirling contents. She was about to ask what he'd been conjuring when he addressed her again.

"I suppose I've grown used to seeing you move about un-encumbered. More importantly, we don't worry about such things here. You may wear what you wish, if you prefer the leggings after all."

Aubria was about to snap that she didn't require his permission to wear whatever she chose, but for once she exercised a modicum of discernment to guess what he really meant: he wanted her to be comfortable, since they'd be working together longer hours than they ever had before, and he didn't want her to feel ashamed in the city he'd invited her to visit with him.

"I'll keep that in mind," she said instead of abandoning her composure over nothing. "What are you working on, and how can I help?"

Terran raised his eyebrows at her, perhaps caught off guard that she hadn't snapped at him. Sliding his current project to the side, he gestured for her to approach his work table as he began telling her about what he planned for them to make.

And to work they went, spending most of the morning and early afternoon hours crafting potions.

More important than anything else, she began to realize with delighted surprise that Terran had been right about her, even if she hadn't had the guts to take notice herself. Aubria was *really* good at potion craft, and it gave her significant joy to practice a talent that she hadn't known she possessed. She'd always been gifted at the little things like organizing, seeing the bigger picture, and knowing when to listen. In the instance of potion making, these aspects of her nature aided her more than she'd expected: reorganizing the walls and walls of potion bottles Terran kept in his multipurpose vault and workroom helped her make connections that gave her new ideas for helpful mixtures—even toxic ones—that he hadn't thought of on his own. Soon her cramped handwriting decorated the labels of a modest array of potions throughout the room; she liked to think that they were tiny pieces of herself, so if she were to leave them to cure and not return here he would have something to remember her by.

The fruits and herbs from the orchard that she'd brought in her small wooden chest also helped, and she fancied that by *listening* to the potential of her store of ingredients, by imagining what they might want to become, she found some of her best ideas. With her treasured store of thornbells and a few of Terran's carefully categorized ingredients she crafted a tincture similar to the one he'd had her make for Sir Bor's supposedly unfaithful wife, one that wouldn't make anyone sick. Then, using dried nespola, aged hawthorn blossoms, essence of jasper, and the unlikely addition of raspberry cordial, she crafted a recipe for the idea she'd described to Terran in Eldacre's stables.

I might have to use this one myself, she thought grimly as Terran passed her the raspberry cordial he'd helpfully fetched from his stores of liquor and wine. *I still have things to tell him, even if I'm too much of a coward to confess now.*

Pausing with her hand poised over the copper mixing bowl, she hesitated to dump the not inexpensive cordial into the complicated assortment of ingredients as uneasiness made her stomach turn over.

"How do we know when it's ready? If it's safe?" she asked him as a drop of the dark cordial mingled with the brightly colored slew of other ingredients. "I'd hate to find someone to test this on in case it doesn't work…"

Terran passed her a blank label with a string tied through it so she could mark down the name and properties of the potion before setting it in a new place on the shelf to rest and grow more potent.

"We who work with potions have instincts that people without our gifts simply do not. These instincts require honing, usually, but when there's a satisfactory amount of natural talent it's no bad thing to hope for the best."

"That seems rather cavalier," she muttered as she stared at her new potion warily. Terran shrugged.

"It might seem that way, and in the case of making potions involving various poisons I usually conduct more tests that you'll learn about as we go on. But for this one, I think trusting both of our instincts will be sufficient. Sometimes even I never know exactly how a potion will work…but ingredients don't deceive, not really."

Aubria nodded along with him as she poured a measure of the cordial into the bowl and picked up a clean copper spoon from the table to mix it together. Then she paused as Terran drew close, not only from his unexpected proximity, but from the realization he'd expected her to discern without surprise.

"Wait, Terran. You're confirming I have magic?"

"Haven't I been saying that all along? Now stir, and pay attention." He didn't directly answer her, but she couldn't berate him for his cryptic reply: he stood close to her to watch her stir the sludgy, discolored potion, and she shifted her weight to get away from him so she could concentrate. His clean yet somehow always smoky scent and the less than mortal heat drifting off of his skin had proved time and time again that he was far too much of a distraction for her, and she tried to listen to whatever magic lay within her instead of thinking about that as he began to chant a circular quintet of words in the language she hadn't been able to identify.

He hadn't exactly been concealing his magic before, but she realized too late that she'd passed a test the day before when he'd summoned the tea tray and told her that the king required his Potioner and wizard to display his magic as often as he could for the safety of the kingdom. They'd worked together in his little shop in Eldacre several times, but each time he'd made his potions as any herbalist would assemble the rarest or strangest of ingredients found in any of the four corners of the world without more than one word of power or other suspicious waves of his hand.

This time, as he allowed her to craft something independently with only a little of his help, she found herself chanting the words of power alongside him, each syllable coating her tongue with a layer of oil that made her speak both more clearly and in a sibilant tone she hadn't known her voice was capable of. The bowl wobbled as she found herself caught up in one of the most unusual things she'd experienced in her lifetime, and with the person who was helping her channel magic into her potion. Terran steadied the bowl by placing one of his hands over hers, and the contents sloshed around much less with his warm grip holding them both stable.

By the time they finished she was flustered enough to pray he would notice neither her blush nor her discombobulation, and the potion in the bowl had settled into the faintest of shimmers. Her instincts, if she had the gleanings of magic that he'd hinted he'd sensed in her, told her that this was a fine brew, even if in the end it might not quite work for the purpose she'd hoped.

"Don't forget the water, if that's what you choose for your medium. I use wine as often as not, or strong whisky depending on the tincture, but in this case I think the purity of water would suffice," he reminded her, stepping away and bringing her a decanter of fresh water from the end of the second table. Wondering if she would be better served splashing the cool water over her face instead of into the potion, she obeyed and poured the decanter into the bowl until the potion settled into an almost ordinary looking mixture. Without a doubt she knew that it was finished.

Terran picked the bowl up from the table and poured it into a fresh blue bottle through a clean funnel. Most of it fit into one bottle, but he had another one ready as he divided the mixture between the two and corked both as soon as he was done pouring. Passing her one of the bottles, he gave her a side-glance to make sure she was still watching as he pressed his thumb against the middle of the bottle and spoke a word in that language she was beginning to realize she'd have to learn. When he set the bottle down on the table, she saw the engraving marking the formerly blank canister.

Doubting that anything would happen, she mimicked him down to the way he held the bottle and the last syllable of the word he'd spoken. To her surprise, the symbol she now knew was magical rather than carved by human hands into the bottle itself appeared without one bit of fuss. She set the bottle down next to Terran's, staring at it as if it might turn into a snake.

"We label our bottles the mundane way, of course, but these symbols ensure that the contents remain fresh until their time of use. Many potions would be worthless if they expired at a natural time, after all." He smiled at her, a teacher pleased by a diligent student, but she hesitated before returning the gesture.

All the while, she still wanted to ask him *why* he teaching her all this, why he was taking the time to teach her at all. She now had faith that she was as talented as he'd hoped and guessed, but the notion that he might want to help her purely out of the goodness of his heart simply would not calculate. Veritas had challenged her to find out why Terran had returned to Oseren, to discover what urgent business had brought him back to this city that he hated, but she had no earthly idea of how to get him to confide in her when she was so terrified of revealing her continuing interest in him.

Get a hold of yourself, she commanded her weak knees and sweaty palms. *There's more at stake than just you.*

"Terran, I—"

But Terran didn't hear, since he was gazing up at the sun through the skylight instead of at her. Whatever moment had lingered between them, whatever shared spark she'd imagined, had passed; she knew he was about to leave before he told her so. He picked up a leather bag from the far end of one of the tables where none of their complicated work had stretched; she heard the clink of bottles as he slung it over his shoulder.

"I will have business around the city for most of today, and I won't be back until late in the evening," he said, walking to the door. "Don't wait for me, and in the meantime feel free to explore; bring a servant with you, if you need to. Madam Herst should be able to tell you which places are safe and which are not. Obviously, no more potion making until tomorrow morning when we work again."

"But—"

If he'd sensed the question about why he'd come to the city at all, he'd chosen a good time to flee. Intent on reaching his destination, he was halfway out the door before he paused.

"I suppose it would be irresponsible of me to tell you that if I do not return, you should return home without delay."

Aubria's stomach lurched uncomfortably at the solemn tone of his voice. She dashed forward, holding the door open as he began to walk down the stairs.

"If what you're doing is dangerous, you should tell me. Maybe I could help." She refused to allow him to leave on such a tense, cryptic note, and if he didn't tell her all of what was going on, she might be able to glean some information from him.

Terran looked up at her from several steps down, tilting his head to the side thoughtfully. "You could help, yes. But this isn't something I'd ask anyone else to do. Someday, when I can, I'll tell you why I've come here."

"Not today?" she asked, bitterness curdling her expression as she took a single step down the stairs.

"No. Not today." He waited for her to turn away, but when she did not he shrugged and continued his path down the stairs to leave the tower. Perhaps it was a show of trust that he'd left her with access to the workroom without his supervision, but for now frustrated Aubria couldn't view that trust as any sort of privilege.

Veritas had told her to find out what she could, and hinted that if she garnered enough truth from the hearsay, either he or Terran might be able to tell her what had really happened to the younger prince. Yet if Terran was going to be gone for most of the time, what could she do?

I'll find a way to make him confide in me, she thought, renewed determination lifting her spirits as she walked back into the workroom. She told herself that she only wanted him to confide in her for her multiple quests, but there was no part of Aubria that believed that to be true.

Before she left to make her way to the royal library, she pocketed the bottle of potion she and Terran had made. He'd told her on the way into the city that she could keep a portion of any potion she made, as long as it wasn't any type of poison—she'd need special authorization from the king to carry those types of concoctions—and as long as she took enough for only one dose.

I don't know when I'll need this, but I know it'll come in handy at some point, she thought as she closed the door behind her. Maybe whatever magical instincts Terran had claimed she possessed were awakening from all the time she spent around him and the potions and the miraculous ingredients. As soon as the latch clicked into place the wooden beams of the door glowed faintly before fading. Aubria hadn't known that there was magic keeping the room and its highly valuable contents secure, but it made sense, really, to use locks no ordinary thief would be able to break.

It took a little time for her to track down the housekeeper, partially because she had no desire to interact with the snobbish woman whatsoever, but once Aubria found her it was easy to obtain directions to Oseren's public library via paths safe for an unaccompanied woman to walk. She was out the door in less time than she'd guessed; her hat lay forgotten in her room, but she reasoned that with it on her head she might look too much the part of a country peasant on holiday.

Aubria made a point of not wandering through the main market square, but there were plenty of shops lining the cobblestone streets where she could browse whatever goods the city could offer as well as purchase an afternoon repast. Most of the products displayed in the windows—jewelry, silks, hand-carved house wares, exotic pets, and glamorous clothing—were well beyond her means even for a girl considered wealthy by orchard standards, but she purchased a memento or two before her better judgment took hold. She wrapped a goldenrod colored shawl meant to enhance the topaz tints in her honey brown eyes around her shoulders as soon as she'd handed over her two silvers, and a copper and a half bought her a matching spool of ribbon for her hat and the waistband of a dress. She wanted to bring back gifts for her father and Cerise and Viola—even if she waited to give them these gifts until Yule—but she didn't want to buy them anything that might reveal where she'd actually travelled instead of Eldacre. So, parting with a less comfortable amount of her savings, she bought her father a handkerchief the same color as an autumn pumpkin, and for her friends spools of satin ribbon in both pale pink and rich blue.

If asked, she could say that a merchant had come into Eldacre when she was there and she'd availed herself of his merchandise.

When she finally passed all of the crowds and shops and entered the royal district, she looked up and up at the towers of the aesthetically pleasing keep where King Barric and many of his nobles and courtiers dwelled. Aubria reasoned that she must have seen this castle when she was a child, but the majesty took her breath away and almost made her drop the crisp pork sausage wrapped in a fresh crust of fluffy, frivolous bread that she'd purchased for her midday meal. Even Terran's fine tower, an anomaly in his area of the city which was a good four mile's walk from the castle, didn't hold a candle to the white marble towers topped with gleaming silver domes that caught the sunlight and reflected it impressively over the rest of the city. Statues of majestic birds of prey, carved from pale gray or white stone and set atop strategic towers throughout the vast castle, watched over everyone and everything with eyes detailed down to each bird's eye feathers.

To the right of the castle and significantly lower, a building with a pointed steeple advertised its purpose with the letters carved above its entryway by a skilled stonemason: LIBRARY.

Renewed in purpose now that she'd come to her destination, she eagerly quickened her steps and hurried out of the sun and into the cool shade of the library. She was already beginning to recognize the thrill of magic at work in the short period of time she'd been exposed to it, but when the gilded silver doors opened under her hand with a touch she genuinely couldn't tell whether or not the workings were of magic or man-made means.

Her sense of wonder vanished once the doors closed behind her. True, the library was magnificent with its high ceiling and velvet cushions and the rows upon rows of books—some requiring wheeled ladders to reach their upper shelves—but as far as she could see there were only men present in this building. Old men in distinguished clothing a little less moth-eaten than the cushions, some with gray beards long enough to mark their pages as they turned them over the leather bound manuscripts of old, and young men clad in scholars robes who stared at her with the usual mix of disdain or outright lechery.

Aubria wanted to leave before anyone saw her, but reason won out over fear: the library was public to *everyone*, not just old men and scholars, and anyone harassing people attempting to learn and better themselves were punished according to the law set out by the royal family and the current king, elderly though he was. Most importantly, she had work to do, and standing in the doorway wringing her hands in her apron accomplished not a thing.

There was a desk near the front, though she hadn't noticed it at first since it was stacked high with books and parchments so the man standing behind it had been partially obscured from her sight.

"I would like to see everything you have regarding the lore of faerykind and about the origins of the king's orchard," she whispered politely to the librarian stacking loose rolls of parchment together alongside a half-filled ledger of notes regarding the content of the rolls.

He barely glanced her way when he responded, his mustache puffing up indignantly at her perceived cheek. "This is a place of *learning*, not superstition. We are all busy here, and if it's foolish, wasteful legends that you want you had better return to your grandmother's knee and get back to your embroidery."

Guarding her temper, she raised her brows and deepened her voice just enough to make her sound like less of a girl. "Are you saying that Oseren's great library has nothing about the ancient tales?"

"Of course we have the lore, but that doesn't mean—"

"Well if you have it, I'd like to see it. *All* of it. Would you hinder one of the king's own citizens from using the library he and his forefathers gave to the people?" She smiled sweetly at him as his gaunt face reddened underneath his scholar's cap. He took several moments to come up with a decent argument, one that would allow him to turn her away, but he didn't have one and they both knew it. As a librarian he was obligated to help anyone who came into the building and asked him for assistance.

"Right this way, *madam*," he muttered through his teeth as Aubria hid her triumph with another pleasant smile. She couldn't remember the last time she'd won an argument with a stranger, since *she* was usually the one who surrendered first.

Aubria followed the crotchety librarian around as he grumbled both to her and to his rheumatic joints as he assembled a collection of the material she'd requested. Once he'd gathered a sizeable stack made of books and parchments both, he guided her to an empty table near the back of the library where no one would "disturb" her. Most likely he didn't want any of his more prestigious colleagues to spot her, but she didn't mind now that she had what she'd asked for. The scholars who'd started at her so unpleasantly began to ignore her as soon as the librarian gave her his attention. Apparently, however grumpy he seemed, he was a figure few dared cross.

With everything else out of the way and her stack of research within arm's reach, Aubria found that she no longer had an excuse to put off what she'd come to do. She pulled the nearest, oldest roll of parchment from the top of the stack in front of her, the smooth back of it slick against the carefully polished tabletop, and all the promise of knowledge she had yet to obtain whispered its literary magic as she unfolded it and began to read the sumptuous calligraphy.

From that parchment, she learned that there had been a princess in the olden days who had bartered with one of the faerykind for a child for her womb, and who had eventually died horribly for trying to thwart the creature its payment. Nothing more.

It took her six books and two more patchy scrolls before she found something remotely useful. Aubria was a novice researcher, but thus far her search had resulted in three stacks: useless, slightly less useless or worth another look, and helpful. The stack of helpful materials was, of course, empty. A fourth stack was comprised of materials the librarian brought to her periodically: apparently her request had intrigued him enough to search the stacks more diligently. That or his practical habits had won out and he was accustomed to bringing people any titles he thought of after their initial search.

Aubria finally found something potentially worthwhile in a tome detailing faerykind history in flowery, sugar-coated terms.

"They *gave* magic to the orchard, and that must be why they want it back so badly," she whispered to herself as she traced her fingertips over the multihued painting adorning the page opposite the passage she'd just read. "They gave of themselves to save it…but why entrust it to humans at all? If they loved it enough to sacrifice some of their magic to save it, why give it over after all of that?"

More and more questions, she continued in her head as she tried and failed to stifle a yawn; the subject had ended with the close of that chapter, and there was no indication that that vein of the story would continue in the rest of the book. *When will I find the answers?*

"Are you tired so soon, Aubria?" Terran's voice startled her, and she jumped in her chair. The top of her knee crashed against the underside of the table with a bang, upsetting the antique book she'd been reading, and a few of the graybeards and snobby scholars deigned present her with their glares of disapproval before returning to their own work.

Terran caught the book as it slid off the table, moving with speed too swift for a mortal. But she guessed that it wasn't Terran who visited her; sure enough, when he set the book back on her table with less noise with which she'd propped it open, she saw Veritas's eyes glowing faintly as if lit by some other force.

"You're late," she accused, slipping her hand beneath the table to rub her bruised knee as surreptitiously as she could.

"I left…where I was as soon as I could. Terran is…busy, these days."

Aubria groaned, not taking the bait. Her head ached too much for games, and she already knew that if she asked him what the Potioner was about she'd get riddles for answers. Stifling another yawn, she wove her hands into the crown of braids she'd assembled that morning and pulled out the pins so her hair could fall freely instead of weighing her down.

"You look like you should still be in the orchard, barefoot and picking plump fruit from the trees when you do that," Veritas told her, his voice a murmur so no one else would object to their conversation.

"Yes, I'm quite aware that there's not a single person in this city who doesn't view me as an ignorant peasant, unworthy to tread the stones of their precious streets," she snapped. "Can we get to work now?"

"Of course," he bowed sarcastically as he picked up one of the books from the tall stack beside her. "We have more than one binding to undo, as you know."

It was a compliment, he told her, whispering into her mind as he took the seat opposite hers and opened the book on the table. Unbidden and orchestrated not by her own mind, a picture of him standing behind her and sweeping her hair to the side so he could inhale her scent and press a kiss to the sensitive place just beneath her ear filled her consciousness and she blushed before she could hide it.

Before, when she'd first encountered Veritas, she would have submitted to the seduction with confused attraction. After she'd gained confidence with her potion craft and the wild, mad idea that she possessed magic of her own—however miniscule the amount, however strangely she'd come by it—she found that she had the will to resist such a siren call.

"None of that," she insisted, tilting her chin up defiantly instead of burying her gaze into her latest book. "I can't use my head to think if you're rummaging around inside it. We have more than one binding to undo, as you know."

It shouldn't have felt like she'd won, but it did. Veritas nodded to her in grudging yet not ill-humored respect before he studied the book he'd chosen from the titles she'd gathered. She noted that he'd picked up one of the books the librarian had brought most recently, and that the title etched into the spine read only *CURSES*.

The distraction Veritas had provided proved beneficial after all, since she found a tiny, cramped paragraph near the end of her current book which referenced the passage she'd read earlier that had intrigued her so much. It took her time to pick apart the overly embellished language, but once she had the meaning she sat back in her chair.

They gave their power to the orchard to nourish it, to make it undying like they were, but something went wrong.

That sounds true, Veritas interjected, and for once she welcomed his input. *All faerykind revere their sacred lands.*

"Then the lands are theirs by right. We were only stewards after all," she said, almost forgetting to lower her voice. "How am I supposed to save the orchard from them if they own it? Are we all supposed to just…leave? Start life somewhere else?"

"Not necessarily," Veritas said aloud, following her example. "The world is ruled by victors, and whatever else happened, the kindness of the faerykind is never as straightforward as it seems. If you can find a way to keep them from the orchard, that wouldn't necessarily be an evil thing. Your people have lived there for centuries."

Aubria stared at him. "Aren't *you* technically one of them?"

Instead of replying, he gave her a look that brooked no further comments of that nature; she moved on to her next thought.

"It doesn't say exactly how they *gave* their power to the orchard. It's phrased in a way that implies they gave something they couldn't get back…or, something went wrong so they couldn't take it back. That sounds important, right?" Aubria smoothed her fingertips over her eyebrows, a nervous habit she'd thought she'd left in her childhood. "Somewhere in one of these books there has to be more about faerykind and their magic, how it works…if I find that, maybe—"

She fell silent as the librarian puttered closer to drop off another book. Veritas motioned for the man to approach; as soon as the librarian recognized the Potioner he bowed, his temper improved by leaps and bounds.

"Lady Aubria will require this table for the next few days, and she will not want any of her research disturbed. See to it," he commanded. The librarian gave Aubria an astonished look which quickly morphed into suspicion. The ladies he was familiar with clearly did not dress in village clothes, nor did they wander about on foot unaccompanied; she also doubted that he'd ever witness the Potioner taking up anyone else's cause before, let alone someone like her. Still, he refrained from protesting and honored them both with another obsequious bow before he took his leave.

Once he was gone, Veritas passed her two much thinner books. "I think you've read enough for now. Take these two books home with you and read them tonight, or at least read as much of them as you can stand. I will take responsibility for them with the librarian, so have no fear."

"I thought it was forbidden to remove books from the library."

"Not for me, Aubria Haight." Veritas used Terran's mouth to gift her with a crooked smile as he pushed away from the table and offered her his hand to help her to her feet like a proper gentleman.

"Leaving so soon?" she asked, warily accepting his help; he let her go with no shenanigans as he began to lead her out through the stacks. "I thought you showed up to help me, not hand me a couple of books before you left again."

Veritas paused when they reached the doors, fixing her in his gaze like a startled rabbit. "There is more at stake during this time than our binding and your orchard. You'll find out what soon enough."

Aubria spluttered a protest, but Veritas was already through the doors and out in the street, wending his way through the everyday traffic and soon passing out of sight.

Clutching the books he'd bid her take back to her room as if someone would accuse her of stealing them like a common thief at any moment, she hurried out of the library into the glow of the setting sun.

13

The following four days marched forward much the same as the first one had with a few exceptions. In the morning she awoke early, endured the disapproving glares from Madam Herst while she scarfed down a quick breakfast and refused to let the maid tend to her hair and dress, and spent several hours practicing potion craft with Terran. For once in her life she was glad she was a quick learner: in the village school she'd finished her reading or her assignments early and then sat around in boredom waiting for the others to finish. This had gained her a reputation through the well-meaning villagers of Loracre that she was a smart child, but the truth was that she only read well and it took less time to teach her. When it came to some equations beyond her scope of understanding—the sort required for certain types of orchard work regarding planting seasons and measuring areas—she'd left her elders puzzled and a little disappointed by her lack.

Terran was a good teacher, one she wanted to impress, and in those morning hours they spent basking in the sunbeams let in by the tower sky light, she learned more about potion and magic than she'd ever thought possible. Most of the time Aubria even forgot her uncomfortable feelings regarding Terran, since learning the properties of chemicals and spirits and matter both natural and supernatural took up the entirety of her fascination. Her own burgeoning magic—awakened, he'd told her, unusually since the latent magic resting in all creatures preferred to lay quietly most of the time—glowed through her skin as she worked and added colorful luminosity to both her dreams and her waking hours. The incomprehensible language Terran used for crafting and other showy bits of magic began to make sense under his careful tutelage.

"Your magic is strange to me," he told her on the third day after she'd crafted a potion with oil from red olives, marjoram for wisdom, and partly fresh leaves from the summer apple trees nearest to her own cottage; Aubria hadn't had a direct purpose in mind for the deep green brew, but her instincts told her to add one of her own tears taken with a glass dropper. After that the whole mixture made a lot more sense.

"How so?" she asked as she bottled the potion with the skill of an expert. "This is a wellness potion, by the way. My friend Viola's mother tends to have low spirits, often staying abed for days at a time because she doesn't have the will to rise. I wouldn't promise that it would lift her mood indefinitely, but—"

"It's the orchard!" Terran exclaimed, interrupting her. Aubria would have chastised him, in spite of how ridiculous she probably looked with one eye swollen from the tear she'd forced out of it and her hair sliding noticeably from the bounds of the braided crown she'd pinned it into.

"What is?"

"The orchard. We've always known it was magic, or built on magical ground, since on its soil you and your ancestors have grown many exotic and miraculous harvests over the centuries. I never thought to examine what effect this charged air, or the land itself, might have on people who dwell under those trees."

Aubria moved away to set the fresh brew with the others lining the green wall of various potions. It would take her years to learn all there was about even basic magic, but her own gifts that stirred within her like a dormant bear emerging from hibernation convinced her to agree.

"Is my magic really so dissimilar to yours? I'm no great wizard, obviously, but is it really so unusual?" she asked.

"I mislike the term 'dissimilar,'" Terran returned to a potion he'd set aside for most of the morning as he spoke; she could hear the contemplation in his voice, as if he were trying to solve a riddle aloud. "All magic is connected in its own way. I suppose your magic is like that of the hearth witches of old, and mine is more show and flash in comparison."

"I think that's more flattering to me than to you."

"Maybe it is," he took her teasing in stride, murmuring spell words over his own potion and taking longer to continue his thread of ideas. "But for a hearth witch to have talents in potion craft...it's not just the ingredients that make potions work, not entirely. It takes a touch of magic, or sometimes more than a touch, to activate properties both hidden and known."

They'd had further discussions about magic and its differences over their stay in the city, and Aubria noticed that Terran spoke to her like she was an equal, an ally in his efforts rather than merely a student. The notion of his respect belonging to her felt like a tangible thing, like some heirloom she could tuck into the pocket of her dress and pull out to look at whenever she wished. It was a bizarre—given their fraught relationship—that she could feel such happiness in his company, but she could only preen so long. They were friends, good friends now, and that would have to be enough.

In the afternoons after Terran departed, she headed for the library and bullied the keepers into giving her the books she'd reserved at the beginning of her stay in Oseren. It wasn't fair to say that she found no further useful information after the first day, since she learned more than she'd ever cared to about faerykind legends, old spirit tales, ancient remedies for curses, and even demonkind, but her frustration mounted each time she found something masquerading as beneficial when in the end it proved useless. Veritas only met her in the library once more, since Terran's business was so pressing that if he wandered away more often it would be noticed. His company always renewed her energy enough to get through the rest of the afternoon.

She spent her evenings alone for the most part, which she both loved and hated. Most of the time Terran didn't return until the late hours, and the one time she'd peeked out of her rooms to greet him she'd been taken aback by how dead-on-his-feet he looked. The gaze he'd turned on her had been intense, barely human though Veritas was nowhere in sight, and her new instincts told her that this was the result of using magic to the edge of endurance.

Aubria prayed the blood on his clothes wasn't his.

"Are you all right?" she asked him, her throat dry as she tucked her new shawl tighter around her shoulders and followed him into the main room. She offered fervent thanks to whatever god had arranged for Madam Herst and her associates to find it unnecessary to greet their master whenever he returned later than the dinner hour. "The blood—"

"Not mine." Terran reassured her softly, "But you should be abed. Why are you still up?"

Biting her lip, she held back other words she wanted to say in favor of wiser ones. "I offered you my help before, Terran, and the offer stands. Forgive me, but you look…well, you look as if you could use it. Is there anything you'd like to tell me?"

Aubria thought she had him, then, that he might spill his mysteries at last right there in that ridiculously ornate sitting room with a fire burning down to embers in the polished hearth. He looked as if he wanted to, as if sitting down to tell her everything that was happening would be one of his dearest wishes.

But he didn't. He said nothing at all: he merely looked up at her like a man trapped in a cage, like a prisoner who had guessed that she'd hidden the key to his cell from him and he was silently begging her to set him free.

Aubria had no answers, nothing to offer other than her help if he told her what to do, and he would not. She had only the reluctant feelings of her own heart, and that source of magic in her essence that she barely knew what to do with…but perhaps that would suffice.

Tentatively, she approached him with her hand outstretched and her fingers curled into a beckoning gesture she hoped wouldn't scare him off. She didn't think he'd take the offer, an offer she barely understood herself, but he met her gaze and held it as he offered his own hand in return. When their skin touched, she murmured a few of the words of power that she'd gleaned from him so far. Light glimmered through the pores of their skin, no brighter than a candle's end, and Aubria felt a tug on the magic that had slept so long within her.

Some of Terran's weariness faded from his face as she passed him what little she could of her magic. He had said the two types were dissimilar, and that he didn't understand her particular brand of power…but they joined together easily enough, their golden magic entwining like their fingers linked together in a firm grasp.

Aubria felt Terran sever the connection between them like scissors gliding through paper. His skin had gained more color while the blood had drained from hers, and she felt more ready for sleep than she had before. All in all she'd gifted him only a little from her well of power. He had yet to release her hand, and she could do nothing to aid the conflicted balance of emotions she saw warring in his face.

"Aubria…" he began, though he said nothing else after her name.

She didn't know what she'd done, or why she'd done it. So she bid his silent figure goodnight and returned to her bed. The hand that had performed the secret magic was clutched tight to her chest under her shawl, not because of the magic, but because of the way he'd held it…as if she were the lifeline tethering him to reality. As if she mattered the most.

But she couldn't sleep yet. The books Veritas had helped her borrow from the library—perhaps illegally—shed some light on the other topics she'd promised she'd help with. On bindings she found nothing specifically related to the one she'd unwittingly place on Veritas or the one that had bound him to the Caird bloodline, but on curses in general it had told her a great deal. One needed the consent and often blood or a lock of hair from both parties of the accursed if there were multiple, and because such magic was often dark and performed in darkness, the curse would have to be broken under the same type of moon it had been cast. If the nature of the curse involved some evil or a sacred clause, a sacrifice could be required...but this fact she couldn't be sure of, since the page on which she found this information was splotched distractingly with what looked like the blood of someone who'd given this method a courageous effort.

Aubria knew none of these facts organically since she hadn't been aware of binding Veritas to her in the first place the night she'd performed the ritual. She had yet to get Terran's consent in working on his bloodline binding in the first place. In frustration she'd slammed that particular book shut, sending a cloud of dust flying into the air and provoking a fit of sneezing...but a few minutes later she forced herself to open it again.

After another hour during which the candle in her bedroom burned lower and lower, she discovered something that could be useful. A section on the book theorized on how curses were constructed, after a long-winded chapter written by a contributing scholar, and she'd almost missed the information altogether. Maiden's blood and the dark of the moon were particularly valid tools for casting a binding in the first place, but the nature of the spell relied entirely on the maiden whose blood had been used and the season in which the moon hung in the sky.

Aubria puzzled out what that meant, thinking back in time to when she'd stood in the orchard near her cottage and awaited the spirit she'd summoned. As a maiden she'd been seeking...seeking what? Veritas had come to tell her that she wanted freedom, and that her latest heart's desire was for the chance to be with someone who would expect nothing of her. That in addition to the new moon of spring...could that have forced the binding?

She'd have to tell Veritas in the morning, if she could get to him without alerting Terran. He'd handed her the two books she'd brought back to her room in the Potioner's tower on the first day almost at random, except for their titles which were self-explanatory regarding their content: *A Treatise on Magic* and *Magic in the Blood.* She'd brought more home with her over the next few days, sometimes by herself now that the librarian knew who she was and who her patron was, but her instincts kept telling her that these were the books that might aid her the most in her quests.

Ready to surrender to slumber, she shifted the tomes resting comfortably atop her bed and pulled *Magic in the Blood* into her lap. She'd already been through this one several times, skimming the passages again and again in the hopes of discovering something she hadn't read and dismissed before, but this time a side note written in a carefully looped script that didn't belong to the original author caught her attention. Squinting to see it better, she read the passage aloud.

"It is said that though the royal bloodline possesses traces of magic long since dormant, the Caird stewards have been blessed either by the gods or their dark counterparts with bountiful gifts in this area. Always has the eldest Caird heir served the king and his family with their craft, whether it be in the official position of esteemed Potioner or as a sword and shield to the crown in times of strife. Yet in recent times, it has been evidenced that the Caird line has not always served the best interests of the crown, for with the murder of the younger prince—"

Slamming the book shut didn't keep the words she'd read from spiraling through Aubria's mind like the skin of a perfectly pared apple trailing from a fruit stained with blood from the knife that had slipped.

I haven't met a single soul who doesn't think he's responsible, she thought, a trickle of despair making her exhaustion sink into her bones. *Could that mean that he did it? That he's a murderer?*

The younger prince had only been a few years older than her when he'd visited the village with his retinue to give heart to the orchard villages after a difficult yet successful harvest. It had been years ago, when she was still a child, but he'd had had all the makings of a kind, caring king who would be brave when required but more intent on caring for his people than starting outlandish disputes with foreign countries. She'd been just another peasant child bowing before a royal, but that moment had given her cause to mourn the younger prince, though she hadn't understood what his death meant at the time or the wildfire rumors of how it had come about.

Terran may have killed him, she decided as she leaned over to blow out the stub of her candle; it had been tall and white in its youth, but it made her miss the sweet-scented beeswax tapers they made in Loracre. *But I don't know the reason, or all of the facts.*

She'd have to ask, and soon. Whether or not he wanted to tell her…they were friends now, and though she couldn't deny that her confused feelings wanted more from him than that, she decided that since they were friends he *should* tell her.

On the fourth day, Terran told her that they'd be starting the return journey to Eldacre and Loracre the next morning. Aubria almost dropped the funnel she was cleaning in a basin of water at the end of the second table in the tower room; water splashed on her apron regardless of her care. She hadn't forgotten her home—how could she, when she spent the second greater part of every day searching through stuffy book after voluminous tome for a solution that would save it from destruction?—but here in the city the orchard seemed distant and out of reach.

"Tomorrow?"

"Yes. Unless you wanted to stay longer?" Terran gave her a pitying look, knowing as they both did that she could afford to stay no longer in case someone went to Eldacre looking for her. "We've been gone seven days already, and we've three more on the road."

"I know," she told him, defensive; the funnel dropped into the basin again and this time she left it as she faced him with her damp hands on her hips. "I had some things I wanted to discuss with you before we went back."

Terran's penetrating gaze made her feel like she was about to burst aflame with guilt, and she had to take her mental self by the hand and force her to stand firm. *He has things he needs to tell me as well, whether he'll readily admit that or not.*

"I remember," he said, surprising her. "You told me back in Eldacre that there was something you wanted to tell me, but that you wanted assurance of my trust first. You have it, Aubria, but it will have to wait until we're on the road again. I promise I'll listen then."

Then, while she was still frozen, he smiled benignly at her and departed.

You can't run away from me forever, Terran Caird, she thought, leaning back against one of the sturdy tables as her adrenaline began to fade.

Before she left for the library, she tore a corner of paper from one of Terran's record keeping books and picked up a quill to write him a note. Before she lost her nerve she copied the message in her head onto the paper and set it under the bottle of their latest potion where he'd be sure to see it if he came looking.

If it's our last night in the city, I'd like to enjoy it. Meet me in the Gifted Magpie for a drink when you return this evening, if you come back at your normal time. I'll wait for you in the tavern.

She had no idea if he'd heed her words, or if he enjoyed the atmosphere found at most taverns, but she decided that her burst of courage hadn't been a bad thing. After all, the tavern was the closest one she'd seen to the tower, so he'd probably be familiar with it. From the outside it looked like a clean, respectable sort of place.

Her afternoon in the library proved as fruitless as the other times she'd been there apart from a few exceptions. The librarian that had grown used to her hadn't grown kinder, but he'd developed a respect for her timeliness and the hours she spent researching a seemingly obscure topic.

As an added distraction, her mind kept worrying at the memory of a conversation she'd had with Veritas the other day. The library windows were never opened for fear the damp would destroy the books and scrolls over time, and given that midsummer approached with heat waves increasing in frequency, Aubria felt overwarm and sluggish as she rested her chin on her hand and paged through a book she'd perused more than once.

"Terran knows *of* you, you said," Aubria had asked him. The day had been just as balmy, and even in the city of marble and stone she'd glimpsed a stray butterfly the color of the sky meandering through the streets on a wayward breeze. "How can he know of you, and yet not what you do or how often you take over his body?"

"Until you, I didn't do it often. I'd intervene when he'd fall as a child, or get himself into trouble it would be best for me to take care of. His father had put up with me holding the reins for much of his adolescent and adult life, once he made choices that informed me that he was neither honorable nor good, and when the curse passed me to his son he never trusted Terran again," Veritas answered, his unusual good humor making him talkative without any tricks as he lazily leaned on the back legs of the sturdy wooden chair; his thoughtful expression made him look more like Terran than himself. "I can't say I raised him, but I talked to him through our minds when he let me, which was rare, and through notes I'd leave behind when necessary. I was more like a secret brother or an imaginary friend. His father refused to tell him the truth of the matter until I forced his hand. I'd rather not say how."

"How did he react?" she asked.

"As…well as one can expect. He liked me from his childhood, but once he understood we were bound for his lifetime until he had a child—a son, for the firstborn Caird is always a boy child—he searched everywhere for any clue that would tell him how to free himself from me. Then his father died, he inherited the position of Potioner and moved from the castle to this tower, and…"

"And?" Aubria wondered if she'd stumbled close enough to the truth for him to tell her what had really happened with the two princes.

Veritas gave her a sideways look as he sat up; the front legs of his chair thumped against the floor. "You've not found anything else out yet, have you?"

"No…" she had sighed, admitting defeat. "No, I haven't. But I've been busy either with potion craft or researching our various bindings. I haven't exactly had time to interrogate city dwellers for the latest gossip."

"Well then, you had better get to it. The truth won't wait forever, you know."

With that, he'd left her alone in the library. She realized belatedly that she'd forgotten to tell him about the information she'd found in her nightly reading that might lead them to the solution for their binding…but no matter. She would tell him when she saw him next time.

Back in the present, Aubria sighed as she absently traced the outline of an illustration with a finger covered in the light cotton gloves anyone who meant to read in the library was required to wear. The dark faerykind depicted in the artwork glared up at her with wooden teeth bared, tormenting her for her failure. Dust motes drifted in the sun streaming in through the high windows: natural light could destroy books worse than careless hands, but candles weren't permitted either. The librarian had grumbled daily about the light, like an aged mole better used to scratching out a living underground.

It was no use: she could do nothing more, and her mind refused to cooperate. Desperation coupled with endless hours of mental labor for one accustomed to mainly physical toil had dulled her senses and even her inquisitiveness. Glaring down at books she'd already read and found wanting helped no one and only made her more exhausted. Aubria surrendered at last, relief rejuvenating the aching muscles of her neck and shoulders.

Still, she couldn't give up entirely. Wondering if she was going regret this theft as much as she had stealing from the Potioner, Aubria peered around the stacks for the crouching shadow of the elderly librarian before she snatched up a thin book with a green linen cover from the edge of her table and stuffed it into the pocket she'd sewn into her pine green dress. This volume was new to her, delivered as a begrudging afterthought from the librarian, and it looked neither important to anyone else nor like it would be missed. Something about the apple green linen cover embellished only with a design painted with brown ink called to her as she stood—called to the magical instincts she was learning to trust—and she slipped the book into her pocket before she lost her nerve.

Something for later, she told herself as she bid farewell to the librarian at his desk and told him that she wouldn't be requiring the research table any longer. Rather than looking relieved, his glare softened.

"Did you find what you were searching for, my lady?" he asked, and when she shook her head in negative he sighed as his spectacles drooped forlornly on his nose. "Few of us ever do."

Aubria had cut off her hours in the library only a little short, for the sunlight streaming through the library windows had borne the last light of day as the afternoon began to fade into dusk. Once she'd made her way back to her room in the Potioner's imposing tower, she took a little extra time preparing for her night out in front of the clear, spotless mirror the full length of her body that stood in the corner of her room.

After freshening up with a basin of water, she'd gathered portions of her hair into a braided crown that she'd embellished with a strand of the goldenrod ribbon she'd purchased on her first solo foray into the city; the rest of it swung unbound down her back. Feeling particularly bold, she'd crept upstairs into the potion workroom to treat herself to a single sip of one of the "vanity potions" Terran had said were so popular with the ladies. Because she'd taken such a small dose the effects weren't immediately obvious, but the topaz shades of her eyes stood out more strikingly than they had before, and her cheeks blushed a lingering, natural pink that she decided looked quite flattering.

Her blue dress would have to do, spruced up with her new shawl instead of the brown apron and revitalized as far as scent with a few drops of the tuberose oil she'd also borrowed from the workroom. She'd laid the book she'd taken from the library atop her neatly packed satchel, which she'd transfer into Clearwater's saddle bags when they picked the horse up from the stables tomorrow. The books Veritas had claimed for her had been returned earlier that morning, most likely by the truth spirit himself through Terran's body.

Why she was taking this trouble she didn't want to say. Aubria truly expected nothing from this evening other than a few drinks with the Potioner before they began their return journey. She'd come to value their friendship too much to risk it again by declaring her infatuation—in part because she feared his disdain almost above all else—but even though a secret part of her heart whispered that tonight could be miraculous, she forced her stronger mind into more realistic expectations.

When she arrived at the Gifted Magpie she found it both more and less crowded than she'd hoped: there weren't enough people yet to distract from her arrival, but enough of a crowd had gathered to make finding a seat without strangers around impossible. More people trickled in behind her, intent on purchasing their libations.

"Picking up a pint for your man, are you? We have a fine selection of golden ale and imported spirits—" The barkeep greeted her good-naturedly as she approached the bar after dodging a rowdy trio of young men.

"I'll take your reddest of wines, good sir, as soon as you can bring it to me," Aubria waved her hand imperiously as she straightened her spine; the barman stared at her, taken aback both by her interruption and her brazen demand, but when the cup he was pouring almost overflowed his shock changed into a scowl.

"Put it on the Potioner's account, will you?" she added as imperiously as she dared, imitating Madam Herst's utter disdain for those beneath her while trying *not* to look like her nose had been shoved into animal refuse. "He will be joining me shortly."

The barman looked suspicious, like he wanted to argue with her or protest that she had no business invoking the Potioner's name and trying to use his money. Aubria held his gaze until he grumbled something under his breath and gestured for one of the barmaids to bring her the wine she'd asked for. The girl did so with wide eyes, her hands trembling as she passed over a chalice filled almost to the brim with ruby red wine. Aubria smiled kindly at her and moved away so she wouldn't continue to make her nervous.

Aubria wrapped her hands around the goblet and carried it to the least crowded table near the back of the room. A local gathering of would-be minstrels had struck up a tune, but the night was still young: there wouldn't be much dancing or sport until most of the tavern attendees had more than a couple of drinks in them, and by then she'd probably be back in the Potioner's tower.

"You're the Potioner's woman?" One of the ladies clinging to the arm of her man leaned around his bulky figure to ask Aubria. He looked as if he would thump the woman—who had chosen to dress in the style of the local courtesans even if a tavern of this respectability frowned on such obvious displays of lewd behavior—on the back of the head to hush her, but curiosity won out in the end and he let the comment stand.

"Is it true?" the man asked. "Has he told you?"

"Told me what?" Aubria asked, sipping from her chalice as nonchalantly as she could.

"They say he was in league with the elder prince to off the younger," the silly girl who had been so concerned with the sordid affair of who the Potioner might be sleeping with laughed. "My brother said that there was rumors of Prince Mardin quarreling with his brother for Barric's favor, and that the Potioner decided to side with the elder after a little friendly coaxing at the edge of a knife."

"You're daft," the girl's companion scoffed, though his tone sounded more indulgent than contrary. "The Potioner saw an opportunity and he took it, it's as plain as day. It's just a shame the old king's never been the same—"

"—and that we have a good forty or so years to put up with the crown prince once he kicks it," the girl finished for him, laughing as she guzzled a few more swallows of her almost empty tankard.

"Is the crown prince really so terrible?" Aubria asked, hating how naïve she must sound. She knew of course that those who lived in Lyrassan frowned often in the direction of the royal heir, since even the orchard folk knew well the stories of the prince's wilder escapades, but aside from those tales she'd heard very little.

"You're not from around here, are you?" The girl snorted, leaving her companion to clap her on the back as she choked before she could be bothered to explain her comment.

"The crown prince has been the one instigating all the conflict on the border in hopes of a war that will bring him glory. *He's* the one responsible for our painful taxes."

"Hush, Kay. That's treasonous," the man next to her muttered, giving Aubria a suspicious glance.

Perhaps he's remembered that I associate with the Potioner, who might be in line with the crown prince, she realized, a little amused.

The woman called Kay ignored her friend's warnings and continued in the same rambling vein. "The Potioner practically fled the city, after the death of the younger prince. They say he's travelled the whole continent selling his wares and avoiding the king, just in case the doddering fool were to guess who exactly was responsible for the death of a young prince healthy and entering the prime of his life. No one's seen him in Oseren for years until now…"

Kay's mouth drooped open as she stared at Aubria with panic making her bovine face look more than a little silly. It had taken a minute, but her companion's warning had finally made it through her thick skull.

"I'm no talebearer, friends. Potioner Caird will hear no gossip from me," Aubria told them, trying to adopt a conspiratorial tone a she leaned forward on her elbows, but the damage had been done. Without so much as a by your leave the sodden couple scooted away from her down the community bench of the table she'd chosen to sit at, leaving her alone.

Aubria downed her cup of wine over the next few minutes, lost in her not so pleasant musings. *Four days in the city, and I've found out so little. Four days, and he's told me nothing. I'm not even sure if he'll deign to join me tonight.*

She decided as she mulled over the tangy bite of the dry wine that she was going to try not to care about that. It was her last night before a three day journey and a return to the endless work at the orchard. For once, Aubria wanted to enjoy herself for once without a mountain of reserve blocking her path.

"Will you sing, lass?" A group of middle-aged drinkers hailed her as she went up to the bar for her first taste of the golden ale the innkeeper had boasted about, and she turned towards them with her full flagon sloshing in her two hands. She was surprised they'd dared speak to her, let alone to ask for a song, given the deference people tended to give her once they realized her time was commissioned by the Potioner himself.

"You want me to sing?" she asked them, relaxing once she noticed that there were women in the group as well as men, all in the same graying age group, and that there was no malice or cruelty in their bearing.

"Aye," the man who'd hailed her before answered as she approached their corner table. "You have the look of an orchard lass, and I haven't been to either of those pretty villages in some years. I've a hankering to hear one of their clever ditties tonight, if you're willing."

"The old fool's grown sentimental in his dotage, I'm afraid," the woman sitting next to him rested a broad-fingered hand on his arm with no small degree of affection. "We've been thinking about visiting again once he passes on the forge to the apprentice."

Aubria stared around at the hopeful faces: both the men and women had hardened looks about them, the type she noticed that most people who lived in the city for most if not all of their lives had, and though she'd been inside the imposing gates for less than a week she found that she shared some of their nostalgia for a country filled with greenery and life instead of cold stone.

"I'm sorry," she began to make her excuses in spite of her sympathy, but the words caught in her throat. Shyness hadn't been familiar to her before her betrothal to Lane, and her uncertainty had developed in tandem with her indecision about her future. It would be good, maybe, to return to her roots and remember how it had felt to be Aubria Haight before the handfasting wheel and the arrival of the Potioner had changed her life for good or ill.

"I'm sorry," she started again as a slow smile lit up her face, "but if I'm going to sing I'll need one of you gentlemen to come up there with me."

One of the older men rumbled to his feet, already grinning. Hoping to take heart from the drink, Aubria guzzled a good half of her tankard and made a face as it burned all the way down as the sour wine had not. It was good ale nonetheless, yeasty and savoring of summer wheat, and she showed her appreciation by wiping the foam from her mouth with the back of her hand.

Fortified, she led her new friend across the room to the corner with the minstrels and addressed them with one hand on her hip to lend her figure a bold, jaunty curve. "I don't suppose you lads would mind if I sang a little song for some entertainment?"

One of the boys dropped his complicated stringed instrument with a clatter; thankfully it wasn't damaged, though another man holding a villager's version of a flute gave him an evil look before turning his attention to Aubria as the leader.

"Depends on the song, lass. If it's one of your fancy court tunes—"

He must have assumed she'd spent time in court with the Potioner. "No court tunes for this crowd, I think. I had an orchard song in mind."

"Aye?"

"Do you know 'The Fairest of the Apples,' by any chance?" She'd captured his interest with the familiar ballad from Loracre, and now he scoffed at her doubt.

"Of course we know it, don't we? We've played for your villages often enough, haven't we?" Aubria smiled wider, choosing not to mention that they only would have played in Eldacre, since superstitious folk like minstrels and bards and troubadours rarely ventured deeper into the orchard to entertain the villagers of Loracre.

"Wonderful! I don't suppose you also know the alteration, then, with two singers instead of one—"

"You and the graybeard go up and sing, lass, and we'll take care of the rest." The leader of the local troupe waved her away carelessly, whispering instructions to his comrades, and Aubria turned to her graybeard companion.

"'The Fairest of the Apples?'" I believe I know this one, though my memory's a bit dim. Isn't that where—"

"I promised you a tiny piece of the orchard, didn't I?" Aubria laughed as he grimaced good-naturedly. "You play along, and I'll do the rest."

Aubria removed her shawl and tied it around her waist for better ease of movement. With nothing left to prepare, she inhaled and exhaled to calm her nerves and strode with as much confidence as she could muster to the front of the room. Most of the tavern crowd was still drinking and talking amongst themselves, but often in the evening various guests liked to perform the entertainment, and some of them had journeyed through Oseren to the Gifted Magpie for that very reason. The troupe leader in the corner caught Aubria's eye and nodded, and she launched into the opening verses of the lengthy orchard ditty with her voice strong and clear.

In days past, she'd sung "The Fairest of the Apples" with Cerise and Viola, and then Cerise and Nathan, who were naturally gifted in music. Her voice had never sung the loudest or the strongest, and she was no honey-tongued castle bard, but her notes carried pure and true in a fashion enough people had found pleasant. People stopped talking to listen as Aubria sang her part of the song before gesturing to the man standing next to her to continue. Luckily his voice was almost as fine as hers, though smokier and far deeper, and people began to clap in time to the song or thump their cups against the tables in rhythm to the music.

The older man singing with her responded well to her coaching, echoing the phrases with the true talent of a jester as he capered about in imitation of either the old witch woman or the "handsome" prince who accompanied the "beautiful maid" in the story of the song. Aubria supposed that neither the witch nor the prince in the tale would quaff great quantities of ale during the harrowing rescue of the maid or her temptation to doubt the prince's honor and risk both the lives of the whole kingdom and her own, but this was something she could forgive. During a break in the song she snagged her own half-full tankard from the table where she'd left it, and sipping when she could saved her mouth from going dry as both the song and the clapping picked up speed.

Halfway through the song but before the culminating verses, a disturbance made Aubria glance towards the doors in time to see Terran's entrance. Her already flushed cheeks bloomed with fresh hue as she saw him as strangers must have seen him for the first time in a while. He did not dress in the glamorous styles of the court, but his clothes were cleaner than most and black as midnight, and the way he carried himself revealed more than anything else his noble blood. His eyes found hers right away, the effort made easy because of where she stood, and she felt imprisoned in their depths from across the room.

The music had stopped for his entrance, along with the clapping and thumping of tankards. Everyone who had been invested in the amusement stared at the Potioner, who she now realized must never have graced this establishment with his presence before. His expression had been mild enough when he'd entered, but it grew stony and aloof as he stood straighter and approached the bar with the clear intent of ordering a drink.

How must all of them—how must *she*—look in his eyes? She'd been singing and dancing and drinking like a common peasant without regard for her dignity aside from performing well.

I was having fun, she thought, *just for the joy of it. What could be wrong with that?*

Nothing at all, she realized. So she broke her gaze from the Potioner's and nodded for the minstrels to continue as she picked up the song where her new friend had dropped it. Following her lead, the man playing the part of the witch challenged her to dance for her life as the tale of the song decreed the lovely maid must dance her way out of the underworld to prevent the wights from stealing the prince's soul away forever.

This was the part of the song Aubria had struggled with in the past, given that the crowd decided who the better dancer was and then that would determine the course of the tale. Cerise had been the better dancer then with her swift, steady feet and flair for the dramatic, but by channeling her energy Aubria managed to pick up her steps along with the weight of her skirts and dance as if her life might really depend on it.

By the time the song was over and the crowd declared her the winner she was out of breath, red in the face, and totally exhilarated. She concealed her pleasure in their reaction by downing the last of her now lukewarm tankard, and before she could debate getting another, one of the tavern girls brought one to her with a wink and a smile.

Behind her, Aubria saw Terran had found a seat for himself at the crowded bar and was watching her, an amused smile on his face as she toasted him with her cup. He didn't look angry, or embarrassed, and she wondered if it was only the wine and ale she'd imbibed making her feel so weightless and euphoric.

"Let's have some dancing!" Someone called from the back of the room before she could go to Terran, and before she knew it the men in the room were pushing the tables to the edges of the room to clear a large swathe of the floor. The barman who'd been surly to her had come around the bar to help, grinning under his bushy mustache at the prospect of how much coin the parched dancing folk might be persuaded to spend on his ale.

A boy Aubria's age that smelled of clean horses and hoppy beer seized her arm and pulled her into a line of dancers, and knowing that she was being watched she went along with the flow. She'd kicked off the evening with her orchard rendition of a popular country song, and now it seemed the crowd wanted to reward her by treating her as the guest of honor in the Gifted Magpie for the rest of the night.

Time passed, but she wasn't aware of how much until she happened to glance out of the tavern window to see the reflection of the moon hanging high in the sky. It would be a hard journey the next morning if she went to bed late, but she didn't want the night to end. So she said yes to the next young man who asked her to dance, and even dared to flirt with him as they wove in and out of a line of people in the steps of a reel.

Eventually there was a pause, one she thought was a natural break for the troupe to catch their breath and rest their playing hands until she realized that Terran had made his way into crowd; it parted for him until he reached her.

"I don't suppose you'd care to dance, Lord Potioner?" Aubria curtsied low in front of him, catching her breath. Her current partner stepped away from her as if association with her would get him in trouble. There was no humility in her gesture, since she awaited Terran's scorn with a single look; he had no place to act in such a way, of course, but that didn't change how she'd feel once she looked up and saw for certain his disdain for everything she was about. He'd smiled at her, and sent her an ale…but was that to make fun of her or to congratulate her?

"I would, actually."

Terran shocked her completely as he swept her up into his arms. She had doubted him, but his hold on her was sure. The music picked up again as soon as the minstrels realized that he wasn't going to stop their performance, and Aubria's laughter overflowed from within her as he spun her with expert skill into the movements of the dancers circling the empty floor.

"I didn't know you could dance!" she exclaimed over the noise, failing to hide her delight as she swung her hair back over her shoulders.

"Of course I can dance," Terran scoffed. "I've picked up a thing or two from villages around this country and beyond."

"Really? You never let on!"

Terran's hands caught hers as he spun her into him, as all the other men did with their partners. "I've never let on to a lot of things, Aubria."

Trying not to lower her spirits by wondering if his phrasing had a double meaning in her favor, she spun out of his reach and called to the minstrels to play a different, more challenging type of song. This tune required the men to lift their partners into the air every so often with a great shout, and while she doubted Terran knew all of the steps she didn't doubt that he'd be able to pick her up with ease.

Sure enough, as the village flute carried the melody for the strings and the makeshift drums someone had found in a back room of the tavern, he lifted her with ease and a valiant shout as the music carried them into happy oblivion. Aubria would feel the exhaustion in her bones and the soreness of her muscles on the morrow, but for now the buoyant feeling grew, and she laughed as she danced with the Potioner.

Until the last time he set her down, and failed to let her go as the song ended.

Breathless from more than the complicated reel, Aubria waited for him to let her go. Yet his hands lingered on her waist where he'd lifted her up in time with the song. The world seemed to fade away, falling into silence as she gazed up at him with her hands resting on his chest.

But the music *had* stopped, and once again all eyes rested on the Potioner and the orchard lass.

"Kiss her, boy!" the man who'd asked Aubria to sing in the first place hollered from across the room, much further into his cups than when their interaction had taken place. Apparently the rumor that she was the Potioner's cousin hadn't won out in the slightest, and the tipsy people who had witnessed their light-hearted dancing were more interested in a little show than a tale no one had believed in the first place.

"I shouldn't," Terran said, low enough so the whole room wouldn't hear. But then he did, soft enough that she could only just feel his lips on hers; their touch sent warmth as golden as the ale she'd consumed through her limbs and made her feel like her hair was standing on end. She'd never felt this way with Lane, and the pleasant hunger that demanded more refused to settle for less. Aubria grabbed him by the front of his tunic and stood on her tiptoes to kiss him like she wanted to be kissed.

Around them the tavern crowd howled, either with laughter or hooting encouragement, but she scarcely heard them. Terran responded to her fervor with hesitant enthusiasm, pausing like he'd been frozen before he tightened his grip on her waist and kissed her like a man should kiss a woman.

Whatever else happens on the road, tomorrow or days after, Aubria told herself when they parted and she lost herself in the siren pull of his orchard green eyes bright with a smile meant for her, *we'll have had this.*

"You'll never finish a bloody song if you keep stopping like that!" she called to the local troupe once she and Terran broke apart, smiling fit to blind the sun.

14

Clearwater and Cloud ambled down the path leading to Loracre days later, when they were almost home from their sojourn in the Oseren. The three days along with the nights under the stars or at the inn had passed in a careful silence between them, broken only by casual conversation that touched on either potion craft or nothing of any import whatsoever.

The kiss had done it. Whatever uncertainty Terran had felt about why he'd brought her with him or why he cared about coaxing out her dormant magic must have transformed into something more concrete. Aubria spent most of their time on the road worrying about what conclusions he'd drawn after their night of dancing and music in the Gifted Magpie. She knew she'd done nothing wrong, that she'd neither encouraged nor discouraged his actions after their one and only kiss, but she wondered if what she had yet to tell him would be made worse by the happy memories they now shared.

Veritas had kept to himself. Aubria had tried a couple of times to think towards him to start a dialogue, but the answering silence had made her feel too idiotic to continue. Though she'd loved Oseren and would like to return someday, enough homesickness had troubled her to make returning to the ordinary tasks of the orchard much easier. A break in favor of the mundane might do her good, grieved though she was to leave the Potioner's tower behind. Maybe once her tired brain recovered she'd be able to draw some useful conclusions from the information she'd earned in her travels.

Eldacre approached, and then Loracre. She recognized more and more landmarks and tree types as their horses carried them down familiar roads, and she glimpsed the recognizable backs of the peculiar orange orchard bees drifting in and out amongst the trees that still flowered or were just flowering. Something was always blooming in the orchard or approaching its harvest time, and the bees often gathered pollen during winter as well since their deeply furry coats protected them from all but the most extreme temperatures.

Aubria had one more chance to tell him, and with her stomach churning in her gut she forced herself to speak. "We should stop, Terran."

"Why? We're not far from the villages...are you so tired already?"

He teased her, yet he drew his horse to a stop when she did. Cloud was the bigger horse compared to Clearwater, but he typically followed her mare's lead after the time they'd spent together on the road and in Oseren's stables.

"Walk with me a little?" she asked, tossing her sun hat onto the saddle as she jumped down from Clearwater's back. "There's plenty of clover to graze nearby, so the horses shouldn't wander far."

He dismounted as well and let Aubria lead the way to the shelter of a tree that had the least amount of bees buzzing around its high branches. A few mendacia vines bedecked with dark green blossoms near their tails swayed above them with the weight of bees intent on harvesting their nectar, but the insects didn't bother them. Temporarily overwhelmed with the honeyed scent in the air and the hypnotizing buzzing, Aubria stared up at Terran as they stopped walking. Her heart stuck in her throat as she memorized the swirling pattern of the tattoo over his eye in lieu of finding her words.

"Did you want to tell me something, Aubria?" Terran broke her trance by speaking first, after clearing his throat in a fashion that could only be called awkward. Perhaps he feared her seeking commitment from him after their kiss in the tavern; in this case she'd prove him wrong.

The potion meant to help her say the impossible things rested uncomfortably in her pocket, like a weight that would have drowned her had she stumbled into deep water. She'd held it like a charmed amulet during their journey, wondering when she'd be brave enough to use it. But facing him now with his expression open to hers, as if he trusted her even though he was wary of the feelings that lay between them, she wondered if the true bravery was telling him the truth without the aid of magic.

Courage. She bolstered her resolve before she began, speaking as calmly as she could as she traced her thumb over the potion bottle in her pocket.

"I told you that there were some things I had to tell you, and I made you promise to hear me out in full."

"I did wonder whether you were going to tell me anything. When you said nothing during our journey, I assumed you were waiting to share what you needed to until you had another pie to offer me," he said. The teasing tone was still in his voice as a summery breeze swirled through the leaves of the trees surrounding him and his hair, but since she knew him a little better now she heard the layer of panic crackling under his words like a crumbling crust.

This did not give her heart, but she forged ahead anyway, putting aside all excuses and distractions. "When you gave me the ritual and the spiritual potion to summon Veritas, he came to me and told me what I wanted and gave me something I greatly desired. He told me that I longed for more than a life in the orchard, which has only become truer the more time I've spent away from it. But he also…Terran, I didn't know it was you at all when he let me give my…maidenhead to a person of my choosing who wouldn't demand I share a life with them. I'd summoned a spirit, and he was kind to me, and—"

"*Veritas.*" Terran spoke the name like it was the blackest of curses, like it was the omen that spelled out his doom. Aubria shrunk back, half-wishing that she'd given in and drank the potion that would have guided her into saying whatever words would waylay any hurt he might feel. The venom in the words, thus far directed elsewhere though she was sure it would point in her direction all too soon, had her steeling herself against retreat even as it had frozen the Potioner into a statue of shock. But maybe there was still hope that she could alleviate the situation…or she'd make it worse by revealing the rest of what she had to tell him.

"You gave me the ritual to help me when I needed it most, and I'll forever be grateful. Neither one of us knew what the ritual would entail, just like I didn't know myself well enough to guess what I wanted…I needed someone to speak the truth to me because I didn't know what I wanted for myself in the slightest, and no one I knew would've understood. Veritas himself said he didn't guess what would happen, that I took him by surprise, but now that we're bound—"

"You're *bound?*"

Aubria caught her mistake too late as Terran's fevered eyes locked on hers; his hands came up to grip her shoulders as if he would squeeze the truth out of her faster than she could speak, and she realized that what was merely an inconvenient accidental binding to her would mean so much more to someone who had been enslaved to a faerykind spirit since his birth.

"Accidentally, yes, but we're going to break it. I discovered a fair amount during my research in the city, and we're also trying to undo the binding that chains you and Veritas together. But the faerykind are trying to destroy the orchard, so there's only so much I can do with so little time—"

Terran interrupted her again, annoying her even though she knew he had every right to treat her with blunt rudeness. "You've spoken to Veritas outside of the original ritual?"

"Yes of course, seeing that he's the only one who can…help me…" she trailed off as his fingers tightened on her shoulders enough to leave bruises before he let her go and stepped back with his nostrils flared.

No, he's not. Terran could have helped, and Veritas or not, you should have told him much *sooner, Aubria Haight.* The thought tormented her because it came too late, and because she would never know now whether or not it would have been better to tell him instead of heeding Veritas's wishes.

"How often have you...interacted?"

"Terran—" she tried to placate him, raising her hands in surrender; sweat had gathered in a small puddle in her armpits, but she ignored it. She had never once suspected that he'd physically harm her for any reason, but the glitter of madness behind his eyes reminded her that she was alone in the orchard out of reach of crying for help.

"How often?"

"Once for the ritual, and once again later...during Beltane. I hadn't meant to call him, but somehow I'd bound him to me during the original meeting. Other than that we've spoken in person a handful of times, and through our minds only a little more."

"Through your minds?" Terran paled, his breath coming in pants as he retreated, his hands lifting to scrape through his hair as if he could remove Veritas by crushing his own skull. Aubria hated this, hated seeing him losing control to panic, but she wasn't sure her gentling touch would be welcome. So she watched as he fought to regain control, trembling as adrenaline coursed through her veins.

"You couldn't let me have this, let alone anything you hadn't touched," Terran finally spoke, though not to her; his eyes were closed as if he could direct their poisonous gaze inward. "I have cursed you for your interference before. How should I now let you know that I'm serious about my threat?"

Without warning, he turned and smashed his fist into the nearest tree as hard as he could. The unusual strength she'd glimpsed from afar made the tree groan down to its roots, and Aubria stifled a scream as she heard the crunch of bone in Terran's hand as blood sheeted out from broken skin. The Potioner made not a sound aside from an involuntary grunt of pain as his closed fist connected with the solid trunk, and she saw a bitter smile of satisfaction twist his face as his skin parted over his bone. No ordinary man could have hit so hard, and it was a miracle that he wasn't bent over in pain from the harm he'd inflicted on himself.

But a miracle it was not. Terran watched with detached interest as his hand began to glow while skin and tendon and bone knit back together before their eyes. Aubria would have been glad, but the tight-lipped fury silencing him as he watched an otherworldly force heal the body he'd damaged filled her with dread rather than relief.

"You won't let me destroy your *vessel*," Terran whispered, half to himself and half to Veritas. "But I know that you can feel pain, and that as long as I fight back I can sometimes take control. There is so much more I can do to remind you that your machinations will not be tolerated."

"Terran, stop!" Aubria couldn't watch without interfering any longer, not when she knew that he might hurt himself to get revenge on Veritas; she stepped forward, reaching out to take his hand while the glow faded. "We can free you from this, I know we can. If we work together—"

"If we work together? Hasn't it occurred to you that many, *many* people have tried to break the Caird curse in the past? What makes you think that a peasant girl and a disgraced Potioner can do any better?" Terran pushed her away.

"You told me before that my magic is different from yours, and that I think differently from other wizards. Might that make me a help rather than a hindrance?" In the spirit of tolerance Aubria let the hurt of him calling her a peasant girl once again fade into the background as she pleaded with him to accept her help.

Terran didn't grace her offered insight with an acknowledgement; his back was to her now as he stared into the depths of the orchard like a man trapped half in one world and half in another; when he addressed her, his half-turned profile appeared razor sharp under a blaze of sun through the leaves of the canopy. "So, Aubria. You've spoken—well, more than spoken—with my cursed spirit. There are many questions you must have, so you should ask them now. I'm sure we have much to discuss."

"*You* gave me the ritual. *You* told me about it in the first place," she pointed out in response to his dramatic and loaded offer of answers to some of her questions. "Why tell me about it at all if you didn't trust him?"

"Veritas must still act in accordance to the rules with that ritual, for true bindings, even temporary ones, can pull a spirit out of its vassal for a short time. He…used to tell me about those times, and they were always otherworldly and decidedly out of the realm of the physical. I suppose it's my fault for trusting him even that far after what he's done, and now you're involved. Now you're *bound*."

"Why help me at all? If you knew there was a risk, why even *give* me the tools to tamper with magic that was no good for me?" Aubria knew his answer in part already, but she wanted to hear what he might say before she judged further. Her temper was rising, harder to bring to heel due to the exhaustion of travelling, but she wrestled with it anyway.

Terran faced her, smiling a little as if anything about their conversation amused him. "You keep asking me variations of that same question, you know. Why did I help you? Why have I attempted to train you in potion craft and the innate magic that I sensed in you as soon as we met? Why did I kiss you in the tavern?"

"I never asked you that," she said, her voice almost failing as the golden, euphoric memory flickered like a dying candle in her head before going out.

"I've asked myself, though. I haven't found any answers that I'm willing to live with. And now that you know for certain about Veritas and the curse on my bloodline…I suppose it's for the best. I can end this now."

End this? Aubria failed this time not to be hurt by the naked relief relaxing his features, even if it was accompanied by something that looked like pain. *Who are you to decide that?*

"I don't care about any of that, Terran! I would've helped you both regardless, because—" The words she couldn't say caught in her throat so she choked on them. She hadn't admitted the truth to herself, not yet...how could she tell him something she wasn't sure she believed in?

"Because *what*, Aubria?" His voice softened in volume, but the rancor snapped free to spite her; his fragile control threatened to break at any moment, but the tenuous cord stretched tighter now than it had before. "Because you're fascinated with the exotic Potioner with the troubled past and the magical binding? Is it the excitement of life outside your home village or is it only my body that drew you in?"

"Terran Caird, you know very well—" she began to tell him off, but he cut in again in such a way as to make her want to tear her hair out in frustration.

"Is this what he told you you wanted? Life on the road, forever estranged from your precious orchard, with some drifter who can't recall half of his own life? Who at any time could be taken over by a spirit for good? Or maybe that's what you really wanted..."

"No! That's *not* what I want, and Veritas wouldn't do that!" Aubria was infuriated enough to stomp her foot on the ground, and she was sure her freckled cheeks were blotchy with anger.

"*Do not* presume to tell me about the creature who I've been bound to since my birth! I know what he is capable of, despite whatever upside-down 'truths' he decided to spin for someone as gullible as you. How can you trust someone—some *thing*—that killed the younger prince, who was our friend and ally at the time? Who used me and my skills to do it and then abandoned me to deal with the fact that now I'm no better than a murderer?"

She'd known—she'd guessed—that Veritas had killed the younger prince at the behest of the elder. Yet the outright confession sent a pang of regret throughout her whole being, as if she'd lost the chance to stop such a horrendous thing from taking place even though she'd had nothing to do with it. She'd had faith, somehow, that there had been a good reason for the heinous act.

"He did?" she asked, her voice making her sound as small as she felt.

"Of course he did. Mardin ordered me to kill his younger brother, and I refused. Veritas said we should just kill Mardin, and again I refused because I didn't want to murder anyone in the royal family...the king's trust meant something to me, then. I wanted the Potioner's title to become synonymous with healing and progress rather than poison and murder as it had been in my ancestors' time. Veritas decided he knew what was best and poisoned Mardin's cup...but Phillip returned early from the hunt instead of Mardin, and availed himself of the fatal chalice."

Aubria covered her mouth with her hands, feeling as sick at heart as if she'd been the one to imbibe poison. *No.*

"Veritas found him. He'd meant to watch the murder happen, but something called me away so he let us leave, assured that Phillip would neither return first nor indulge in the chalice when he preferred fresh water after hunting. By the time he returned, the younger prince had died...and Mardin stood over him, grinning like a fiend." Terran halted his dreadful story, looking out into the horizon and letting the horror of those moments replay in his mind. "Not wanting to reveal himself, Veritas abandoned me to accept Prince Mardin's congratulations and reap the rewards. I myself would have killed him then, but I knew already that Lyrassan and King Barric both could not afford to lose another heir, even a bad one. Regardless...Veritas took over my body and my mind, he engineered the death of one of my closest friends and the man who would have been one of the best kings Lyrassan had ever seen, and he made me responsible for the strife this kingdom will have to endure once Mardin is crowned." His bitterness was palpable: she imagined she could see the black hole in his heart that had eaten away at him for years, and she could taste the sour regret like spoiled grapes in the back of her throat.

What could she say to assuage that emptiness, that guilt? Who was she to absolve someone, even someone cursed, of such a crime?

I did it to save him, Veritas told her, finally interjecting. *The elder prince would have killed him had he not changed sides. The Potioner is a powerful figure and a wizard in his own right, but the elder prince had and has many, many allies ravenous for power and favor. It would have been no difficult thing to stick a cursed knife in his back at the soonest opportunity, or any other weapon enchanted with anti-healing properties. I never meant to kill Phillip, and I wouldn't have attempted to kill Mardin if he hadn't threatened Terran. I failed all of them. Condemn us...me...for the act if you must, but know the whole truth if you do.*

"Is he talking to you now? Is he trying to free himself from your condemnation with twisted truths?" Terran laughed, the sound hollow. "He hasn't spoken to me since, but I can *feel* him in my head. Who knows how much he's taken from me, or how many people he's hurt or killed? Who knows how much of my life he's stolen, especially now that he's hoodwinked you?"

"Even if he did do any of that—which I doubt, aside from the prince—you are not to blame," she said as soon as she could speak again. She approached him as she would a cornered wolf with an injured paw: warily, but with soothing sounds she hoped would begin to ease his pain. "You're under a curse, Terran, one your ancestors got you into with no thought for the future. I believe that the one they bound you to is no evil spirit. I believe...I believe he did what he did to protect you, even though he failed. He cannot lie, and since he cares about you I don't think he'd twist the truth."

Terran laughed, the sound as harsh as his lethal glare. "It must have been phenomenal, what he did for you during the ritual and then again during Beltane. Tell me, were *we* any good? You came back for more, so I assume you liked how *we* treated you—"

"Terran—" she had to stop him, she didn't want him to say such ugly things, but her voice choked with unshed tears as she clenched her hands into her skirts for empty comfort. "It wasn't like that. I did let him...lie with me, but if I'd known I *never* would have used you in such a way."

"Would you not have?" he taunted her, disbelief ringing in his mocking laughter. "Here I am now, Aubria! Make use of me how you will."

Terran wasn't shouting, but the poison in his words made her retreat a couple of steps. Yet he pursued her, and he seized her roughly by the shoulders and kissed her hard enough to wound. She resisted, and their teeth clinked together as he forced her mouth open with his tongue for the most violent kiss she'd ever received. His hands gripped her tight enough to leave marks, and she pushed against his chest with a muffled screech of protest as he kissed her as if he owned her, like he would rather use her than be used by her.

But he didn't have it in him to continue the cruelty, and she didn't have the will to resist him. His expression, white with rage with his eyes burning like malachite, lingered in her mind as he kissed her. His mouth softened against hers as he perhaps realized that now that he had her at his mercy, he didn't really want to hurt her at all. Aubria in turn melted into him, sighing as his hands moved from her shoulders to her back to hold her against him with more tenderness than she'd experienced from him before. Throwing aside the reservations she'd restrained herself with the whole time they'd been in the city, she allowed herself to have this moment.

Terran didn't resist as she slid her hands up his chest, where before she'd tried to push him away. Nor did he stop her from running her fingers through his hair, from using it to pull him closer so no empty space parted the two of them. She could feel him, every muscle in every line of his figure, through her loose shirt and fitted leggings. As if he knew what gave her pleasure, he maneuvered a hand between them and with agonizing slowness, with practiced teasing, he slid it under her tunic but above her undershirt. She could feel the heat of him through the cloth, and she gasped into their kiss as his fingertips brushed the peak of her breast and pinched together.

Then he pulled away, as if his delight in her desire for him had caught him off guard. She couldn't look away from him, and she didn't want to.

Aubria loves Terran.

The words came to her of their own volition, and though she knew they would hurt her later because nothing had been fixed and he would hate her for this as well later, she let them etch themselves into her heart with a mark that would last forever. Nothing else in the world might have been right, but this was. She'd never been more certain of her own heart before, and as she leaned forward to renew their kiss a few tears streamed down her face savoring of the regret she would have to face later, when he inevitably left her alone.

It's too soon, it's the stupidest thing I've ever stumbled into but…it's true.

What shocked her was the return of her anger when he pushed her away, which she felt like she didn't have the right to experience in the face of what she'd done to him, wittingly or not.

"Veritas or not, it's *you* who desires me, Potioner. I think there's more between us than you're willing to admit. I think you care about me. I think you—"

"Stop. I know."

He let her go, putting space between them. The wild-eyed anger she'd seen that had almost consumed them both hadn't faded, not altogether, but some of its heat had been directed into desire that had him clenching his jaw as if it took huge effort for him not to continue what he'd started by kissing her in the first place. Aubria hated to see him this on edge, and she would've given anything to close the distance between them to offer him words of comfort.

Then he broke her heart.

"When you get home, send Clearwater in the direction of Eldacre. She knows the way. I think it's best if we don't see each other anymore."

There was so much she could've answered. *What was all of this for, then? Am I to struggle against the faerykind alone, without even Veritas to aid me? Why befriend me if this was how it had to end all along?*

He means to leave you, yes, but I will help you from afar when I can, Veritas's voice intruded into her despair. *For now he's determined to shut you out. I think you should let him, Aubria. He needs time.*

"I think that it's best too." Aubria hadn't expected any of this to go well, but to never see him again, or to only see him as Veritas whenever he could get away to help her…she pitied the truth spirit, too. It had been obvious from the beginning, even when he'd pinned her down and held a knife to her tender throat, that he'd cared about Terran from the first, like some sort of twisted older brother. How terrible to be trapped in a body that wasn't yours, to someone who resented your presence even when you were keeping yourself small or only trying to help.

I wish I could have freed you, she thought, though she spoke more to herself than Veritas, if he was listening at all. *But at least I can choose to not use our binding.*

Terran's lengthy stride had carried him to Cloud's side much faster than she could walk even if she hadn't stood like a frightened wood sprite under the draping mendacia vines. He mounted his horse and cantered off without a backward glance. As if she was baggage he was relieved to leave behind.

Aubria trudged back to Clearwater's side and hauled herself into the saddle. Now more than ever it would be a relief to her to go home, though in a few short days that comfort would transform into the bars of a cozy cage. As the mare trudged towards her home village at her own pace without any urging from her rider, Aubria stroked the sun-warmed fur of her mount to soothe them both.

I was a burden all along. One he sought out, for a time…but in the end, still a burden he'd do anything to be rid of.

By the time her cottage came in sight, Aubria felt as worn out as a limp rag. She'd expected to cry, but her eyes had thwarted her with their dryness as the rest of her fought the onset of numb, weary acceptance of the fate she'd so thoroughly bungled. Clearwater, gentle horse that she was, tried to console her once Aubria dismounted; her soothing whickering and the nudge of her velvety nose against her shoulder almost broke the dam against her sorrow, but Aubria held the pieces of herself together with the fragments of her will as she patted the mare on her rump to send her back to Eldacre. The satchel she'd repacked with a haphazard slew of her items was no worse for the wear since the saddle bags had taken most of the abuse from the journey, but it weighed on her far more heavily than it should have.

251

As she walked down the lane leading to her front door, her father swung the door open and stood waiting for her, the cat in his arms purring as if to let Aubria know that it had taken her place as the favorite in her absence. Darragh's expression, punctuated by the thunderous downturn of his mouth underneath the dark beard accentuating the lower half of his face, formed its own paradox of anger mingled with relief. She remembered that when she'd left home he'd been suffering under the burden of the seasonal sickness, but the potion Terran had given her had done its work; no puffy, watery eyes or continuous sniffing met her attention.

He said nothing while she approached, choosing to let her suffer under the weight of his silent accusation until she reached the bottom of the trio of steps leading up to their door. Aubria could hardly bear to look up at him, but when she did she saw his anger soften into parental concern.

"You didn't go to Eldacre," he said, making a statement rather than an accusation as he had clearly planned.

"No. I was in Oseren...but now I'm back." The explanation, simple almost to the point of deceit, felt like rocks tumbling down from the top of an impending landslide. Eventually, she might tell him what had happened...but she couldn't. Not yet.

Darragh's jaw worked as if it cost him physical effort to keep his interrogation at bay. But he looked kindly at her rather than with wrath, and underneath the concern of his stare the shattered armor lying in pieces around Aubria's exposed, raw heartache disintegrated into ashes.

"I'm back now," she repeated, the tears she'd dismissed gaining the victory at last.

Darragh sighed as he urged the cat to leap from his arms to the ground so he could pull Aubria in for a hug. The creature rubbed against Aubria's ankles—easily accessible rather than curtained by the folds of a dress—to show its unusually charitable mood in response to her suffering. Later, she assumed, it would take revenge for its demotion back to second favorite with a hairball outside her bedroom door.

"Hush now," Darragh told her. "Whatever it is, it's over now."

15

*M*idsummer approached its zenith, meaning Litha and the next turn of the handfasting wheel drew near. Aubria found that as the weeks after her time in the city passed that she could feel both love and loathing for the place she'd grown up in and the person who'd showed her that there was more.

Spring was a busy time in the orchard, for both fruits and their flowers were of considerable value in any market, but the first half of summer provided its own unique mountain of work for everyone who lived in Loracre or Eldacre. The villagers of Loracre especially had their hands full, since many of their magical harvests developed in late spring and early summer. Anything with magical properties—citrus fruits in bold shades or orange and yellow and blushing violet in particular—needed to be gathered and treated with care. The Guide of Rites was an exacting task master when it came to honoring the gods with the daily harvest rites and the weekly sacrifices of something from each bounty.

Aubria avoided helping in the village or with their neighbors as much as she could. Darragh had assured her that no one knew that she hadn't been in Eldacre for so many days, but gossip spread fast and she wanted to keep to herself. There was work aplenty for their own side of the orchard, and she and her father kept themselves occupied with tending to their own harvests—nothing magical enough to require the presence of the Guide of Rites grew around their cottage and the acres they owned—and caring for their own livestock.

Aubria stifled any recent longings and her own bewildered sadness with the abundance of labor and her father's soothing company. As before, when she hadn't yet travelled to the city in the Potioner's company, she took solace in her work and with plucking fresh fruit from the trees and packaging it in their humble barn so her father could cart it into Loracre when they had enough. At night she collapsed into bed smelling of the pink or yellow lemons from the trees a few acres to the left of their cottage, and by day her skin was sticky with sweat or with tantalizing, honey sweetened lemonade that she bottled by the gallon and stored in their chilly cellar for the rest of the summer. Her father loved lemonade above mead or beer, and doting on him by making his favorite drink or food and helping him work made her feel less alone.

And alone she felt, when she wasn't keeping busy. Aubria paid closer attention to her father than she had before, wondering how he had coped after her mother's death when she was a young child. Staring at him through the branches at the top of her ladder that helped her reach the fruit dangling from the tops of the trees gave her no answers, but she was hesitant to ask him anything in case she renewed any old pains. Many years had passed since her mother had died, and any grief had been soothed by time so that he no longer mourned as he once had in her earliest and dimmest memories. Though he had not remarried by choice, he kept himself busy and happy with his community and with her, since until recently when she'd gone to the city their relationship had been close and mostly void of secrets.

Now that she knew she loved Terran—loved him to the point of being consumed by it even though she realized that this wasn't exactly a healthy way to feel about anyone—she doubted that she'd experience anything quite like this again. She'd sacrificed her heart and her mental well-being to the Potioner, and now that whatever relationship they'd had had gone up in flames thanks to her poor decision making, his denial of his feelings for her, and supernatural forces, she had to pay the price for her folly.

The potions she'd filled her case with by her own intuition and by Terran's guidance lay tucked away under her bed. Aubria loathed herself for her weakness every night when she rose from her sleepless bed and unlatched the box just to take each enameled bottle in her hand and list off the ingredients and the crafting process in her head. She missed potion craft already; in the Potioner's tower she had felt more complete than she had in years, as if working with the secret shards of her magic made her feel whole.

Worse than that, she had done enough introspection to know that it was Terran she missed the most.

You pulled away from Lane and the orchard and everyone else because you didn't want your heart beholden to anyone, she scolded herself over and over, forcing herself to appreciate the irony of the decisions that had led her to this heartache. *Then you sold your heart to the Potioner and expected nothing ill to come of it. Foolish, sad Aubria.*

As for the book she told herself she'd borrowed, she hadn't had the heart to open it. Every time she looked at it she imagined that it was a key to the empty feeling locked away behind bars she'd constructed so carefully around her heart, and that if she opened the book those feelings would escape. Maybe it was irresponsible to wait for so long…but wait it would have to.

The orchard struggled still. No new faerykind attacks had taken place—Darragh would have told her so the day she'd arrived back home—but the crops that had suffered were too slow in returning to a profitable state. Terran's tree healing potion had helped, but there wasn't enough of it to go around now that more than the thornbells had been destroyed, and Aubria felt a fresh sense of guilt in not convincing him to make more while they were in Oseren.

He wouldn't have agreed. Not without payment, she reminded herself whenever she couldn't sleep. *And I'm done offering him anything at all.*

At least the thornbells were thriving. The trees weren't fully healed, and the seeds and saplings they'd planted to grow new trees required mindful tending, but the larger trees that had escaped some of the damage had produced a small quantity of fresh, white thornbells well out of season and bedecked with velvety fur rather than thorns. Aubria had taken one of them home with her, and it rested on her night table as a reminder that everything in nature could be healed with a little nurturing, even if sometimes it was never quite the same afterwards.

Her father had noticed upon her return from her journey that her spirits were in a worse state than when she'd left. Yet he did not press her for answers she wouldn't tell anyone, and though the rest of her suffered under the burden of her regrets, his silent attentiveness comforted her more than she could say. He'd never commented on her tendency to work herself to the bone whenever she was unhappy, but he made sure she was never without company for too long, whether that meant sipping tea in the kitchen while she baked or helping her weed their modest vegetable garden.

After weeks had passed without her straying farther from the boundaries of their cottage or their orchard land than she had to, Darragh finally spoke of something other than the fine summer weather or the delicious new seven grain and herb bread she'd baked.

"I saw Cerise and Viola in the village today. They asked when they could stop by and visit you. I told them you've been unwell, but I don't think they believed me. With the amount of our crops I've been bringing into the village for the communal tally they know that there's no way I've been getting this amount of work done all on my own." There was no reproach in his words, but Aubria didn't fail to catch his meaning: he'd grown weary of her moping, and he thought the best cure would be to see her old friends.

Yet the thought of talking to any of them—of trying to explain what had happened that had changed her—made her feel nauseous, so she bent over pile of mending she'd been tending by the fireside and pretended that she hadn't heard.

Two days later, Aubria was tending to the chickens in their coop and fetching the morning's eggs when she heard the distinct sound of people approaching their cottage from the road leading to Loracre proper. Her nerves, successfully deadened by routine and her resolution that she would recover from her heartache on her own, slammed upward into total anxiety as she nearly dropped the egg she'd forcefully wrested from their most ornery chicken. The bird was still clucking like a demon in the corner, glaring at Aubria's scratched hands from its nest.

What are they doing here? Aubria thought once she recognized the voices talking amongst themselves: Cerise and Viola, who'd taken time out of their busy days to come and see her.

A fortnight or so had passed since Aubria had returned home, and in that time she'd seen no other living souls besides her father and the animals they tended. So she didn't really blame herself for being silly when she hugged her half full basket of eggs to her chest and dashed out the door of the chicken coop and around to their barn in a mad hurry not to be seen.

It was too much to hope for, she knew, that her father would cover for her and send her friends away without speaking to her. He could be sensitive and caring, but he was also the one who'd set her down one day and refused to pick her up again until she'd learned to walk on her own. So she was resigned rather than shocked when the familiar pattern of footsteps—Cerise's unhurried but purposeful, Viola's light and quick—drew closer to the barn. Giving in to the impulse to hide once more, Aubria ducked behind Toby's stall and gave the horse a pat with her free hand to hush his welcoming snuffles.

"Do you suppose she'll be angry with me?" Viola asked as she followed Cerise through the wide open door of the Haight's barn. "I want to tell her, but if it makes her pull away again—"

"Leave it to me, Vi, I told you," Cerise's louder voice broke the quiet of the barn like a whip cracking in the open air. "She has more explaining to do than us…we'll handle the rest later."

Curious against her better judgment, Aubria took a steadying breath and patted Toby's muzzle one last time before she stepped out of his stall; later he'd go back out to wander their land and graze, as he spent most of his days, but for now she was glad she'd neglected to let him out until after she'd gathered the eggs.

"Handle what later?" she asked, smiling as casually as she could, as if she wasn't at all worried about their meeting after everything that had happened.

"Aubria! How we've missed you!" Viola's innocent exuberance overwhelmed Aubria as the redhead embraced her; she barely had time to set her gathering basket on the ground before Viola was upon her. As always, she smelled fresh and clean even after any work either with tree tending, planting, harvesting, or packing, and when she pulled away after the tight embrace her blue eyes were bright with fond regard.

Cerise glared at Aubria from behind Viola, her sharp eyes and her rod straight stance full of command.

"I've...missed you too." Aubria obliged them both by answering, and was surprised that she still possessed enough feeling to mean it. She'd been missing her friends for some time, she realized, but how could she still call them her friends when she'd been cutting them off at every turn for months now? How could they still care about her once they found out how many secrets she'd been keeping?

"We went to Eldacre to find you," Cerise said once the awkward pleasantries were out of the way; her waterfall of dark hair had been tamed into a tight braid that draped over her shoulder, and the severe style made her look like the sternest of the three instead of the most mischievous. "Viola and I had decided that you'd hidden from us long enough after Lane. We were going to find you and make you tell us what was really wrong this time. Imagine our surprise when we discovered that you weren't in town and hadn't been there at all."

"We came here after that, assuming that Squire Haight had told us you were in Eldacre so you could have some peace and quiet at home. But he was as surprised as we were to learn that you weren't in Eldacre," Viola continued Cerise's speech with her own mild form of accusation. She looked guilty for doubting Aubria, though she wasn't so mild-tempered to not be a little angry at the deception.

"Darragh almost brought together a search party for you, but when he went into Eldacre himself to look for you and make sure we weren't mistaken, someone told him that Potioner Caird had departed for the city with his new apprentice…the blonde Loracre girl he was going out of his way to pick up and bring with him."

Oh. Aubria winced, biting the chapped corner of her lip as she realized that her father knew more of her story than she would've guessed. She'd told him next to nothing, taking advantage of his longsuffering patience, but after this interview by her old friends she'd have to make her explanations to him at last.

She couldn't look any longer at Cerise with her austere accusations borne out of love, or Viola with her nurturing concern that had her wringing her hands with anxiety. If she kept looking them and truly absorbed the fact that they'd spent so much time searching for her and had been genuinely worried, she might crack the armor she'd been rebuilding around herself piece by piece, and then where would she be?

"What do you want to know?" she asked instead in a hollow voice as she picked up her basket of eggs and led the way out of the barn and back to the cottage. Cerise stopped her, coming up from behind and turning her around by grabbing her shoulder to make her stop walking.

"We want to know what happened to you. We want to know why you've shut us out, and why you're trying to ruin your life by running around with the Potioner like nothing bad will come of it. We—"

"Cerise," Viola admonished, turning the other girl's name into an admonishment before she faced Aubria again. "We have things to tell you as well, Aubria."

I'm sure you do, Aubria thought. *And I have something to tell you, Viola, that you will hate me for knowing.* Though much had taken place since her Queen's Night in the orchard, Aubria hadn't forgotten the heavy feel of Merek pawing under her dress and trying to take something she was unwilling to give. She shuddered in the present, leaning against the doorway of the barn as she relived the terror and the repugnance of that moment.

Aubria discovered then that she was too tired to argue and too tired to keep secrets that didn't matter anymore now that Terran was effectively out of her life. They all came spilling out of her, like a spray of lemonade that she'd choked on. Some she couldn't tell, like anything with Veritas or her predicament over saving the orchard, but the rest were enough to shock them both.

"The Potioner has been training me in potion craft and more since I have a…knack for it. When he had business in the city he invited me to come along. I did, and it went well…but I did something to ruin it. So yes, Cerise, something ill did come of it. And more might come of my foolishness besides."

Aubria remembered that to the other girls Terran was still a nearly mythical figure, a character in some story just like the king and the nobility in the city felt unreachable and irrelevant to their daily lives. The fact that she'd befriended him and travelled with him and learned from him like he was a normal person instead of someone with access to magic that was forbidden to the rest of Lyrassan couldn't be anything but shocking, but her friends returned the favor by choosing to believe her rather than doubt the explanation she'd given them.

"Oh," Cerise said at last, her voice diminishing as she looked at Aubria with pity in her onyx eyes. "You fell in love with him, didn't you?"

Cerise had always known her best, aside from her father, so Aubria didn't see the point in denying the obvious. She nodded an admission and gestured for the girls to follow her out of the barn and into the early morning sunlight.

"I did," she confessed as she led the way to her cottage; if Darragh knew what was good for him, he would've made himself scarce by the time she entered with her friends. "But that doesn't matter now. I…Lane wasn't right for me, for what I wanted. I love this orchard and I love my home like it was my own heart, but I don't want to be bound to it as someone's wife for the rest of my days. I don't think...I think my freedom is worth a little sacrifice, even if I bungled the whole thing. There are a few things I would alter, but I wouldn't change my decision. And someday I'll find what I'm looking for."

Once she led them to the door she found that she didn't want to take them inside, or to linger indoors herself out of the warm breath of the morning air and the refreshing sunlight that hadn't yet begun to burn hot with the blaze of a summer day. Aubria avoided their stares, waiting for them to cast judgment upon her as she flopped down onto the stairs leading up to her cottage door. Her work dress would be covered in dust from the stoop she hadn't swept in several days, but that didn't matter when her friends were on the cusp of casting her aside forever. She creased the hem of her apron in her fingers as she belatedly remembered that she had gifts from the city to give them, though now she might never be able to.

"Aubria Haight, you are without argument a foolish girl," Cerise began, looking down her nose at Aubria once the latter risked looking up. "But you're only foolish because you didn't tell us any of this. How long have you been carrying this burden alone?"

"We used to share everything," Viola added, sinking onto the step beside Aubria and slipping her left arm around her waist in the universal gesture of girlhood solidarity. "Everything. Why would you feel that you had to keep this from us? Did you think we would stop being your friends if you wanted something different from us?"

"I suppose...well yes, I did. I didn't think you'd understand me, and that you'd shun me for thinking I was too good for our way of life here in the orchard," Aubria admitted, completely bemused as Cerise took a seat on the step below hers and released a long-suffering sigh. "As far as Terran goes, I didn't think anyone would forgive me for befriending an outsider."

"Terran, hm?" Cerise rolled her eyes; plucking a greenish brown egg from Aubria's basket, she rolled it back and forth between her two hands as if the motion helped her think. "We've known each other since our birth, Aubria, all of us. We know you best, if not better than you do yourself. I knew for a while that Lane wasn't making you happy, not for lack of effort...but because he wasn't what you wanted."

"You've seemed...lost. I'm not sure for how long, now I think about it, but when we were all going through the handfasting wheel together, I wondered if—well, I really shouldn't be saying any of these things, because—" Viola trailed off, her encouragement falling short as she blushed and lowered her head, slipping her arm free from Aubria's waist. Cerise gave her a warning look, but Aubria almost missed it as fresh guilt moistened her eyes. If her friends were choosing to try to understand her even after she'd ignored them and treated them rudely for so long, then there was more still that she could tell them to perhaps heal the breach she'd caused.

"Lane wasn't right for me, Vi, and I've learned to be all right with that," she started as she set her basket aside and tipped Viola's downcast face up to hers with a gentle touch. "But Merek isn't right for you, and I think you need to know this for certain. He doesn't treat you kindly, and he abandoned you at Beltane. I was willing to let things be as long as you seemed happy with him...but he tried to hurt me on Queen's Night. He would've taken advantage of me if I hadn't managed to outrun him. I don't think you should finish the handfasting wheel with him as a partner, least of all marry him at the end."

Aubria's stomach churned as she awaited the outrage and the disbelief, the anger that she'd kept something so important to herself for all these months. Yet the girls surprised her again, and this time when Viola's wide blue eyes slid to the side to exchange a look with Cerise she caught on.

"What's happened?" she asked, turning to Cerise.

"You've been out of the village for some time, so you wouldn't know this yet; Darragh wouldn't have told you before we could. Merek's gone missing, but he severed his binding with Viola before he left to wherever he was going," Cerise said, her disgust apparent in the way she squeezed the fragile egg in her hands; it almost cracked, but she caught herself in time to save it. "Not before he hurt her, though, in the same way I suppose he tried to hurt you."

"Is this true?" Aubria asked Viola, cursing herself yet again for holding her silence. She'd been quiet too often of late, and kept too many things to herself. If she'd failed to prevent Merek from hurting Viola, she resolved to guard her secrets a little less tightly.

Viola nodded, briefly unable to speak as she clasped her hands in her lap and bowed her head as if in prayer to the nature gods. "I...I knew it wasn't me he wanted, and that he liked behaving roughly with me more than he should. But I had no idea he'd—Aubria, I'm so sorry for anything he did to you—"

"Hush now," Cerise soothed her by resting a hand on her knee. "It's over now, and he's gone. You're safe, remember? So is Aubria."

Viola agreed with another nod, but she looked no less uneasy as she stared down at her hands as if she could still see the bruises Merek would have left around her wrists. "There's something else."

"Yes?" What else could there be? What could be worse than Merek taking advantage of Viola and then abandoning her? Unbidden, the memory of Terran's lips crushing hers when he'd been seeking to hurt her had her clenching her hands into fists as the feelings of both rage and desire that she'd tried to stifle overwhelmed her for half a second.

"Lane invited me to continue the handfasting wheel with him and then marry him during the Yuletide season. I accepted." Viola revealed the steel in her backbone by looking up at Aubria and daring her to condemn her choice.

Lane and Viola...Aubria's mind tied their names together in a tidy bow, perhaps realizing before she did that it would be a good match. Though her heart belonged to another who had rejected it, the news still knocked the wind out of her. She pressed her hand over her heart as if that would remind it to beat properly instead of stuttering to a stop. Viola hadn't stolen something from her, not really, and though part of her regretted how she'd left Lane she would not have sought him out again.

Cerise frowned at Aubria, but there was no judgment as she

awaited whatever reaction came forth from the well of confusion within Aubria. Viola paled as Aubria stared at her.

"I'm happy for you, Vi. Really. I wish you bliss," Aubria said at last, and meant it. She was adult enough to know that she had no right to care whether or not Lane had moved on from her so quickly, but she knew both of her friends well enough to know that it would take more time than what had passed for their loyal hearts to turn completely from their past loves towards the future of their heart. Surprisingly, that was enough for her: she meant her well wishes for Viola.

Cerise smiled at her in approval like an older sibling might smile at a younger one who'd done something good, and Viola's eyes welled with tears as she threw her arms around Aubria with a small cry of joy.

"I'm so glad you understand," she blubbered. "If you had hated me for this I wouldn't have been able to bear it."

Aubria exhaled as both of her friends embraced her, the sound coming from somewhere deep within her body, from a place that had been locked in painful tension without her notice. But she'd let it go at last, and wounds she hadn't known were there ceased bleeding and began to heal.

I'm not alone, not really, she thought, closing her eyes as Cerise and Viola let go and stared at each other with smiles hinting at approaching laughter. *I might be all right now.*

The three of them looked up as they heard someone running towards the Haight's cottage from farther down the road. Few people ran in the orchard unless they had to, for conserving energy for all the work was paramount in their lifestyle. But someone was running towards them, and Aubria saw that it was her father and a boy she'd seen at play around the village rushing towards them as if something chased them.

"What on earth?" Viola asked, snuffling back her tears so she'd look presentable. Aubria rose to her feet when Cerise did, and they hurried off her front step and down the road to meet her father and the boy accompanying him.

"I was going into town to let the girls say their piece to you, but he waylaid me on the road to let us know that there's been another incident," Darragh told them, out of breath from his swift jog. "This one's happened right outside the village, the closest one yet."

"We should go," Cerise said, worry creasing her brow; her family's home and their beekeeping business rested closer to Loracre proper than Aubria's cottage, and she seemed to be anxious about if her family's land had been struck.

"There's more," Darragh said, gesturing for the boy who'd volunteered as messenger to speak while he caught his breath.

"Something was seen last night, though not by me. And it's left a message."

Aubria hadn't seen the destruction sites of the orchard in some

time. The sight of her beloved trees cast hither and thither with their roots scorched where they weren't torn and all the felled leaves and blossoms laying about in homage to chaos nearly made her weep. This crop had been one of their more symbolic, ornamental harvests: pale pink blossoms gave way every summer's end to fragile, spiraling fruit with a similar scent to jasmine and rich cherry blossoms that induced euphoric feelings often supplementing medicines given to those who were grieving and soldiers returning from the front lines. She'd hoped to craft many potions with this harvest, for its single use of bringing a small measure of happiness with its scent could help many people, even if the cost was high.

But no more, or at least not for several years if they could coax the remaining trees into prosperity once again. Viola choked back a sob as they wandered the land now open to the sky, all of them feeling lost.

On their journey from the Haight's cottage through Loracre and deeper into the orchard, the messenger boy had given them the bare bones of what had happened the night before, when the attack had been discovered. Squire Krag's son had been up early to hunt, and he'd seen a strange light beckoning him through the trees into the crop that had been chosen for destruction by some unknown force. When he'd come too close the light had temporarily blinded him, and when he'd been able to see again he'd been standing right on the edge of the runes carved into the ground within a circle of toadstools. He'd returned at once to inform the village and summon the Guide to translate the message.

"Who would do such a thing?" Viola mourned as Cerise comforted her with a light hug. "And why?"

I will make them stop, Aubria vowed, the resolution she'd abandoned in the face of her heartache and the helplessness she'd experienced when both Terran and Veritas had abandoned her. She tucked a small branch of pink blossoms in her pocket for preservation later, a charm for her renewed dedication.

Eventually they reached the center of the new wasteland, where the Guide of Rites held his own little court in the middle of the afflicted area, the fallen trees around him functioning as a makeshift barrier. Clearly, someone who had almost witnessed the attack taking place in a decidedly supernatural fashion had made him feel more important than ever.

"Three times now has our blessed land been destroyed by forces beyond our control. How long shall we tolerate this woe before we turn to the gods and repent? The gods are patient, but fickle as well. They will only suffer our disrespect for so long before they destroy all of these lands once and for all as punishment!"

Darragh snorted audibly enough to draw the eyes of the sizeable press of villagers surrounding the Guide. "I'll grant you that there's some funny business happening, given what Krag's son saw. But to assume that one among us is to blame is—"

"It's not all that unusual," one of the other Loracre committee members interrupted, more rudely than he should have when a fellow member was speaking. "How many attacks like this will we allow until the ruin beggars us?"

"There are other things we can do to prevent attacks now that we know for certain no out of season storm has destroyed our crops," Darragh argued, speaking over the wagging heads and the mutters of those who didn't want to agree with his rational ideas. "We grew lax in the watch we set, so we can renew it with regulated vigilance. During the nights we can send men that can ride through the orchard and report anything strange, and if we go to the king with our plight he is obligated to protect these lands."

"We *will* summon the king," the Guide interjected, surprising everyone by agreeing with Darragh Haight for the first time in his life. "But only to bid him partake in our rituals of repentance. For the message left by the gods was clear: if we do not repent of our transgressions and our lack of piety, if we do not cast aside both our arrogance and the one who has betrayed both the gods and our village, we in turn will be cast out of our orchard by the children of the gods themselves."

Aubria tried not to flinch as the Guide's baleful gaze swept over her and lingered a moment too long. Though no one knew that she'd partaken in a forbidden ritual and used magic outside of the sanction of the king and the gods, she felt guiltier than she should have. Could the Guide see her potential sin? Veritas had told her—and the research she'd done had confirmed this—that the faerykind had little to do with the gods themselves, and that they were probably more intent on recovering their ancient lands rather than punishing a village girl who'd supposedly transgressed.

The Guide was a man of power in the orchard, as was her father, who opposed him at every turn and kept the villagers from falling too far into ignorant superstition. Aubria knew that her father *did* respect the gods...but the Guide viewed only prostration before the village altar on a regular basis as devotion to the divine, and it would behoove him well to find a way to punish either the squire who opposed him or his daughter by proxy.

"That's an exact translation, I take it?" Darragh strode forward, skepticism wrinkling his brow as he challenged the pompous, robe-clad Guide both with his approach and his superior height. "Those are the exact words left by the so-called messenger of the gods?"

The Guide backed away a step or two as Darragh approached; Aubria trailed behind him, wishing to view the message the faerykind had left more than she wanted to hide in the background.

"There is no *exact* way to read the runes of the gods or their children, but the basic translation says that the sacred trees are not our own, and that we will remember who they belong to before the end." The Guide gestured to the ground behind him as Darragh nudged past with a disdainful glare. Aubria restrained a gasp as she saw the message scratched into the dirt with what looked like a slender branch that had been set on fire and burned into the ground.

Terran's tattoo? But how? Now that she looked she could see the differences: the script had the same swirling loops and slashes, but it was a different rune in spite of the similarities. She wished she'd found a book in the library that could translate runes like these, and she'd even looked for one based on Terran's tattoo, but no luck. She was as unskilled as anyone else in the village when it came to antique languages and lore. Defeated, she traced her finger over the edge of a loop on the left and futilely willed it to tell her its meaning.

"I noticed that you daughter has been away for some time, Squire Haight," the Guide whispered to her father behind her back as she traced her fingertips over the charred, swirling pattern left in the grass. "The possibility that she might have something to do with our troubles has crossed my mind often. Do not think that I will not whisper this knowledge into the right ears if you continue to express your doubt so shamelessly."

Aubria leapt to her feet, abandoning her scrutiny of the faerykind message as she faced the Guide, her mouth opening to protest her innocence and to decry his manipulation. But her father stopped her, laying a restraining hand on her arm. Astonished, her eyebrows shot heavenward as she turned to stare at her father. Darragh looked as angry as she felt, absolutely white-lipped with rage, but he held his silence and stared into the cold gray eyes of the Guide.

"That would imply that you did anything but bellow your every thought to the public as soon as you had one," her father snapped, but he'd lowered his voice, and he broke dominant eye contact as he glanced around at the crowd of people milling through the remains of the ripped up trees and blossoms that had been trodden on.

He's afraid, Aubria realized. *He's afraid because if the people listen to the Guide as they've been encouraged to do their whole lives, they might believe him if he makes an accusation against me. They might punish me for my "sins," and who knows where that would lead.*

Darragh had mentioned before that the Guide wanted to discipline whoever had brought the wrath of the gods upon them by letting them burn in the lightning field. Did he truly fear what would befall his daughter if the Guide pointed the finger in her direction?

"Let us pray to the gods for guidance in this matter before we toss accusations about. Let us send word to the king that we require his aid, and the aid of his soldiers in defending our homeland," Darragh said at last after the Guide gave him another poisonous, knowing look. "Let us petition the Potioner in Eldacre for help, for more of the potion that healed the thornbell trees. If he understands our plight I'm sure we can work out a reasonable trade of services."

The Guide didn't look happy with the final addition, but he could hardly protest now that Darragh had garnered the attention of the group at large once more and had most of their heads nodding in agreement. A few—more than a few, more than made Aubria comfortable—were staring at her and her father with suspicion in their eyes, as if they too were trying to puzzle out why the Guide had involved them. As if they too suspected that Aubria Haight was at the heart of the matter concerning the whole orchard.

Aubria ignored them, and so did Darragh. She gave her friends a farewell wave as her father stormed from the orchard back towards the village and beyond to their cottage. She started to speak to him, but the words she wanted to say held their distance, and he looked too distracted to hear her.

Once they were some distance from the ruined site, Darragh addressed her in a rapid undertone, as if anyone could be spying on their exchange. "The Guide is a proud man, Aubria, and now he has too much power and the ear of everyone in Loracre. I know you went to Oseren, and I want you to leave Loracre and go back there if he threatens you again. At least until all of this blows over."

"Really, Da?" she questioned. "How could I leave you? How could I—"

"You will leave when I tell you to, and that's final. I will not sacrifice my daughter on the altar of pagan superstition and the word of an old man afraid of his own shadow," Darragh cast her a sideways glance full of thunder as he took hold of her arm and pulled her along with him. It would rain today, Aubria could feel it: the orchard could always use a healing rain, but today the gray clouds that blocked the morning sunlight for good offered her little solace.

One way or another, time was running out for her and for her orchard home. Aubria had no choice but to set aside her misgivings and read the book she'd stolen, returning to her research with earnest.

What she dreaded most was calling on Veritas again, and she knew she would have to. The Guide had told them what the symbol meant, but the symbol was linked to Terran's tattoo in some way and she needed to figure out how that could be.

He said he would answer, if you needed him, she reminded herself. *The fact that you don't want to need him is irrelevant.*

But it wasn't meeting Veritas she feared, and her heart knew the difference.

16

Aubria lounged underneath the shade of the ember tree, staring up at the clouds through the huge, draping leaves that maintained their red and orange hues all the year round. The pure white fruit pods wouldn't be ready for harvest until Samhain, since ember tree fruit was one of the most delicate crops in the whole orchard, but it was worth the wait. Emberpods were called so partially because of their bright leaves and their rich red blossoms that smelled like they were kin to roses, but the white fruit was ideal for healing burns caused by fire or the sun. The whole crop was popular with blacksmiths and the southern portion of the kingdom.

For once she wasn't thinking about fruit or the properties that made it valuable or beautiful. She wasn't even imagining what sort of potion she could make with the milky pods once they were ripe for the harvest. This was the first afternoon rest she'd had in several days, and probably the last she'd have until after Litha and the Doorway ceremony coming within the next few sunrises.

Two more attacks had befallen the orchard, and she wanted to dedicate this resting time to worrying about the future of her homeland and for reading the book she could now admit to herself she'd stolen from the city library. She'd brought it with her and tossed it carelessly on the soft grass that she'd used as a napping place time and time again, since her fingers tingled when she held it for too long as if in accusation either of her theft or her irresponsibility for leaving it locked in her potion's chest for so long.

It was good, too, to get away from the others in Loracre who were suspicious of her involvement with the attacks. Her absence from both villages was still the talk of the town now that word had spread of it, and only the preparations for Litha and the distraction among her peers for their Doorway rites had diverted them enough to leave her be for now. Even Viola and Lane, considerate though both had been, had begun to wear on her patience whenever she witnessed proof of their growing happiness in each other's company and the blossoming seeds of genuine love between them. She had wanted Lane to find happiness with another, and Viola had always deserved the best…but with her heart still in tatters she didn't want to witness the tentative joy they nurtured for their future together.

She had looked forward to the Doorway ceremony more than most, back when Lane had claimed her during Yule. The men who had chosen the land for their future dwelling on the allotment of acres assigned by the orchard council and the king's land committee had begun building their cottages during the early spring, and now together with his betrothed they would select a tall sapling from the orchard and replant it near their home as their chosen dedication to the land and to each other. Then, working together, they'd carve and make a broom from the same type of wood of whatever tree they'd chosen, hang it above the doorway when they wed.

Aubria's parents had chosen a lemon tree for their Doorway ceremony, and the faint scent of lemons still breezed through the front door of their cottage now and again from the broom hanging in its spot above the door. Every time she caught the scent from the broom it felt like a hello from the woman she knew as a foggy memory, and the bittersweet feeling of missing someone you knew you would've loved most in the world struck her like a blow each time.

She supposed she would still learn what Lane would have chosen once he and Viola completed their ceremony in the bones of their future home, but she had no idea what she would have chosen on her own. Right now she imagined that the vibrant, tri-colored wood of the ember tree might make a fine ceremonial broom, but her mind had changed before.

For now, as she stared up at the clouds and toyed with a leaf she'd plucked from the lower branch of the tree that shaded her now, she tried not to think about what Terran might have chosen.

Aubria groaned, setting the book aside as she rolled onto her stomach and rested her chin on her hands to observe a furry caterpillar traversing the jungle of the grass leading to the raised roots of the tree. Though this was a mild summer compared to past seasons, the heat wore heavily enough through her work leggings and the not-so-clean tunic of her father's that she wore now that she felt lazy rather than productive. She would have liked nothing more than to rest her sore muscles and take a nap here and now.

Come on, Aubria. It won't tell you what it's hiding without a look, she thought as she forced herself to take up the book again. With a meditative inhale she turned back the linen cover...

...and startled as the same symbol as the tattoo that lay over Terran's left eye stared back at her.

It wasn't the same, not quite, though it took her a moment to note the differences: she could spot the curl of leaves in the tangling script, which Terran's tattoo lacked, and though her human mind could barely comprehend the swirling dance of ancient text she could *feel* that this book was telling her its name.

A Guide on Faerykind. Had she found a path to the truth and a solution for her beloved orchard at last? Her heart jumped at the idea, and her mind buzzed with so much speculation that she could hardly focus on the next page once she turned it over.

The book, she learned through a casual perusal of the first few pages, was its own generic Guide of Rites. Except that it wasn't, for within the pages lay not the basic tenets of pagan worship that

Loracre's Guide swore by, but ritual after ritual for interacting with the children of the old gods: the faerykind.

Aubria marveled at how the author—whose name she could find not one single mention of—seemed to know more about the faerykind than she'd read in the king's whole library, as if he'd known many of them personally. He had seen them, too, when they hadn't bothered with possessing any humans, and his description of them as beings of light unbound by the rules of the physical world reminded her of Veritas's light seeping through Terran's skin. Was that his true form, since the faerykind could no longer bind their spirits to bodies of their own creation? But he had shown that he could feel and express things like any other human, even though he wasn't one. What was it like, she wondered, being bound to the spirit realm when you spoke and thought like a mortal built of flesh and blood?

It hurt to think about Veritas, who hadn't shown his or Terran's face since they'd abandoned her outside of her Loracre. They may even have moved on from Eldacre already, though she hoped that they hadn't. So she put him out of her mind as best she could—along with her painful pity for him and the Potioner—and tried to focus on the book she'd brought with her to the grove.

The faerykind, Aubria read with increasing interest, *are prone to mischief, but more inclined to toy with humankind during the heavy, playful months of summer. They will answer those who call them if summoned respectfully on ancient, sacred ground, and a clever human might bargain with them for whatever they wish. Be warned, however, that the faerykind are capricious, and any words that are not carefully considered before they are spoken can be used to bind the petitioner in turn.*

She acknowledged the warning as she snapped the book shut with a thump that fluttered the thin pages, her mind whirling as she realized what she had to do next. But Aubria wasn't as excited as she thought she'd be at discovering her next clue, and she bit her lip in concentration as her brow furrowed with doubt.

I need to summon the faerykind soon, on the days of the summer solstice. I'll need Veritas to help me so I don't bind either of us or the orchard any further with my lack of knowledge on how to treat with them. I have to go to him, she realized with a sinking feeling in her stomach as she closed the thin volume and lay back down on the cool grass. *He hasn't come to me, and I doubt he wants to see me at all, but it's time. I can't wait any longer for Veritas to break away, now that I know for certain that I can break our binding and contact the faerykind.*

She'd wasted too much time. She had to find him in Eldacre today, and now was the best time even if she still had work to do in the later part of the day. The Loracre villagers still had ruins to clear from the parts of the orchard that had been attacked, and they would tend to those areas after harvesting and managing the crops they needed to take care of during the day. None of the recent attacks had left any messages other than the one that had already been dispatched, and Aubria imagined that a bird flying overhead would see the empty patches in the orchard like holes in a threadbare quilt.

If she didn't stop the faerykind from pushing them out of the orchard, soon they might not have much of an orchard to tend. As vast as the reach of the fruit and nut and pod bearing trees stretched over the western reaches of Lyrassan, she had no doubts that they could ruin most of the orchard before anyone could stop them. Loracre had sent an envoy from the orchard to the king after the first message.

Aubria clambered to her feet and stood on her tiptoes in a stretch that made her joints pop and her sore shoulders tingle. Clutching her treasure of a book tightly, she galloped with little grace out of the ember tree grove and towards the winding orchard road that had led her there. Her shirt flapped in the breeze created by her movement as she jogged, cooling her for a few seconds before she reached the road that younger orchard workers cleared of branches for an easier passage by trimming the tree branches once or twice a year. Fresh beads of sweat dotted her skin as the summer sun beat down on her head and hair, which had lightened a shade or two from its naturally pale hue thanks to all of her time outdoors.

Given her location in the ember tree copse, she planned on a long walk back into Loracre and then on to Eldacre, since her father had required Toby for work today and she had no access to a horse. Aubria wished she'd thought to bring her hat, but if she grew too warm she could diverge from the road into the trees to get out of the sun as she walked. Her hand grew sweaty on the possibly priceless book she held, and she fretted over the possible damage until she reached Loracre and snagged an empty potato sack to keep it in so she could take it to Veritas without it touching her bare skin the whole time.

As she left Loracre after treating herself to a long draught of water from the well, more worrisome thoughts consumed her while she walked. Any time she wasn't keeping quiet and working herself to the bone the other villagers often cast sideways glances her way or stared at her outright with both questions and sometimes accusations curdling their formerly friendly expressions into looks she'd grown to dread. The Guide of Rites had only threatened to tell the village that he suspected Aubria Haight of being the sinner amongst them whom the gods demanded they punish. But had he circulated the rumors all the same to spite his most vocal opposition over who held the true rule of Loracre?

Aubria stumbled over a raised root that she'd missed during her contemplation on the woes of living in a world of men. She'd diverged from the main road, beaten by the sun's rays at last, and she barely caught herself with her hands as she fell to her knees in the loam underneath the tree. The ground was soft, and she took in her surroundings anew as she sat down to give her bruised knees a chance to recover. Her palms had been scraped by twigs ground into the dirt, but the red flowers that bloomed every year in time for Litha had left a full carpet of silky petals on the ground. Her dingy tunic had patches of red on it now where the petals had clung when she'd fallen, and the sweet smell tinged with the faintest note of natural rot had her senses in overload as she looked up at the trees.

Litha buds bring sweetness to any dish, and the flowers help smaller infants grow hearty, she recited the properties of the fallen petals she held up to her nose with both hands as she sat like an urchin in the patchy grass underneath the tree that had tripped her with its roots. *Not much can be said about the tiny, hard nuts that grow from the dead buds in the winter, but they can fortify anyone for some time if they're on a long journey with no other food.*

Aubria reluctantly recalled another aspect of the Doorway ritual: laying next to one's partner of the wheel under the canopy of Litha blossoms, couples would promise their love for good. After Litha, anyone who wanted to step out of the handfasting wheel would be breaking their promise, and they'd be hard pressed to find another partner at all since everyone would see them as untrustworthy. Everyone still saw Aubria that way after she'd broken things off with Lane, but Merek's abandonment had stolen the show in that regard.

Litha flowers were red like the holly berries associated with Yule, when all of the betrothed couples would bind themselves together in marriage. Holly from the year before had been preserved as carefully as the orchard workers could manage, and before crafting the broom that would bless the doorway of their future home, the couples would wind Litha flowers and the holly around two separate branches of oak to symbolize the strength of their commitment and their upcoming marriage. Then both staffs and their adornments would be cast into a hearth fire to release its sweet scent and signify the approaching unity of the individual spirits.

Aubria paused alongside the road, her dour concentration broken by the sounds of approach from further down the path. The temptation to run and hide further in the shelter of the trees warred with her curiosity, and she ended up standing frozen in the path without making a decision until the sounds of wheels driving along the smooth road and the clops of horse hooves drew close enough for her to react. She dashed behind the refuge of a wide tree just in time for the cart and its driver to come up over the little hill that had concealed her long enough to get away.

Terran Caird drove down the road in a cart laden with cauldrons that had their lids tied on with sturdy twine in crisscrossing strands. Aubria recognized Cloud by his sleek gray coat, noting that the horse looked less than pleased to be bound to a cart again after their journey during which he had only needed to carry his rider, but the horse obeyed easily enough and didn't look like he struggled with the weight of the heavy pots.

What's he *doing here?* She wondered as she flipped her braid over her shoulder and peered around the tree at the Potioner. Enough time had passed for him to have altered slightly in appearance: she observed the shadows under his eyes and the hollow cast to his cheeks, like he'd avoided both sleep and healthy quantities of food since that last time she'd seen him. Both were signs that he was anxious, and Aubria felt an all too familiar pang of regret for her part in causing him pain.

He'd hurt her too, though, and she remembered how shattered she'd felt after he'd abandoned her outside of Loracre. She had done worse things that she didn't want to make excuses for, but now that she saw him again as he drove closer to her hiding place she found that her uncontrollable elation over seeing him again couldn't quite mask her anger over the vicious things he'd said and done at their last meeting.

She'd been going to see him anyway, however, and her business couldn't wait. Aubria was also curious about the full cauldrons sloshing with great quantities of potion; her father had mentioned that they should send someone to the Potioner for help, but she'd doubted anyone had been willing to go almost more than she doubted that Terran would help without sufficient payment. So she brushed the fragments of dirt and bark from the tree she'd leaned against off her tunic and took a steadying breath before she walked out of the trees and into the path with her hand raised in greeting.

Aubria knew that she'd surprised the Potioner more than once in recent months, but it still sent a tickle of satisfaction through her bones when she saw Terran's pensive expression transform into shock. He sat straighter in the seat of his cart and tugged on Cloud's reins a little harder than necessary to signal him to pause; the horse turned to roll its dark, intelligent eyes at him, but Terran paid him no heed as he stared at Aubria.

"What are you doing in Loracre?" she asked when the silence dragged on long enough to make both of them more uncomfortable than they already were. For once, she wasn't concerned with not seeming like a boorish peasant, since she looked too much the part in her less than clean tunic and her work worn trousers. The sun filtering down through the trees was bright enough to make her squint, and doubtless she looked exactly like the shifty thief he'd expected her to be after she'd stolen the hare potion from his shop.

Terran, noticing that she had to squint to look up at him, gallantly swung down from his higher seat so she wouldn't have to look into the sun. "I have business here. I heard about the other attacks, and since I'm a citizen of these villages now I thought I might as well help. A messenger from Loracre came to me not long ago begging for help, so I rushed the growing potions to make them ready for repairing the orchard. They might be a little testier now…but they'll do their job."

"Oh." Aubria could accept the explanation as a reasonable one, but the other things she'd thought to be true clouded the air between them like invisible mist. *I thought you'd have left Eldacre and all of us behind by now. I didn't expect to see you again, though I had to try. I expected…I don't know what.*

"I didn't expect to run into you so soon," Terran broke into the weave of her thoughts so she'd look up at him again instead of inspecting the state of the road to avoid meeting his eyes. "I knew I might see you in the village when I came here…no. I counted on seeing you, Aubria, and if I hadn't been able to find you I would've come to your cottage."

"For what?" Aubria crossed her arms over her chest as she waited for an explanation that would inevitably disappoint her.

Terran shifted his weight onto his other foot, looking more and more like an errant school boy caught in a transgression by the second. "I wanted to apologize. My behavior and the words I spoke to you were said out of misplaced hurt and spite, and though I can't unsay them or…take back any pain I inflicted on you, I'm offering my apologies all the same."

She weighed his words on a mental scale, balancing them against the hurt and sleeplessness and the pain she'd felt for weeks after he'd left her. Aubria had imagined that they'd bonded during their time in Oseren crafting potions, and perhaps especially after their evening at the Gifted Magpie. In the following summer days overshadowed by both her guilt and her grief she'd realized that she still didn't know him as well as she thought she had. He hadn't even told her why he'd returned to the city, and he hadn't given her time to tell Veritas that she might know how to solve his binding to her. The charged tension between them filled with secrets that he'd clearly wanted to tell her that other night in the Potioner's tower had gone unexplained as well.

"Did you rehearse that on your way here?" she asked after letting him stew a little. Terran chuckled, more with chagrin than humor.

"Did it sound that stiff?"

Aubria nodded, fighting back a tiny smile of her own because she didn't want to forgive him yet for reasons she was just learning herself. "It's the most starched apology I've ever received."

"I'll apologize again, then. I'm unused to saying sorry for much of anything in my life, and now that I care for the opinions of the person I'm apologizing to..." Terran trailed off, the courtier's mask he'd worn since he saw her on the road leading into Loracre slipping long enough for her to see that he really did fear her rejection. "I mean every word, Aubria. Perhaps it's no one's fault what happened, and that you and Veritas were drawn together in spite of me to bring an end to the Caird curse, or the power the faerykind have over your orchard. Regardless, I had no right to treat you as I did, to...handle you so boorishly, and I am truly, profoundly sorry for however I might have hurt you. I'm here to help, if you'll let me. Surely a Potioner's magic may come of use in saving the orchard and its villages."

If it helps, Veritas interjected between his mind within Terran and Aubria's consciousness, *he really is sorry. He's been moping for weeks.*

"I'm sorry too," she said after another pause, during which she tried not to show how moved she was by his sincere apology. "I'm sorry for not telling you sooner, and for...for everything that's happened. I never once meant to hurt you, and had I known the truth from the beginning I never would've—"

"It's all right," Terran interjected as she blushed like the maiden she no longer was. "I was the one who baited you with the ritual to keep you coming back to Eldacre since I was deeply curious about the current of magic I sensed in you, and even you didn't know what you would ask of Veritas until it happened. After that...well, you were bound and didn't realize it, and I believe you when you say you wouldn't have called on him had you known...everything."

Wincing, Aubria couldn't look at him again both because of her embarrassment over how he'd phrased the events of her recent past as well as her shame that she'd let it happen in the first place.

"I should have told you sooner," she apologized again, voicing one of the many thoughts that had tormented her since she'd last seen him. "Veritas asked me to keep quiet to guarantee that you'd bring me into the city with you, so we could work together...but I should've told you."

The two of them faced each other in silence, Aubria's blonde hair and the golden strands in Terran's hair shining in the sunlight as the air around them shimmered with warmth that only reigned during summer. It was harder to see in the sun, but she glimpsed Veritas's light gleaming through Terran's skin for a split second, reminding her in his own way that he was there too. For a horrible moment she wondered if she'd ruined it again, if her treacherous feelings had widened the rift that kept them apart. But no, that couldn't be, since he'd come here ready to own his wrongdoing and attempt to make it right.

Then Terran spoke, tucking his hands into his pockets in a show of nonchalance. "I want to help, and I want you to come back as you did before to learn potion craft. Everything else aside, it would be a shame for you to let your talent with potions languish for good. Now that everything between us is out in the open...are we at peace?"

Are we? Aubria felt better than she had in days, but with Terran's return all of the painful feelings she'd recognized as somewhat unhealthy due to their all-consuming nature had come back with him.

I don't know how to be friends with you when I feel like this, she thought, not caring whether Veritas heard.

Yet she voiced none of her misgivings as she sighed and walked closer to him in an obvious move of relenting. "I can't have you and Veritas at odds while we try to find a solution. You'll have to learn to work together until we find they key that will free you both."

"We've...spoken again, since we saw you last. That shouldn't be a problem." Terran tried and failed to hide the relief her brusque acceptance brought him as he leaned back against his wooden cart, which somehow still looked finer than any of the other work carts throughout Eldacre and Loracre. Aubria took her confidence a step further as she added more instructions.

"I think I know how to break the binding on me and Veritas, and I know our next task in trying to free our orchard. We're running out of time, I think, since the faerykind have attacked us more and more of late...which is why you will stay with me and my father during Litha, or until you return to Eldacre. Loracre doesn't have an inn, and I don't want to wander around the village looking for you whenever I need you."

"As you wish," Terran conceded. "Shall I give you a ride back to town?"

Aubria shook her head. "No. I'm going to walk back through the orchard. The villagers suspect me of being involved in the destruction of the orchard...like I'm the only sinner in Loracre who could've called the wrath of the gods down upon us. It will be better if I'm not seen with you again so the gossips gain no fodder for their wagging tongues."

"When should I come to your cottage?"

"Whenever you're finished in Loracre. I will be home first so I can tell my father what to expect and prepare a space for you. The next turn of the handfasting wheel is tomorrow, so most of my friends will be busy with their partners, and any parents will be in the village already celebrating Litha in their own ways. We should have the cottage to ourselves so I can show you the book I found."

They may have apologized to each other and healed the breach keeping them apart, but Aubria sensed that the awkwardness between them would retain its power for some time yet. It occurred to her that he might have misunderstood her confession that the house would be empty for most of the day tomorrow, and the maidenly blush she had hoped she'd outgrow in rapid time returned long enough for him to notice.

Aubria tentatively smiled at him in farewell before she turned to walk away. Terran's hand gently grabbed one of her wrists and turned her back to him. He looked like he was about to say something else, his lips parting and his breath inhaled to form words, but nothing came out as he looked down at her. They stood fairly close together, much closer than Aubria could stand given how his proximity scrambled all rational thought on her end. It was such a paradoxical feeling, the urge to press closer mingling with the strong desire to pull away and remove all chance of embarrassment or heartache.

Terran spoke a single word in the language of wizards that she had learned to recognize before they'd left the city. A swirl of Litha flowers danced towards them both from their branches on the trees, their blowsy petals fluttering like the skirts of twirling ladies. He caught one by its stem in the hand not holding her wrist, and in one fluid motion he tucked it behind her ear, the one not covered by the plait she'd swung over her shoulder. Its heady scent, reminiscent of bitter herbs and gardenia, enveloped her and she wondered if her body would burst into flames under the power of the Potioner's greenest eyes.

"Litha flowers symbolize commitment, Terran Caird," she told him once she could breathe again. She expected him to let her go, to say something about it only being a flower, or anything else to stabilize the tension resonating between them, but he did none of those things.

"I know what it symbolizes. I can't offer you that, and I may never be able to. But...how I want to, Aubria Haight. You should know how much I want to." For the first time, he allowed her to glimpse a piece of the heart he'd kept locked away and out of her reach. It wasn't much, and he let her go and looked away before she could see the true depth of his emotion, but she saw enough to make her want to beg for him to kiss her.

But she didn't, and he didn't, and she watched him depart in a lingering swirl of Litha blossoms as he hopped on his cart and rode towards Loracre to help repair the destruction the faerykind had brought upon the orchard.

17

Doorway

Darragh didn't react immediately when she'd told him that the Potioner would be staying with them for a day or two. He must have noticed that she looked more at peace than she had in weeks, and that the flower she hadn't had the heart to remove from her braid might not have been placed there by her hand. Aubria had withheld a few of the more sensitive details of her journey from her father, but he knew enough for his cognac brown eyes to narrow with suspicion at the mention of their guest.

"The Potioner will be staying here?" he clarified with Aubria as she stood before him, her hands tucked into the pockets of her apron. She'd changed out of her grubby clothes into her cleanest work dress upon her arrival at home and freshened up over the chipped wash basin in her room. After what Terran had said to her it had suddenly become more important to look like a welcoming hostess rather than the disheveled girl who'd met him on the road from Loracre.

"Yes. He brought a great quantity of potion for the wreckage in the orchard at his own personal cost...I thought it was fitting that we gave him a place to stay. Even with his generous help I'm not sure anyone else in the village would offer him somewhere to stay given their suspicions—"

"Enough, Aubria," Darragh cut her off. "You told me of Terran Caird's poor treatment of you, and I myself have witnessed you labor to pull yourself out of the gloom he cast over you. I will need far more of an explanation than that before I allow him to set foot in my house."

Aubria stared at her father as he gave her the look that had had her instantly repenting of any wrongdoing throughout her childhood. He'd been so understanding about everything lately that she'd forgotten that as well as caring for her in place of a mother that he'd also been the disciplinarian she'd feared whenever she'd mouthed off to a village elder or gotten herself into any other trouble. Apparently his forbearance had come to an end.

"I need him, Da. It's not just my...my heart at stake. He has magic and knowledge that I need access to, because of the orchard," she said, confessing as much as she dared. If the Guide called with a host of villagers brandishing torches and pitchforks, she wanted Darragh's proclaimed innocence to ring true.

"The orchard?" Darragh asked.

"Yes. I can't say any more, but...I know something about what's going on with the orchard, and I'm trying to save it. Please believe me when I say that I wish I could tell you more, but I can't. You're going to have to trust me, and I'll tell you everything that I know when it's over."

"Aubria Haight—"

"Time's running out! The attacks tearing apart our livelihood and the homes of both our villages are getting worse and I have to stop them. We have to stop them, Terran and me. I think we're the only ones who can." Aubria held firm in spite of her sweaty palms and the nauseous feeling that defiance always brought her. She lifted her chin up in a challenge for him to argue further with her, letting him know that she had set her path to this course and wouldn't be deterred.

Darragh matched her stare with his own, guarded calculations lining his forehead and making his merry face—much like her own with the exception of his eyes—more somber than she'd seen it in some time. Yet he relented first, and she exhaled a pent-up breath as he took a seat at their table.

"I see that arguing with you won't change your mind...but if I don't like what I see when I meet this man again, then he won't be allowed under my roof," he said, and Aubria avoided his reproachful study as she left the room to prepare a space for Terran to sleep.

They didn't have a sitting room, as most people in Loracre did not, but their kitchen was larger than most to provide a more spacious area for baking and socializing, and in days long past Aubria, Cerise, and Viola had had sleepovers in her cottage with the table and chairs pushed against the walls so their pile of quilts and other bedding had room to spread. She supposed she could duplicate that effect after dinner with a spare quilt or two for Terran and a plump pillow as well, though there was supper to prepare and the rest of the cottage to tidy...

"Aubria," Darragh interrupted her flurry of activity as she re-entered the room with the work broom she kept tucked into the tiny closet in the hall dividing her bedroom from her father's. She looked up at him and blew a strand of her hair out of her eyes as she waited for him to speak.

"Be careful. I would not like to see you hurt again, not like you were when you came home."

I can't promise that, she thought back at him, though of course she knew better than to speak her thoughts aloud. She smiled at him weakly before she returned to her mental list of tasks.

By the time Terran finally arrived a couple of hours later she'd completed almost everything she'd set out to do, with the exception of preparing dinner. She'd been so busy accomplishing one thing in time to dart back and forth between her work and the window in her kitchen that she'd forgotten that her father was watching her, and he gained a full view of her pressing her hands to her flushed cheeks and whirling away from the window as if it was the elder prince himself coming to call rather than someone she knew well enough to consider a friend.

"I'll go out and speak to him," Darragh offered, relenting from his austere pose by the door—arms crossed and the pipe he was most fond of between his lips—long enough to cast a sympathetic look her way. Aubria nodded gratefully, torn between wishing to tidy herself one last time and between wanting desperately to hear the first exchange between her father and the Potioner now that both of them knew some of the nature of her heart towards the latter. But Darragh had stepped outside and was walking down the path towards where Terran rode towards their cottage, ostensibly having entrusted the care of his cauldron filled cart to the villagers in Loracre, so her choice had been decided for her.

Aubria lingered in the kitchen, craning her neck to look out the window without being seen by either of the men outside as she unknotted the apron strings behind her back and unbraided her hair, combing it with her fingers. Terran dismounted as soon as Darragh drew close enough, she saw, and he offered his hand in greeting. She had to dash to her bedroom to rinse her face in the washbasin again and pat it dry with a clean cloth, so she missed anything that happened after her father took Terran's hand and shook it gravely. Feeling foolish as she did so, she dabbed a few drops of scented oil made in the orchard from a mix of local flowers and cedarwood oil onto her wrists and neck, with a drop or three to spare for her brush so that her hair would shine like the palest of riches and smell of home. As for the flower Terran had tucked into her hair—wilting a little now—she set the stem into a small tin cup filled a little with water and brought it out to the kitchen table to bring some cheer to the room.

By the time she'd finished and darted back to her post at the kitchen window, Darragh and Terran had concluded whatever sober discussion kept them occupied, and her father was leading the Potioner to the barn to care for his horse. Relieved, Aubria made an effort to slow her hurried movements and the racing of her heart as she stirred a pitcher of summer tea sweetened with precious sugar and rose petals that she'd strained out after they gifted their flavor to the tea. By the time the door swung open again and she caught the scent of Darragh's familiar smoke, she told herself that she had composed herself enough to appear serene as she turned around to face her father and their guest.

Anything she might have said, anything witty or welcoming vanished from her head as she looked up at Terran, who had changed from his fine black Potioner's garb into clothes normally worn by orchard workers. Both his trousers and tunic were new, or only lightly used, but they fit well; the warm brown and cool gray fabric made his tan skin look inviting. Aubria met his gaze before it slid away to see the flower he'd picked for her by magic resting on the table they were to eat at.

"You know my daughter, of course," Darragh remarked dryly, smoke puffing from his mouth as he broke the tension holding both his daughter and the Potioner mute. Aubria blushed and looked down, quite embarrassed as she occupied herself with pouring some of the tea into two cups and offering one each to the two men. Yet she wasn't so embarrassed that she couldn't smile a little at the sight of the Potioner looking so at home in the clothes of her fellow villagers, and she wondered how he'd come to wear them in the first place.

"I told him that he could stay here for as long as you allowed him, Aubria," her father spoke again, and she saw him roll his eyes at the shyness between the two of them. "But if you don't speak I fear that he'll think you're unwilling to welcome him after all."

Aubria cast Darragh a murderous glance that she hoped was subtle rather than believed it to be. Then all at once the comedy of their situation struck her, and the smile she turned towards Terran as he took the cup of tea from her was genuine.

"Welcome, Potioner Caird," she said. Their fingers brushed together before she withdrew, and the embarrassing tension hanging over them both faded into memory so she wondered if it had been present in the first place.

All awkwardness aside, Aubria dared to relax while Darragh

291

graciously tossed forth a line of conversation regarding current events in the kingdom so Terran could take the bait. She even smiled to herself a little as she began to prepare a normal dinner of fresh bread scraped with herbed butter, savory vegetables from their small family garden, and a cozy chicken soup. She hadn't planned on a dessert, but Darragh had brought home a basket of strawberries from a neighbor and she sliced and mixed them together with honeyed goat's milk.

To her surprise Terran made himself useful while she cooked without interrupting the conversation he carried on with her father. It wasn't that her father never helped her in the kitchen or prepared food on his own, but he was as hopeless with any sort of baking or cooking as she was with woodwork and figures. As soon as Aubria had been old enough to run her own kitchen she'd encouraged him to focus on orchard work and council business so she could take care of their household in peace. With Terran by her side chopping the vegetables or mixing the butter it felt almost like they were back in his tower working on a potion, and Aubria was hard-pressed to focus on the tasks at hand rather than his presence.

Darragh watched the proceedings with a calculating eye, though he extended nothing but courtesy and then a certain measure of respect towards their guest as their conversation progressed and they found themselves to be like-minded on any number of things. The cat loved Terran too, of course, and Aubria tried not to glare at it too obviously whenever it wove around the Potioner's legs, meowing imperiously for attention and pets. Once, her father caught her glaring at the creature when it leaped into Terran's arms, and he coughed back an amused chuckle as he scooped another bite of the strawberries into his mouth. He was right, of course, though he hadn't directly said anything: it was ridiculous proof of her feelings that she was jealous of a cat.

By the time the evening drew to a close with the setting of the sun and all of the dishes had been washed and dried, Aubria found herself drowsy rather than alert as she rested in her chair at the table. She and Terran hadn't had any time to talk, which should have vexed her, but she was more relieved that her father liked Terran well enough to try to find common ground with him. Try as she might to fight it, part of her couldn't help but picture their life in the future, should they ever have one: she and Terran at peace in their own kitchen when they weren't travelling Lyrassan and the lands beyond those borders, with her father visiting for dinner now and then to talk about anything and nothing as the sun set over the orchard. Whatever else might happen, it was a pretty picture that she wanted to hold on to for just a little longer…

"You're tired, Aubria," Darragh's voice broke through her stupor, and she awoke with a huff of surprise as his hand landed gently on her arm.

"Did I fall asleep?" she asked, embarrassed anew as she stifled a yawn. She hadn't realized it, but she'd leaned forward on her arms until she'd practically curled up on the surface of their table, her head lolling on her arms as she dreamed restlessly.

"For a little while. I think it can be forgiven," said Darragh, exchanging a glance with Terran that Aubria couldn't miss as she stood and pushed her chair in to stir some life back into her sleepy muscles.

"I should go to bed. There will be much to do tomorrow," she said, trying to lead her father away with another pointed look.

But Darragh wouldn't be deterred from whatever purpose he had in mind, and he lifted his eyebrows in mild challenge as if reminding her that she couldn't gainsay him in this matter would be enough to banish her to her room. Unfortunately for her it was, and she sighed as she surrendered. Terran showcased his courtly manners when he stood to bid her goodnight with an incline of his head in her direction, and her cheeks warmed when their eyes met again.

"We'll talk tomorrow," Aubria promised him in a whisper as Darragh glowered at her from across the table. She'd wasted time loitering about with tidying the kitchen, but her father clearly didn't want her to spend any of the rest of her evening alone in the Potioner's company—either as a test for her or for Terran—so she resigned herself to her fate and trudged down the hall towards her bedroom.

Yet Darragh lingered in the main room without taking leave for his own bed, and he waited with the Potioner in silence until he assumed that Aubria had gone to bed and wouldn't hear anything of the conversation about to take place. But she was smarter than that, and she stood stock still in her own open doorway as she strained her ears to hear what he'd say.

"My daughter is…fond of you, Caird," Darragh began, his familiar voice low both with intent and warning. "You're aware of this?"

"Yes." Terran's clipped reply bit at her, more so because he didn't elaborate.

"You're aware that my daughter is smitten with you, and you're choosing to meddle with her heart rather than committing to her or leaving so she can move on?"

Terran was silent for a moment too long before he replied, the accusation provoking no ire in his voice. "I'm aware, but I can promise neither my heart nor my protection as a husband. She knows this, and we are both trying to maintain our friendship."

"Then—" Darragh's boots scuffed against the ground as if he approached Terran in order to grab his scruff and throw him out into the night.

"I want to offer her the world, even my world. But I'm not free, Squire Haight, though not because of my pride or another woman. I…let me say that my fate is bound to hers and to my…craft in more ways than one. Until I am bound by such chains no longer, I cannot promise anyone even a day of my life."

"You might never be free, though," Darragh observed, ever practical. "You might never be free, and she will pine for you until you let her go. I don't believe in telling my grown daughter how to live her life, for she has wisdom of her own in spite of her youth. But I know her better than you, *Potioner,* and you will have to break her loyalty to you if you want her to move on and be happy."

Terran didn't speak again for some time, and all Aubria wanted to do was run out to the kitchen and tell both of them that they had no right to discuss her future and her decisions without her as if she was a child requiring the guidance of a firm hand. The progress she thought they'd gained with each other over the dinner she'd labored over had been a sham, and for the first time in years she resented her father for his subterfuge.

"If I cannot free myself, be assured that I will leave and not return. Aubria is cleverer than people give her credit for, I think, with you as the exception of course. But if I choose to go there is no corner of this earth that she would be able to find me if I do not wish to be found." Terran promised Darragh, sounding as if he was speaking the oath to himself as well as to her father.

"I don't want her to need to search all the world for you. If you can't make her happy, then—"

"I can, I think, make her happy. I could try my best, at least, once I am...no longer bound in the ways that I'm bound," Terran interrupted, "but I need a little more time. If we do not come to an understanding by the end of the year I will go and not return."

Silence, then; Aubria imagined she could hear them staring each other down.

"You have it," Darragh sighed, his unyielding tone changing into something more normal as she heard the thump of his chair as he moved it. "I don't think I could change her mind regardless. She's stubborn, you know...but her mother was just the same."

The rest of their conversation cut in and out as Aubria heard them moving the chairs and the table against the wall so Terran would have a place to sleep, and she gave up after a minute or two of silence to prepare for bed. When she was climbing under the covers she heard her father's heavy tread pass her door as he made his way to the room he'd shared with her mother before she'd passed.

Part of her wanted to get up and go to Terran then, to see what he had to say about her father and what else they had discussed. She wondered, as she stretched out in her narrow bed so her fingertips hung over the sides, if he was waiting for her to come to him. A shiver ran through her body as she imagined him coming to her room instead, though not to talk. For once wisdom won out over impulse in spite of the heat coursing through her sun-weary body, and she forced herself to sleep after a few minutes of restless tossing and turning.

Darragh didn't wake Aubria as usual the next morning, and she awoke well after sunrise with the luxurious, rare feeling of being well-rested. Since the sun was up and she wasn't working, she assumed that Darragh had graciously broken character and decided to tend to the cottage chores himself. Then she rose from her bed to get herself together for the day to come. She couldn't forget that today held all the promise of a handfasting wheel event without any participation on her part, but thankfully she had other things to occupy her that would keep her from feeling any regret at staying away.

Duplicating her nervousness of the evening before, Aubria tended to her daily toilette with extra care as she donned her light green frock and began to pin her hair up. At the last moment, while the triple strands of her halfway assembled braid were still twined within her fingers, she let them go and instead brushed her hair vigorously and styled herself the braided crown with the rest of her hair loose, as she'd worn it at the Gifted Magpie. Maybe it was foolish, to remind him of their first real kiss…but she wanted to see what he'd think.

Finally prepared, Aubria picked up the book from Oseren's library and left her room at last. The Potioner was waiting for her as she padded out to the kitchen in her soft, deerskin slippers instead of her sturdy work boots. Maybe that was why he didn't hear her right away, and he didn't see her either since his eyes were closed. He stood in the oddest fashion in the doorway of the cottage as he muttered various spells to himself and the room around him spun with a confusion of magic. The blankets and the furniture they'd moved the night before settled back into their usual places, with the quilts folded neatly in a spare chair with the pillow resting on top. The cupboard doors flew open and two plates glided through the air from their places onto the table, and the leftover loaf of bread from dinner the night before sprung free from the cloth wrapped basket she stored it in. An invisible knife sliced it into pieces, and as each piece descended onto the waiting plates the bread transformed into fresh eggs neatly scrambled, piles of bacon, and small breakfast cakes drizzled with syrup. At the smell of these Aubria's stomach began to grumble in protest of her patient watching.

She noticed, too, that his magic had left its traces over the whole room: gold dust similar to pollen blanketed every surface as if her cottage had been transported into a faerykind realm. Terran surveyed the repast he'd conjured with a critical frown. At the last, he pointed at the cup functioning as a vase for the Litha flower that he'd given her yesterday and spoke another spell. The flower bloomed anew, vivid color flushing its fading petals, and three more identical flowers grew from within the depths of the cup to bring their brazen color to the centerpiece as a whole.

All this for me? Aubria pressed her hands over the butterflies in her stomach, the corner of the book she held knocking against her ribs. Terran had vowed time and time again that he could promise her nothing, and he had scarcely hinted that he loved her in return. But were these not the actions of a man experiencing at least the highs of infatuation?

"Good morning, Potioner Caird," Aubria said as she stepped out of the shadow of the hall, hiding the grin on her face with supreme effort. Terran startled, but recovered his composure as the magic in the room dissipated on contact with the real world. The food he'd arranged remained along with the rest of his conjurings, and though Aubria was amused she couldn't help but be touched by his efforts to please her.

"Your father left to oversee the distribution of the potion I brought to Loracre yesterday, I believe. Apparently the older men are in charge of that since most of the village will be occupied with holiday preparation today," Terran explained, his speech only a little more rushed than normal as he stepped forward and pulled out Aubria's chair for her. "Yesterday I didn't think he'd leave me alone with you, but apparently he found me trustworthy enough after all."

"I suppose so, but I did tell him a little of what we have to do. Not all of it, but enough so that he would understand why I brought you to our cottage," she replied. She could have teased him further, but she decided against it as she took the seat he offered and pushed her chair back in.

"What's all this?" she asked instead.

"It's better to feed the mind than to starve it in favor of working hard," Terran spoke what sounded like a new platitude with his characteristic smoothness as whatever equanimity she'd disturbed by surprising him returned. Aubria smiled to herself again as she looked down at the place he'd set for her and the delicious food he'd brought into reality.

"You forgot the cutlery," she reminded him as she watched the syrup pool underneath the spiced breakfast cake before making its way to the pile of bacon she doubted she'd be able to finish. Did magical food taste like regular food? Could it sustain a body the same way? Aubria's mind prodded at the new notion of this sort of magic, and she hesitated as one of the words Terran had spoken while she'd watched him unseen surfaced in her mind like a fish peeping out of a pond. On impulse she spoke the word with her eyes half-closed as she pictured the cupboard door opening to release the forks so they could float on an invisible breeze to rest on the table next to their plates.

It happened just like that...almost. The cupboard doors slammed open, their hinges creaking in protest to such rough use as the forks flew like daggers towards the table and clattered against the wood as if an angry spirit had tossed them down in a fit of rage. Still, her magic had worked, and she picked up her utensil with no small measure of awe. Potion craft had been one thing: the assembling of ingredients, even magical ones, could only be so wondrous. But magic from nothing, she who had thought that she was the most ordinary of everyone...

"You're a quick study," Terran murmured, almost to himself as he picked up the three tined fork she'd summoned with her own reserve of magic as if it was an object infinitely more wondrous than. "Most magic requires far more study and practice than what you've had. Yours, though...it mystifies me."

Their work called, and while they ate Aubria gave him the book to peruse so they could discuss what she'd found. She wasn't sure if she was ready, besides, to admit that the strange magic had been her own. Her hands trembled from unknown strain, and her lungs itched, as if the air she breathed might was full of needles. Her will had always been strong, and she remembered Terran mentioning in the past that a steady will was a requirement of even the simplest spells...but her magic seemed to function on will and concentration alone, and that couldn't be normal compared with everything else she'd learned about the gift of power.

That was a conundrum that could wait, she decided. After he'd read enough to catch up with her, she told him what she'd found out about duplicating the events of the first ritual to break the binding.

"So you see, the binding linking me and Veritas is a relatively simple one. I don't know much yet about how bindings of this nature work, if there's pain in breaking one or if the one who holds the binding can hurt the other if they don't obey...but the important thing is that I know a way to try to break it." Aubria paused so he could think it all over; he'd listened to her intently enough, leaning his labor toned forearms on the surface of her kitchen table as he scanned the passages she'd marked with scraps of ribbon between the pages. He'd returned again and again to the introductory sigils similar to the ones tattooed over his eye, but tracing his fingertips over the patterns and muttering spells of revealing hadn't gained him anything but a significant dose of frustration.

"I agree: if you replicate most of the conditions of the ritual and speak the correct words the connection might break. It was a...consensual binding, of sorts," Terran glanced at her from his peripheral, the tips of his ears reddening. "You may not have to replicate *all* of what took place that night, and since you are...no longer a maiden, you won't have that blood to access."

Aubria leaned back in her chair so her own elbows were off the table, seeking distance between herself and the Potioner; it took work, but she pushed her embarrassment aside long enough to reply. "The new moon is tomorrow night. Veritas and I can tend to our binding then. Tonight...well, Litha is the summer solstice, and I know it's maybe earlier than you prepared, but if I can talk to the faerykind troubling the orchard myself—"

"Tonight you may use both of us to contact the faerykind to persuade them to leave," Terran finished her sentence; his jaw clenched his tight enough to make a muscle jump. Aubria started to slide her hand over the smooth tabletop towards him, but decided against touching him when he looked up at the ceiling as if begging the gods for a better solution. He'd agreed to cooperate with Veritas to help her, but after so many years living with the torment of sharing the only body you had with another spirit who could erase you at the slightest whim—and had on one occasion to kill the younger prince by mistake—she couldn't imagine that it would be easy to submit to that same spirit taking over your body at any time.

We talked, Aubria, in our way, Veritas interjected into her anxious musings as she pulled her hands back to herself and rested them in her lap. *He doesn't trust me yet, but he knows that I would rather be free of him for both of our sakes.*

"Thank you," she said anyway, grateful for his help in ways she couldn't express. "I hate to burden you, either of you, but I think I'd hate even more if I had to do this myself. The last time I interacted with one of the faerykind it didn't really go well."

Her bit of humor fell flat as he turned the pages of the linen covered book back to the passage detailing the summoning and read it again. *"'On these grounds we summon you to bargain.'* It sounds simple enough, although such things are rarely how they appear to be. But sacred ground—"

"Anywhere on these lands should suffice. All of the orchard is sacred to faerykind, so I'm told," she clarified. *Told by Veritas.* Perhaps he knew who'd told her, for he fell silent again as he traced the outline of one of the summoning symbols dotting the page he considered.

"My tattoo bears these same lines. Have you guessed why?" he asked, looking straight at her so she could compare the two; Aubria

300

shook her head, and he continued. "It's not really a tattoo, you know. It's a birthmark of sorts, one that has appeared somewhere on the bodies of my ancestors since they bound Veritas to the Caird bloodline. I happened to be unlucky enough for it to manifest on my face rather than anywhere else."

The information wasn't really that much to go on, since Terran had clearly guessed this already, but new ideas exploded in Aubria's mind along with a crazed uprising of hope that made her lean forward to stare at him in earnest. She reached out to trace the lines with her fingertips as she glanced between the book and his birthmark for reference.

"Could this be what binds the two of you? If we could find a way to remove the mark—"

"No, though it's a logical guess. I know it's connected, and now that we have this book I might be able to find out a little more about it…though I searched through the royal library a hundred times over and never found this volume before or laid eyes on it once. The librarian must have favored you to grant you access to such a rare book," Terran said. Aubria cleared her throat awkwardly and directed the subject down another route.

"But the birthmark! If we remove it, won't that free you?" Some of her desperation cracked through the surface, and Terran's fingers closed around her wrist with sympathetic gentleness. She'd traced the last curl of the mark up to his hairline and he hadn't stopped her until then.

"No. As far as I know, every single one of the Cairds has tried removing the mark in some way, and Veritas always gave them enough control to try. He tried, too, using magic none of us could comprehend. My father's mark was on the back of his shoulder, and he tried slicing it off. I tried burning it. Others tried much more, and it always returned, and the scars healed without a trace." He told her this without inflection, but her palms prickled with empathy as she imagined Terran taking a fire poker to his face to burn the mark away for good.

"I'm sorry," she said, for it was all she could say. Terran's eyes held hers for a heartbeat longer before he let go of her wrist and looked away, as if ashamed.

"Have we been here all morning?" he asked as he leaned back in his chair, reminding her of further of Veritas with his posture.

"Yes, but that's all right. I'd rather not go out today as it is," she answered as stretched. She and the Potioner had been hunched over the ritual book for so long that she felt stiff after so many days of long labor culminating in a day of rest that her body no longer felt used to.

"Why is that?" he said, surprising her by asking in the first place. She blinked at him, stifling a yawn to hide both her sleepiness and her discomfort.

"Tomorrow is Litha, as we've discussed. But the day before is the next event in the handfasting wheel, which is today. It's called the Doorway rite, since the couple visits their almost built cottage in the morning to build the broom hanging that will hang over their threshold and plant the seedling tree that they've chosen to honor the gods, among other things."

"Ah, I heard something about this. You wished to avoid all of that?"

Aubria refrained from giving him an incredulous look. *Of course I do. If I can't enjoy the rite without the only person I'd consider as my partner for the wheel, I don't want to partake at all.*

Would you like me to tell him that? Veritas's ridicule lacked the edge of callousness that might have wounded her pride, but she refused to acknowledge him as she toyed with the fraying edge of the ribbon she'd used to mark her page in the library book she'd "borrowed."

No, she replied curtly. *That won't be necessary.*

"I've heard that the rest of the couples meet in the town square afterwards to dance and drink their early portion of Litha wine until dark, when the bonfire will be lit for tomorrow," Terran surprised her again with his knowledge…along with the hesitant manner with which he caught her eye and held it with his gaze. "I think it would be a shame for either one of us to miss the festivities, since we can do nothing further until after moonrise tonight."

Aubria opened and closed her mouth like a fish before she regained her dignity. Was he asking her to attend the festival—the indubitably *romantic* festival—with him? Should she be thinking this way? Other issues crowded in like a mother hen gathering all of her chicks together.

"I…there are some people I would rather not see me associating with the Potioner, even if Loracre is grateful to you for your help," she told him, reluctant now to conceal any relevant information from him.

"Because they suspect you of bringing the gods' wrath upon the orchard?"

"Some do. Some will if the Guide finds them anything like proof. Others might defend me, but if the word of the Guide is against me, neither my father nor my friends will be able to protect me." Aubria hadn't spoken this thought aloud yet, which she realized now as the fear struck her. If the Guide truly believed that her death—he'd call it a sacrifice—would save the orchard, if she couldn't scare off the faerykind or bargain with them to leave in time for the bulk of their summer crops to be spared any destruction…

"Do you fear the Guide of Rites, Aubria?" Terran broke into her reverie, and somehow his voice reminded her that she wasn't alone in this dreaded task after all.

Not alone, Veritas's voice—more honeyed than Terran's and only in her mind—interjected into the fear that had cooled her skin and paralyzed her. *Never alone. And were the Guide to dare this thing…well, he would be far from the first mortal I have slain.*

"I don't fear him," she decided, the words coming true as she rose from the table and picked up their dirty dishes to set them where they belonged. "Not really. We have time to repair everything, and I have to have faith that we will. Besides…if the gods were as angry with me as he said, I think they would've struck me down by now rather than punishing the whole of the orchard. These trees are sacred to them, so I'm told."

"Have they not struck you with misfortune?" Terran asked, his fingertips drumming against the edge of the table as the only sign of his doubts. Aubria frowned at him, narrowing her eyes.

"Don't say that. I don't think they have anything to do with this, really, and you shouldn't either. Just like I don't think *you* have anything to do with my misfortunes, or the misfortune of this orchard."

Terran didn't answer her, but his reservations were known to her even if he did her the courtesy of keeping them to himself. She wanted to ask him why he thought so little of himself, and indirectly so little of *her,* that he would assume that he was the only complication in her life that otherwise would've been blissful and boring as she became Lane's wife.

No, Potioner, she thought as she tidied the kitchen without using her magic again, *I wouldn't have chosen the easy path even if I'd had the choice.*

Aubria packed an afternoon picnic as fast as she could with whatever she could gather from their cellar and food stores: a fresh loaf of bread sliced and layered with aged olive oil, sour vinegar, bitter greens, seasoned meat, and a bit of cheese that she decided her family could spare for a Doorway luncheon. At the last moment, she hurried down to the cellar and snagged an expensive bottle of honeysuckle and rose accented mead for them to share, if the opportunity came.

Terran took down a basket for her from a hook on the ceiling, and she packed their victuals into a patchy but clean blanket before she tucked the whole package inside the basket and declared that they were ready to depart.

Somehow all of the doubts and troubles of the future—however urgently they'd pressed minutes before—evaporated under the heat of the sun, which turned towards early afternoon as they walked. Aubria cajoled Terran out of his usually taciturn mood, and soon both of them were laughing over shared acquaintances in either of the orchard villages, which Aubria knew several stories about both flattering and unflattering to the subject. He in turn told her about some of his past clients and their humorous foibles while they passed into and through Loracre.

The village swarmed with activity as the couples who had completed their ceremonies in the earlier hours of the morning wandered among their friends and the Litha preparations with the languid grace of youth enjoying itself. Aubria had contemplated the attention she and the Potioner would garner, especially by those who disliked her family for their prosperity and her father's outspoken support of innovation over tradition, but with Terran beside her carrying their picnic basket as they walked she found that she didn't regret her pointed boldness at all.

"I wonder if they're still afraid of you," Aubria mused aloud. "All the villagers know is that you are the Potioner that served King Barric before deciding to travel rather than stay at the keep…well, that and the other rumors. Now you've helped them without demanding too high of a payment for your services…what do they say about you, I wonder?"

"Shouldn't you know that better than I? This is your home, after all," Terran replied.

I suppose I should, she thought instead of answering; a scene caused by a couple serving each other fresh water from the town well distracted her, and she couldn't help but smile as the girl dumped an entire bucket of water over her lover's head.

"Most everyone in Loracre treats me the same, in a way…but it's not really the same. They're starting to treat me how I imagine they treat you," she said as she watched the young couple run off, chasing each other and hooting with merriment.

"I wouldn't say that, not yet…though, if that is your Guide of Rites who is staring at us, I would imagine that to be true in his case," Terran nodded, not really with respect, but at least acknowledgment for the Guide as Aubria followed his gaze. The bald man in his robes—white, as always, though made of lighter fabric so their wearer could cope with the heat—had stopped what he was doing to watch them pass, and nothing about his face looked pleased with their situation. The couple he'd been laying a blessing on had also turned to look, but their idle curiosity changed to surprise and then hostility as they took in the sight of scandalous Aubria Haight walking side by side with the king's Potioner.

"Regardless," Aubria said, telling herself that her face had gone red from the weather rather than any embarrassment. "I'm glad I didn't hide in my cottage all day."

"Good," Terran answered, and they said nothing more until they came to the Litha grove. She had intended to move past it, turning east into the orchard so they could have their picnic by the river running through the land, but she changed her mind and slowed to a stop. Around them, she heard tale of the distant sounds of the couples lounging around, far from each other for privacy but close enough to hear faint laughter or speech.

Aubria paused and looked up at the multitude of red flowers; her heart soared with inexplicable hope.

"Wait," she told Terran, tapping his arm so he'd stop too. He faced her, quizzical, and she smiled at him as she glanced around to make sure no one saw them. Then, hesitating, she spoke two of the easier spell words she'd gleaned from his teachings with her purpose clear in her mind. Lifting up her hands to catch what she'd summoned, she waited patiently as several whole blossoms with all of their scarlet petals still intact drifted down into her open palms. Improvising, she whispered a set of words she mostly knew the meaning to and watched in amazement as several of the blossoms obeyed her will and wound their short stems into her long hair until she knew that she looked like the perfect midsummer maid she'd had in mind.

"Good," Terran said again as she beamed up at him, but his face was serious as he cleared his throat and looked away from her. "I don't think you should be experimenting with words you haven't officially been taught yet…but this orchard knows you, and I think it wants to do as you ask. Maybe that's why your magic functions so well on will and imagination alone."

Aubria would've been hurt that he'd looked away, and some of that feeling lingered even though she knew why he wouldn't look at her with the flowers woven like faerykind locks into her hair. Feeling bold, she stepped forward and tucked one of the flowers into the button-hole of Terran's outer tunic; he hadn't yet donned his Potioner's clothes again since he'd shown up at her cottage, and though part of her missed the powerful, imposing presence she'd come to know when he wore his Potioner's mask, she found that most of the time she preferred him looking as at ease as he did now.

She led the way to a shady spot under an unoccupied copse of the trees and gestured for him to set down the basket. She set up their picnic in silence, avoiding his gaze even though she could feel his eyes on her as she went about her business. They'd set out for a simple luncheon outdoors before their possibly deadly summoning later that night, but the tension in the air made her feel like they'd both committed to more without realizing it at the time.

Aubria ventured forth a topic of conversation or two as they ate, but his replies were less elaborate than she'd hoped, and they ended up sitting on the grass and eating in silence. Terran did notice an ant crawling on the blanket she'd laid out for the two of them, and one spell later any insects in the orchard made a wide berth of their little camp.

Aubria didn't mourn sitting in silence and watching the breeze make the leaves in the trees sway and dance and shed a whirl of red petals every so often. Her belly was full from the delicious meal she'd assembled, and she and Terran passed the pleasantly warm bottle of mead back and forth between them for some time until the drink did its work and made her light and tipsy enough to laugh easily if anyone gave her the opportunity.

Aubria didn't remember when she'd made the conscious decision to do so, but she set the empty basket down past their feet and pushed the blanket aside so she could lie on the cool grass and feel the bristles of it against her hands and arms. Terran lay down beside her, and though he held his drink much better as a larger person and a man at that, she could see the faint glaze of tipsiness in his eyes that had coaxed him to recline next to her.

For a time, in silence, they looked up and watched the clouds pass over the sun through the trees as if nothing else in the world would ever bother them again. She felt one with the earth, almost like she did when she used magic, and the buzzing bees gliding through the trees sounded like whimsical spirits blessing the moment with their presence.

Perhaps it was the drink, or perhaps it was the fact that Aubria felt closer to Terran than she had before, but the question she asked next came from her heart. "How do you feel right now?"

If he said "good" again she intended to laugh at him, but his answer knocked her off kilter.

"I feel...at home here, as I have not before in the course of my life. I accepted long ago that this is something that I can't have, and there will always be a part of me that would wish for the freedom to wander the world without anything tying me down. But once a thought like that gets in your head, it clings like a burr under the saddle," he told her. "I can't stay now, and I wouldn't in the long run...but it would be nice to have a place to return to, to always have somewhere to go." Terran's expression was thoughtful, as if this idea had never occurred to him before, or because the prospect of having someone to listen to these thoughts and care about them was so new.

"That's what having a home means," she replied, rolling onto her side and propping her head up on her hand as she looked down at him. "Home doesn't force you to stay in place, and neither do people you love. They just give you something to come back to, or someone to share the journey with."

"You're right," he agreed, turning his head so his green eyes could look at her face and make her feel dizzy with longing. "As you are about so many things."

She kissed him for that, hesitating briefly before she closed the small distance between them. She tasted the honeysuckle mead on his mouth, sweet and syrupy. It occurred to her before the rest of her rational thoughts fled that this was the first time they'd kissed with no secrets between them, no lies…and Veritas kept himself closed off, so she couldn't sense him in her mind aside from the tie that bound them.

"How do you feel now?" she asked when she leaned back to breathe.

"Good," Terran said, his eyes half-closed and his mouth quirked up in a smile before he pulled her head back down with his hand lost in her hair so they could continue the kiss she'd paused.

For a time they remained, both of them pretending that this sun-soaked yet shade blessed eve of Litha was the only time that would ever be. If his hands studied the lines of her body as if he would know them more intimately later, if she in turn rested her hand on the part of him that responded so readily to her touch, well…that was all right, because they were only summer lovers, and tomorrow would never matter because it wasn't going to happen. They paused for breath eventually; both of their faces flushed and eyes overbright. Looking down at him, Aubria saw that his pupils were dilated more than she'd seen them before.

"What have you done to me?" he wondered aloud, reaching up to trace his fingers over the line of her cheek. She had no answer for him, because in truth she didn't know what he'd done to her either. Nothing within her, nothing she'd been raised to believe or do had led her to believe in the reality of this aching, bittersweet thing that had changed her forever. She had seen her father mourn her mother, and that had taught her the nature of grief…but what could you do when the person you loved was almost in reach, but could possibly never be yours?

"We should go back," Terran said, his brusque closing of the door against the sunlit intimacy they'd shared—almost shared—making her mournful thoughts fill her with sorrow. He sat up, watching her rise as well and touch her lips as if she could preserve the taste and feel of him there forever. He looked away and stood, holding out a hand to help her up.

She wanted to be offended, anything rather than this hurt. But this was different from before, from when he'd kissed her out of spite and then left her alone on the road. Now she knew that he shared some of her feelings, though he'd never say so unless he was free from all other ties.

"I'm sorry, Terran," she told him instead as she took his hand and let him help her up. She didn't lean against him, because suddenly it was important to not cause him any more hurt. She could hurt, and welcome, but the prospect of his pain made her want to weep.

"Don't be sorry, Aubria," he told her, sounding like he meant it. "Don't ever be sorry because of me."

He led the way back to her cottage, refusing to look at her again.

18

The warmth of the summer night couldn't burn as hot as it did under the eye of the sun during the day, but Aubria grumbled to herself about the heat anyway as she used the tips of her fingers to pull her work tunic away from her perspiration slick back. Sneaking out of her window without detection from her father in spite of its creaking had been easy enough, and she didn't doubt that Terran could take the few steps from the kitchen to the front door without alerting a soul to his movements. They'd agreed to meet in the grove of lemon trees near her cottage but far enough to not alert her father or her neighbors to any of their doings. The walk took a little longer, but she didn't mind the journey.

She spotted Terran immediately when she reached the grove, crowded though the land was with trees unintentionally planted just close enough together to block any clear path. At night the orchard became the ancient grounds of those who were not mortal, and she and the Potioner were only two more madcap things gamboling along secret paths under the dark of the moon. The smell of trees past fruiting, the lingering odor of natural decay, and the tang of citrus underlying the whole assaulted her nose; she stifled a sneeze.

"Are you ready?" Terran asked, his words strident in the silence though he'd barely spoken above a whisper. For answer Aubria took the piece of charcoal she'd brought and knelt on the patch of grassless dirt Terran had cleared with a spell. He had one as well, and together they sketched the sigils they'd seen in the book over and over on the ground, aligning the five points of a star until the image was complete. She stood up again after brushing her hands against the grass outside the star to remove any trace of the charcoal. Terran had drawn his side under the light of a wizard's flame held aloft in his left hand, the magical source providing enough light for the both of them.

"Is that all?" He stepped closer as she tossed the remaining shard of charcoal into the darkness beyond their pool of light. They'd memorized all that they could about this particular ritual that morning, but she'd brought the book for reference. It would be disastrous if they neglected even the slightest step.

"We have words to say over the sigils to persuade them to protect us...the book said that the faerykind would try to lead us out of the star, but that we shouldn't listen to them. Apparently a truth spirit like Veritas is an anomaly, and they will twist words to their own ends."

Aubria pulled the book out of her pocket and flipped the pages until she reached the one she'd marked with a spare scrap of twine. It was too dark to see properly, but the pillar of fire hovering like a living candle in Terran's open palm made the inky words dance under its light. She opened her mouth to begin the reading, breathless with faith that this ritual would be enough to call any faerykind to them, but instead of reading she spoke a name.

"Veritas."

He was there for her as soon as she'd called him, as she'd known he would be. He would have had to show himself to interact with his own kind anyway, but first she had something to say to him. Something she wanted to hear his answer to out loud, rather than just in her head where it was harder to hold onto.

"If it looks like they mean to harm or kill either of us, let them have me. You can get Terran out of the orchard unscathed, I'm sure of it. Promise me."

"No."

"Please, Veritas," she continued, ignoring his protest, "I'm tempted to use my binding on you for the first and only time to make you do this. I know your word is binding, and I would rather you swear it without me needing to force you. I never wanted to do that, not to you or anyone else...but I want him safe."

Veritas's reply was a long time coming, and she risked looking up into his face. But he didn't look angry; his face displayed some emotion she couldn't guess, with his lips pressed together in a thin line and his brow furrowed in thought.

"I will protect you both. I will promise only that. Terran's soul is tied to mine, and I consider him the only brother I've ever known, even among the whole of his ancestors and the entirety of my own. But you...you're something different, and it isn't in me to let that fade away. That will have to be enough for you."

Here in the orchard that was sacred to faerykind Aubria wished to show her strength rather than her weaknesses and doubts...but what Veritas had said unnerved her with its tenderness.

Returning to the task at hand, she pushed all distractions from her mind before she turned to her book, ready at last to recite the words of the summoning.

"We call to you in welcome, spirits of wind and earth, creatures of tree and root. We bid you come to us freely and without fear, as we are without fear here in this star on the earth. On these grounds we summon you to speak, to sing, to bargain in good faith. A third time we call to you, we bid you welcome, and we beg your indulgence this night on this good, sacred earth. Come, see how the earth greets the season with joy in her heart, and let us share that joy in your presence," she read. Then, passing Veritas the book, she listened and repeated after him the words she hadn't been able to read, the words that the unknown author of the book from the Oseren's library had somehow captured and traced onto the page for mortals to discover.

The final word spilled from her lips like a precious jewel, weaving its own light into the air as the other words of power had done.

Veritas had told her before through their thoughts that she could only speak the words right after him, else the spike of power might hurt or kill her depending on how many she dared to speak.

After, they waited for their summoning to take effect. The night bore the heavy perfume of magic all on its own, and the ritual instructions declared any solstice time distinctly magical throughout the world. That was what the ritual relied on, after all, that and a spirit of friendship between the faerykind and the one who'd dared ask for their help.

When they came, Aubria wanted to breathe in their beauty as if it too was as necessary as the air that filled her lungs.

The thrumming pressure in the air that made her eardrums feel like they were clogged with her own blood droned on, but it was in the background rather than at the forefront of her threshold for pain. She'd retreated into the center of the star, her back against Veritas's chest. No breeze stirred the branches any longer, since the whole orchard seemed to have fallen into a gap in the world in which no leaf moved and no creature moved or breathed.

Lights winked into existence all around their sphere of protection. Perhaps they had been there for some time, watching in the quiet as she and Terran had laid out the star and summoned them. The star didn't bind them, and they could've chosen not to answer at all...but Aubria had wagered they'd take the bait, and she hoped above hope that she could save her orchard here and now with only her own wits and Veritas's knowledge.

The lights in every shade of yellow and gold held no true form other than as oval columns of luminescence that drifted in and out of the surrounding trees as if they were lost and seeking the road that led homeward. All of the uncountable faerykind surrounded them with the slow grace of a cat waiting for a mouse to poke its head out of its hole. One, larger than the rest, drew the closest; Aubria had the distinct notion that it was staring right at her.

"Who calls us?" They spoke in one voice, yet the echo was filled with voices as innumerable as the elongated pillars of light that dotted the lemon grove like stars descended from the heavens.

Aubria stepped forward a little, taking care to stay within the boundaries of the star they'd traced on the ground; Veritas had offered her some tutelage on what one should and should not say to a wild faerykind. "Names are a gift. I would give you mine in good faith, but you must make an oath that you will not use it against me at any time."

The faerykind she addressed hovered closer, right up to the edge of the first point of the star; she expected it to talk to her again, using a voice without any lips or tongue with which to speak, but it only drifted back and forth in the smallest of patterns, reminding her a little of a stubborn honeybee intent on a particular flower.

The fond association disappeared as she realized with a dull pulse of fear that it was inspecting the edges of their star, seeking any weakness. She knew that they'd drawn the runes accurately down to the last sweeping arch…but her mind whispered *please hold, please hold,* to no one over and over again.

Steady, Veritas whispered into her mind. *We are not in danger yet.*

"We will make no such vow," the creature finally said, "for there is another with you whose name we already know. Well met under this moon, *Veritas Daemonae."*

How do they know your name? Aubria asked through their minds, alarmed.

Faerykind always know each other's names. It's one of the reasons we trust only our own kind, because we cannot use our names against each other without reciprocation of the same betrayal, Veritas explained as he bowed contemptuously from within Terran's body to the leader interacting with them.

"Well met, Noblynn. I have not seen you for an age. How do you come to trouble our old sacred lands with your kinfolk?"

"Is that why you came here? We thought you had come to your senses and decided to seek our help in undoing the chains linking you to that sorcerer's ilk." Noblynn's glow changed color, the golden hue of him cooling to silver that somehow made his distinct voice stand

315

out from the rest of the faerykind, as if the silver marked him for a wise graybeard among their number.

Veritas's glow through Terran's body altered as well so that the sun yellow luminosity gleaming through the Potioner's eyes darkened to rich, buttery gold. "The price I would have to pay for your help is worth another hundred years or so of enslavement to this line."

Aubria didn't understand a bit of this exchange, but even if she hadn't been in danger and horribly worried for Terran and herself she decided she never would have gotten along with Noblynn. She pictured him as a human as she tilted her head to the side, imagining an austere, slender figure clad in rich, jewel toned robes with a silver goatee that concealed not the arrogant upturn of a strong chin and an even stronger will.

The rest of the faerykind, silent unless Noblynn used their voices to speak, pressed closer to the edges of the carved star as their spokesman continued to coax Veritas into friendship. "We know what you have not yet learned. You are young, Veritas, by our standards. We know the secret that will unbind you from the human's bloodline...only name the girl to us, and scratch out these foolish runes. You are faerykind, a prince among us and a son of the king in the ether, and you may return to us at long last."

For a moment—just an instant—Aubria saw Veritas falter. Naked under the influence of the other faerykind who were his kin, perhaps his subjects if he was indeed the prince Noblynn had named him, she saw his longing through Terran's changed, eagle gold eyes. Not for the first time she pitied him for his plight, and as she laid a hand on his arm in unspoken sympathy she wondered if there was so easy a way for Veritas to break free of the chains he chafed under while still saving the orchard and Terran himself.

Then Veritas looked down at her, at her hand resting on his arm. Frightened by the blank look that made him look as ancient and timeless as the bodiless faerykind all around them under the trees, she tried to withdraw...but his hand landed on top of hers, warm and compassionate as if it was Terran who held her still.

"You have always misjudged mortals, Noblynn, and resented them for what we cannot have. I will not let you use me to punish them for the crime of being locked into the physical world and its cycles of time...and I will not give you the name of this one for my own ends. Let her speak with you as the summoning allows, and then be gone." He didn't look at Noblynn or any of the faerykind as he stared down at Aubria as if nothing else mattered.

The leader of this gathering of faerykind hadn't changed or moved, but if Aubria had pictured him in a mortal body again, his face would have borne a sneer.

"What would you ask of us, child of dirt?" he asked, his multilayered voice frosty.

Some manners, first, she thought, but instead she got right to the point, though her language was a little more formal than usual.

"You are destroying the orchard is my home, and the home of all the humans who lived here now and in the past. I don't know which of you gave the orchard to my people, if you were there when it happened...but we love this land, all of us, and we have tended it faithfully over the years. Can you not leave us in peace and let us continue doing what we were born to do? We would be happy to share the fruits of our labor with the beings who gave us our home in the first place."

Noblynn and the other faerykind froze in place, all hovering and whispering coming to a standstill as their leader froze at the point of the star on the ground. Then he laughed, and they laughed too: vicious, erratic amusement that cut the inner workings of her ears like brittle steel.

"*Share* with us? Share the bounty of what is rightfully ours, what should have always been ours? Share with the children of dirt that we had to teach out of necessity?" he mocked her. "No, child. We may toy with your kind, we may use them, some of us may breed with them for amusement, but *never* will we bow to you or accept you as our equals. How could those who live only a few turnings of the sun match our power, our beauty, our wisdom?"

317

"You cannot tend the orchard yourselves, even with your power," Veritas interjected, his anger breaking through his calm. "You cannot possess these mortals unless they invite you, which is the only reason most of you have gone without form for so long. It has always been so, and that will not change merely because you wish it. Why take— *Aubria, no!*"

Aubria stumbled, and that was her undoing. For she'd made the mistake of looking into Noblynn's heart of light as he'd spoken, looked without realizing that that had been his intent. He lured her out of the safety of the star with the ease of an adult tempting a child with a shiny toy, and as soon as the tip of her foot left the shelter of their magic he had her. The faerykind all around brightened, their murmurs rising to a painful pitch now that Noblynn had trapped her with magic that she couldn't escape.

Fool, she told herself in the instant before he was in her head, rooting around for anything useful. *That is all you ever were.*

"Let her go, Noblynn!" Veritas shouted, stepping forward as if he would lay his mortal hands on the being that held her and wring the light from him forever. "Let her go, or I will see you extinguished in the dark!"

"No!" Aubria managed to shout around the collar of fire—which burned her without tarnishing her skin—before it tightened slowly to not only cut off her air, but do it slow enough to increase her pain. The faerykind couldn't hurt Veritas, she was mostly certain, but it was Terran's body that he used, and she didn't doubt that they could hurt that. She bit back a scream as tendrils of light wrapped around and around her and Noblynn's voice bit into her mind like a snake dispelling venom.

So you are Aubria, child of the orchard. True *child of the orchard, for you have been blessed with its magic in ways others in your village were not.* His voice sounded in her head, different without the echoes of the other faerykind in the background. *That is of no consequence. We will take it and then some, for we have need of power even now—*

"What price would you name?" Aubria half-screeched from her

choked throat, her wits fading as Noblynn's collar threatened to overwhelm her. "The solstice is a night of bargaining, Faerykind Noblynn, and I summoned you in good faith. Name the price you would have for my orchard, and I will see it done by the end of the season!"

She'd done it; she'd surprised him enough to relent, and Aubria coughed loudly and without much relief as the grip around her throat lessened. Noblynn had no eyes to stare, but she sensed his gaze upon her as if it would burn her worse than the collar had.

"You would promise such a thing to one of the faerykind? Such an open-ended offer is without price, were you to fulfill your end of the bargain," he said, the voices of the other spheres underlying his words.

"She didn't mean to promise that!" Veritas interceded for her, sounding desperate as he paced within the confines of the star. Aubria gave him a look once she'd finished coughing, but he ignored her. "No mortal would promise such a thing!"

"No?" Noblynn said, with a chuckle that sounded almost indulgent. "You wound me. Whenever we make bargains with mortals, it is our custom to take their firstborn and raise them as a sacrifice so one of us may live in a physical form for some years. We can no longer keep them immortal…but no matter. We have other plans for this one now she's given her bond."

Aubria hadn't looked ahead to whether or not she looked forward to bearing children, but Noblynn's words struck fear deeper into her soul. Her gaze drifted over to Terran, and through the pain of the faerykind fire burning her skin she imagined briefly what a child of the two of them might look like. Later, if she survived this peril, she knew she'd wish that she'd never imagined her future in this way. But if she was going to die at the hands of this faerykind, perhaps it was good to imagine what her life could've been like…

You are mine, Aubria, as you have promised me and my kind. For I know your name, the name I found when I lured you to me…and I know your heart better than you do yourself, Noblynn laughed to himself, the malice in his

319

words distinct and personal. If he were human, the eyes she pictured as wintry chips of gray ice without empathy or mercy would cut her to the bone.

"Say what you would have of me or let me go," she dared to say as the probe in her mind twisted painfully, making her squint against any light in the darkness of the orchard at night. "I can't help unless I know what you want."

The faerykind around her tittered with glee as they spiraled around her and Noblynn and Veritas in the summoning star in a weaving dance. "How practical. Very well: Aubria Haight, we charge you with finding the power we lost centuries ago, that we may return to our homeland across the sea and mingle with humans no more. In return, we will leave your orchard in peace and bless you and yours with long life. The trade is fair."

Caught in his ethereal grip though she was—he held her wrists, too, with chains of light that made the veins in her arms visible through her skin—Aubria's curiosity sent question after question tumbling through her mind. *This isn't as powerful as they could be? They're not native to our lands? How many more faerykind are there in the world than the legion that lives in our kingdom, in our orchards and greenwoods? What made them lose their power?*

"*That* is your price?" Veritas cried out, his poise shattered as he laughed; the vibrations of the sound made the faerykind surrounding them sway in their places, either out of amusement or indignation. "That's a myth! Ancient as you are, you should know better. We have been as we are now for millennia. How can a girl such as this offer you power you never had to return to a home that never existed?"

Aubria choked as Noblynn's fiery collar around her throat tightened, the other faerykind no brighter than the stars of approaching oblivion dancing behind her eyes. The cuffs around her wrist tightened as well, making her bones creak with strain. Both had turned red, crimson like the embers of a powerful bonfire, and the faerykind around them glowed with an equally infernal light.

"We will not hear your blasphemy, undoubtedly brought about by your willful link to the mortal wizard, magic-blessed though he is." Noblynn's ridicule hurt her with every syllable, pulsing through the bond he'd entrapped her in, but he didn't seem to be paying attention to her as much as he had before. His voice grew distant, and she felt like his eyes were turned on the horizon through the trees as he elaborated.

"We have searched season upon season for what this land stole from us," Noblynn intoned, and Aubria heard anew the tones of every other faerykind in the grove echoing beneath his words, like the swell of waves distant from shore but ever oncoming. "We have searched among storms and through the mountains of fire that lay far to the east, we have delved beneath the earth to the cold roots below…and though those powers resonate with us, they cannot restore what we've lost. For a time we settled, ready to begin our lives anew and forget the past we lost…yet our power has ever dwindled so that the orchard we built in our youth is beyond the reach of our care. We nurtured the fruit to restore us, and so it can…but only through destruction. If we do not find our power soon we will be lost, as we were before, and the ether will not await our return as our spirits fade."

Even Veritas listened in silence, hypnotized by the enchanting hum of the Noblynn's voice.

"Mayhap a mortal, even a lowly child of dirt, will be able to find they key that we could not. But make no mistake, daughter of earth: if you think to escape us by letting our power dwindle, know that we are strong enough yet to bring this land crumbling down into the void. If you fail there is nothing that will save you from our wrath, neither you nor the orchard we allowed your ancestors to borrow."

"You've struck your bargain, Noblynn. Release her," Veritas ordered, and when she looked at him she saw that he had paced to the absolute edge of the star, and the wildness vibrating through his form as if the Potioner's body couldn't contain him frightened her further. Then the collar and chains of light holding her in thrall disappeared along with Noblynn's presence in her mind.

Aubria swayed on her feet, trying not to crumple to the ground as Noblynn released her. Whatever hooks he'd sunk into her brain withdrew with the intent of causing her pain, and her eyelashes fluttered with the effort of staying conscious. Thankfully she wasn't so far from the star that Veritas couldn't catch her: in her state of half-conscious awareness, she thought it was Terran who'd caught her as she'd fallen. But the same light as the other faerykind shone through his mortal skin, and she knew it was Veritas.

"Hurting her won't make her work at her task any faster," Veritas said, a growl reminiscent somehow of the liquid voices of the other faerykind rumbling beneath his words. "You have made it impossible enough. If I could break the rites of bargaining or undo this night, I would. If slaying you would end her bargain, I would, and without a shred of regret. You were wise once, Noblynn...but that wouldn't save you."

"No, I don't suppose you would regret it. We know that you are bound to speak the truth or not at all, *Veritas Daemonae*. Through this you reveal too much of yourself, as you always have." Noblynn drifted back from the edge of the star, his strange beauty working on Aubria's mortal mind as she looked at him again. She would curse herself later for falling prey to his fatal lure, the lure of all his kind, but in this moment she understood how impossible it had been to resist, even with what she knew now.

"You promised us a season, fair Aubria, and you have until autumn to end our exile. On Mabon's dawn we will come for you, if you do not summon us again before then."

So soon? Dismay filled her, but she forced herself to stand on her own two feet.

"In the meantime, I would like you to leave our orchard in peace."

"The fruit is our due, child, and we will not do without so you may dither over your failure in peace," Noblynn replied, flaring red again at her audacity before he settled into his usual color. Unpredictable as his kind were, his rage faded as quickly as a summer storm, and in less than a second he was—they all were—as beautiful as they could make themselves. With her internal mind raging against her frailty, she couldn't help but gasp in wonder as they made a show of their departure, spinning out of the lemon tree grove owned by her father in wheels of flame that couldn't be anything but lovely, fatal as they were.

Yet there was lingering enchantment even in the disaster of what she'd seen. All around them lay marks of the faerykind they'd summoned: the tops of dewy toadstools in red and other colors springing up from the earth in a ring around their summoning star.

What have I promised? She wondered, numb as she stared down at the ring trailing over the ground.

19

Litha

erran refrained from asking her questions when they reached the boundaries of her cottage. He merely looked at her, waiting for a retelling of what had taken place during the summoning. Veritas had taken control of him for the entirety of it, so he knew nothing of what she had promised Noblynn and the rest of the faerykind. Now that he looked at her with hope rendering his grim face a little friendlier, however, Aubria choked on the words she knew she had to say. She'd failed once again, and the faerykind had lured her in and forced her to promise her life and possibly the orchard away by the end of the season if she couldn't find their power and restore it to them.

Also, Veritas had known, perhaps as he'd always known, that he could convince the rest of faerykind in this country to help free him...but he hadn't in the past, and he hadn't tried tonight. Aubria couldn't grasp all of the reasons why not, but she'd assumed the price meant service to Noblynn that involved killing or enslaving a great many humans. In spite of the rest of her troubles she had to be a little grateful for his refusal.

She wasn't sure Terran would see that in the same light.

"Well?" he asked when she took too long to explain, hovering as she did under the shade of the trees questioning all of her decisions yet again. He held the wizard's flame in his hand aloft, the better to see both her and where he was going, and she wondered if someday she too could conjure such a tame fire.

But she could only think of what she'd just done, and it tormented her as she remembered it in the seconds before she had to speak or risk Terran's suspicion of her truthfulness.

"Don't tell him," Aubria had begged Veritas in the dark of the orchard minutes before. "Not until I think of how."

"Have you not learned your lesson?" he'd chastised her, the anger that had slammed through him when confronting Noblynn now turned in part against her. "We have concealed things from him before. Not once has that gone well."

They still stood in the star carved with charcoal on the ground, but Veritas no longer held her; he'd pushed her away as soon as her wooziness had passed.

"He will try to stop me, or make you try to undo the bargain I've made. I can't have that."

"You have no idea how to accomplish the task they've set for you, and you still want to shut out Terran's help to shelter him from your failure? Are you really such a fool?" Veritas pruned his words with care, as if he was holding back worse terminology for her sake, but Aubria took a few steps back regardless. She'd wrapped her arms around herself in a futile method of protection; it was a summer night, but now she was cold.

"How can you bring back the so-called lost power of faerykind if they themselves couldn't do it? They've had eons of time before you were even born to find it, and they never did," he continued.

I don't know, she thought, but didn't say aloud. "Noblynn said that I might be able to find things they couldn't. I may not have any ideas now, but I found out how to undo our binding already—"

"We don't know for certain if our binding will break! Though our binding is a true one, it is minor compared to anything that might have been done to my kind that they didn't bring on themselves." Veritas stretched out a hand over the ground and obliterated the star they were standing in with what looked like no effort; his skin had ceased glowing as much as it had in the presence of his own kind, but the magic he used brightened it again long enough for her to watch the grass grow over their marks quicker than nature intended.

"That's simple magic, and you can't even do that. All you have is the touch of magic you inherited from the orchard. That won't be enough," he told her, his anger colder than she'd experienced it before; she couldn't look at him, so she focused on the toadstools arranged in a ring that the faerykind had left behind.

"What else could I do? What else *can* I do?" she asked him, for once unconcerned with appearing strong and fearless. "I *am* afraid, Veritas. I'm afraid of failing everyone I love along with the land that has been my home and my father's home and his father's home. I am afraid of my own failings and anything I might do to make things worse, afraid every minute of every day. But should I let Terran carry my burden as well? Is it fair to weigh him down with my troubles when he believes that he can't care about me because of you? Is it fair to—"

"None of this is fair, Aubria, but Terran wouldn't want to be spared from that," Veritas insisted, more kindly than he had in the past. "I wouldn't lie to him, even if I could, and I strongly urge you to refrain from deceiving him as well. He is strong enough to handle this. You shouldn't doubt him."

All at once Aubria deflated, her shoulders slumping once his candor proved more than a match for her timorous soul. She gave herself a second or two to rally her forces so she could honor his honesty by matching it.

"You're right. As you are all too often. But I hate to tell him this. I don't want him to know that I fear what I promised to the faerykind...to both of you."

Veritas sighed, finished with chastising her; his tone changed, the anger sparking under the surface melting into nothing like foam against the shoreline. "Thrice-bound Aubria Haight: first to me by blood, then to the Potioner by the ties of your heart, and now to all of faerykind by sacred vow. Three is a powerful number, but…though you are stubborn and flawed, it is difficult to stay angry with you. Even I can never manage it for long."

"I *am* stubborn," she said, able to laugh at the absurdity a little now, though her bruised throat objected to the abuse. "Maybe through sheer force of will I'll be able to succeed. Or it'll get me killed along with my homeland. I doubt Noblynn will be content to own and drain the power from the orchard alone."

Veritas hadn't been listening. He'd watched her laugh, the sound ringing with scarce humor, and she realized belatedly that'd he'd closed the distance between them. It felt familiar, now, when he tilted her face up towards his own with his forefinger and thumb. The tattoo—the birthmark—marring his left eye had mesmerized her before, but that was nothing now to the power of his gaze drawing her to him now.

"What is it you've done to me?" he murmured, more to himself as his eyes hovered closed and he leaned in to brush his lips against hers. The echo of his rhetorical question in the shadow of the very same thing Terran had asked earlier that day threw her, crumbling her resistance. And she had resisted at first, pushing him away purely out of habit, but his touch was so achingly gentle as he cupped her face in his hands—but they were *Terran's* hands—she let herself receive his kiss.

When they connected, kissing under the same type of moon that had linked them together in the first place, Aubria felt more than the glow of intimacy spreading through her veins. Somehow, it felt like there'd been a knot in her mind, a knot tied by someone beyond even the faerykind, and when they kissed it began to unwind and then come undone completely. The sense of never quite being alone in her head when Veritas was within range faded slowly…but fade it did until she was kissing only a man who had no presence in her head whatsoever.

Veritas felt it too, and they broke apart to stare at each other as pain briefly shot through her body. Aubria looked down and saw that one of the super fine cuts on her arm from Noblynn's ill treatment—he'd burned her without leaving a mark, aside from the thin lashes his cuffs of fire had left behind—had trickled a small stream of blood down her wrist without her knowledge.

"My magic...its arbitrary nature must have allowed the binding to come about in the first place. I didn't guess I had any, never mind knowing how to use it...the first time we came together, I think I clung to you more than physically because I feared the future." The puzzle pieces slid into place for her all at once. "The moon is new. There must have been enough magic here tonight to replenish the orchard for days. I wasn't sure, not entirely...but Noblynn cut me too, and I suppose it's fitting that what was created by accident ends in one as well..."

Aubria trailed off as Veritas traced his thumb over her lips as he had so long ago, in a dream she could hardly remember.

"I kissed you because I wanted to, not to hasten the undoing of our link. Don't cheapen what I've done because you think I didn't mean it," he told her, his words a rebuke despite his gentle manner. His eyes—*Terran's* eyes, gold though they were now—danced with stars that couldn't be seen in so dark a sky under the refuge of trees in the grove.

"What do you want me to say?" she asked him; a cool breeze ruffled her clothing, and when she quivered in the unseasonal zephyr; he chafed his hands against her arms for warmth in a mild gesture of intimacy. "You know the truth of my feelings better than I do. I—Veritas, I don't know what you want from me."

"So say nothing," he suggested, "and listen. Listen to me this once, in this voice that isn't only mine, and let me say what I need to. Because I care for you, Aubria. I care for you—I have grown to care for you—as no faerykind has cared for a human since the enchanted days of old. I think...Terran proved to me that I had a heart, because I've never truly had a family before. But you reminded me that the heart is a human thing. Independent of any binding, I care for you, and for the first time I am…happy. Happy as I have not been in all the lengthy days of my existence."

"Veritas…" Aubria said his name before she remembered that her best gift to him was listening now even if she could offer nothing else. Her lashes felt damp, as if she had wept, but who could refrain from weeping in the face of such devotion? Not she, especially since she knew the answer she'd have to give.

"Don't weep, orchard girl…not for me. I have faith, whether I express it well or not, that you will be able to free all of us from the things that hold us captive. Even if it pains me that you will choose him, and that you are as mortal as I am eternal, I am grateful that we have this time. Because that's all we really have, you know. We have moments, and days all too brief in their shades of happiness or sorrow. And I treasure the ones I'm able to spend with you, even from afar," Veritas said. She saw him smile with Terran's features and expressions. Yet for a moment she thought she could see the real Veritas behind the mask he'd been forced to wear for longer than the length of her life. Then she couldn't see, because the tears she had tried so hard to deny spilled down her cheeks and sparkled in her peripheral under the light shining through Terran's skin.

"Kiss me again," she told him. "I would give you a memory of me that doesn't bring you sadness."

So he did, and Aubria once again told herself that there was no tomorrow or anything past this moment, so she could give Veritas a similar experience to the one she'd gifted to Terran under the Litha trees.

When he withdrew and deliberately set her out of reach, their preserved slice of time ended. He looked no worse for wear, since faerykind couldn't weep through human eyes, but she felt the rend in the human heart he'd claimed as if it was her own. She cared for him too, she knew…but Terran was *hers,* hers to love without return if need be, and she was his.

"Enjoy your Litha with him, but know that he's leaving by the end of it. He may tell you why, if you ask him…but that's not my tale to tell." Veritas told her. He didn't sound bitter, but his voice carried some shades of it that made her wonder what had upset him.

Then he'd disappeared, and Terran had stood in his place expectant and ready to hear what had taken place during his absence.

Back in the present, back outside her sleepy cottage with Terran awaiting her answer, Aubria decided what to tell him.

"They came, Terran, and they were beautiful and terrible all at once. I can't tell you what they said, not tonight. I won't lie to you again. But I think I would break if I told you now. Tomorrow, after Litha…"

The Potioner contemplated her as the call of crickets in the grass serenaded them. Aubria steeled herself for his protests, for his insistence that he had a right to whatever knowledge she'd gained during their summoning. She was weary to the bone as she hadn't been in days, as if the magic that ran rampant in the presence of the faerykind had drained her to a husk, but in this matter she intended to fight him.

But he didn't fight her.

"I will tell you some of my own tale, then, if you're willing to hear it," Terran spoke at last, his spine no less rigid and as tense as if he'd started an argument after all. "Tomorrow. After Litha."

She nodded, weary, and they parted to sneak back into her cottage in the silence of a night almost ended.

It never ceased to amaze her how even a little rest could summon a brighter outlook on anything sad or hopeless. Aubria had promised to complete an impossible task to a malicious faerykind who would brook no failure, and she may have sworn her heart to someone who couldn't in good conscience take it, but the sun shining over her as she fed the chickens, tended the goats, and sent Toby out to graze somehow shone brighter even than that light drenched afternoon with Terran that she'd never forget.

Darragh came out to speak with her in the barn as she was leading Toby out, and he didn't look pleased.

"I heard much talk of your afternoon with the Potioner last evening at the village council meeting. A meeting we held to discuss the return of our messenger to Oseren," he said as he patted Toby's soft muzzle when the horse passed him.

"He returned? What did the king tell him?" Aubria changed the subject, but she knew that wouldn't delay the inevitable.

"Old Barric is sending an envoy to us in a few weeks with a suitable escort to investigate the disturbances in the orchard and to punish those responsible. I need not tell you, especially after yesterday, how many whisperers will point in your direction. Soon they might not be whispers alone, and with the king's envoy here the Guide may have more power than usual."

"The people in the city hardly remember the gods at all, let alone worship them," Aubria heard Darragh following her as she led Toby out and set him free in the nearest grove. Toby was a good horse who always came back for his dinner, and he was really too big to steal and not of much worth outside the orchard. Her father didn't speak again until they'd begun strolling back to their cottage.

"That doesn't matter. I know...Aubria, I know you've set your heart upon the Potioner. I don't dislike him myself, man to man. He's educated, courteous, and not offensive to those beneath him. But I don't think he's for you, and you traipsing about the village on his arm does you no favors."

"Da—" she spluttered furiously, her distress outpacing her sense until she forced herself to pause. *How can I tell him that I might not have much time left, and that I'd like to spend it with Terran before the world comes crashing down around my ears?*

"I will try to be more discreet," she said, making it a promise, "but

I still need him and we still have business to attend to that is…that is more important than ever." They had come to the doorway, and spoke in normal voices since Terran had departed for the village in the early morning to find out what was left of the growing potion and to ensure its potency. Aubria picked up the basket of fresh eggs that she'd left outside the door and cradled it, her brow furrowed with worry.

"I am trying to trust you, sweetheart," Darragh said, "but you are making it difficult for me to do so. Is there nothing else you can tell me? I hate to hear your name muddied all about the village when the Potioner might leave you behind to start your life anew in the ashes of his wake."

She opened the door and hesitated to enter, though she didn't look back at him. Terran *could* leave her and not return: the orchard was not his battle to fight, and he'd lived with Veritas long enough to grow used to the intrusion and go on living with it if he chose not to fight for her or himself or anyone else.

But yesterday he'd kissed her, and all but told her that she was the only home he'd ever known. Aubria didn't believe he'd just leave.

She turned her profile to her father, nothing more; she couldn't bear to see his disappointment, as she felt like she couldn't bear so many things of late. "I have a quest, father, like a knight in the olden days. We do, the Potioner and I. Nothing can be decided about my future until it's complete…or it isn't, and then every single one of us will have bigger problems than my fate."

"What keeps you from sharing this burden? Why will you not tell me what troubles you?" Darragh demanded, his voice struggling to stay mild. For an instant she had an inkling of the self-control he had as a parent to not force her to look at him head on and speak all of the truth or risk punishment. Most fathers treated their daughters so, after all, even in prosperous Loracre.

"I don't think I'm supposed to tell you," she said. "I think I'm supposed to do this on my own, me and Terran, because we're involved."

"Who did you bargain with?" Darragh asked, but he'd already

333

guessed. She turned at last and tried to erase the bitter smile off of her face.

"I used to dream of them, do you remember? I wanted to dance with them in a toadstool ring and ask them to grant my wishes. I would've wished for mother, you know."

"I know," said Darragh, sorrow softening his tension hardened eyes. "I told you then that they were dangerous, and the wishes they would grant you if they let you leave the ring would be double-edged. Come to think of it, you always found those rings more often than anyone else...once, your mother found one right outside your bedroom window."

All strength gone with their exchange, Aubria sighed and impulsively hugged her father; he held her tightly, as if she was still small enough to scold and carry to bed for a soothing nap. "You were right, Da. But I'm grown now, and I will do what I've promised. And...my life is different, in the wake of this and how I've come to feel about Terran. Even if I don't get my heart's desire, my future will be...not like we've planned."

They parted, and Aubria went about the household tasks and ate a quick breakfast while she dressed for Litha. She didn't take nearly as much care as she had the day before, but she did remember to bring her hat and rubbed a little emberpod paste over her nose and cheeks— tanned a little brown now and freckled from the season and so many hours per day spent outdoors—to prevent sunburn. She wore her blue dress without the shawl as well, and she'd threaded a pale blue ribbon through her hat for a change from the green days before. Her stomach fluttered nervously with the prospect of meeting Terran, and with what she'd eventually have to tell him by eveningtide.

Then, decked out for the festival, she met her father in the kitchen and they walked together towards Loracre.

Fire was a treacherous master at the best of times, and in a land of wood and things that would burn with too great ease it was perilous to trust it. So Loracre—and Eldacre too, and all the other villages scattered throughout the orchard—formed a careful procession of torches led through the village while the Guide extolled the gods for their favor and beseeched them for continuing esteem.

When they reached the village, a number of people had already gathered around the town well while they waited for the Guide to finish his preparations. Darragh had told her that the king's temporary envoy that had returned with Loracre's messenger had been invited to participate in today's events, but he'd declined and began his journey back to Oseren almost at once. So at least she wouldn't have one more person brought in to share the suspicions of the Guide. Curiously, she saw Terran nowhere in sight, and she'd expected to meet up with him, her reluctant father or no. Even Cerise and Nathan and Viola and Lane weren't there yet.

She had time to think as she waited, which she didn't really want...so she turned her mind to other things other than what had occupied it the most often in recent days. Many of their ceremonies had similarities, which Aubria noticed again as she had since she'd grown older. Most of them seemed to start or end with a bonfire, even the events in the handfasting wheel. Yet Litha was different, in its own way, as all the events in the wheel of the year had their quirks. The torch procession would march under the sun and through the orchard until they reached the river, where the Guide and his volunteers would pass out the dried berries from last year's Litha ceremony. A few people at a time would approach the river and offer it blessing and the sustenance of the berries in hopes of a prosperous year. It was common for other wishes to be made on the handful of berries as well...but it would be ill luck to speak those aloud.

Eventually, as Aubria sweated under the hot sun, Cerise and Nathan found her and her father and made small conversation with them while they waited. They couldn't talk about anything serious even if they wanted to, and Aubria fought back the fleeting urge to tell Cerise everything, knowing that of course Cerise would judge her harshly but in the end help her rationalize things into something more bearable. Nathan was docile and would go with whatever plan Cerise presented—when they were wed, Nathan would most likely keep the house while Cerise preferred the orchard work—but it would be a boon to rely on her friends again instead of just herself.

The moment passed with the arrival of the Guide. He had donned his robes of state—pure white, as fit his station—and for Litha he'd added a garland of the scarlet flowers around his neck. He was a plump man by orchard standards, where most everyone was slender from the sheer amount of work they undertook day by day, but his face held an air of sallow greediness that had always given Aubria chills. Most of the children liked the Guide of Rites, for he was kind to them and always had some sweet to offer. But he'd never liked her because of her father, and she'd steered clear of him most of her life.

But none of that was important now, for out of the Guide's humble house had come the Potioner, and Aubria gasped with everyone else at the shock of it. Not only did Terran cut a miraculous, almost mythical figure with his rumored skill with magic and poisons, but he'd made himself a paradoxically likeable fellow by helping repair the ruined parts of the orchard with his magic without hope of sufficient repayment. The Loracre villagers still clutched their suspicions like pearls to their necks, she knew from listening to the gossip, and the people of Eldacre were hardly any better. But he'd gone a long way to helping his own reputation…aside from associating with her, she supposed with a wry smile.

Terran standing with the Guide looking so short and inconsequential beside him gave her a dizzy feeling, as if something wasn't right with the world. The Potioner could appear imposing even to Aubria, who had kissed him under the summer sun. He'd donned his Potioner's clothes again, all in black even in this heat, but he didn't look sweaty or sick. She knew without giving much thought to it that he'd worked a spell or taken a potion to keep him cool, though for what purpose she had yet to find.

"Fellow villagers!" The Guide called, and his sonorous voice quieted the muttering crowd at once. "Today is Litha, and we will honor the gods and our blessed river as one people. We are doubly blessed that the king's Potioner has decided to aid us in making reparations for our transgressions against the gods. We may be better stewards of this sanctified orchard thanks to his help, wherever it may have come from. I have granted his request to celebrate this Litha festival alongside us, and I hope each of you will show him the hospitality that is a reflection of our favor from the gods."

His lip curled at that last part out of its saccharine smile, as if he suspected more than he let on that the gods withdrawn their favor. The Guide scanned the crowd until his eyes found Darragh and Aubria, and within the dark irises she read deep enough to glimpse his focused intent that they be brought to "justice" for their crimes against the nature deities.

Not so, old man, Aubria jibed him mentally, though of course he couldn't hear her. *But I will save even you from what the faerykind have planned for the land that is no longer theirs.*

Terran bowed to the crowd of villagers as they applauded with enthusiasm—mixed unmistakably with bemusement—before he left the Guide's side and nudged his way through the crush of people towards the knot of people that made up Aubria's group. She exchanged looks with Cerise, who raised her eyebrows, and her father, who glared resolutely at Terran until he came close enough to notice. Seeing both that glare and Aubria's frantic and hopefully surreptitious signals that he should cease, he paused and then nodded at her, just once. Then, changing directions, he stood by a quartet of women who, though they were betrothed, looked upon him with far more interest than was proper.

Later, she called with her mind to Veritas before she remembered that the link between them had been broken.

Aubria followed her friends and family and the people she'd grown up with as they took their torches and the handfuls of berries passed out by the Guide's volunteers and made their way through the orchard towards the river. It was not a short walk, and the weather was far from forgiving, but she and her friends always found a way to enjoy themselves. In a short while, everyone was singing their hallowed songs to celebrate the holiday, and not even the most dauntless of curmudgeons could resist the cheerful call of working men at rest for the purpose of honoring their gods for long.

The deep river should have been much bigger for the purpose it served, but this perhaps above most things in the orchard possessed more magic than anyone could guess. It was a large enough river, traversed by wide bridges here and there for the purpose of transporting fruit to and fro, but it was gentle enough for children to play and swim in. The level of the cool, eternally blue water never varied through drought or flood. Water from this river tasted clean and sweet throughout the year, for not once did it freeze no matter how cold winter blasted the land. The villagers in both Loracre and Eldacre praised this fountain of life for the orchard and revered it to the point that polluting its waters bore their highest penalty, which was exile if they couldn't get the king to approve an execution.

After the singing, when Aubria stood before the river waiting her turn to cast her berries into the water and make her wish, she breathed in the fresh smell of the green trees and clear water and tried to imagine what she should wish for. The obvious answer was a solution to her dilemma with the faerykind, or for Terran to realize that it was worth being with her whether he was free from his curse or not…but she didn't want to wish those things, not now. Here in the orchard she loved among people who she'd always known she wanted to wish for something more profound in its own way.

I wish for this place to always be as it is now, or better, she thought as she drew close to the banks of the river and dropped the blackened dried berries in one by one. *I wish for you to thrive, river of the orchard, and continue providing life to the roots below the earth forevermore. Even if we cannot tend you any longer…I wish for you to be well, always.*

Maybe she imagined it, but Aubria thought the water surged as she murmured her wish aloud under her breath so not a soul besides herself could make out her words.

After, when she stepped aside to make way for the next villager— this one bore a torch that he would douse in the river as a sign of sacrifice to the gods—Terran was there, and he pulled her aside and led her away from the crowd. The nettles of his magic pricked at her pores, giving her cause for alarm until she realized that no one was looking at either of them as they passed back the way they'd come and to the left. He'd enchanted the both of them with a temporary spell of distraction so they could get away, and an unexpected though far from malicious shock of jealousy burrowed under her skin at the idea of having the power to make herself unnoticed at any time for the purpose of a clean get-away.

"What are you thinking, antagonizing the Guide?" Aubria demanded as soon as they got far enough out of earshot for even the most attentive eavesdropper. "He's dangerous for you too if he decides you are unworthy to stay in our villages. You could lose your shop and the piece of land you bought."

"I don't fear your Guide, any more than I fear the people he thinks he rules over. Your governor may think he's too good to live in the orchard with the rest of the workers, but I know where he lives in the city if I wish to obtain the papers I would require to stay. The king decides who gets the land, and my influence isn't yet so small that I can't go or stay where I wish," he shrugged. His flippant answer would have ordinarily annoyed her, but she let go of the sleeve she'd grabbed to get his attention and tried to compose herself.

"You have magic, so you're safe. For now you're seen as a help rather than a hindrance, so I don't think he'll go after you. But don't forget that magic is still frowned upon in these parts, if it's seen as unnatural and stolen from the gods. And if the king perishes any time soon from his age, I hear the elder prince might not look favorably on you." Aubria scolded more than she intended to, but Terran took her ire without complaint as merely watched her with his face stony and impassive. She'd come to recognize this mask, which he had a propensity to wear whenever he was feeling more than he wanted, and this time it gave her pause as she trailed off and simply looked up at him with all her thoughts scattered like feed for the chickens.

"I'm leaving, Aubria. I don't know for certain when I'll be back. Word has reached me...well. I haven't told you." He looked at her, up through his lashes as if she was taller than him though of course she was far from that, and his regret didn't lessen the irrational hurt his declaration had brought her. It felt like the time a horse had accidentally kicked her hard enough to crack a rib and bruise her for weeks.

"Leaving?"

"Yes. Not just to Eldacre, back to Oseren. I left business there unfinished, and I've dallied for far too long...events are moving apace, and I should be there to help, if I can." He looked almost as he had that one night she'd come upon him in the tower when he'd returned, but this time a thinner barrier rested between them. She steeled herself against any coming shock or pain, pushing the injury of his departure aside so she could think as she squared her shoulders and rested her hands on her hips.

"Tell me. Then I will tell you what happened last night with the faerykind."

Terran hesitated, battling his usual state of mistrust before he crossed his arms in front of his chest and continued. "The price of this information is my life if you choose betray me and tell another living soul. I would be captured and put to death by the other wizards in Lyrassan, if I couldn't leave soon enough and enforce my own exile. It was some of their number who conspired with the elder prince to murder the younger...but that won't matter if I tell the ones who weren't involved, for at that point I wouldn't be believed."

Aubria winced at the thought of more wizards, more people with Terran's power who still served the king and would eventually serve the corrupt elder prince.

"Tell me," she insisted again.

"I have been helping a small faction of rebels plan a coup that will remove the Prince Mardin from power as soon as King Barric dies. When I went into Oseren, it was to tend to the victims of a too-early skirmish between the prince's personal soldiers and help them plan a way to overthrow the prince without bloodshed. Without creating a vacancy of power that would lead to civil war. They wanted more from me as a Potioner and a wizard, and they wanted my help to choose the prince's replacement...but I've refused to offer that. Do you understand?"

"I understand," she whispered. *Magic wrought to cause death unmatched. Magic and poison combined.*

They wanted him to poison the prince, because in theory he'd done it before. Yet how could they—whoever these rebels lurking in the shadows of court were—trust him if *he* was the one who'd supposedly murdered the younger prince in the first place? Prince Phillip, by all accounts, had been as temperate and just as could be wished for in a future king. If he'd told them that it hadn't been him, if he'd shared with them anything about himself or Veritas, then how could they ask him to murder the king's only remaining heir?

Aubria pressed her fingertips against her temple, wishing she had magic to cool herself down. *Too many questions.*

"Word reached me that the rebels want to act *now*, before Prince Mardin launches his next attacks on the border kingdoms to gain more territory, and before they've even decided on a candidate for the throne. I'm going to tell them that their choices will lead to a bloody civil war between the king's councilors and relatives and themselves, which at the beginning of this venture everyone swore they opposed. I..." Terran trailed off, the fervor that had alighted in his eyes flaring and then fading in equal turns; now he seemed at a loss for words. "For my part, I feel responsible for the fate of Lyrassan...if it weren't for me, for the Caird curse and the spirit bound to me, Phillip would still be alive and Mardin could be dealt with. I never wanted to involve you in any of this, Aubria. But you, as you know, have a way of making yourself present in my life as no one else has done before...and who knows, you may have a part in this when all is said and done."

More than ever Aubria realized that she was an inexperienced girl of nineteen who knew nothing of the politics of the land other than that war brought destruction and hunger and disease, and that she didn't want any part of that for herself or those she knew or the kingdom at large. She dropped her hands to her sides, tucking them into her pockets to hide their trembling. Terran was the Potioner, and seven years her elder. He'd seen more of the world than she had, been better educated, and had a wizard's strength and wits. What could she do, even if she wanted to help him save Lyrassan from a terrible ruler?

All she could do was defend the orchard with her vow and her life, if need be. So she swallowed her anxiety and her irrational anger with Terran for putting himself in danger and told him what she needed to.

"The faerykind exacted a promise from me. I have until Mabon to return the power they lost, or the whole orchard will be theirs to destroy. If any humans survive we'll have to migrate elsewhere and start our lives anew," she said, praying that her voice wouldn't crack and reveal the savage fear that surged within her breast like a tide that couldn't be quelled by any mortal hand. "We know nothing of living outside of these trees, not really, and most of us who didn't die defending the orchard would perish soon enough. I have ideas on where to search for this power, but Terran…I'm afraid, and doubly so after what you've told me awaits you."

She watched as Terran passed through an array of emotions similar to what she'd experienced: he narrowed his eyes, questioning the fool's bargain she'd made, and he clenched his hands into fists as she told him of her fear, either from the desire to fight those who would harm her, or to shake her for putting herself in this position in the first place. If she hadn't known before, this alone would have let her know that he did care for her enough to worry after all. But he had no right to argue, after what he'd signed up for himself: court was treacherous and full of lying snakes, even peasant girls knew. Any whisper of rebellion could be quelled within a day, if the king or his retinue caught wind of it.

So he said nothing, instead reaching into his pocket to pull out something which he then handed to her. He held it close to his chest for a time, as if overcome with indecision, but then his mouth curved in a small smile that let her know he'd been thinking of something else.

"I'd thought it was complicated before, you know. I've never shared my magic or my secrets with another soul…yet there I was, baiting a stubborn village girl with her own secrets to visit me again because I saw magic behind her eyes like the silhouette of a cat sitting in a window. Then I thought the worst I'd have to do was learn to keep my distance and teach only what I should to one who had the potential for such talent...then, I thought the hardest thing was hiding how much you fascinated me," he told her.

"I fascinated you?" she scoffed, remembering with a slight cringe how she'd behaved the first few times they'd encountered each other. Terran's smile widened.

"Of course. When you tried to flirt with me to persuade me to give you the ritual guide and the potion to summon Veritas...well, that almost worked. If you'd kept at it long enough I might've given it to you in the hope that you'd warm my bed that night."

Blushing as she laughed from the startled realization that he'd been attracted to her from the beginning, Aubria ducked her head and tried to forget her embarrassment. They'd both laughed, but even their better memories couldn't dull the realization that they were saying farewell for an unknown length of time. She had been focused on him, on the pallor of his tanned face, but when she took the object he set in both of her hands, she looked down and gasped. He'd given her a bottle full of starlight, or captured a bit of moonlight just to amuse her. It didn't shine so brightly as she imagined it could because of the bright midday sun, but the enchanting warmth spreading from her fingers in waves through the rest of her body made her feel stronger than she had in weeks.

"What *is* this?" she asked, a little breathless as she made a cradle of her hands to hold the potion bottle. That too was unlike anything else she'd seen, even in the Potioner's tower: the translucent surface bore a shape she hadn't known anyone would be able to craft with so fragile a medium as enchanter's glass. No ordinary glass could be molded into a seven pointed star with not a single flaw in sight, and stoppered with a glass lid sealed in pale blue wax and stamped with archaic symbols she didn't recognize.

Aubria held it up to the light and inspected the glimmer peeping through the glass with no lack of awe. "How does it not break? I feel like my grip could shatter it to pieces!"

"It's a magical artifact that I've carried around for most of my life, as my father and his father carried it around for their lives. I don't know how they came by it, since often the most beautiful of ancient potions lay hidden away in eldritch caves and other secret places, but there was a message found beside it that's been passed down."

"What was the message?" she asked, cradling the sharp-edged bottle shaped like a captured star to her bosom as if she could protect the gorgeous heirloom that way.

"No one is sure what this potion does, only that it's valuable beyond reckoning and that those who unstopper the bottle and drink of the contents without great need or true purpose will suffer a death beyond the pale of pain," he told her. "That was the general idea when my family found it, anyway, and my father never liked to talk to me long enough to convey any particulars. I haven't dared remove the wax, because nothing felt important enough to risk such a fate. But you...you treat with the faerykind, and maybe even the old gods too before all of this is over. My heart tells me that you should carry this potion, at least for a while. I suspect that it has faerykind essence in its contents, judging by its glow."

Aubria would have protested that this gift was too much, that she would rather have him than any potion worth the ransom of a king. But he was leaving, because he had to, and she was staying because she had to.

"I bid you safe travels, Terran Caird," she told the Potioner as she clutched the star bottle tighter, unwilling to let it go as she let it rest in her pocket so no one would see its light when she returned from this meeting to the village crowd. He stared down at her, surprised at her straightforward dismissal as if he too had hoped a little for a drawn out goodbye. But he'd been right, before; he couldn't promise himself to her, not with Veritas hanging over him, however well-intentioned the faerykind spirit may be. And now she couldn't offer anything, for her fate had been promised to the faerykind, and beyond Mabon she couldn't see a way forward.

"Goodbye, Aubria Haight. I will search for as much information as I can in the public and royal libraries and send word if I find anything," he promised, his words halting where they'd once run smooth. They stood facing each other, close enough to imply intimacy but not enough to express the deep feelings Aubria felt were strangling her with their ties.

Terran spared her her dignity as he ended their meeting and began to walk away.

"My binding to Veritas is gone as well," she blurted before he moved out of hearing. "It was as you said. The new moon, a bit of blood, the will to break the binding, and...a kiss. Nothing more."

Terran half-turned, and she saw him smiling at little as if from relief.

"Good," he replied, and nothing else. She watched him disappear between the trees towards Loracre, where he'd find Cloud in the stables and return to Eldacre before making his way back into Oseren.

ria slept fitfully, the unique potion bottle firmly in her grip despite the sharp edges cutting into her palm, but it couldn't protect her from what she saw when she awoke and dressed and walked out her door to tend to her daily tasks. For it seemed that the Litha grove had journeyed through the whole of the orchard to come to her house, and the petals that had rained down on her and Terran not so long ago but also an eternity in the past now covered her yard and her front stoop like a massacre.

We will not do without so you may dither over your failure in peace,

Noblynn had told her in his multilayered voice. Even now, his message was clear.

Time was running out, and she had no other choice but to do the thing she'd vowed or suffer the consequences.

20

Darragh packed her travelling bag as soon as she returned inside after watching the Litha flower petals drift over their doorstep. Aubria would have helped, but the prospect of running away daunted her too greatly to fetch her bearings in an instant.

"You want me to run away?" she asked as she sank into a seat at the table.

"Not yet. Loracre and the king's men would surely hunt you. If it comes to it I will send you as deep into the orchard as I can…I think you know enough to evade them for a time there, and they will assume you fled elsewhere in Lyrassan instead of remaining close to home," Darragh explained, the light in his eyes feverish as he darted through the house and into her bedroom; she trailed after him, a little lost until he continued. "If you are asked, you will tell the Guide and anyone else that you spent Litha night in the Potioner's company before spending the night with the Erdenweds. You'll stay there until—"

"Until what?" Aubria asked. She was glad now that she'd already prepared for her day—a day that would no longer proceed according her usual plans—as she watched her father unceremoniously shove her nightdress, orchard work clothes, and other odds and ends that she'd usually bring for a stay with Cerise's family into the satchel. "Until all of this blows over? No, Da. This won't end until I find a way to end it, and I'm not sure if I can do that in town…besides. They'll suspect *you* instead of me, and I won't have that."

"You will. You will let them suspect me instead of you, and if I hear you do anything but deny your involvement with the plague of destruction hanging over the orchard I'll come to town and tan your hide as I never did before." Darragh's threat rang sincere despite the fact that he'd never beat her, but Aubria could hear what lay beneath his words: fear, fear for her sake and for the orchard itself. No one who cared for these trees and their harvests year after year could deny the tie of their heart to every leaf and bough…but she couldn't bear to think about that, because then her resolve might waver. So she clung to her determination that her father wouldn't take the fall for the Guide's dangerous suspicions.

"I won't let you do it," she declared, speaking quietly as she stood in the doorway with her hands on her hips.

Darragh ignored her as he shoved her harvest gold shawl into the bag and knotted it closed. He didn't speak again until he reached the door, where she blocked his path. He made a study of her face, of the stubborn tilt of her chin and the purplish circles under her eyes, and Aubria noted with surprise that they were both of the same height. Perhaps he'd noticed the same thing, and in a moment of wondering when it had happened that she'd grown so much, his desperate ire softened into a will no less strong, but more reasonable.

"Your mother was always a wee little thing, and I'm not among the tallest of men. It's nice to see that you take after me in one or two ways," he chuckled, though his gaze carried no less weariness; then he told her a story she hadn't heard before. "The Guide was in love with your mother, once upon a time. He knew he was too old for her and that she was interested in me, but he loved her from afar for years. When we wed, he almost refused to bless our union, and…when she died in the winter sickness that came over the orchard when you were a child—she and her parents, who she'd visited long enough to pass on the ailment, and my father as well—I don't think he ever forgave me for losing her. I know I had nothing to do with it, as does he, and out of our family only me and your grandmother lived...but he's never forgiven me."

"That makes him petty and beneath our deceit," she told him, touched by the shadow of sorrowful memory darkening his contemplative gaze as they lingered in the hall of their cottage. "I won't leave you to take the fall for his superstition or for his misplaced grudge."

"You will," Darragh insisted, breaking their stand-off by drawing her in for an embrace that felt like saying goodbye. "I expect your Potioner to come back seeking my approval to partake in the handfasting wheel with you. What shall I tell him if the Guide arrests you and has you tried for heresy?"

Aubria relented at last, for how could she not? Darragh was determined to save her, as any decent parent would be, and she tried to mimic his strength as he took the heavy bag he passed to her and walked her to the door. He checked out the window to make sure no one had come to their cottage in the early dawn hours to follow the trail of scarlet petals. Once his keen eyes had scanned the trees and the road for sign of any surprise visitors—or villagers with pitchforks—he ushered her outside and stood in the doorway to watch her depart.

One thing more occurred to Aubria as she shouldered her satchel and deliberated the sneakiest way to slip through the orchard and the village to reach the Erdenwed's back door unnoticed.

"They'll call me a whore, Da. For dallying with the Potioner without regard for the handfasting wheel, as if I fancied myself too good for our own orchard lads. Loracre in particular does not look favorably on relationships outside of our own people," Aubria's voice shook at last over this insignificant sliver of straw from a stack big enough to cripple her. She had grown distant from her friends and fellow villagers over time, since a little before she and Lane had entered their betrothal; her decisions after that had only led them to think of her as a foolish oddity. She was not so calloused, however, that she could shake off any regrets for those who would see her as someone beneath their notice, worthy of nothing but their scorn. It seemed so long ago that she had sorted through the crops listening to tales from the older women, or sang with her village sisters as they plucked fruit straight from the branch.

"I know my daughter. I know that I raised her to think for herself and make her own choices so she wouldn't be dependent on anyone unless she decided that they were worthy. I raised you to accept your own consequences, and I can see that you are the wise young woman your mother and I hoped you would become," Darragh said from behind her as she faced him; this hurt far too much for her poor conscience to handle as she struggled with guilt over what she couldn't yet fix and love for the father that had always believed in her. "It's more important to live to brush off their insults and live a better life than they dreamed."

A better life, Aubria turned the phrase over and over in her head as she left her home behind and made her way down the rambling paths she imagined were known only to her. *Is it possible?*

Cerise and her mother had no way of knowing anything about what was going on, but when Aubria knocked at their back door some time later, they accepted her without question as she stumbled inside and tried not to crumble from the burden of everything that had passed in the last few seasons crashed down on her shoulders all at once.

"There, there," Mary Erdenwed, Cerise's mother, soothed Aubria with a maternal embrace. "There's no trouble and no heartache that time won't erase."

She was right, in a sense, but Aubria knew now that some things would not submit to time's ebb and flow. It was precisely those things that she had to fix, and Cerise regarded Aubria with a mixture of sympathy and poorly concealed curiosity as she passed over a cup of strong herbal tea accented with a spoonful of honey and a dried sliver of orange peel.

oon enough Litha faded into memory, but the collective, impotent pain of watching their orchard suffer wouldn't pass for a single villager for the rest of their days. Eldacre had suffered attacks too, though fewer in number. Aubria suffered the helpless feeling of hearing how the villagers turned their backs on her father once a number of them followed the trail of petals leading right to their doorstep. They'd refused to help him clean up the damage, which would've been understandable given the destruction of the main grove itself except for the fact that the Haight land also had several large trees torn from their roots and cast over their land.

At least Darragh didn't have to clean up alone: Lane and some of his friends and their fathers who didn't outright support the agenda of the Guide of Rites came after their work of the day was complete to help him clear the area.

Aubria proved less immune to the scorn of the people who were afraid of what would become of them should the orchard attacks increase. She'd told anyone who'd asked what her father had suggested: she had found an alibi for any of the attacks, even if she had to use Terran as an excuse, and she'd come to stay with the Erdenweds to erase further suspicion.

It didn't seem to be working, though, not as well as either she or her father had hoped. The watch Darragh had suggested still patrolled the orchard in their designated areas night after night—paying particular care now to watch the Haight's land for suspicious activity—but as the weeks passed none of the men who'd been chosen for their vigilance spotted anything, not even when there was another attack on a copse of walnut trees that dealt the commerce of the orchard yet another blow.

After that attack, Cerise's mother suggested in her gentle yet firm way that Aubria stick to their work on the Erdenwed family land rather than venture into Loracre where heads made hot with anger that had no outlet might bring her to harm. Aubria was glad to obey: the Guide's ever-constant group of followers grew by the day, and every single one of them glared at her or her father when they came into town. One or two of them had spat at her heels when she'd walked by in quest for the Erdenwed's weekly supply of flour for bread, and the gob of salvia congealed like an accusation in the dirt. She had turned and fixed them in her glare as sweat trickled down her back under her work tunic, and part of her wished that she had magic enough to crush these close-minded fools under her heel.

They'd stalked off, chagrined, but even that had had unfortunate consequences. The Guide suspected her father as well, following Darragh's plan to eventually force the Guide to focus on him alone so Aubria had time to do what she needed to do, but people in the street didn't spit in the dirt at the sight of him or make angular signs against evil with their hands when he passed.

Aubria missed her father, with his quiet ways and steady spirit much like their squire horse, and she missed having her own home and tending to her own work. She missed Terran, too, more than she wanted to think about. She fell asleep clutching the mysterious potion bottle every night either in Cerise's little sister's bed or in the kitchen with a room temperature cup of tea that she could nurse for hours late into the night. He had left her, and the days and weeks and nearly a month passed with no word. He could have been discovered and killed along with the rebels, and she'd never know.

No, she told herself as she knelt in the Erdenwed's garden pruning an ample crop of weeds. *We would've heard something, even here in the orchard, about the rebel coup falling to pieces. Or I...I would know, I think. I would know if he was gone.*

Summer stretched on and on, almost like it would never end as the season climbed up and up towards the sun. Lammas approached what felt like an eternity after Litha, meaning more and more crops needed to be plucked and packed and shipped. As much as Aubria looked forward to a short rest from work brought by an autumn still too far off to imagine, she could only help the Erdenweds with their chores and their orchard land when community crops weren't ready yet, and dread the coming season when the faerykind would return to take back what had once been theirs. Her pride and her sense that they would want her to work on her promise alone faltered after a week; surely Noblynn and the others would rather her succeed than waste resources that would help her find the power the land had taken from them.

Besides, she had thought she'd have Terran for this, both him and Veritas. She had neither, so at long last she pulled Cerise aside and confessed absolutely everything to her in a whispered flurry of words that had shocked both of them.

Cerise had her own life to live, and for once Aubria hadn't minded looking on as an afterthought. The time of betrothal in the handfasting wheel was unlike any other time of life, she knew from what little experience she'd enjoyed with Lane, and somehow it was comforting to watch Cerise's relationship with Nathan progress into the sickening phase where, to them, they were the only people that mattered in the world. But Cerise made time for her, as— understandably—Viola did not, given that her betrothed was Lane after Merek's disappearance, and though Aubria missed her other friend she couldn't help but feel relieved that she didn't have to explain everything a second time to Viola. Besides, this knowledge could endanger either of them, and Cerise was smart enough to lie and look honest whereas Aubria doubted Viola had ever told a falsehood in her life.

The Erdenweds—along with a few other families—had both the privilege and the burden of tending to the Loracre bee hives during the months of summer. The curious orange orchard bees were studious workers, but at times they were languourous and friendly, and something about the magic in the air of the orchard made them more sentient than any bee had the right to act. It was during these slow afternoons tending to the hives and making sure all the bees were cared for that Aubria spent time with Cerise, and together they put their minds to the task Noblynn had set.

"Their power is here, in this land," Aubria puzzled aloud as she watched a cluster of bees visit a spray of quince flowers she and Cerise had set out for the purpose of flavoring a batch of honey; the blossoms would give the bees a taste for that flower, and for the next few days those would be the flowers they would set out to pollinate the most. "That's the only thing I know for sure. I don't know whether or not to search for caves under the earth or anywhere else, because all Noblynn told me was that they'd searched high and low for their power already. The natural forces they'd searched resonated with them but did not hold their power."

"Natural forces," Cerise mused aloud, pausing the song she'd hummed for the bees as she shook a stubborn, pollen-coated creature from her sleeve; the bees rarely stung, if at all, and never the people who cared for them long enough. "What makes up a natural force? Rain is a natural force, and so is the current in our river. Have they looked there?"

"I don't know! There's no way for me to know, because I'd have to risk summoning them again without Veritas alongside me, and I'm not certain it would be Noblynn and his followers who would show up. He spoke of a 'king in the ether,' who sounds like someone I would really, *really* hate to summon." The veil Aubria wore—to keep the bees focused on their work rather than investigating faces—fluttered as she exhaled in frustration.

"I've wondered whether or not the source of their power is in the orchard itself. That maybe in giving life to the orchard, they gave a part of themselves that has been draining them over time…"

"The cursed field," Cerise guessed, accurately predicting Aubria's direction as she led both of them into the shade to sip water from the bucket and ladle they'd carried with them.

"I can't imagine that they didn't search for their own power in the lightning field, since it seems the obvious choice. Even we mortals know that such an eerie place can't be normal."

"Have you found anything in the book you stole that might help us?" Cerise asked, ending her rambling.

"No. It only tells stories of rituals and the legends we know about faerykind. I'm inclined to believe most of them, but there's nothing to imply that the faerykind lost any power at all. The orchard isn't even mentioned," said Aubria; then she paused, mentally flipping through the pages she'd mostly memorized as she held the half-full ladle close to her lips without drinking, since she'd forgotten all about the water. "I wonder…the faerykind don't know how they lost their power, and they haven't been able to simply reclaim it. I once thought the orchard was draining their power, but they said nothing about that. Our world is governed by rites and rituals and the gods who laid them down for us to follow, which must have happened before the faerykind found our country."

"Is there a ritual that might return their magic?" Cerise asked; it was hot, even in the shade, and she lifted her hair and veil to splash some of the water on her neck.

"Maybe. I'll have to look when we return to your cottage to be sure. I don't think there's anything specific, but if I can find out more…" Aubria felt the high of hope returning before it crashed down again. "But I'm still a mortal. I can't set foot in the lightning field without it striking me down. How can I investigate if I can't even take the book into the field and try out my theories?"

Aubria finally remembered the ladle and dropped it into the bucket of water with a splash, her frustration threatening to get the better of her. Cerise glanced down at the small puddle the splash had made and remained silent long enough to increase Aubria's sense of hopelessness. If sensible, witty Cerise couldn't come up with anything to help, if the faerykind themselves couldn't control their own power and bring back what they'd lost, then what could *she* do?

"Don't despair," Cerise said as she tore off her hat and brushed back the sweaty strands of dark hair away from her high forehead; the gauzy veils that they'd attached to the brims of their older hats with careful stitching were fragile, but she took no heed for hers. "We have time yet. Something will come to us!"

"It's almost Lammas, Cerise. You'll be celebrating the next part of the handfasting wheel with Nathan in a few days. Mabon comes all too soon after that...and I don't have any answers. Terran, if he's safe, hasn't sent me word on any findings that might help us, and he has the prince to consider..." Aubria paused. She'd told Cerise everything that was hers to tell, but not this; Terran's business with the royal family wasn't hers to share, so she'd only hinted to her friend that Terran had left her for something important to the whole of Lyrassan, as the orchard was important to the kingdom in a different way.

"Either way, you have me. I will help until the end," Cerise replied, stepping around one of the busy hives to take Aubria by the shoulders and offer the strength of her friendship. They stared at each other, then Aubria reached up her gloved hands to formally grasp Cerise by the elbows in the universal gesture of unending loyalty.

"Thank you," she said, speaking lower than she'd meant to.

Later, much later in the day after most of the work was finished and everyone was making their way home, Aubria left the nest of humming bee hives behind as she and Cerise ventured back through Loracre to go home to the Erdenwed's cottage. She spotted Cerise's younger brother—he was eleven with a hooked nose like his father had had and Cerise's black hair and eyes—running past them, red-faced and out of breath. Following his direction, she noticed the bluster of people gathering in a huddle on either side of the road, their mutterings growing clamorous as the two of them approached.

"—he's here, he came with the envoy—"

"But why? Someone like him wouldn't fuss about our orchard—"

Cerise ignored the snatches of words carried to them on the wind and seized her brother as he passed, her fingers sinking into his shoulders like talons.

"What's happened?" she asked him, the authority of an elder sibling in her voice. "What did you do now?"

"Nothing!" the boy protested, wriggling free. "I was talking a walk with the other lads and we saw the king's envoy returning…with the elder prince leading them on!"

The prince is here? Aubria's whole body tensed; she'd tucked the veil up around her hat so she could feel the breeze on her face, but now she was tempted to pull it down again so no one could read her. She'd known the envoy would return, of course, as had the rest of Loracre. Preparations for the representatives sent by the king to investigate the crimes against the orchard had been underway since after Litha. Livestock had been selected for meat, a ration of the best of the fresh harvests had been set aside each day so that the king's men would have an appropriate feast—and therefore have nothing to complain to their sovereign about when they eventually returned to Oseren—and the villagers had repaired the odds and ends of their houses so that Loracre looked its best. The men had trimmed their beards or shaved altogether, and the women had set their best dresses aside and cleaned their work clothes until not a stain remained.

But if the prince had come, none of that would be enough. His preference of finery in victuals and people and his surroundings was well known throughout the whole kingdom. Aubria wondered what had persuaded him to come: these days the king was too infirm to force him to do anything, and the prince wouldn't have taken such a mundane task as orchard care if he didn't view it as a way to increase his reputation.

Moving to stand with the crowd and helping Cerise unceremoniously shove people out of the way until they reached the front of the group, Aubria gained the privilege of being one of the first to see Prince Mardin and his company of at least thirty guards, all of them gleaming in their casual, lightweight armor.

Where will we put them all? Aubria wondered, practicality winning out before she noticed who else rode with the company. *I suppose we can put them in the meeting hall if we clear it out and bring every bit of bedding we have to spare in the rest of the village, and the long tables should serve as the best place to serve the kind of food and drink the prince will require…*

357

"Aubria!" Cerise's exclamation, shouted over the tumult of the crowd half-heartedly cheering to welcome the prince they feared rather than revered, shook her out of her reverie. "Isn't that—"

"Terran?" Aubria lost track of everything else, of anything but the sight of Terran riding a black beast of a horse that wasn't Cloud at the prince's side as if he belonged there. He'd trimmed his hair in the style of court and shaved any stubble from his face, which somehow made his green eyes more haunting, more otherworldly as he scanned the crowd of villagers as if he'd never interacted with any of them before. His tan skin had paled a little after more weeks spent indoors than outdoors as he had been wont to do during his time in the orchard community, but his white smile would have flashed in the sun in contrast with his sun-browned skin if he'd been inclined to greet them with joy. Both his somber features and the severe cut of his black Potioner's garb gave him the exact air of the person everyone had feared when he'd first decided to stay in Eldacre: the king's Poisoner, not the man Aubria had come to know.

Cerise clutched Aubria's arm as they passed, or perhaps Aubria clutched her so she could stay upright and not become woozy from the heat of the day, the people pressing around them, and the shock itself. Though she stood at the front of the crowd, Terran's eyes didn't seek her once as he stared straight ahead and let the prince take the lead.

Desperate enough to try, desperate enough to call on what little magic she had to knock at the door of the Potioner's mind, Aubria searched for Veritas to try to see what had happened to bring him back here in the company of his greatest enemy.

But Veritas couldn't hear or simply didn't answer, and she looked instead to the prince to try to gauge what had taken place in Oseren.

He was a handsome enough man, all burnished golden hair and leonine aristocratic features, but the satisfied smile he turned upon the villagers as they greeted him didn't illuminate his face with any real emotion. Given what she knew about the fratricide he'd forced

Terran to help with through Veritas, she imagined the black swirl of evil floating under his skin like a dark tide.

His eyes fell on her, as they fell upon all the young women who were within eyesight, and those gorgeous lips curved upwards. Aubria winced, wondering rather than disbelieving that the prince would refrain from summoning one of them to whatever bedchamber they cobbled together for him. She prayed that it wouldn't be her...or Cerise, or beautiful Viola, who had suffered enough at the hands of Merek before he'd run off. Of course she rather hoped he didn't call on any of the woman to "tend to his needs" at all, but hoping wouldn't make her wish come true.

Terran wouldn't let that happen, she thought, and then she wondered. She knew too little about what had taken place in the city to guess at what he would do in this new arena for his rebellion.

Her questions would have to wait, and so would Terran. The elder prince had stopped at the edge of Loracre, and had lifted his hand for silence as his red horse danced nervously beneath him.

"Greetings, people of Loracre!" he called in an agreeably tenor voice full of authority. "My father, King Barric, has sent me with his envoy to investigate whatever brigands or creatures plague our orchard. It pleases me to come and meet my future subjects, you who toil so stubbornly in our realm, and to remove what ails you at the soonest opportunity. Until then, come and show me your community, for I would make merry with you and yours as your next festival draws near!"

The crowd cheered, relieved that he'd asked no more of them yet. The Guide made himself known to the prince with a waved hand and a deep bow.

A pretty speech, Aubria thought as she watched the two of them interact with wary suspicion. *But who knows what that will entail?*

The people of Loracre flowed into the village to hasten their preparations while the Guide set about the task of giving the prince and his company a local tour to buy the villagers time; Aubria followed with the rest. She hoped to catch Terran's eye while everyone darted about like rabbits, so she could somehow tell him that she wanted to meet once it was dark, but all pretense stopped when Cerise began to drag her away. For the prince's eye had fallen on her—on both of them—as she slowed, and the greedy look in his eyes conveyed anything but the nobility of his words in the speech he'd fed everyone else.

21

Aubria expected Terran to sneak away from the prince to come
and see her that night. He had little way of knowing that she had been
staying with the Erdenweds almost since he'd left to go back to the
city, so she'd kept herself busy baking and cleaning late into the night
so she could look out of the front window as often as she chose, in
case she saw him pass by in time to hail him down. But few people
slept peacefully that night, for the prince and his company kept awake
in the improved meeting hall for long hours making merry and
drinking more cider and beer than was good for them.

She finally went to bed a few hours before dawn, and awoke shortly
after to Cerise shaking her awake.

"We're going to set up our table in the market early, since some of
the prince's men who didn't drink and sing themselves hoarse have
ventured out to wander the village," she told Aubria, her dark hair wild
out of the confines of its braid.

"I thought we were supposed to harvest the early figs and apricots
today?" Aubria asked, bleary from sleep as she staggered to her bare
feet and rolled her shoulders to coax herself into wakefulness.

"Some of us are, especially those who don't live in Loracre proper
like your da. But most of us must stay in the village to entertain our

guests," Cerise said. Her nose curled a little as she referred to their visitors, since she had always looked poorly on people who couldn't hold their liquor and yet refused to moderate their consumption of the liquids that took time and effort for the orchard workers to make.

"How much did they go through?" Aubria groaned.

Cerise sighed as she ripped her brush through her puffy hair and moved to dress in the dark purple gown she usually wore for market. "More than any of us wanted to give them."

Aubria said nothing as she tamed her own hair and slipped into her cleanest dress. She'd taken to carrying around the green book filled with ritual guides and faerykind lore in her pocket, no matter where she went or what she was doing, but today she gave Cerise a guarded look and tucked it into the heirloom wardrobe that held both her clothes and Cerise's and her little sister's.

I'll read it again once everyone has gone back to drinking or preparing for the Evening of Games, she promised herself. It hurt like a sliver of bark under her nails that she couldn't devote every minute of her time to figuring out how to save herself and the orchard from the faerykind—especially now that she felt so close and yet so far from the solution thanks to Cerise's help—but she couldn't afford to shirk work or act any differently from normal to the many eyes trained on her doings. She couldn't save anyone if she was accused of heresy or witchcraft and burnt to death.

Now that Terran was back...if she could find a time to talk to him, to tell him what she'd guessed and to hear what had persuaded him to travel with the prince he'd sworn was his enemy...

It was fortuitous for the royal gathering that they'd arrived in time for market day. The village might be able to entertain him and his men a little, and after that both the Evening of Games—the next event for the handfasting couples—and Lammas a few days later awaited all of them. The usual festival spirit that held sway in Loracre could tide them over for the few days it took for the prince to become bored with the office he'd undertaken and perhaps choose to leave them be. The envoy who'd arrived with him as the more serious counterpart to the royal influence looked to be a sour, business-like man more in tune with the Guide's personality, and once all of the prince's merry-making and frivolity was spent everyone could get down to business and entreat the envoy to investigate.

So she had to be glad, in her way, that she had a few more days to ponder out the riddle of the faerykind's lost power before the official envoy began investigating everyone and everything in the orchard for any secrecy. The city dwellers might worship the sun god when they chose to, and scoff at all the other gods who never affected them in their halls and buildings of stone, but heresy from any source wouldn't be tolerated even by them.

As she and Cerise and the rest of the Erdenweds left their town cottage carrying Aubria's baked goods and both the new and aged honey their family had gathered the past three seasons, Aubria marveled at the number of people milling through the square alongside the prince's men as they stumbled out of the cool shadows of the meeting hall and into the bright sun of the late summer morning. The arrival of the prince had cured some of the snobbery of the Eldacre folk, and many of them had ventured out to Loracre in the early hours to see the honored visitors with their own eyes. Some of them had capitalized on the opportunity by bringing carts and tables of their own to sell the wares they brought from home, which would have angered those of Loracre if collectively they hadn't been so determined to keep things friendly while Prince Mardin was present.

Cerise's little brother had gone hunting and had a generous brace of conies butchered and wrapped up in a dish reserved for the market table, but even the raw smell from those didn't make her feel as nauseous as she did when she saw the way the royal retinue treated the villagers and their wares. Knowing the city guards that travelled through the villages on a cycle to "keep the peace and do the king's will" as they did, no one was really surprised at how the guards treated the local folk.

These guards weren't quite as bad as the ones Aubria had met before, but they treated everyone who had the misfortune of crossing their path as far beneath their notice. When someone offered them food or drink or other wares, they paid as little as they could since the people were too timid to barter with the prince so nearby. They mocked the men for not being brave enough to join the army or smart enough to make a living in Oseren or beyond it, revealing their own ignorance as they spoke these untruths with boisterous conviction and ogled the women enough to almost start a few fights.

Aubria took a proactive method of selling the Erdenwed's goods by arranging jars of honey and preserves into a basket and carrying it through the town, though she never strayed too far from Cerise and her mother's watchful eyes. If she'd hoped that the prince would put a stop to the casual waste of food and commerce—and the general ill behavior of his men—then she would've been disappointed when he emerged last from the hall with Terran by his side and one or two of his equally handsome close friends. These friends kept a few respectful steps behind the prince, so that he could walk with the Potioner uninhibited by their company. All of them were dressed in finer clothes than they'd been the day before, in rich tones befitting royalty that dazzled the eyes of the villagers and set them to speculation about how much the oiled boots of one or the pure white silk as fine as the feathers of a swan of another might cost.

Suspecting that her magic based instincts taught her this, Aubria knew beyond the shadow of a doubt that these men weren't exactly what they seemed. Were they the wizards Terran had said were loyal to Prince Mardin?

Terran trailed after the elder prince in silence, a shadow clad in formal black that made him look like a herald of war. Neither he nor the prince showed any signs of perspiration or discomfort in the heat, no doubt due to the potion that Terran had used before, or an enchantment on the prince's clothes. But the villagers were discomfited, and the market quieted as the prince began to walk through it as if he was a god descending upon the world to bless the mortals below with his mere presence.

Showing some fitting royal behavior at last, Prince Mardin stopped at each table and made conversation with the merchant keeping it. He wasn't the attentive ruler his father had aspired—and failed, though at least he'd tried—to be, for his arrogance was too plain to disregard, but it wasn't everyday that a villager could interact with a future monarch. Most of them were grateful for the attention even if the prince bought nothing himself. If there was anything he wanted, he had merely to arch his groomed eyebrows at the merchant for them to stammer out their offer of the item as a gift, and one of the men behind the prince would step up and carry the item away.

Aubria wove through the crowd with her eyes trained on the small group, which was no easy feat considering how many people were watching the prince pass through the market. She'd sold more than she'd expected for the Erdenweds given the holiday atmosphere lingering in the air like the cloud of humidity that would make the insects swarm in the orchard, but she couldn't remember making any sales due to her distraction. Since she had the benefit of no such potion or spell like the ones keeping the prince and the Potioner cool, perspiration dotted her skin and made her long for the bath she would indulge in later—before Cerise, since the Erdenweds always treated her like an honored guest—after the market closed.

Sweaty and uncomfortable as she was, she was grateful to her mind for coming up with the idea that would serve her purposes the best.

If I can get close enough to Terran I might be able to call Veritas's attention, she thought, her feet already moving to accomplish her plan. *Maybe he'll give me a sign.*

Aubria set her jaw with determination and evaded a tipsy guard who'd nearly bumped into her; carrying her basket like a shield, she made her way over to Terran and the prince. One or two people stopped her to buy honey, but she waved them off and moved forward as stealthily as she could. Finally, she crept close enough to see the blue stitching on the prince's collar and to hear some of his conversation with Terran.

"—too soon, Caird, it's too soon for that. If you think that I intend to let you out of my sight..." Mardin was saying as she walked up to the table they'd just passed and inspected a nest of linens as if they interested her. The merchant—someone from Eldacre—gave her a flabbergasted look when she hushed him as he tried to butter her up to buy his wares.

"I don't have what you seek, and I have told you before that you mistook my loyalty for blind faith. I respect you too greatly to deceive you, my prince, and you should know that this misunderstanding has gone on long enough," Terran replied to the prince, not even glancing at the goods on the next table—jewelry and totems carved from orchard wood and fitted with polished stones—as he argued. Aubria could only see the back of his head—of both their heads—but she doubted that he'd altered his expression.

"Has it? On the contrary, Potioner. You will be free when I have what I've demanded. Your friends in Oseren will go free not a minute sooner, and only after I'm sure of their...renewed loyalty," the prince replied. They'd both been speaking in undertones—the merchants, who wouldn't have understood even if they'd listened, happily feigned deafness until they were spoken to—and Aubria drew as close as she dared to hear better.

So he was caught? They were caught? Her heart sank as she absorbed the implication of the conversation she'd overheard. *And the prince wants something from him, something Terran isn't willing to give...*

The prince had turned to face Terran instead of walking forward, and Aubria quickly averted her gaze and feigned interest in the linens again. Too late: he'd noticed her watching, and possibly eavesdropping. Aubria tried to drudge up an excuse for her intrusion, but in the panic of the moment nothing came.

Prince Mardin waved her over, smiling in a satisfied way that made her skin crawl even if his expression was friendly and welcoming. Caught in his attention, Aubria made the split second decision to play as stupid as could be as she grinned like a blushing fool and approached to duck down into a clumsy curtsy.

"What's your name, lovely maiden?" he asked her, granting her a mordant bow that was far more graceful and gallant than her wobbling curtsy.

She told him. "Aubria Haight, Your Highness. I was instructed to make you a gift of our orchard honey in gratitude for your visit to our humble village."

"Is that so?" Mardin exchanged a look with Terran, his eyes narrowing with cunning. "And are you betrothed, Aubria Haight, so that you may take part in the Evening of Games and the handfasting wheel I've heard tell of already?"

She tried not to look at Terran, to not give herself away. "No, Your Highness."

She hadn't known why the prince had asked such a question, but she was about to learn and regret approaching the two of them at all. Aubria called with her mind to Veritas, but her mental voice reverberated in her skull like a bat in a cave.

"You spent time in these villages, Caird. What say you regarding the ladies of the orchard? In particular, this lady?" Prince Mardin smiled at Aubria in a way that made her feel unclean. It wasn't that he leered at her like a common lech: far from it. In all things the elder prince carried himself with dignity and good manners, she could see that. Yet his cold eyes didn't lie when he studied her like a traveler looking over a horse he wanted to purchase.

Terran didn't stop him, and Aubria felt like crumpling up into a pile of mightily embarrassed skirts as he made a show of looking over her body like he owned it. Maybe it was a common practice in court to treat women this way, as mere objects ready for the taking, and maybe those fine ladies smiled and accepted the gesture for praise rather than a demeaning practice. All *she* wanted to do was take the jars of honey from her basket and hurl them at both of their heads.

"She's pretty enough, I suppose, in the way peasants are. But she's far too tan and freckled from her work, and her hands would undoubtedly be rough and blunted," Terran said in a voice that carried, making her flush with mortification; she chanced looking at him, and mostly wished she hadn't as his green eyes as deep as a forest pool that reflected the trees above flattened with censure. "In time her back will be bowed from labor, and her face as wrinkly as an old peach."

Then he turned away, back to the table of leather goods he and the prince had been inspecting before she'd walked by. Aubria remembered the moment she'd decided to walk past in the hopes that Terran or Veritas would speak to her and tell her something— anything—that would explain the company he'd arrived with and his secrecy, and she cursed her past self with vigor.

Prince Mardin was laughing when the red haze masking her vision and hearing cleared, and he smacked Terran on the back with a gesture of camaraderie that somehow came across as hollow. "How ungallant, Potioner! I never suspected you of such ruthlessness."

Terran laughed with him, the sound painfully familiar and ringing of genuine humor as his teeth flashed in the sun with his smile. "Did you not?"

Am I imagining the edge to his words? Aubria thought, as she was forced to stand there in silence until the prince addressed her again or dismissed her. The smiles the two men exchanged in front of her reminded her more of hunting cats circling each other in preparation for a fight over territory rather than two friends having fun at a peasant woman's expense.

"No," Prince Mardin said, his laughter vanishing as a curious sorrow softened his voice. "I did not."

They moved on, forgetting her entirely and the village-wide humiliation they'd inflicted on her. Aubria forced herself to walk, not run, back past all the market tables and carts and people to the safety of the Erdenwed's cottage. She glimpsed Lane and Viola watching her with real pity. Viola reached out a hand with the impulse to comfort that always came so naturally to her, but Aubria passed them by.

When she finally made it into the cool shade of the cottage, which would have felt stuffy under ordinary circumstances, she slammed the door behind her and stood with her back pressed against it. She hadn't run, she hadn't made a further fool of herself, but her knees wobbled with sudden exhaustion as she sank down and sat on the floor to catch her breath.

Terran, what happened to you?

22

Evening of Games

By the following evening Aubria felt ready to pull her hair out from the roots and run screaming through the streets like a madwoman. Terran had laughed at her, jeered at her, and she'd let him only because she'd seen the paradox of calculation mingled with panic in his eyes as he'd followed the prince through the market like a dog called to heel. Though less important than the rest, he'd solidified the villagers' opinions that she was a whore who had slept with the venerable Potioner and gotten burned, and she burned with shame at the recollection of the pitying, revolted looks many had cast her way as she'd fled the market with as much dignity as she could muster.

He'll come to you soon, she told herself, *he just can't get away.* She surmised that he'd humiliated her to offer a thin shield of protection between her in the prince. If the prince suspected anything of his Potioner and knew that he favored her, he might fix his gaze on her so steadfastly that she'd never be able to wriggle free of it again.

Even after everything she trusted Terran enough to not doubt his loyalty to her. When her faith threatened to fade, she brought out her potion's case and trailed her fingers over each lid, and each of the seven points of the star shaped bottle he'd given her.

After spending the day inside—eschewing work and everything but the book she'd stolen and read so often from cover to cover that she imagined her fingers had left their own imprint on the pages forever— due to the rational and acceptable excuse that everyone would assume she avoided company to lessen her mortification, she'd discovered one more useful piece of information she'd nearly missed.

Everything in the joined world of faerykind and mortalkind operated on a system of threes. Her binding to Veritas had needed her virgin's blood, a new moon, and words spoken by the light of a specific candle, and to break it they'd used that same moon, some of her blood, and the candle of flame in Veritas's hand when they'd kissed to make her blood as close to the maiden's issue as possible. She hadn't figured out the pieces needed to break Terran's curse, but she knew the birthmark over his eye had to be one of them, and if she could ask Veritas what he remembered about the first time the Caird ancestor had summoned him she might find more clues there. Most rituals, she realized with a flash of insight as she turned the pages faster and faster and narrowly avoided inflicting a paper cut on her palm, always had the number three involved.

But what would the faerykind need to find their power again? She guessed that the power of the lightning storm perpetually swirling over the scorched, gray field deep in the orchard would be one of those things, though she could only pray to gods she wasn't sure were listening that she was right. The other two things were a mystery to her.

For today, she'd run out of time. All day people had passed by the cottage with the feast tables and torches that would be lit when night fell. All the meadowsweet garlands and crowns had been prepared for the competitors in the Evening of Games. She couldn't let Cerise go alone, since her mother and siblings had gone ahead to help set up the feast and finish up the harvest work that could never quite be put off. The young men hadn't been seen by anyone all day, since it was their right and privilege to disappear as a group into the orchard to train for the upcoming mock fights that would help them prove their strength to the woman of their choice. It wouldn't all be fighting, necessarily, and Cerise's Nathan would most likely choose to exert his skills in craftsmanship or his agility rather than his fighting strength, along with a few others who were built slighter than the rest.

Respecting Aubria's distraction and knowing what was at stake as she did, Cerise had borrowed her mother's room to prepare for the Evening of Games. Everyone in the house had bathed the night before, starting with Aubria and then her, but even if they had refrained from washing the piquant aroma of meadowsweet would've covered most of any odor. It felt good to be clean, though, and as Aubria rushed through dressing in her Beltane dress and brushing her long hair she tried to quiet the dizzying thoughts and questions that evaded all answers as they danced around her head.

When she finally exited the quiet room into the even quieter house in search of Cerise, she found her in the main room of the cottage, and not alone. Viola had come to visit, and together in their red dresses, festival dancing slippers, and their crowns and garlands of meadowsweet and ivy they made a contrasting and beautiful picture in the same way a white swan would look equally as lovely as the black swan gliding beside her.

Aubria, unattached and thus not bedecked with greenery, froze at the edge of the room without any idea how to proceed or what to say. After yesterday, after how Terran had rejected her for the world to see, how could anyone who didn't know the truth speak to her again?

Viola didn't know what burden lay on Aubria's—and now Cerise's—shoulders, and she couldn't know. But she'd come to the Erdenweds with her bluest eyes warm with friendship and pity for Aubria that somehow didn't injure her like everyone else had.

"I don't know the details of your tale," said Viola as she came forward and took Aubria's hand in both of her own; her long red hair trailed down her back and over her shoulders like a fall of hearth fire. "But I *am* your friend regardless of whatever else has happened or will yet happen. I won't leave you behind because I've learned to be happy."

"Viola…" Aubria began before trailing off to look at the object Viola had pressed into her palm. It was an uncomplicated charm, a net of wood woven with twine that extended into a long loop so it could be worn about her neck. The whole thing smelled strong and sweet and clean, thanks to the meadowsweet woven into the net of twine in the wooden ring so it looked like a basket full to the brim with the little white blossoms.

"You may not be betrothed, the Potioner may have scorned you, but *I* love you," Viola continued as Aubria, moved by the small gift, refrained from speaking. "Lane loved you once, and he still thinks you are a person of honor and beauty. I have never persuaded him otherwise."

Still at a loss for words, Aubria slipped the necklace of twine and wood and bloom over her head and let the pendant rest over her heart. The three of them then left the cottage behind and ventured out into the mostly vacant town as the sun sank lower in the sky. The games would begin soon, and in the hawthorn clearing—much bigger now after the destruction wreaked by the faerykind—made over for the evening, the ladies of Loracre would be occupied blessing the primary torch with their humble prayers before lighting the other torches one by one.

Aubria, Cerise, and Viola said little as they journeyed through the orchard, though Viola made the brave effort of conversation more than once. She had much to tell about Lane and herself, and her excitement over how he'd prove himself worthy of her—worthy of marriage to anyone in the orchard community—would have been contagious if Aubria hadn't been so lost in her thoughts.

Three things are necessary, she mused as she walked under the trees as the sun set and Cerise pointed out the distant light of the torches. *Three things. I guessed one. What are the others?*

Despite her distraction, Aubria had to look upon the arena arranged by the men in the morning and spruced up by the women in the afternoon with anticipation. More people than usual attended the Evening of Games for its sport compared to the other events in the handfasting wheel, and often the not so old men would spar with the younger ones fresh to the experience for fun. The hawthorn clearing was so big now that hundreds instead of dozens of torches surrounded the area to offer sufficient light for what was to come—and a bucket brimming with well water under each torch in case any of them cast embers too vigorously—and the prince must have allowed the long feast tables to be carried out from the meeting hall after all. Each one had been decorated with trails and piles of meadowsweet and mint leaves, and the pitchers of mint and honey infused river water were covered with cloths so as to attract no insects. After the games, the greenery crowned girls would bring the first of this water to their partners regardless of victory or defeat, for the water was meant to enhance a well-earned victory or to sweeten the bitterest defeat.

This was a festival close to Lammas, so there was fresh wheat bread aplenty, and the smell of savory, gamey meats cooked over a fire and seasoned with a variety of strong herbs made Aubria's stomach grumble with hunger she'd forgotten about earlier. Though it wasn't the shortest of walks, many people had carried chairs from their houses to set on the grass around the arena so that the ones being honored—the women actually participating in the handfasting wheel with their menfolk, who wouldn't join them until all of the games were over—would have a better place to sit and watch the proceedings. Everyone else had brought blankets out to sit on as they gathered around to eat and mingle with one another and watch the men in their sport.

So far only the women and those who were married or too young for a betrothal had arrived; the men would march in later en masse, carrying their weapons of choice or the beautiful things they'd crafted for their love in their own time if they chose not to compete physically. Cerise led the way to the chairs for the women to sit, and challenged anyone who looked askance at Aubria with a stern frown, as if reminding them that she had a place here too. Cerise above anyone else knew the tales of Aubria's heart, and who she might as well have been betrothed to.

The usual pageantry proceeded at length, halted only by the arrival of the prince and his company. Chairs had been arranged for them in front of the clearing, closest to the action as well as the food, and the royal retinue arranged themselves into the chairs with much boisterous laughter, as if they were about to witness a bear-baiting or something involving more cruelty. Aubria hid a grin of satisfaction at the thought of their upcoming disappointment: the object of the night was not to injure anyone too badly, and thus only quarterstaffs and blunted knives were approved, and of course one's fists. Anyone coming to view bloodshed had no place here.

The Guide of Rites arrived with the young men of the orchard in tow: most of them had shed their tunics, since the evening was balmy and it would be easier to spar without cumbersome fabric in the way. Aubria admired the assembly as a whole and cheered along with the women sitting all around her as the Guide intoned blessing upon blessing for the men about to fight for the honor of their promised ladies. Yet even he could only extend the ponderous, ceremonial part of the evening for so long, and once the men had lined up around the arena and were ready to begin, the Guide moved to his own chair next to the royal party and raised his hands in benediction.

"Begin!" he shouted, and the pair of men who'd agreed to wrestle for dominance first stepped into the center of the arena to compete.

Relieved to relax for the evening with her friends on either side of her—until Lane and Nathan came to claim them—Aubria cheered and booed good-naturedly with the people of her village as they watched match after match of boxing and staff wielding and so on. It was a night for celebration, and oft times one of the men who had been slighted by defeat would challenge the victor to a duel that usually ended in comedy and exaggerated blows that had everyone laughing.

Even the prince and his men looked like they were enjoying themselves, smiling almost against their will after a particularly ostentatious mockery of battle between Lane and one of the other lads. Aubria hadn't realized it, but she'd lifted her hands to trace the edge of her meadowsweet pendant as if it were a protection amulet every time she glanced their way. It was a sadness always to her when beautiful flowers wilted away so soon, as these would, but that sorrow couldn't match the feeling in her heart when she looked at Terran sitting next to the prince with his back rigid and straight while his eyes remained locked on the arena as if bound there.

I'm going to save you, she thought before she could stop it; would she ever stop making promises she wasn't sure she could keep? *I'm going to save you, both from your curse and from whatever the elder prince holds over you.*

He couldn't possibly have heard her, but to her perception even from a distance and with only the light of the torches to see by he looked as if he'd glanced her way. If it was a coincidence she was still grateful, but if he'd heard...

All sound had stopped, and not due to anything Aubria had done. While she'd been distracted the prince had stood from his chair and held up his hand for silence. One of the courtly men near him looked put out, as if the prince had bypassed convention to act for himself, but the sour man said not a word as the prince waited for the villagers to notice him.

"What's he plotting?" Cerise asked Aubria, hissing the words under her breath so no one else would overhear and possibly tattle on her for her disrespect. "Royal or not, he shouldn't intervene in the games!"

"I'm with you," Aubria replied, shrinking back into her chair as the prince's eyes passed over the young women in their red dresses and crowns of greenery. "It can't be good, whatever it is."

Prince Mardin lowered his hand as the crowd quieted long enough to hear the rustle of a faint breeze through the trees around them, away from the arena. He smiled, the sort of doting gesture a benevolent father bestowed upon an entertaining child.

"You have amused me with your banter and your country way of life," he told the group at large. "I wish to compete in the games."

Everyone had already cloaked their thoughts in silence, but somehow the quiet grew into a profound, living thing heavy with speculation and shock. The *prince* compete? How could anyone compete with him when any injury to the royal person meant exile or death?

Looking around at the gathering, Aubria studied the faces of all the men competing and wondered which one would have the misfortune of contesting the prince. Would one of them volunteer to save the rest, or would the prince simply single out a man for the deed? Seeing Lane and Nathan and the others she'd grown up with, she clutched the meadowsweet medallion in her hands and sent a fervent prayer to the gods for protection for all of them.

The Guide recovered his composure first, and he stood from his solitary chair a little ways off from the royal retinue to answer the prince's demand.

"Our ways are simple, Your Highness, but we have a rule or two I would bring to your attention." He bowed, humble for once, or putting on the appearance of it like a robe he could discard at will.

"Name them," the prince said, readily offering mercy for the Guide not immediately capitulating to his will. "I would hate to anger your gods by breaking the rules you have so carefully attended to."

"We do not kill or seriously injure on the Evening of Games. For most of us work awaits on the morrow, and it is rare that we can afford to lose one of our strapping young men in the orchard. And…" here the Guide hesitated, as if sure his last point would bring further offense. "There must be a lady that you fight for, if you are of the age, for even our older men have wives in this clearing who accept the honor paid to them in contest this night."

Laughing, the prince stepped away from his retinue with one sideways glance towards Terran. "Is that all? Fear not, my dear Guide. I would hate to injure any of your fine men too badly, and if one of them were to overcome me I would waive any royal penalty for the duration of the contest. As for the lady…"

A collective sigh of relief had swept through the people like a pent-up breath finally exhaled, but Aubria knew that the worst wasn't over when she saw the prince walking towards the gathering of women she sat with. If he hadn't already seen her—how did his eyes find her out of a group each and every time they were in the same area?—she would've hid behind tall Cerise and her imposing expression. Perhaps everyone else knew what he was doing, since the group he approached was made up of all promised women aside from Aubria. When he stopped in front of her with his hand on the hilt of the sword he always carried, grinning as if her discomfort gave him utmost pleasure, she rose with the others and curtsied with them almost as one entity as her heart pounded in her chest.

"Would you let one such as myself fight for your favor, lady? A kiss from you would be something to tell of, I am sure."

Prince Mardin stared at her expectantly, no doubt anticipating more of the tittering and flirtatious laughter the single girls in Oseren's court had offered him. Aubria, trapped in his attention and his gaze, stammered out the first excuse she could think of.

"M-My lord—that is to say, Your Highness, I am but a peasant girl. I would hate for you to endanger your person just to earn a kiss from me."

"Surely not just a kiss? I have heard tell of you since I've come to your village," the prince said in a voice that carried, and several unkind voices laughed as she flushed. Mardin had spoken in a sultry, seductive tone as he'd bowed low before her, lower than any royal should have to bow to another in a gesture that conveyed respect for her about as much as a slap in the face would.

Aubria clenched her fists in her lap as she ducked her head to hide the fury in her eyes that could get her punished or killed. "I will not attest to the truth of what you've heard, but you should know, dearest Prince Mardin, that there isn't a man here who would compete against you for my honor."

It wounded her that this was true, to the extent that anyone who *would* have vouched for her was taken—like Lane and Nathan—and was thus ineligible to fight for her sake. Viola reached over as surreptitiously as she could to squeeze Aubria's hand in offer of reassurance, but then she gasped along with everyone else as Terran rose from his seat from the chair in the royal section and spoke at long last.

"I would," he said simply, and the muttering crowd went silent as he stared at the prince and Aubria with icy resolve hardening his face to stone.

No, Aubria thought at him, at Veritas as the prince turned towards Terran. She didn't have the true story of what had happened to put the Potioner at the prince's mercy, but she doubted him standing up for her would help. If revealing that he cared for her and her honor would endanger him, she'd rather the whole village call her a whore and throw rocks and rotten fruit at her now and be done with it rather than see him hurt.

"Would you?" the prince asked, the words sibilant in his mouth as his handsomely round eyes narrowed in another false smile. "Would you challenge me?"

"I would," Terran repeated, his declaration as solid as the rest of him. Aubria saw his throat bob up and down as he swallowed, but other than that he betrayed no other misgivings as he stared the prince down and nodded in a third promise that he would meet the prince in the arena. In the relatively early hours of the night when more men still had the opportunity to prove themselves, the arena was emptying even now of all competitors in preparation for the duel about to take place. Any weapons—the quarterstaffs, the blunted knives, the wraps for boxing—left behind were hurriedly set aside, as if everyone guessed that the noblemen wouldn't require them.

Prince Mardin clapped his leather gloved hands together and laughed as he addressed the crowd at large. "Well then! This should provide more sport than I anticipated. Though none of you are skilled in swordplay, Potioner Caird and myself are. It will be swords, then, that decide who will receive the winner's kiss! If the lady is willing?"

Aubria didn't really have a choice, but that didn't stop her from trying to put off this fight that she had a horrible, horrible feeling would go wrong. "I have prepared no crown of greenery for the winner, Your Highness. It would be dishonorable of me to accept any game on my behalf without a proper favor to bestow."

"Caird?" the prince commanded imperiously, speaking over her as he summoned Terran to his side with one lazy wave of his hand. "The lady is in need of something you can provide."

Terran walked over from the men's side, still not looking at her or anyone other than the prince as he approached. When he drew close enough for her to stretch out her arm to trace the lines of his birthmark with her index finger, he paused and finally, *finally* looked at her. Her breath threatened to stop in her lungs, trapped there forever as his gaze arrested her, and now she knew for certain—as, unfortunately, the whole world did now—that he hadn't meant a word of what he'd said about her yesterday. Aubria looked down as quickly as she had yesterday when the prince had spotted her snooping, hoping that this time she wasn't too late; Mardin was no doubt studying them both, searching for weaknesses, and here he would find a multitude to wield against Terran if he caught the devotion making her eyes burn.

She stared up at Terran through her eyelashes, and saw him pick up a fallen meadowsweet leaf from the ground. Then, raising his hands imperiously over her head with the leaf cupped between them, he spoke a stream of spell words that flowed like the orchard's river. Aubria felt the weight of a crown that shouldn't have weighed much of anything, and Viola and Cerise both gasped behind her.

"It's *gold!*" someone else exclaimed, and the cry spread through the gathering like wildfire.

"Are those emeralds? *True* emeralds?" Someone else sounded angry: a woman's voice acrid with jealousy and avarice that Aubria couldn't recognize hissed in the background.

"Would you look upon what I've cast for you, my lady, that you may approve the favor you now have to give?" Terran spoke to her kindly, more than he had in days, and when she risked looking up with her heart full of something she didn't want to think about now, she saw the hovering surface of silver that he'd summoned without words

381

so that she could see the crown. It was beautiful, an artistic marvel: he'd enchanted the gold into the same crown of blooming meadowsweet all the other betrothed women wore, and numerous small emeralds winked in the torchlight under the petals that looked as delicate as real flowers.

"Thank you," she said, and nothing more as she sat down as demurely as she could, the weight of the crown heavier now that she'd seen it. Internally, she was shouting to him, and to Veritas and praying that they could hear.

If it will not cost your life, you must lose! You must let him win! She told him, hoping Veritas heard her even if Terran could not. *It is only a kiss, after all. Do not provoke him further!*

She thought she sensed something, right at the edge of her awareness: it could have been the brush of a moth's wing against her cheek, except she'd felt it in her mind. Nothing more came, however, and she began to despair.

"You are indeed favored to have earned the…admiration of our Potioner," Prince Mardin said, his mask of amusement taunting her. Aubria knew by now to fear the artifice; he added a second part to his address, quiet enough so no one else, not even Cerise or Viola, could hear him. "What could you have done to earn such a gift?"

Terran lured the prince away from her with a brisk challenge; he'd entered the arena alone and was already shrugging off his outer tunic and his crisp black shirt until he stood bare-chested under the amber light of the torches. Aubria told herself that she wasn't looking at him to witness the smooth flow of his muscles outlined in the light, though most of the women around her sighed with admiration they failed to conceal. Terran Caird was an attractive man, and would've been more so to others if he'd been friendlier, but none of that mattered to Aubria. She loved him for more reasons than just that, though at the moment his pigheaded stubbornness aggravated her more than she could accept with any grace.

The prince's attendants hurried forward as Mardin began to remove his own top garments and his leather gloves, overeager to help undo the many buttons and unsheathe the golden sword to present to their prince on bended knee. One of them took the belt and scabbard along with the clothes away, apparently willing to miss the fight in favor of returning to the meeting hall with the expensive apparel so not a thread would be stained or damaged.

While he waited, Terran spoke a quartet of spell words in a voice that carried, channeling his inner magic to bring into reality a sword fit to clash blades with the prince. As it materialized into being in a haze of silver light, Aubria decided that the sword suited him, as the unadorned longsword decorated with a black leather wrapped hilt and nothing more would suit anyone who preferred an elegant style. The metal gleamed brighter than any ordinary silver, though, and this sword wouldn't bear the stain of time or the slightest hint of rust.

"What are the conditions?" Terran asked, his lips a thin line of resolve as he stood as if this were only a casual practice session, with his sword tip level against the flattened grass.

"Shall we say the first to make three marks?" Prince Mardin replied, his own skin pale as any aristocrat's, though the muscular structure it covered was no less imposing than the Potioner's, even if he was leaner. He held his golden sword at the ready, its crossguard and hilt dotted with garnets and far more ornate than anything Aubria had seen with the exception of the crown she wore now. Gold was not a strong metal, so she assumed that it was an enchanted sword that was a relic of the royal house the prince had inherited, but the repeating mantra of threes on threes this night gave her pause so for a moment she lost concentration for the present events.

Are the gods confirming my suspicions? Is it three things that I need to free the faerykind and the rest of us? She wondered long enough to miss the rest of the lead up to the fight.

What followed as the two combatants touched swords and prepared to duel with graceful bows, Aubria could hardly bear to watch. Both were skilled swordsmen and almost equal in height and bulk, enough so that neither had a surety of victory. Though they both had agreed to three hits before victory, she doubted in her heart that the enmity between the two would allow any of those hits to be glancing. If the prince were to accidentally slay the Potioner, well then…what could be done?

He has something the prince wants, Aubria reminded herself, repeating the words like a mantra. *He's in no immediate danger.*

Terran attacked first, diving forward with his conjured sword gripped tight in his hands as he tested the prince with a blow to the side. Mardin parried easily enough, and pressed the attack himself with a flourish of his blade that Terran in turn blocked from slicing his left forearm. They continued in this fashion for some time, parrying with skill trained into them over a lifetime at court with the best swordmasters in the land. Their opposite blades flashed in the glow of the torches as each of the combatants moved, the prince like a dancing flame with his sinuous evasions and sweeping strikes that more than once made Aubria think that he'd struck the first mark. But Terran seemed impervious to damage, and he pressed forward like a river flooding its banks and flowing inexorably forward.

Evenly matched though they were, Terran managed to draw a thin line of blood from the prince's shoulder as they burst apart after a particularly furious series of blows. Someone in the crowd whooped before they could catch themselves, and the prince revealed a little of his true nature by casting a dark, murderously irritated glance in the shouter's direction.

"Well done, my friend," Mardin said to Terran, hardly loud enough for anyone else to overhear before he renewed his attack and arced his blade downward in a sudden slashing motion that the Potioner barely dodged. Aubria wished she could tear the golden crown off her head and jump into the arena to stop them, though neither that nor her grinding her teeth together to keep from yelling for them to halt would work. The prince may have engaged her as the lady of this fight out of spite for Terran, since somehow he'd guessed that the Potioner cared for her to some degree, but he'd expected to win without taking a mark, apparently. Aubria saw his increased fury and determination with unrest, and knew to fear that wrath.

The prince made his first mark on Terran when he took an opportunity to break Terran's guard with a punch in the face with his hilt and a low slash over the Potioner's stomach. Without breaking his stride—though he turned his head to cough out a gobbet of blood from his bitten tongue—Terran shoved him back and slashed upwards as more blood sheeted from the too deep wound over his gut.

Veritas could do this, and lose for both their sakes without letting on that it was on purpose, she thought, the idea occurring to her in time for Terran to strike his second mark, this one a thin line on the prince's forearm; faerykind were unpredictable, and the truth spirit no less so, but he was smarter about letting his arrogance get in his way. *Why won't he act?*

The elder prince no longer smiled as easily as he had before, and though he and the Potioner were not uneven in their skill and their chances, he perhaps hadn't bargained on Terran's cold fury during their contest. Or maybe he had, and hoped his Potioner would defy him and give him an excuse for later revenge…Aubria couldn't think, she couldn't guess, because finally the prince struck a second blow and it was far less glancing than the ones Terran had left on him. This one landed with a heavy strike of the blade into his shoulder, where the golden edge bit deep into the muscle. It would've slashed deeper, but Terran had blocked the fullness of the strike and countered with another push as he leapt backwards and out of reach.

Each of them had only to strike one more blow against the other, and though the audience dared not cheer for anyone but their prince, tensions escalated enough to make the air crackle with hidden electricity. The fight, though swift in its pace, had carried on long enough to show the sweat-slicked backs and the exhaustion of each combatant, and it was anyone's guess who would strike the final blow.

Until the prince extended too far, having taken a chance with a complicated series of maneuvers that left him vulnerable to Terran's sword. Terran said nothing as he lifted his blade up almost lazily and scored the prince's cheekbone with the tip of his silver sword.

"Match!" The Guide cried, ending the duel and thus reminding everyone of the significance of his presence at the same time; he could only feign humility for so long.

"The honor is mine, my prince," Terran said, grinning through a bloody mouth where he'd bitten his tongue before he sank to one knee. Aubria couldn't be sure if it was from his wounds or if he was showing obeisance to the prince, but she could intervene now: it was her right as the lady who had been fought for to enter the arena and crown her victor. She had time to see the prince reach up slowly to touch the thin slash adoring his high cheekbone, as if he'd never been injured before.

"You idiot!" she whispered to Terran as quietly as she could as she knelt in front of him and tried to heave his bulk to his feet. If she could get someone to help her carry him out of the arena and back to Loracre it would be easier to tend his wounds...

"Finish the contest!" The Guide said to her, looking on with disapproval from his vantage point behind Terran's shoulder. She'd accidentally upstaged him again, for upon a contest's conclusion the Guide of Rites was supposed to lift up the hands of both the winner and the loser and pray to the gods before the ladies of the hour came to fetch their men. Even he knew this hadn't been an ordinary fight, and it would be better for everyone and the other combatants who had the rest of the night to compete—though how they'd match up to the swordplay Aubria didn't know—if the whole affair ended here and now.

Terran grinned up at her, making her want to slap him rather than give him what the contest had decided he deserved; she stood so she could look down at him from a higher position.

"I name you my victor, Terran Caird, and offer the favor of my crown and my kiss to you with the joy of my heart," Aubria smiled through her bared teeth as she lifted the crown from her tumble of hair and jammed it onto Terran's head, where it rested at a jaunty angle she hadn't intended. Then she kissed him, leaning down to press her closed mouth hard against his in a quick peck. When she pulled away and knelt beside him again to try to help him to his feet he looked straight through her eyes into her soul. He said nothing more, since the prince was still nearby with his remaining attendants, but she felt rather than heard all the things he couldn't say.

"Can you heal yourself?" she asked, more gently now that she found her anger couldn't be sustained under the weight of the things between them. Terran shook his head.

"No. The prince's sword is enchanted to make wounds resists magic, and even then I would need some of my potions. If I can get back to Loracre—" he began to stagger to his feet, and poor Aubria tried to carry as much of his weight as she could, but he was too heavy…

…then other hands came to help, and she looked up to see that Lane had come over from his side of the field still wearing Viola's meadowsweet crown to help her, to help them.

Aubria and Terran and Lane made their way step by step back through the orchard towards the village. She and Lane exchanged little to no conversation, and Terran wasn't talkative himself, but when they reached the Erdenwed's door and entered to deposit Terran on Cerise's bed she managed to speak after all.

"Thank you," she told Lane, meaning it with all her heart. He only nodded and left her alone with the Potioner to tend his wounds.

23

"It *was* foolish," Terran agreed, coughing around the blood in his mouth as she unceremoniously pushed him back onto the bed and inspected his injury with little regard for his modesty. She'd have to see if the punch to the face had loosened any of his teeth later, but that could wait. The wound in his stomach had looked glancing, and it hadn't slowed him at all, but the prince's sword had cut deeper than she'd originally thought. A simple cleaning and skin salve wouldn't do the trick after all; she'd have to stitch him up.

"I'm a fool," Terran continued as she pressed at the edges of the laceration to see how many stitches she'd need to use. They would be clumsy, but while Terran couldn't heal the wound, he could eventually vanish a scar with much less effort. "I've endangered you and myself and everyone on our side by winning against the prince."

Aubria listened as he laughed, a bizarre sound that held absolutely zero humor.

"Yes. You're a fool, and now I'm the fool with you," she said, keeping her tone neutral as he winced from the pressure of her prodding. "Do you have anything useful to say? Anything you want to tell me before I give you the pain easing potion?"

"I don't need the potion," Terran said before he groaned: her fingers had slipped too close to the cut, and she withdrew before her nails did more damage; he continued to resume the conversation. "I did hear you calling for me, somehow, or Veritas did. We can't...well, he heard you, but I didn't want to let Mardin win. I didn't want him to kiss you, or demand anything that he would have punished you for refusing."

Aubria looked up into Terran's pain clouded eyes, searching for the delusion that would have made him put his logical nature aside in her favor. But she couldn't find any such thing, and any thoughts of exchanging the information they needed to temporarily flew out of her head like birds on the wing.

"Oh," she said at last, knowing she should have just thanked him and been done with it as she left his side to wash the blood off her hands in the basin of water she'd fetched only a few hours ago. The water was still clear and cool, since she'd only splashed her face with it earlier, and she dipped a clean cloth that she'd grabbed from the kitchen into the bowl so she could wash away blood that had oozed from his wounds. Aubria paused, and after a moment's consideration she walked to her bed and pulled out her potion case from underneath the frame; once she'd gathered what she needed, she returned to the basin and stirred in a mixture of thornbell salve and diluted rose oil before dipping the rag in again.

She still had to have a look at his shoulder, too, where the prince's sword had bit too deeply. It wasn't easy to see as much as she needed, since she only had the four candles she'd lit in their rustic sconces around the room to see by, but she would have to make do.

Terran watched Aubria work as she set about cleaning his wounds before she gathered the needle and stitching threads from the Erdenwed's all-purpose cabinet in the kitchen. His spell-crafted crown flickered with the reflections of the candles. He hadn't looked at her for days, let alone so intently as he did now, and she found that in this case she didn't want to sit through a single minute of his precise scrutiny after all. She opened her mouth to speak as she sat on the other side of the bed to clean the blood from his shoulder and assess the damage, but he did too and they both waited for the other to speak…except in their waiting they both forgot to.

"I'm sorry," Terran said at last, wincing as the damp and now bloodstained cloth scraped over his wound no matter how cautiously she cleaned it. "For those things I said yesterday. I didn't mean a word."

"No?" Aubria smiled enough to let him know that she spoke in jest. "Maybe you'll have to fight a duel for me to lend truth to your apology."

"Of course," he promised, smiling back with his teeth gritted against the pain. "As soon as you patch me up I'll return to the arena and challenge Mardin again. Will that suffice?"

"Mm, I suppose so…but you'll have to take off that ridiculous crown first. I won't accept an apology from you in that." Aubria stood again, the bed rustling beneath her as she returned to the wash basin for fresh rags. "Why a golden crown, anyway? Isn't that a little on the nose?"

Terran laughed, and then grimaced as the cut on his belly stretched. "That was the point. If he seeks to goad me by insulting or endangering you, then I will bait him in return."

"Why, though?" Aubria wondered aloud, puzzling out the riddle he hadn't yet answered as she left the room to gather what she needed before returning. She lifted a green bottle of crafted anesthetic from her box to offer him, but he waved her away again.

"I don't need any of that. I can't heal the wound, but I can deaden the sensation around the area long enough for you to work," he told her. She shrugged and sat down on the bed again.

"He looked like he wanted to kill you, Terran. I doubt anything other than his own rage and petty displeasure crossed his mind." Aubria bit her lip as she prodded the cut she'd cleaned; his shoulder would be fine after she stitched it up, but he shouldn't do much work for several days. She looked up at him to tell him so, but his piercing gaze together with the calligraphic lines of his tattoo-like birthmark and the feverish glow of his skin made him look more like the mystical creature his ancestor had bound to him.

"It would please him to kill me, yes. I'm a loose end he would much rather tie up so I can never tell who ordered his brother killed. To his knowledge I have never defied him before…until now. I would have, of course, but Veritas…"

Aubria shushed him as she dipped another clean cloth into the thornbell and rose infused water and began to wipe the blood off of his recently clean-shaven face. "Veritas wanted to protect you. I'm only sorry that the wrong prince drank the poison. But you both have been circumventing his plans for years, as best you could…the king still lives, along with his wiser councilors. Few could do more than that in the face of such corruption."

Terran gazed up at her without flinching, unperturbed by her closeness. "I'm not sure if I like you knowing everything. At least, I'm not used to sharing that burden with anyone else."

"There's no harm in sharing a burden, I've had to learn. Why would you be the exception?" Aubria would have been annoyed, but with him injured and in pain in front of her, she found that the well of her patience ran deep enough to sustain her tenderness. "You've told me more than once that I'm clever and resourceful. I know it took some time to trust me, but I could've been helping all along, you know."

"I'm sure you're right," he murmured as he lifted his hands to trap both of her wrists in his own. He was tall enough to be almost of an even height with her even though he reclined in Cerise's bed, but he had to look up at her still as he caught her attention along with her hands. "But you are of value to me, Aubria, as more than my assistant or my friend…and above all else, I am loathe to risk losing you."

How could he be saying these things to her now, she wondered, when he'd never risked doing so before? How could he hold her captive with his strong hands and tell her exactly what she wanted to hear when so much remained unsaid between them? The timing wasn't right, her mind shouted while her heart thundered in her chest like a swift cavalry. She wanted to kiss him, but she forced herself to gently withdraw her wrists and push him back onto the stack of pillows so she could stitch him up.

"Are you ready?" she asked. He nodded and coughed a jumble of words with the deepness of his voice, closing his eyes to concentrate. Then, helpfully, he held up his hands and conjured a weak spell light for her to work by, and she murmured her gratitude as she threaded her needle and pinched the edges of the wound closer together. The needle made a faint popping sound as it pierced his skin, and she tried not to gag; she'd stitched up a few wounds on her father once or twice, and in Loracre people were known to come for her for help with wounds like these that weren't life-threatening, but that sound always made her nauseous.

"How does he know about me, let alone my connection to you at all?" she asked as she worked.

"He's been spying on me, of course. I thought I had him fooled with my spells and tricks, but he hired one of the other mages to work against me by giving one of the spies a rare, expensive object that negates magical concealment. I was caught...*we* were caught."

"We?"

"Me and the others. The prince found us conspiring and threw my allies in the dungeons of the keep. I thought he'd kill us, and though I could've escaped the wizards under his command he locked the others up and told me I could save them if I gave him something he wanted. Something he desires above all else."

In the way that she had thanks to the magic awakening within her like a tree budding into flower, she guessed what he wanted with a chill that had nothing to do with her nausea over stitching flesh back together.

"He wants Veritas."

Terran nodded and leaned his head back to exhale a rushed breath of air; he had numbed the pain of her work, but the effort obviously taxed him a great deal. "Yes. He's been researching ways to gain power much in the manner my ancestors did. The Caird bloodline curse has been the gossip of court for decades, even if no one's ever looked too closely before or known what that might entail. My father in particular did much to quash that rumor as soon as Veritas left him by power of the binding to possess me."

"What does he know for certain? Does he know how to break the curse, or to change the binding over to his bloodline? I hadn't thought of that as a solution, but I assume neither one of us would want to burden someone else with Veritas's consciousness let alone grant them access to his power whenever he chose not to use them..." Aubria trailed off, her fingers still with the needle stuck fast in Terran's skin; she hurried back to work as soon as she realized she'd paused. "If the prince somehow took Veritas from you, could his wizards suppress him or—"

"I don't know, and I don't know. He's...bound me to him, for now, so that I can't leave his side for too long. I could've broken the tie, but that would mean the death of everyone in the rebellion as soon as I did so, since one of the wizards with him would send a message back to Oseren to execute the prisoners in their cells," he waylaid her rambling questions. "I can't leave him yet, even for a rescue mission, and I had to see...I feel as if our fates are tied in some way, Aubria, you and your orchard and me and my quest to bring the throne back to the king."

Aubria finished bringing together the long, deep gash on his stomach. The same feeling he spoke of had built in her for some time, brushing against the edge of her thoughts like a feather tracing the length of her spine, but she hadn't known it for what it was until he named it.

"I don't know how, and I only have suspicions about what it will take to save the orchard, but I know...I know that both our fates are joined, somehow, in a way the gods ordained that I can't understand."

They looked up at each other in mutual understanding, both of their expressions bleak. Aubria had to move to his shoulder now, leaning in with her hair swept back over her shoulders so she could do her best work. His attention on her felt warmer than the flame he held close enough to offer more light without singeing her hair or skin or the thread she worked with. She waited until he coughed those same spell words again before she began, taking the time to force her brain to function properly with him so near to her.

"No matter what happens, I can't let him have Veritas," Terran was saying once she found she could concentrate again. "I would rather him stay bound to me forever than bound to the royal line through a prince that promises to be both more cruel and more corrupt than any monarch we've had in this kingdom before."

"Couldn't Veritas bind him? Couldn't he take the prince over forever, and—"

"He could, for a time, but the royal wizards might know the difference and seek to exploit or punish the entity controlling him. Veritas is powerful, and there's a chance he could go on without detection indefinitely...but it's a risk, and if he fails there's little hope for the future of Lyrassan and the kingdoms across our border." Terran explained.

"He's powerful enough to wreak havoc, but weak enough to not overthrow any of his oppressors if they all were to rise against him. That's why Veritas has been hiding," she realized as she spoke. "One of the wizards might have sensed him, or sensed him through you, and then—" Aubria didn't know precisely what, then, but it couldn't have been good. The tragedy of Veritas as an independent spirit forever bound to a mortal form struck her all over again, a landslide against the mountainside of her grief for everything bad that had befallen and would befall if even one of the steps they took was the wrong one.

"We have to free him. Free him in such a way that he can't ever be bound again." she announced, jabbing the needle in a little too roughly in her fervor; thankfully Terran couldn't feel the jab with his nerves deadened. "I'm slowly figuring out how your binding works, I think, and—"

"Aubria." Terran stopped her, saying her name in such a way as to make her look into his face with surprise. The rugged beauty of him, even injured, struck her as he watched her, half-reclined and shirtless in the bed she'd slept fitfully in for weeks. He'd looked healthy and strong, all sinuous muscle and trained efficiency in the arena as he'd battled the prince with swords that sang a song of steel as they clashed together. Now the light casting shadows in the hollows of his cheeks and the dark eyebrows and the dip between his collarbones reminded her that he was a man she desired just when she didn't need that recollection to trouble her at all.

More importantly, he looked like he wanted to say the thing he'd started when he'd trapped her wrists in his hands, and if she heard what she'd wanted to hear for all this time, *now* of all times, she thought she'd break. She could scarcely breathe in this little room, trapped where she could catch the dusk and amber scent of him she'd hoped she'd grow immune to over time.

"I would like to meet them," Aubria said as she drew the wound to a close at last and clipped the thread; with both injuries cleaned and closed he looked much better, though still exhausted. "Your friends in Oseren. Someday."

"Good," he said. They were in a room lit only by candles and the moon streaming through the window, but it felt like she was basking in a halo of warmth as he pulled her down to kiss her.

The kiss was as unlike as what they'd shared in that sunlit afternoon a month previously as a trickle of water streaming down a leaf was to a river's powerful current, and she found that she didn't want to breathe after all as he sat up to crush her body against his. Heedless of his stitches, he pulled Aubria further onto the bed with him and surrendered to the urgency she'd never experienced from him before; his hands wove into her hair, pulling her closer as he made a sound she'd never heard him make that made her whole body feel like she was melting into him, pure ore ready to be forged anew.

Aubria sat astride Terran before she'd realized it, held like precious though definitely not fragile treasure in his arms as he kissed her with all the vigor she'd missed when he'd been holding himself back. Tasting the residue of blood in his mouth, she broke apart to speak a concern she almost couldn't recall.

"Y-Your stitches, Terran, they'll—"

He growled, the first time she'd heard him make such a sound as he tipped her head back by the grip he had on her hair and kissed his way from her mouth down to the place where her shoulder met her neck.

"They won't," he promised against her skin. Her legs tightened around him by instinct as her eyelids fluttered when the unexpected delight transformed her whole figure into one tense knot that she knew he'd take pleasure in unraveling. He was still technically injured, and she expected him to tire at any moment and withdraw from her, but when he began to pull up her skirts she found herself mentally begging him to hurry.

She was directly on him aside from her thin seasonal undergarments, though they hadn't had time yet to undress him fully, and the heat and hardness of him between her legs made her want to lose her sanity. All the time he was kissing her, and when her arms got stuck embarrassingly in her dress she heard a short tearing sound as he yanked it off and tossed it onto the floor. She caught her own scent from the gardenia oil she'd "borrowed" from Terran's store of potions in his tower and sprinkled on her dresses, which reminded her of other things.

"What changed your mind?" she asked, speaking around his kisses as he slid his hands up her outer thighs, moving inwards before he teased her by trailing them up to where her shift strained to cover her breasts. "You said you couldn't give me anything, and this—"

"Didn't you hear? I was a fool, and I still am one now," he interrupted, impatient with her protests as he gripped the bottom hem of her shift and started to pull that up too. He made it halfway up her chest before her meaning broke through the haze of his desire and he slowed; she'd lifted her arms to help him remove it, but she lowered them back to her sides when he paused.

Don't stop, Aubria begged in her head, knowing she couldn't say these things aloud. She pictured herself naked on top of him, then with him, and how it would feel to finally become one with him at last. She moved her hips against him, arching her back for him to see more of her through what little of the shift she still wore before she made herself cease. He'd been holding his breath as he rocked against her in return, but it couldn't continue.

"But…" She'd known it was coming, knew that this moment was too good to be true, and when she heard their ending in his voice a little part of her hoped that he'd keep being foolish and change his mind back again.

They parted, each panting for air. His grip was still tight around her waist as she cupped his face in her hands with their foreheads resting against each other.

"One of them will be here, soon, to check on me. I doubt he will send anyone else but one of the wizards to act as my jailer," Terran told her; she was already obliging, extracting herself and climbing off of him and off the bed to ostensibly check his stitches again. We'll have to finish our conversation and…other things elsewhere, at another time."

"Tomorrow," she insisted. "The orchard can't wait, Terran. Not for much longer."

"I know," he told her. Then he watched in silence as she collected her dress from the floor to put it back on. If it had torn, she'd have to fix it another time. Once she was done he stood as well, clearing his throat to dispel the awkwardness of him standing there still shirtless and recovering from his arousal.

"Tomorrow," he repeated. We'll meet in the grove by your cottage again, if you're willing."

"Yes," she said, and nothing else. She wanted him to kiss her goodbye, but knew he wouldn't risk it with their desire aching between them and both of their mouths bruised from kisses they had almost been unable to stop.

And, strangely, she realized after the fact, after he'd left her alone in Cerise's room in the Erdenwed's cottage, that when she'd almost made love with Terran, none of it had felt remotely similar to when she'd coupled with Veritas. She hadn't even thought about those nights in the orchard, first by ritual and then by desperate summons, but she'd technically had Terran's body entangled with hers before…yet it had felt so different with him, the actual man she loved, compared to the truth spirit borrowing his form.

Tomorrow, she promised herself, though she didn't know what exactly she was promising.

$\mathcal{L}$ammas was days away, and the town hadn't yet recovered either from the arrival of Prince Mardin and his company or from the chaotic events during the Evening of Games. Indomitable, the Guide waited for no man and insisted that the preparations and the gathering of ripe harvests continue. Ordinarily everyone would've been happy enough to work; the season was a bountiful one hanging on the cusp of the autumn that would arrive with a welcome respite from the constant tumult of summer. Not so for this turn of the wheel: after all the attacks, people had learned to fear the orchard as no one ever had before—save for ignorant city dwellers who called the trees cursed even while enjoying the fruit from their boughs—and they feared the prince as well.

Supposedly Prince Mardin had arrived to help them find who was causing the attacks if it wasn't nature herself unleashing her fury upon them. The envoy accompanying the prince told any of the villagers who dared interact with such a foreboding fellow that the prince intended either to prosecute the criminals himself as his men stood guard in the orchard in a series of watches night after night, or to help the Guide find the sinner causing the gods to turn on them. The Guide repeated the message with an emphasis on the latter part of his speech.

Yet the watch turned up nothing, not a stray leaf or—to Aubria's relief—any signs of faerykind activity. After his duel with Terran, the prince kept to his own company in the meeting hall and rarely left it.

Terran himself was trapped in there with him, since Mardin wouldn't allow him out of his sight again for reasons Terran hadn't yet told her.

Tonight, Aubria told herself over and over as she paced the confines of Cerise's room; given what had happened during the games, she too had thought it wise to keep to her rooms. *I'll see him again tonight, and we'll plan then. If he can get away. If…*

The golden crown sat on Cerise's night table, mocking Aubria with its etched beauty and the curiously deep emeralds set into the leaves and petals of the piece. Knowing what she did, Cerise had still crowed over the exquisite crown Terran had given Aubria as if it were something that brought excitement and intrigue rather than danger. Yet that was her gift, after all, stern though Cerise was on a day to day basis: she could brighten any poor situation with her wit, and though Aubria was sick with worry and preoccupied with the future she managed to crack a smile more than once.

The crown's rich beauty assaulted Aubria's senses like a slap, one meant to wake her from her stupor. The reflection of the gold reminded her of the brilliance of the lightning bolts in the wide gray field deep within her orchard, and also reminded her that she had yet to work out how she was to explore the lightning field without coming to harm. She was only mortal, not one of the faerykind, and she wondered if even they dared trespass in that dreaded place without…

…*without magical help,* Aubria realized, and then could've punched herself for being so dense. Terran was a wizard who could conjure a crown from one stray leaf using a mastery of the elements and other aspects of magic she had yet to learn. Veritas was one of the faerykind, and doubtless had his own type of magic to wield at will. More importantly, though she would need to consult Terran as soon as possible, *she* had some small magic at her disposal that might be enough to grant her access to the forbidding plain. She couldn't wait forever, and if Terran couldn't help her she'd have to take matters into her own hands.

Aubria stared at the emerald laden crown with renewed interest, huffing a few strands of hair out of her face as she picked it up in both of her hands to study it. It had been made of magic, she reasoned as she scratched at a flat gemstone with a fingernail, so might its properties be more conducive to protection spells that would aid her in her quest?

Maybe not, she mused as she set the crown back on the night table with a sigh and resumed pacing the room. *If Terran could craft lasting gold with his magic then I don't think he'd worry so much about making coin from his potion craft. It must drain him of energy, somehow, or over time the gold might fade into dust...*

Once again, she held an assortment of questions in her hands without access to the one person who could give her answers. Before her betrothal, before Terran's arrival in Eldacre, Aubria wouldn't have been able to fathom the true depth of what impotent frustration she'd experience in the seasons to come. Now the answers that were denied her soured in her mouth like early mendacia berries, and even the heart Terran had marked hadn't brought out this pacing madness in her that almost made her wish her world would just end already so she could get it over with.

Cerise found her this way, hunched over on the unmade bed with her open potion case and the magic crafted crown laid in front of her. Uncharacteristically irritable, Aubria opened her mouth to snap at her friend, but when she saw the expression on Cerise's face she paused to listen.

"The prince is coming this way with some of his people. No, not the Potioner. But I think he might be coming to see you," Cerise told her, twisting her fingers together nervously. "Mother doesn't know much of anything about anything, but she knows that bad tidings follow the prince like crows. If it comes down to it, she might—"

"Don't fear, Cerise," Aubria hurriedly packed the colorful bottles and her herbs back into the wooden case and shoved it under the bed; the crown she stuffed unceremoniously behind her pillow. "I'll leave before he tries anything if I need to. I wouldn't have you or your family punished for any vendetta against me or Terran."

Cerise nodded and waited for her to finish tidying up before the two of them rushed, a little out of breath from their panic, into the main room of the cottage. The Haights were wealthy as far as orchard standards were concerned, but the Erdenweds were not since Cerise's father had passed away some years earlier. Thus the room was small, simple, and without much adornment aside from the flowers Cerise brought in on occasion and a collection of interesting acorns and rocks gathered by her younger brother and sister to rest forevermore on the windowsill.

Aubria dared a glance out of the window and almost knocked over a tin cup chock full of bright green acorns in her haste; sure enough, the prince was nearly at their doorstep. Conversing with the other villagers must have slowed his journey, a coincidence for which she was grateful: she would've hated to meet this man unprepared.

"Aubria," Cerise's mother began, laying a bony yet no less maternal hand on her shoulder to lead her away from the window. "Did Cerise tell you—"

"She did, and if he wants something...if it endangers all of you, I'll be gone by morning," Aubria promised, laying her own hand over Mary's in a gesture of solidarity. Mary's eyes softened, the deep brown complimenting the slightly hooked nose and dark skin that she and her children shared.

"I think of you as one of my own, lass. Cerise misjudged me if she thought I would put you out in the cold at the least sign of trouble."

"Mother—" Cerise either protested or apologized, but they were out of time as a closed fist knocked against the cottage door with clear purpose. Mary exchanged glances with Aubria and Cerise, pointing with her eyes towards the chairs at the table. The two of them filled their seats and tried to look busy with the task Mary had abandoned: cleaning empty jars that would later be filled with orchard honey. Then she opened the door, and there was nothing more Aubria could do to stave off this moment.

Prince Mardin entered the Erdenwed's cottage entirely alone, though Aubria glimpsed his attendants waiting for him outside in the heat. He said nothing, at first, waiting a beat of silence too long while she and Cerise and her mother leapt to their feet and bobbed hasty curtsies in his direction.

"Your Highness," Mary stammered, "we had not dreamed of expecting you—that is to say, how may we be of service to you?"

Cerise caught Aubria's eyes and rolled her own as surreptitiously as she could while Mardin nodded with a shade of respect too opaque to be genuine towards her mother.

"You must forgive me my intrusion, madam. I am here to speak to the lady I fought on behalf of last evening, to apologize for my defeat and offer a quest to regain what should've been mine."

His phrasing was odd, as was the amused and frankly disrespectful glance he sent Aubria as he bowed towards her, but none of them could question it. Knowing what she did, Aubria concealed her frown behind an empty smile. The prince wanted Veritas, unknowing of the cost...he was a fool, but a fool born into the royal family with the weight of the crown in the form of the ornate golden circlet he wore granting him authority.

"Of course, Your Highness," Mary gestured to Cerise like a hen about to summon her brood for feeding time. "We will go about our business in town to give you a bit of privacy, if you wish."

Aubria cast a panicked glance towards Cerise, whose own eyes were wide though she didn't know all the particulars of why a solitary meeting might prove disastrous for her friend. But what could she do? The prince had made his requirement for a private audience known, and it would be foolhardy to defy him in so small a matter.

As he damn well knows, Aubria thought, and gritted her teeth in silence.

Once Cerise and her mother were gone, Prince Mardin wasted little time in making the rest of his purpose in visiting the lowly cottage known.

"You are prettier than I expected for the Potioner's infamous whore. Then again, Caird *has* always preferred country blondes...and your hair does glow bewitchingly in the light. Maybe that's how you captivated him," he started without preamble as soon as they were alone in the clean but cluttered, verbena scented kitchen. Under so many conflicting blows—insults wrapped in compliments and tied off with rudeness—Aubria had no idea how to respond, so she said nothing and merely bobbed her head in acknowledgement that he'd addressed her. Her anger—both for Terran, his allies in Oseren, and her own dignity—ebbed and flowed under her placid surface, and she jabbed her hands into her pockets to hide her trembling fury.

Seeing her struggle in spite of how well she tried to hide her true heart, the elder prince laughed and threw himself into one of the chairs the rightful occupants had abandoned at his word.

"Come now," he cajoled as he tipped the chair back on its hind legs so he could rest his dusty boots on the table, "that's as much favor as one such as you can expect from one such as I. You're smarter than I expected as well, does that help? I know you can guess why I've come to you."

Aubria forced herself to curtsy again, though she really wanted to kick the legs of the chair out from under him. "You haven't stated your purpose yet, Your Highness. How could I guess what it is you require of me?"

"Very pretty," Prince Mardin said, nodding appreciatively after she'd demurred. "He taught you how to speak to the nobility, at least. I thought I'd have to decipher your peasant dialect before we could understand one another. I will give you leave to speak freely, this once, without all the honorary titles. You know why I'm here: I want the source of Caird's power for my own, and he has kept it from me. I have wizards aplenty, powerful in their numbers...but they could conspire against me, and only in full force can they contest Terran Caird. Before I leave you will tell me how to gain his power. Though I heard you are his whore—a good one at that, in the way most lusty village maids are—I also heard you are his apprentice. It's usually bad policy to mix business with pleasure...but that doesn't signify now. He will have told you secrets, and you will repeat those to me."

Aubria clasped her hands in front of her, the picture of servile femininity as she smiled at the prince with all the wildness she could summon; if this was how he thought of her, she might be able to stall for time by playing the empty-headed slut he assumed she was. "In truth, he has told me little of anything. Oh, we played at his craft now and again, mostly him showing off for my benefit. But he is a man like any other, my lord prince. Do you really think he would've taken valuable time away from our...physical pursuits to train a silly village maid in a subject she couldn't possibly understand or use practically?"

"Fair point," the prince conceded. "I could see he was...distracted by you from the moment we arrived in your charming little town. It's why I baited him at your market and at the games, you see...he owes me quite a debt, and I've thought of hundreds of ways to ensure that he pays it in full."

"Oh?" she questioned, her blood boiling at his arrogance and assurance that he owned the world and everything in it. "Was losing to him part of your plan, my lord?"

Mardin's comely face—a beautiful mask of arched cheekbones, an aristocratic nose, and blue eyes framed by lashes as golden as his hair—flushed unbecomingly. Otherwise he betrayed none of his anger or annoyance, and Aubria waited for his next demands with her spine rigid and her muscles tight with anxiety. It was too warm in the cottage, as it would be for some weeks yet; dots of sweat decorated the prince's brow under his circlet.

"I lost, yes...but his injuries will be slow to heal, thanks to my sword, and his schemes against me must grind to a halt while he recovers. Potioner and wizard though he may be, he can only flee for so long in his state...but he won't run while I have his allies in our illustrious dungeons. And now I have you." Prince Mardin smiled at her as if his good looks and smooth words would have had her swooning by now if she had misunderstood or ignored his threats. Aubria's mind skittered away like a rabbit trying to free itself from a snare; she forced it back into submission so she could focus on the matter at hand rather than picturing Terran's injuries again or imagining what could be happening to his friends in the dungeons of the royal keep in the city.

"That doesn't concern me, begging your pardon," she lied, her mouth going dry; to curry some goodwill, she closed the distance between herself and one of the kitchen cabinets to bring out a bottle of preserved and spiced apple juice that always made her feel much cooler. After pouring some of it into two wooden cups, she held one out to the prince like a peace offering. He stared at her, one eyebrow arched with disdain.

"You are the Potioner's apprentice," he said to her, speaking as if she was a dimwit. "You will taste both before you offer one to me."

Aubria obeyed, the flavor of the wellspring apples tart and sweet all at once on her tongue. After she didn't drop dead, the prince took one of the cups and availed himself of the cider as well. If she'd been a kinder person she would've taken more of the cooling drink out to his attendants sweltering in the heat, but as of now she wasn't feeling particularly charitable to anyone who arrived in the royal party.

"I admit that Lord Caird fascinated me, perhaps more than he should have. I am under suspicion now from those in my village because of my association with him…but we are finished, as he knows and would tell you himself. He cares for me as much as any man cares for someone he views as his rightful property…which is why he challenged you for me, I believe. But I know nothing of him other than his body and a few paltry tricks he stooped to teach me after our bed play. This secret of power you tell me of is as much news to me as it would be to anyone else."

Her delivery of the package of lies impressed her: she'd been nonchalant and careless, just enough of both to convince the prince that she and Terran had shared a sordid physical relationship and nothing else. Later, if she could get the prince to leave her alone, she could warn Terran that the net around him was closing in all too quickly…

"I have heard of you from multiple sources who say many things, Aubria Haight. It's strange that a lowly orchard girl has so many people uttering her name in either whispers of gossip or declarations of witchcraft. Are you aware that with a few words I could tip the public vote in either direction and have you burned as a heretic and a witch? Your village is laughably superstitious about the gray field in the orchard, calling it besieged by the gods…it wouldn't trouble me to test that theory with you as the sacrifice." Prince Mardin didn't miss her sharp intake of breath at his words, hide it though she would have. But he *did* miss the reason for her shock, since he had no knowledge of her vow to Noblynn and the rest of the faerykind. An inkling of an idea had begun to occur to her, and if the prince would stop talking long enough for her to think outside of this perilous moment, then she could—

"If you do not wish to burn I suggest that you remember the duty you owe your future sovereign. I want the power that Terran Caird denies me, and I will have it just as I will have his life in the end for his defiance," he was saying as soon as she grabbed hold of the present again; the blood drained from her face, and the golden inkling of the idea in the back of her mind was growing and burning to burst free with its truth. "I believe you are the key to unlock his power, one way or another. I will use any key or tool at my disposal to strip my rebellious Potioner of his gifts so that someone far worthier may make better use of them."

He didn't sound angry, or petty, or cruel. Aubria had mistaken him for a hot-headed, reckless boy intent on his own pleasure and power. Now she saw that he was merely ruthless, cold down to the depths of his heart where no living thing would ever reach him. It gave her chills to think about it, and she rubbed at her arms for warmth even in the sweltering cottage kitchen as goose bumps spread over her skin.

"Why would you need such a thing, my prince?" she stalled, though she was genuinely curious. "Are you not the crown prince, and is your father the king not an old, decrepit relic? What need have you for such trappings when you are set to lead the kingdom within the next few years? I know of no such hidden power, nor much of magic itself, but I never would've dreamed that a royal would need such influence to bolster the vast power he has by birth."

Mardin's flat eyes, devoid of something necessary and human, blinked slower than they should have at her audacious question. His hand tightened around the cup of cider he'd already finished, before the white on his knuckles faded in stages.

"You are disposable, so I will share with you what few others on this earth know. My father is old, yes, and would have been foolish enough to make my brother his successor if…fate hadn't stepped in to remove him from my path, the path of the rightful heir. He is old, and I am young and strong, and since he does nothing but grieve I have been running the country for years. Yet he has not officially named me his heir, and due to the nature of our bloodline it is impossible to compel him in this matter…not by natural means," he told her, his voice as flat as his expression in a way that reminded her of the wily dragon that was the royal family's coat of arms. "I mean to have everything. I will be the next king once I find other magic to compel my father into reason. There will not be a corner of this world that doesn't bear my seal and bow to my throne by my life's end."

Aubria wanted to recoil from the blue-eyed royal, the would-be conqueror of the known world. It made sense, suddenly, the constant border disputes that were beginning to reach even into the orchard villages to call men to war. It made sense, too, why Mardin wanted Veritas, and wanted Terran's power for his own as someone who had no magic and saw the means to acquire it just out of reach like a ripe peach dangling from a branch higher than a person could climb to pluck it.

Returning to himself and away from his dreams and ambitions, the prince rose from his chair and gallantly offered her his hand to help her rise as well. She didn't want to touch him at all, nor he her, but she couldn't refuse; his hand didn't feel as cold and reptilian as she'd expected, but she flinched all the same as the prince bowed to her a final time.

"Heed my words. The Potioner trusts you and cares for you as more than an entertaining bedfellow, I am certain. If you exploit his weakness and bring me the secret on how to extract the power from his family curse, not only will I spare you a heretic's execution and a bland life as a peasant, but I will reward you beyond your imaginings. If you do not..." the prince trailed off with a shrug, as if nothing really mattered to him after all. "You know what awaits you."

He turned to depart, and was halfway to the door when she gave in to her reckless desire to threaten him as he had her.

"Please take care, my lord prince. Given what happened to the younger prince, I would hate for one such as you to suffer the same fate as he. All it would take is the right drop falling into the right cup," she told him, smiling as she curtsied lower and with more skill than she ever had before. The threat was as empty as the two cups that they'd drunk from minutes before, which both of them knew. But she'd unsettled him, for though he smiled at her in acknowledgment of her barb, she saw him glance between her and the empty cups with suspicion narrowing his eyes. He had to have tasters, especially given how he'd had his younger brother murdered under Veritas's influence, but even they were fallible to the long-lasting poisons...

When he left, Aubria settled herself back into her chair and pressed her palms to her dry, sleep-deprived eyes so she could recapture the idea the prince had awoken within her at the worst possible time.

The field...a sacrifice in the field...

Her time was short, trimmed further by the menace of the prince's demands, but she might have found another piece of the puzzle that would help her save the orchard from faerykind.

24

Aubria tore through the orchard around her cottage much later that night, long after sunset. She didn't need to run, since she'd taken extra care to be stealthy so anyone following her would lose the trail, but it felt better for the panic swirling within her chest to lend speed to her steps. On her back she carried the satchel bearing the few belongings she'd brought with her to the Erdenweds, along with an extra assortment of food and travelling supplies. For their safety she'd told them that she'd be leaving the orchard and fleeing to Oseren. She couldn't tell Mary much more, but Cerise could explain to her what was relevant later. In reality, Aubria couldn't think of leaving the orchard altogether, especially not now that she was so close to saving it from ruin.

First she had to stop by her own home. In the dead of night her father should have been sleeping, with her knock on the door coming as a surprise. Instead, Aubria saw him sitting outside on their front stop smoking as if he'd been awaiting her arrival for some time.

He was a little shocked to see his daughter fleeing home through the wayward, less known paths of the orchard. The frown under his beard lent lines to his face that she'd forgotten to notice in the frenzy of the past few months.

"What's happened?" he asked her once she reached him. "Are you well? Is Mary well?"

"I have to leave. Tonight," she told him in trim explanation once she caught her breath back.

"Leave?" He'd been the one in the past, when the Litha petals had led a condemning trail to their door, to come up with the idea of her leaving in the first place. She wouldn't have guessed that from how ashen his face looked now in the darkness speared by the tall candles in the sconces hung outside the cottage door.

"I have to, Da," she assured him, feeling like he needed to hear it. "I can't put the orchard at risk by letting the prince decide my fate...he's wicked, and he wants to use me against Terran. I need to stay in the orchard long enough to—"

"No. There's nothing here more important than my daughter's life," Darragh stood up and descended the steps to pull her into an embrace. "Tell me what you need to do and I will see it done. You can travel away from here and start a new life elsewhere."

And leave you behind? Leave behind my home forever? The thoughts would've brought unbearable sadness to her heart had she had the time to process them. But Aubria had little time left, so she pushed her father away so she could look him in the eye.

"I'm not leaving the orchard. I came to say goodbye, for now, because I plan to go so far into the trees that no one will be able to find me unless I want them to. I need...I need to be able to return. To the lightning field."

"The lightning field?" Darragh, thrown off balance by the clue she'd given him, wrinkled his brow in confusion. Aubria nodded and impulsively hugged him again before withdrawing for good.

"Once I leave with Terran the prince will suspect that we've fled the orchard altogether. I don't think he'll guess that we've gone deeper into it than a city dweller like him could guess. He should leave in pursuit of us, and we'll return once I've put together the pieces of the puzzle that will save our homeland," she told him her plan in swift, clipped words that hid her own fears and misgivings. More than ever she wanted to seem capable…though what she really wanted was to come home and sleep in her own bed while the rest of the world sorted out its problems without her aid.

Darragh nodded once or twice, absorbing her information like a squirrel mulling over its winter stores. The lines in his forehead sunk deeper than she'd seen before, and his ashen pallor had yet to fade, but she knew he understood her and wouldn't argue further. There was nothing else to say, really, no advice he could give in this scenario that she would take, and she couldn't yet muster the will to tell him her whole story.

"Be safe, Aubria," he told her after they spent a minute memorizing each other's features in case something horrible befell her before they could meet again. Her words caught in her throat, she nodded and hugged him a final time.

Turning her back on her father, she resumed her jog deep into the trees to meet Terran. She sprinted until she couldn't tolerate the thump of her satchel against her back any longer, and then kept walking until she reached the place they'd agreed to meet. Terran hadn't made it yet, and her taut frown belied her panic until she remembered that he didn't know the same secret paths as she, and would probably take longer to come to the rendezvous location.

Aubria settled in to wait, tossing her belongings aside; the lack of their weight was a relief. She wondered as she waited whether or not something terrible had happened after her unexpected meeting with the prince. The trees had always sheltered her, and the fruits of their harvest had nourished her and given her strength, but their stolid presence and the familiar, spiced scent of the ember trees and their faintly glowing silver fruits couldn't offer her any solace as she paced back and forth. For Terran was not a child of the orchard, and as far as she'd seen the trees didn't trouble themselves to protect things that weren't their own.

"Aubria."

He spoke her name from behind, and without pausing to check her exuberance she abandoned her satchel on the ground and ran towards his voice. Terran caught her as she threw herself into his arms, still favoring the side that hadn't been injured during his duel with the prince. She heard him grunt—he couldn't avoid her weight thumping against the stitched gash on his stomach—and she pulled away to spare him any further pain, but his arms held her fast in an embrace almost too tight for her to breathe through.

"You came," she exhaled the words and struggled to pull in another breath. "Prince Mardin came to the Erdenwed's house to threaten me…said he had your friends and had weakened you so you would surrender Veritas…"

Terran released her—her ribs groaned with relief—but kept one arm wrapped around her waist. "He's told me as much, confident that he has me trapped. But I have more secrets than he or his pack of fledgling, hot-head wizards could dream of…and I've sat on my hands for too long. If its war he wants then its war he'll get, though not on the front he's expecting."

Aubria had never seen him like this, all sharp eyes full of fatal stars and a jaw set like a blade. "You mean to go back to Oseren to free your friends."

"Yes. And you're coming with me."

I can't, she thought. *Veritas, you know I can't.* She imagined her feet growing roots that curled downwards, delving deep into the soil to keep her in place. Though he risked detection he let her feel his presence, and in that she sensed the beginnings of a refusal that might cost her her homeland.

Having released her, Terran shrugged his own small bag of belongings off his shoulder and tossed it onto the grass next to hers.

"I haven't forgotten about your vow to the faerykind. But I think we'll work better away from the menace of the royal guard, once we get a head start back to the city. The Potioner's tower has never fallen even during invasion. I'm weaker now, but I have the means of making us travel much faster with magic. Once we gather my supplies and whatever books you need from the library, we can free our allies—"

Aubria cut in, no longer able to hear out his hopeful planning. "We can't, Terran. I'm so close to breaking the binding…but I have to be here to do that. And the prince…well, you know him better than I. I fear him, and I want to help you find a better candidate for the throne, but I don't want to do so at the cost of a war. A war that will break us, because our orchard is suffering and my time to save it won't go on forever."

Terran stared at her as if she was a deer that had stood up on its hind legs to talk back to him. Immediately the impulse to capitulate, to surrender to the will of someone who most likely knew better than she about almost everything, made her want to take back what she'd said. Aubria stood her ground and looked up at him unflinchingly. His expression mingled frustration and fascination with what she could only call respect, the light of which rendered his green eyes brighter in the darkness than they should've been. They flashed yellow, too, long enough to remind her that he wasn't alone in his head.

"He is considering *making* you run away with him, Aubria. For your protection." Veritas said to her, speaking in an unusual monotone that made goose bumps prickle her skin. "He's decided not to, for now, but be careful how you press him. I can only intervene so much without my power bringing the prince's trackers down on us."

"He wouldn't dare—" Aubria began furiously, her hands flat on her hips in a stance of defiance, but Terran's green replaced the yellow before she could finish her sentence. She segued into her next thought with hardly a pause. "I can't leave! And you can't just return to your tower and begin a war that could cost Lyrassan more lives than we know in a civil war that could draw out for years! You used to know this, and you're far too knowledgeable to pretend otherwise. I know you want to rescue your friends, and we'll get to that…but what changed your mind from pursuing peace?"

He didn't answer her, not at first, and she fully intended to shout— or whisper-shout, because she didn't want to alert any patrolling guards watching the orchard to their meeting—at him again until he gave her a better explanation. Terran looked at her with his face wiped of any emotion; he reached out to trace the ridge of her cheek with the back of his knuckles, a gesture of tenderness belied by the tremor in his fingers.

"Mardin seeks to punish me for my insubordination whether or not he somehow manages to rip the binding linking me and Veritas to shreds," he explained, begging her in his halting silence to put the pieces together so he wouldn't have to say them. "One way or another he intends to see that I pay for my crimes against his crown. He values a price paid by someone else while the transgressor looks on."

Aubria understood, though she wished she didn't. She'd been afraid, before, in the abstract way pressing danger made a person feel like a hunted animal. She'd feared the Guide, too, more than she'd told anyone, for he could have her condemned to execution in the gray field and the protestations of the few wouldn't save her from that painful death. But now the prince had her within reach as well, and there was little he wouldn't do to gain what he sought and punish those who stood against him.

Who could oppose that? She wondered. *I'm only Aubria of the orchard. What can I do if the crown is set on my death and the enslavement or death of the man I love?*

"I know more of what we need to do," she blurted to snap herself out of her paralyzed state of fear as well as breach the matter at hand. "For the bindings, I mean. I know more of what we need for both."

"Tell me," Terran commanded, and so she did. She told him her belief in the power of threes, and that she thought the lightning field was one piece.

"The field represents the power that was taken from them, and it makes sense that a field so unnatural would have been brought into being by wild magical forces," Terran surmised aloud, pacing. "We don't know whether or not it was the gods who limited the faerykinds' power, or what reason they might have had to do so…"

"You believe in the gods now?" Aubria asked when he trailed off to contemplate the information she'd told him. Terran looked at her askance.

"I never disbelieved. I just doubted that they had much of an interest in mortal doings in our age, since all evidence points to them not caring about anything but their own affairs. Regardless…the lightning field is one piece, judging by your theory, and we have only to find the other two. I can help you with another one, I believe."

"You can?"

"I had a little time before the prince closed the net meant to trap me with my friends as the bait. I went to the royal library—not the public one—and searched for as much as I could find about your orchard." Terran groaned with the memory, pressing the heels of his palms against his closed eyes as if staving off a headache. "There was little to find among those books other than stories and fables and harvest ledgers…but many of the tales mentioned the 'first fruits' of the orchard and their significance. The context of the phrase was odd, at times, but I grasped it easily enough. What's the oldest fruit in your orchard?"

"Heart of the gods," she answered, the response as instinctual as it had been when she'd been learning which fruits grew where and in what season in the orchard. "We grow one tree in every grove, for the roots from it encourage the other trees to grow better and produce more. It doesn't taste good, since it's so bitter after the initial sweetness, but—oh. Do we need one of those to free the faerykind?"

Terran gave her the same look he had when she'd answered a question right during the times she'd studied potion craft with him. "I believe so. Thankfully it's plentiful, according to your explanation. But…it seems too easy. I suppose the hard part might be getting the fruit into the field without getting scorched."

Aubria tucked her hands into her pockets and glanced around at the rest of the trees as she considered the store of knowledge she'd gained. *The field, the fruit, the fallen…if that's what that means, I—*

"You said you had two of the pieces, Aubria, and I've given you the second. What's the third?" Terran asked her, as if he knew she'd kept it from him deliberately. Which she had, because if he'd contemplated taking her away from the orchard by force with the threat of only the prince, what would he do when he found out the rest of what she might need to do?

A sacrifice…

"What does Veritas remember about when he was bound?" she asked Terran to stall him."I know your birthmark is one part of the binding, since it's written in a faerykind dialect, but for the rest…"

The green eyes flashed to yellow again, though this time Veritas didn't look on her with much understanding. He closed the distance between them, bold enough now to override Terran's control and risk alerting the prince because somehow he *knew* her secret in the way he'd known things when they were bound.

"I remember faerykind fire burning me, and my own power turning against me as I was called and funneled into the body of the Caird ancestor. I remember the mark they left on me, though I don't remember much else besides the all-consuming fire. But none of that will compare to what I will feel if you lay yourself open to harm that no magic will be able to repair, Aubria."

She stalled again, tilting her head back with her expression wiped of anything but a wry half-smile. "I thought you couldn't read my mind anymore."

The yellow eyes—menacing though they'd been at first, their ocher gleam comforted her now in its own strange way—blinked, shuttered off from the world long enough for him to gather his thoughts. "I can't. But I know you're keeping something from us, and I know enough of the nature of faerykind curses and bindings to realize that you might not come out of this unscathed…if at all. I can't let that happen, least of all without knowing beforehand how to stop you."

Aubria debated what she should tell him, wondering how much he would relay to Terran in the privacy of their linked minds, but the numbed horror tamped down in the depths of her own spirit refused all efforts at communication. She waited for him to let her go, staring up at him with her eyebrows raised, and when he did she turned the subject.

"Fire. You said you remember fire, and pain, and the mark…they must have branded you through the first Caird to bind you. If I'm right, then the next piece for your binding is fire."

"That doesn't matter now! If we all make it through this we can work on the binding later—" Veritas almost shouted at her, his mutinous looks making him look both taller and more imposing, but for once she cut him off before he could continue.

"Don't you see? It's all connected! If we free you from Terran then the prince has no hold over either of you, and you can intercept the rest of the faerykind with Noblynn and persuade them to work with us. They can ensure that we aren't disturbed while we free them and save the orchard, and then—"

"Then the prince would still have us hunted and executed regardless of whether or not I'm still linked to Terran. Did you forget what sort of man he is?"

Aubria's fervor wilted like grass browning in the sun. They stood at an impasse, facing each other in the orchard as they had so many times before; Aubria sighed and resumed her pacing for lack of any other way to breathe life back into the sails of her ideas.

"It would be easier if I simply killed him," Veritas measured each word before he spoke it, as if it were medicine he'd drizzled with honey to make go down more easily. "There would be little anyone could do to stop me. With him dead, you and Terran would be free to save your homeland and live your own lives out of the shadow of this corrupt royal. I know I failed before. That wouldn't happen again."

It would *be easier,* she agreed, though she didn't say this out loud. The wild nature of Veritas—of all faerykind, really—couldn't surprise her as much as it had before everything had started, but seeing the inhuman light seething under Terran's skin like a visible rendition of his spirit and hearing the deadly words uttered so casually gave her pause because she agreed: why not kill the prince and be done?

"It would be easier," she repeated her initial reaction, speaking as contemplatively as he had. "Easier, but not better. His death, as joyous as it would be to some of us, leaves Lyrassan without an heir. King Barric is old, and the country would fall into civil war with little delay.

We have abused the kingdoms around us for too long, and they would push into our lands as well. Some of them are even less favorable to magic than ours. Terran and I might be free for a time…but what would it cost? How many people would die as a result of our vendetta? And the orchard…"

"Peace," Veritas raised his hands in surrender. "I understand. I understand you want to save every single person in this land, including my less than deserving kindred. But…you would save them at the cost of your own life and happiness? You would give your life for these people who would turn on you for something as inconsequential as not acting like everyone else? Not to mention the faerykind themselves, who have committed atrocities against mortalkind in the name of sport for centuries."

"You didn't," she interjected quietly. "It's not so easy as condemning everyone for their mistakes. The faerykind are more difficult to understand, let alone forgive…but should I not save who I can, when I can? Isn't it better to spare people from pain and death whenever possible?"

The yellow eyes blinked green and then back again as Veritas inexplicably relayed everything she'd said to Terran. Then they changed to green for good, and Terran closed the distance between them to enfold her in an embrace only a little less crushing than the one he'd bestowed on her when they'd met in the grove earlier that night.

"You are stubborn and flawed and hasty where you should be patient, Aubria Haight," he murmured into her hair, his breath a warm puff against her ear; then he withdrew far enough to cup her face in his hands and press a tender kiss on her forehead. "But I'm afraid I've fallen entirely in love with you, and I'll be damned if I let you destroy yourself in the name of the dubious greater good."

I've fallen entirely in love with you, he'd said. Aubria swore she heard her heart singing the harmony to those words throughout every chord in her body. She'd guessed that he shared her feelings long ago, and he'd provided more proof each time they'd met. How could she resist a

420

smile, even under such dire circumstances, now that he'd finally said the words?

"Terran—" she looked up at him, ready to confess her own heart in its entirety as she hadn't fully been able to before. He didn't exactly smile down at her, since he was too occupied with her stubborn insistence that killing the prince and starting a war was the worst of their options, but she reached up and traced his jaw with her fingertips anyway; it pleased her when he softened, as if her natural touch possessed magic all its own.

Then the prince's guards swarmed them from the cover of the trees that had been meant to shelter them.

It all happened very quickly, Aubria would remember later. Terran's reactions were almost as fast, though not enough to save them. He lashed out with a burst of power that glowed as bright and amber as fire, though it burned nothing of their surroundings. His strong arms shoved Aubria behind him, protecting her from any attacks with his own body and the strength of his magic. The guards continued to pour into the small clearing regardless of the angry wizard holding them at bay, until fifteen men stood between them and their flight to freedom.

The Potioner, though deprived of the bottles that had given him his title, wasn't an easy man to capture. He called a sword forth from thin air, the same one he'd used to duel the prince. But he was still injured from severe wounds that had been meant to heal according to natural rhythms instead of magical ones, and Aubria feared for him.

The attack had been too much of a surprise, really, even with Terran's own precautions to make sure he hadn't been followed. Veritas had only shown himself for a moment, and aside from a small enchanted light neither one of them had cast magic, so she assumed that one of the wizards must have conjured some other way to keep track of the prince's pet Potioner. Regardless, though Aubria called frantically on her own stores of magic to shield the two of them from any lunging swords or capturing hands, her panic won the day and they separated her from the vengeful, sword-wielding Terran and pulled her kicking and screaming away from him.

In the split second when he was still close enough to grab her back, Aubria saw Terran's eyes shift to brightest gold as the clearing around them vibrated with hints of ground-trembling power. She held his gaze and shook her head, begging with her eyes for him to hold back. The prince's men wouldn't kill either of them, not yet; she was valuable as a bargaining chip against Terran, and Terran himself possessed something the elder prince desired to the point of obsession.

Veritas's presence faded, and though it felt like it was killing her to watch, Aubria looked on while they subdued Terran with their numbers and their bulk. They didn't bother tying her up, since she wasn't strong physically and two guards could hold her as well as any rope, but they pushed Terran to his knees so the conjured sword fell from his grip and wrenched his hands behind his back to tie them together. Their prisoners secured, the steel helmed guards guided them out of the orchard towards where a few men waited for their return out of the misty orchard.

"Well," Prince Mardin greeted them with a dashing grin as his men dragged Terran and Aubria out from the grove they'd lingered in. "I wondered when the two of you would conspire to meet each other."

The light of the torches seemed profane, an attack against the silvery moonlight. Aubria's fury boiled to the surface, and if she could reach the prince atop his magnificent horse she would've spat in his face like the dirty peasant he thought she was.

"So what if we did? Is that a crime?" she asked, biting off the ends of her words.

"You'll keep a civil tongue in your head when you address the prince!" One of the guards not holding her captive stepped forward to slap her face with a flick of his arm that cost him little effort even if it gave her a shocking amount of pain. Her cheek stung as blood rushed to its surface, but the slap had turned her face in Terran's direction, and she saw his eyes darken to ominous evergreen as he muttered a spell that made the guard who'd struck her reel back as if he himself had been slapped.

"Ah, none of that," the prince intervened, gesturing to one of his few mounted attendants with one raised finger. The attendant, older than the rest of the crowd that more or less shared an age with the prince, dismounted in a swirl of dark, jewel-toned robes and fussed with an object in his hand that she couldn't see. Terran struggled as the wizard approached him, but his eyes were on Aubria. She was watching him too, looking on when the wizard snapped a magic suppressing collar around Terran's neck, so it caught her off guard when the guards holding her roughly stretched her arms out while two more approached. One began to fumble at the ties of her leggings around her waist while the other gripped the edges of her shirt with both hands to tear it off.

The appalling nature of the deed they were about to do to her barely had time to sink through her skull, and she had only started to struggle before Terran went perfectly still and looked away from her to face the prince.

"Stop. I'll submit. I can't give you what you seek because it's not something I have…but I won't fight you." Terran's words rang clear through the orchard. He would've made a good prince, Aubria knew, better than this man-child who threw impossible tantrums when he didn't get exactly what he demanded. He would've made a good ally to the younger prince, too…if he'd outlived his elder brother's scheming.

"That's a start, isn't it? I'm so pleased to hear that you'll cooperate with me now. Apparently the rebels I imprisoned weren't valuable enough to earn your obedience." Mardin laughed, the sound echoing an innocent happiness he had no right to imitate. "And you, orchard girl. I have your Potioner. I trust that will ensure your own cooperation?"

Aubria glared at him instead of answering, expecting one of the guards to strike her again for her insolence. Yet the blow never came.

"Did you hear anything useful? Anything to our advantage?" Mardin asked the ten soldiers who had swarmed them. Aubria cursed herself again for her stupidity, for not taking precautions to hide them. Terran couldn't have used much of his magic without alerting the prince to his whereabouts and about Veritas…but she could've. Surely there was something she could've done to avoid this ending?

Maybe, just maybe, there was something she could do now. No one knew that *she* had magic, after all…

"No, my lord. They spoke softly, and acted as lovers do," the most business-like guard said, stepping forward to salute the prince. Aubria stared at him the whole time, biting the inside of her lip hard enough to make it bleed as she concentrated on him with every fiber of her being. It took more work than she'd expected, imposing her will on another, and it left her feeling sick and gray and dirty. But the prince couldn't know about what they'd discussed.

The other guards looked at their captain askance, but a desperate Aubria dealt with them as well. She didn't have enough power of her own, so she drew power from the orchard. Picturing her feet sunk into the earth like roots into soil, she snapped out the same looping thought over and over into the borders of their minds: *we saw nothing but two lovers meeting in the orchard, and we heard nothing but the whisper of the wind.*

Eventually their expressions cleared, and that danger passed. A wet trickle smelling of iron leaked from her nose, and Aubria glanced down as a droplet of blood spilled off her chin and onto her tunic. Disturbed by the caress of her quiet power, the trees stretched their branches towards her as far as they could, as if moved to lift her from the ground and carry her aloft and away from the danger.

"Oh? How disappointing," Prince Mardin flicked his reins to quiet his restless steed, the only one besides Aubria who noticed the disturbance. "I expected witnesses for high treason. I suppose the other charges will have to do."

"Other charges?" Terran questioned, his frantic gaze landing on Aubria again; in his panic, he'd failed to notice her magic surge and then ebb as the trees returned to their natural state. Making a face of disgust, the prince gestured to his pet wizard once more, and the ostentatious man pulled a handkerchief from his pocket and stuffed it in Terran's mouth to gag him.

"Other charges?" Aubria repeated, half out of spite and half out of genuine, fearful curiosity. "You have nothing with which to charge us."

"Do I not? Your community will not share your assessment," the prince said, ridiculing her as his teeth glinted in the amber torch light. "Potioner Caird I will deal with in my own time, in my own way…but you, Aubria Haight, are charged with heresy, consorting with dark spirits, and conspiring in the death of Squire Merek."

Merek? Aubria strained to sift through her memories, back to the last time she'd encountered Viola's erstwhile betrothed. Other than the foggy, purposefully dim recollection of the time he'd tried to force his way under her skirts, she couldn't think of anything at all.

"Merek's dead?" she asked, thrown off guard by the baseless accusation.

"Yes, as I'm sure you know, though predictably you've decided to pretend innocence. They found him in ring of toadstools near your home, gorged on faerykind fruit and dribbling gold."

It looked like she wouldn't be leaving the orchard after all.

25

When they finally came to fetch Aubria from the cramped back closet of the meeting hall, she'd both decided that she loathed tiny, enclosed spaces and resigned herself to the trial that was about to come. For now it served her purposes to wait and see what they'd decide to do with her…but someone had thought to cast a spell on the lock. She had doubted that anyone had known about her magic, paltry thought it was compared to any contracted magic users in the realm, but now these suspicions kept her company in her solitude along with her fears for Terran's and the orchard's sake.

Deep, deep down in her heart, she mourned the boy the faerykind had taken from the world. Merek hadn't always been bully, though he'd grown into one young enough, and she'd never liked his power over Viola in their relationship. Aubria didn't think anyone deserved to die as the faerykind were rumored to kill: stripped and starved and made mockery of for their amusement, then gorged on cursed fruit before being cast back into the mortal realm like rubbish that had served its purpose.

If it was my choice I might not help the faerykind regain their powers after all, she thought as the image of Merek's prone body carried away from wherever they'd found him on the Haight's land in his father's arms materialized in her mind as a product of her imagination. *But if I deny them not only will I forswear myself and lose my own life…but the fate that befell Merek may fall on everyone else as well.*

These thoughts tormented rather than comforted, but she had one thing that helped keep her sane as she sat down on the floor among the dust bunnies and old, brittle gathering baskets with her knees hunched up almost directly against her chest. The prince's men had searched her, more or less, some of them with groping, rude hands and others with bored efficiency, but she'd concealed the one thing that mattered from their grasp with a bit of luck and whatever magic she had to her name.

The pointed star potion bottle emitted a dull glow in her hands, and the faint hum of enchantment that resonated through her bones hadn't yet dampened with exposure. With nothing else to do, she studied it like an artist intent on capturing a likeness; it reminded her, now, of the long-armed, elegant star anise pods from the shrubs they grew in the medley of apple groves. During Mabon many villagers wove garlands of dried star anise with citrus rinds—also carved into stars— and dried rowan berries to separate each star for their windows and doorways and storefronts. The spice was said to ward off the coming negative energy of winter, along with adding its potent, licorice-like scent to any area. Even the least superstitious person in Loracre wore a Mabon garland throughout most of autumn and sometimes well into winter.

Mabon, she mused, thinking back to her memories of the first of the autumn holidays. *Will I ever see another?*

Aubria hastily shoved the bottle back into her pocket and pulled her shirt down over the bulge when they came to fetch her. Though she hadn't explored any further guesses about what such a rare, mysterious potion might be for, Terran's gift was a comfort and she didn't want it taken away.

They brought her out into the large meeting hall between two royal guardsmen, who gripped her by her arms as if she was a feral wildcat that would swipe at them with deadly claws. In reality, Aubria shuffled awkwardly in time with their steps without shrieking curses or attempting to physically fight her way to freedom. She thought about it, imagining breaking free and leaping onto the speaking dais to denounce the royal presence along with her accusers before blasting them aside to find Terran, but her limbs were stiff after a whole night and a good part of the morning spent in the cramped basket closet. Denouncements and freedom would have to wait.

Late morning light streamed through the tall windows of the meeting hall, reflecting off the smooth, cherry wood of the long table and the three chairs behind it. Loracre rarely had cause to use their meeting hall for anything other than council meetings, harvest allotment and scheduling, and announcements, but on occasion someone in the village put forth a grievance that needed to be addressed publically. Then everyone concerned and anyone who wished to see justice served would gather in the hall, and the Guide of Rites, the accuser, and a defender from the council would occupy the three chairs to oversee the proceedings. The accused would stand, usually with cap in hand, before the table and tell his own side of the story, and then depending on the case the three would decide amongst themselves whether or not the council would take action…or, if the public outcry was strong enough, the villagers would persuade the council with their heckling to serve their own brand of justice.

The public meant almost everyone in Loracre and a few visitors from Eldacre today: the meeting hall was packed to the max, and the sweltering heat outside enhanced the warmth from the crush of warm bodies within the high-ceilinged building.

Aubria hadn't been under any delusions about how her case would fare, but it did surprise her to see her father seated in the defender's chair alongside the solemn faced Guide of Rites. Between them both, the prince himself sat resplendent in his fine clothes and his golden circlet. She had wondered, while she tried not to hyperventilate in the basket closet, if they'd taken her father and accused him of the same crimes as well, but it appeared that he was allowed to go free and would be allowed to defend her. He didn't look well, though, and he

429

had a black eye blossoming on his face. Their eyes met, and he tried to smile at her encouragingly; the gesture reminded Aubria of the time she'd broken her wrist and had it set by Loracre's healer, when Darragh had tried to be brave for her sake even though broken bones made him queasy.

She looked all around for Terran, as the guards let her stand on her own two feet before the three seated men, but she didn't see him yet.

Have they hurt him? Has the prince decided to kill him yet? Fear assailed her, and she risked any social capital she had left by breaking tradition and speaking before the Guide addressed her to begin the proceedings.

"Where is Potioner Caird?" she asked, her voice rasping out of her throat as a reminder that she hadn't drank any water since she'd fled the Erdenweds. "I wish to see that he is alive and well before you try me."

"What you wish is of no import, as you are accused of deeds almost too heinous for us to speak of," the Guide snapped back at her, rising from his chair at the right of the trio to loom over her. "The Potioner's welfare is not your concern."

"Terran Caird is alive and will be for some time, to my knowledge," her father intervened in a careful monotone, catching her eye again to convey his sincerity. "They're bringing him here now."

"You are permitted to sit as defense only because you are a councilman, and because not one of your fellows would defend your wayward daughter. Do not forget your place, Squire Haight, nor forget that our own questions regarding your behavior are yet to come," the Guide leaned around the prince to glare at Darragh with all the resentment of his bitter spirit apparent in the twisted lines of his aging face. He was old, she realized, older than she'd thought of him as a child. The combination of aging and enduring the poisonous regrets of past mistakes didn't sit well with many people, let alone the vengeful Guide.

"Enough," the prince intervened before Darragh or the Guide could say anymore. "I've come on behalf of the king to intervene in your troubles with the orchard. I confess that I did not believe, at first, the tales of faerykind mischief and disfavor from the gods from our envoy. Now with such evidence as has been presented to me, I'm inclined to change my mind."

Prince Mardin's hyacinth blue eyes glittered with handsome menace as he studied her, the toe of his boot tapping against the ground once or twice like a gavel calling for attention. Mutters passed throughout the room like smoke from a fire, but they quieted at his words.

She regretted her appearance a little, though it wasn't as if she'd been languishing in a dungeon like Terran's allies. The closet they'd tossed Aubria into had been dusty rather than dank with mildew, and the tunic and leggings she'd worn for the flight that had never come to pass were still clean except for the spots of blood across her sleeve and the lengthy but not yet indecent tear from the guards almost raping her at the prince's command. Her hair, however, was tangled and still half-caught in a braid; this alone made her look like the heretical witch many of the villagers believed her now to be.

Aubria stabilized her weight on both of her feet and tipped her chin upwards, hoping that her assertive posture would lend her the confidence she desperately craved.

"I await the words of my accuser, my defender, and my judge," she declared, pleased with the absence of the dehydrated rasp that had plagued her question about Terran. Darragh tried to catch her eye again, but it hurt her to see him so concerned, and she couldn't afford to show a single shred of weakness. She avoided looking at everyone but the prince, whom she challenged with her forthright gaze.

Then the doors to the hall slammed open behind her, and she turned with everyone else to watch the guards lead Terran down the center of the room to the place of judgment where she herself stood. Lead him they had to, for the marks of the beating they'd given him once the wizards had him bound marred his face for everyone to see.

Breaking protocol and her personal code of showing no weakness again, Aubria gasped audibly and closed the distance between them at a run. Terran's arms were still tied behind his back, he still wore the suppressing collar, and he couldn't speak through the gag they'd tied around his face. His eyes met hers through their halos of bruising and the crusty blood that had streamed from a cut in his left eyebrow to communicate something she didn't understand in her panic over his wellbeing. He still wore his Potioner's clothes, and though the black fabric concealed much of the shocking red blood that oozed from the new or still-healing injuries on his body, there'd been far too much abuse to conceal completely with dark clothing.

Aubria reached him long enough to touch his cheek with her fingertips before the guards who'd brought her into the hall from the closet yanked her away by twisting her own arms painfully behind her back. The two of them marched her back to stand before the trio of men set to judge her guilt or her innocence, and after a moment they led Terran to stand beside her. Aubria doubted he'd be able to stand on his own two feet, but he managed.

I'll find a way to make them pay for what they've done to him, she thought to quell the seething rage making her chest rise and fall like a bellows. She would've directed the promise to Veritas, if she could've reached him, but she knew that the wounds hadn't healed because doing so would reveal Veritas's power and bring about more abuse from the prince.

"Can he defend himself through the gag?" she demanded as she massaged her bruised wrists once the guard let her go; so long as she behaved, he wouldn't manhandle her again until the trial was over. The prince didn't answer, but his tight-lipped nod at one of the other guards was sufficient to convince the soldier to untie the gray kerchief.

"Let's get on with it," the Guide groused, weary of the delays. "Aubria Haight, we accuse you of heresy and magical mischief, along with the contemplated murder of Merek, a scion of Loracre. We have evidence of your crimes, but first we would give you a chance to confess on your own for a more lenient punishment."

Aubria would've snorted with disbelief under ordinary circumstances: the prince would never let her go free with what she knew.

"I've committed no crime. Let me hear your 'evidence,' Guide."

"I support her innocence, not only as her father, but as a councilman and defender. She has committed no crime worthy of this trial," Darragh agreed as he stared stony faced at his daughter. "The evidence you brought to the council is as insupportable as it is contrived."

Irreverent as always, Mardin rolled his eyes. "Contrived, Squire Haight? Who, pray tell, would dare to fabricate evidence under the royal eye?"

Aubria watched her father open his mouth to argue, but a look from her quelled his equally disrespectful words. There was nothing he could say to that except to accuse the prince of corruption, which would cost him his own freedom and possibly his life.

"I would hear the charges," she interrupted the male posturing, crossing her arms to ward off an inexplicable chill. "And I would also remind the council that it is against the law to abuse prisoners unduly. The Potioner's plight should concern all of us." The Guide gave her another acerbic look before he rose again from his chair to recite her crimes for the whole hall to hear.

"The whole village has observed your untoward behavior, Aubria Haight. There is no crime in eccentricity, of course...but your change has been linked to the arrival of the Potioner in Eldacre, and it is known that you consorted with him both to learn his unsanctioned arts and that you have defiled your handfasting bed with his body. Furthermore—"

"The Potioner is a wizard sanctioned by King Barric, and has the necessary license!" she protested. "He's allowed to practice the magic he was born with, and I have no magic to speak of and thus cannot be charged for something not within my power."

"The king withdrew his support from Potioner Caird some time ago," the prince explained to her with a fond smile, as if he was speaking to a child who'd fallen from the trees onto his head one too many times.

Liar, she thought, but didn't say aloud—or scream aloud, as she would've preferred to—because she had no proof to give weight to her accusation.

"You partook in his illegal dealings at his side. Several witnesses reported your comings and goings from the Potioner's dwelling in months past, and when we searched your belongings and your home we found the case full of potions and black arts that you'd concealed. That is enough to condemn you to exile from our number here and now, or surrender you to judgment from the crown itself."

"Too true, my good Guide," the prince picked up the thread where the Guide had let it drop for theatrical effect. "But there are more grievous charges than these. For you have told me that Aubria Haight has conspired with the faerykind to bring about the downfall of the orchard, since her crime of poaching magic brought her low enough to consort with them. How can you prove such a heinous crime?"

"All too easily, sire. Haight was not careful in her dealings, and thus other witnesses noted her absence after several of the attacks on our orchard—be they faerykind mischief or punishments from the gods for her wrongdoing—and her own immortal comrades judged her wanting when they led us to her door on a trail of Litha petals. The prince's guards, noting her suspicious behavior, followed her along with the Potioner when they crept from their beds to meet near her cottage to consort together in the dark arts and bring about another attack on our sacred grounds. Furthermore…it is known that she rejected Merek out of her own sense of ill-placed pride. The boy, imprudent with his thoughts of love, may have gone to see this deceptive witch to woo her further—"

"'Love?'" Aubria mocked, unable to stay silent as the Guide ignorantly referred to Merek's "love" for her. "I did not wish him dead, especially not from the faerykind entrapment and degradation you told me he suffered, but he was a spiteful bully who behaved wickedly toward his former betrothed before he abandoned her to pursue me. And by pursue, I mean literally. He followed me through the orchard on Queen's Night intending to force me to yield my maidenhead to him."

"How easy it is for you to spin that tale, given that you are the only

434

one who can verify its truth now that the other party is dead," the Guide shook his bald head dolefully, gathering his robes about him as if they would protect him from her wicked lies.

Aubria turned around to scan the crowd for anyone who would speak up for her; Viola would have attested to Merek's vicious nature, and since the town viewed her as their saintly May Queen and the betrothed of their golden boy her word might have carried more clout. But she only saw the stern faces of people who clearly thought she'd had a part to play in both the orchard's downfall and the death of one of their own.

"Who are these witnesses? Who are my accusers? Do I not have a right to see who has told tales about me?" she asked at last, willing her voice not to waver; she shared a glance with Terran, who had mysteriously held his silence. His gaze was frantic, his eyes wide as if he truly wished to defend her himself, but...*oh.* A wave of nausea churned in Aubria's empty stomach as she realized that, though they'd removed his physical gag, one of the wizards had seen fit to silence him with magical means as well.

"The witnesses have chosen to speak anonymously, since witchcraft can be directed in vengeance based on a face and a name," the Guide told her smugly; the crowd that had started to jeer at her quieted as he raised his chubby hand for silence. "Merek's father has given me leave to inform you that he is one of the many who have rightfully blackened your name for our judgment. I warned him against it, but he does not fear your faerykind aided mischief."

"Nor do I, Guide, because she has none to speak of." Darragh stood to say his piece, now that the Guide had voiced any and all accusations against her. "My daughter is innocent of all charges except naiveté in following the Potioner's guidance. He, I think, is our ally and someone we should show mercy towards...but we have met today to discuss my daughter, and that's what I intend to do."

"You would speak on her behalf, defender?" the Guide exchanged a look with the muttering crowd, as if it pained him to indulge the ravings of a lunatic.

435

"I would." Darragh refused to take his bait and rose from his own chair. "I would assert that my daughter has innocently been misled by the Potioner, and that she is merely a clever girl seeking to learn healing craft for the benefit of her village. Who among you has not purchased a potion from Terran Caird at one point or another? A potion meant to ease an aching back, or one meant to earn the love of a straying spouse? Have we not all benefited from the potion poured onto the roots of our ruined trees, a potion bought from the Potioner himself with the help of my daughter, and then given freely when he saw our need?"

"Our need made all the greater by your heretical slut of a daughter!" someone cried from the back of the room. Aubria would have whirled around to hurl back an insult of her own, but her new wisdom found in curbing her impulses bade her not fuel the fire.

Darragh looked angry enough for the both of them. His face had paled, making the bruise on his face more lurid, and she imagined she heard his teeth grinding together to keep from challenging the heckler to a fistfight right there during her trial. His steely eyes scanned the gathering of villagers still in their orchard work clothes, as if by mere force of will he could sway them to his way of thinking. Seeing him like this, she couldn't blame him for trying to save her at Terran's expense. Any caring father would have done the same…and she'd already known that she didn't stand a chance as soon as she walked into the main hall.

"That remains to be proven, which I am not convinced of. And as for these 'witnesses…'" her father trailed off, as if too scornful to address these villains properly. "I was not aware it was the policy in our village to tattle on our neighbors like children unable to solve their differences by themselves. Witnesses prone to prejudice, fear, and mindless superstition are not reliable in any situation, and should not be utilized in this judgment. But if that is the case, very well: if my daughter is guilty of working with the Potioner, than so are all of us who have enjoyed the potions he's passed into our hands. I know that there are very, very few here who have not indulged in one at one time or another."

The assembly chattered amongst themselves, some shouting more insults, and others gossiping with their neighbors about what other heinous deeds the Haight girl must have done. Aubria wanted to face them again, since she felt their barbs—the direct ones along with the poisonous, indirect ones—sink into her back like darts, but for now she deemed it more important to face her father.

"And Merek? What have you to say to her inclination to vengeance and murder, Councilman Haight?"

"Hogwash," her father asserted confidently. "Utter hogwash. My daughter was betrothed to Lane during their falling out, and Merek was a boor who pursued women other than his own betrothed until he stumbled upon a faerykind ring and took no precautions against the Fair Folk. The faerykind are more active now, true, and there are other reasons they have decided to work against us. But none of them have anything to do with my daughter, and she has nothing to do with a foolish boy with dark intentions wandering into a toadstool ring and pretending that no danger could be found there. It is known that mainly the weak-minded fall prey to the whims of faerykind."

"Slander! Slander against the dead, no less!" a male voice called from the hubbub of people who'd turned out for the judgment, and Aubria spared another glance for Terran as her father and the Guide set to arguing in earnest. She was extra glad that her mother had shown wisdom in choosing Darragh Haight instead of the Guide—who hadn't held that title yet—for a husband. Unlike her mother, she might never have a chance to choose who her husband would be. She might not live past dusk.

I love you, Terran, she said to no one, locked in her own head. *I wish I could tell you out loud. I wish I could save us both from this.*

All this time during the banter between the Guide of Rites and her father, the prince had held his own counsel and listened. He hadn't exactly slouched in his chair, but his semi-reclined posture had belied a sense of indolent authority, and the coin he flicked back and forth and

437

back again between his knuckles flashed in the warm light streaming into the room. Aubria hadn't forgotten the cloud of his menace resting in the third chair in the center of the trio, but when he did finally open his mouth to speak she felt the knobs of her spine prickling as if they'd been touched by the cold hand of doom.

"What does Aubria Haight have to say for herself? Should we not give her a chance to say something that might earn her a royal pardon and regain the trust of her community?"

Snake, Aubria thought at him, glaring with her hands curled into fists at her sides. He was angling for her to give away Terran's secret to save herself. Worse, she knew there were circumstances that would have persuaded her to speak: if it would have guaranteed Terran's freedom and his life, she would've told. But no one else had figured out the secret to separate Veritas from the Potioner, and she doubted the prince's pet wizards would be able to safely break the binding.

Terran groaned, a soft sound only she could hear. He captured her attention again with that sound, and she turned to look at him as if seeing him for the first time. Back then, he'd dazzled her with his confidence and his birthmark and how he'd looked at her like both a fascinating curiosity and an equal. Aubria had kissed those perfect lips, and held him closer by his untamed hair, and she'd felt both shamed and adored in the halo of his verdant eyes.

Tell him, those eyes begged her now, *tell him whatever he wants to hear so that you live.*

But it wasn't just his eyes saying that. Aubria recognized the hum of power, unbearably dim though it was, echoing in her head as Veritas reached out to her with Terran's desperate message. Perhaps it was his own message, too; he'd confessed his feelings for her an age ago.

We cannot watch you die, Aubria. Not for us, not for this orchard, not for all of faerykind.

One of the wizards stirred from his place with the royal retinue on the eastern side of the room, his eyes narrowed towards the Potioner as if he suspected what had taken place. Aubria didn't want Terran in any more trouble, so she severed the connection with her own unequal store of power and refocused her attention on the three men on the dais.

I'm sorry, Da, she told Darragh in her thoughts as she reached out to take Terran's arm in a gesture of solidarity and affection. Her father couldn't hear her, of course, but she saw his face fall as no parent's should over the fate of their child. Her heart had been broken before, but this far surpassed that, and she battled an upwelling of sorrow.

"I did not consort with faerykind to destroy the orchard, which is as precious to me as my mother was. I did not conspire to kill Merek, foul as he was, because I believe in fate enough to let her deal with cretins such as he. I..." she paused her declaration, her grip tightening around Terran's fever-warm bicep; it felt strange after all this time to speak her heart so freely to the public at large. "Potioner Terran Caird has become my friend as well as my teacher, and he is loyal to Lyrassan and its king. He taught me his craft because I have a talent for it, and I do not believe that the king revoked the license of his most powerful wizard and Potioner...but that may be because I love him, and I trust him in all things. I am innocent of the charges against me, as is he, and may the gods have mercy on us and persuade this gathering of our truth."

Aubria wished it would've made a difference to tell the crowd the rest of her tale, regarding magic and bindings and the faerykind she'd resolved to free from their entrapment so they would spare the orchard from their embittered wrath. But it would have made her sound more crazed than they already believed her to be. Still, it felt good to confess the truths of her heart, meaningless though they were to a crowd and a judge who had already condemned her. Overcome with emotion and unsure whether or not she would ever greet Terran again in this life, she tipped her head onto his shoulder and breathed in his scent—altered with sweat and the metallic aroma of blood from his beating and imprisonment—to memorize him.

An expression equal parts frustrated beauty and thwarted ugliness passed over the aristocratic features of the future king, and with a firm thud he caught the coin he'd been toying with and smacked it down on the table.

"We have passed judgment on you, Aubria Haight. Tonight we will lead you to the gray field which you will enter of your own will or by force. The lightning will decide your fate, and may its fire purge you of your heresy and wrong-doing," the prince intoned, fighting back a smile no one seemed to notice but Aubria. "You will be judged in the sight of your people, but the Potioner has committed crimes against the crown that we cannot ignore. He will return with us to Oseren to await further judgment."

Prince Mardin consulted neither the Guide nor her father in his judgment, though Darragh leapt to his feet with all the blood drained from his face and his whole body trembling with fury and shock. Aubria, even with the foreknowledge that the judgment would follow these terms, swayed on her feet and held onto Terran for balance as the prince pronounced her painful doom.

One way or another, she'd found her way to the lightning field at last.

26

They didn't return her to the closet in the back hall of the meeting room after the trial. Being a councilman's daughter hadn't saved her in the first place, and now they tossed Aubria into the tiny but serviceable prison constructed mainly for petty thieves and the unruly drunks in the village itself and those who visited from Oseren. At least she'd be alone: with the royal excitement in Loracre, no one local or foreign had mustered the courage to act foolishly under the prince's eye.

It was morning still, since the sham trial meant to condemn rather than treat her fairly hadn't taken long to conclude. The prince had declared her execution would take place that very night, but she couldn't wrap her head around the fact that she wouldn't live to see another dawn.

And Terran...*Terran*...

They'd beaten him. Aubria had known they would have, and she'd seen the bruises from pounding fists and cuts from jeweled rings and his older, oozing wounds for herself. Worse, the collar they'd snapped around his neck as if the once great Potioner was merely a dog to be leashed and beaten into submission...if she could have, if she didn't suspect that her life was worth more than just their two futures, she would've disintegrated her spirit into the pure power necessary to blast the prince and his retinue into oblivion.

Aubria had revealed her heart again by crying out for him when they wrenched her away to lead her to the prison and him to wherever they'd kept him in the first place. The people of Loracre and Eldacre, even those who favored her side of the story and could've been talked around to helping in any way they could, believed that she'd enticed the faerykind into taking Merek and practically murdering him herself. Not to mention the acres of destruction, which to them was a clear sign of her wickedness in practicing accursed magic with the Potioner and bringing the gods' disfavor down on them with her heresy.

She'd spend her last hours in this dusty cell, looking out through the bars on her window that overlooked the orchard. The metal bars were scorched from the heat of the sun, but here in this cell Aubria felt only the chill of her despair. The small comfort of a blanket would've been a blessing she wouldn't deny.

What will they do to you, Terran? And Da…I hope they don't punish you for defending me. Her thoughts wandered in the same, tired circle like a set of steps worn smooth over a wooden floor, always returning to the same problems and shying away from her impending execution. She had less time to herself than she'd imagined, though: after only an hour or two pacing in her cell and waiting for nightfall she heard what sounded like a ruckus right outside her small window.

"Aubria! Come to the window!" A familiar voice called to her, and without hesitation she pushed her messy hair that she'd tried in vain to brush with her fingers and re-braid away from her face as she approached the bars. She'd heard Cerise's voice, but it caught her off guard when she saw Nathan, Viola, and Lane accompanying her. All of them carried something meant to break her out of her prison: Viola had a skein of rope slung over her shoulder, Lane carried what looked like a metal hook, and somewhat behind all of them Aubria saw Nathan coaxing a work horse that was bigger than Toby closer to the forbidding building.

"What are you all doing here?" she asked, wanting to confirm what she'd seen before she had to persuade them to leave her be.

"Freeing you, of course!" Cerise whisper-shouted, craning her neck around to make sure they hadn't been followed and the guards tasked with watching over Aubria hadn't come outside. The back of the prison faced the orchard, which would have been a security hazard if anyone other than blind drunks and the occasional troublemaker ever spent time in the solitary cell. Aubria had the distinction of being the most dangerous prisoner Loracre had ever needed to contain, but that didn't change the fact that aside from the barred windows and stone the cell wasn't really secure. She couldn't have broken out without help, even with her depleted magic, but others could help her escape.

Aubria would've laughed, or sighed with relief if she hadn't guessed what she already had to do.

"You shouldn't be here!" she whisper-shouted back at her friends. "I didn't see you in the meeting hall, and that's a good thing because *all of you* should avoid suspicion while the prince is here."

"They wouldn't let us speak for you," Lane said, looking up slightly into Aubria's window. "We tried, but—"

"The Guide made sure no one let us in, so only your father could defend you because *somebody* had to. No one else noticed that we were missing, or they pretended it didn't matter...but we wanted to vouch for you, all of us," Viola told her, accompanied by the nods of Lane, Cerise, and Nathan. "Every single one of us, and our families...well, except for Lane's mother, but she's an overpious bitch and no one likes her at all."

"*Viola!*" Aubria gasped, since this was the first time in her life she'd heard Viola speak unkindly about anyone. Cerise looked at her red-headed friend with shock as well, though Lane did not, since he of all people knew his mother was unpopular.

"It's true! I've always...I've always tried to see the best in people, and to think of them in ways I would like to be thought well of. But...oh Aubria, I don't know how I'd be able to stand living here after what they've decided to do to you! It's not right!"

"It's not, and that's why we've decided—all of us—to free you and go on the run," Cerise patted Viola on the back and exchanged a determined, authoritative look with her betrothed and with Lane. "I love my home, and I love this orchard, but this village is no place for me if everyone else has decided that the best way to deal with someone who thinks differently and acts according to the rules of her heart is to execute them in the barbaric ways of old. The prince is no future king I want to serve, tradition be damned. Besides...the orchard won't be around anymore if we don't free you, Aubria."

Cerise's dark eyes met hers, widening slightly with knowledge of the secret that had linked them for weeks.

"What? What do you mean, Cerise?" Nathan asked, for once sounding awake instead of sleepy with contentment in his love of Cerise. The horse in his charge chuffed at his neck in a way that always tickled, and the shorter boy reached up to pat its muzzle absentmindedly. Aubria hesitated, tempted once again to tell her friends her whole story...but it passed as she looked out at their hopeful, determined faces.

"My father? Have they done anything to him?"

"Not yet. I don't think they mean to, since there's no evidence he had any knowledge of your doings or took part in them himself. Besides, it seems like the Guide is more than willing to let his punishment be watching you suffer the lightning tonight. They've taken him somewhere to wait so he doesn't interfere, but mother is with him so I know he'll be all right." Cerise said, and something clicked into place for Aubria that made her feel a little better about what she had to do.

She'd wondered before if her father had found someone new to love, but he hadn't come to tell her about it yet, and she hadn't wanted to pry like everyone else in the village always did. When she'd returned to her cottage before getting caught, Darragh had asked if Mary Erdenwed was well...and it made sense, really, that a widower and a widow from families who spent so much time together would fall in love. In the past Aubria might have been a little miffed that he'd waited so long to tell her, but now all she could think of was that she didn't have a real chance to say goodbye to her father before tonight.

"I can't leave," she admitted at last. "There's...there's something I have to do, that only I can do. I don't want any of you to risk your own safety for me. Besides, all of you are about to start your lives together as newlyweds! How could I live with you throwing that joy away just for me?"

"How can you say that?" Viola drew as close as she could to the window, reaching up to wrap her hands around the bars as if she could yank them free from the stone wall with her own strength. "We've come to save you, and that's what we're going to do! Lane—"

"Most of that joy won't be worth anything if it comes at the cost of letting you die unjustly, Aubria. You have to come with us. I don't know what's happened to you to make you think that you have to abide by the will of the council—"

Aubria didn't allow Lane to finish, staring only at Cerise as she willed her to understand. "The field, Cerise. I know what I have to do."

She knew she'd won when Cerise's stalwart posture sank into one of defeat, into resignation for what must be. The two of them, friends to the end, locked gazes and exchanged a host of unspoken words the others wouldn't understand. Nathan, sensing Cerise's distress, laid a dark hand on her shoulder to offer support since he couldn't offer anything else.

"No. No! I'm not leaving until she tells me what's going on..." Viola protested violently, her red braid swinging as she shook her head in denial. Her heart shaped face held all the loveliness it usually did, but color splotched the naturally pale cheeks as tears blurred the cornflower irises. Lane gripped her shoulder, a gesture offering the comfort of his stability, but instead of leading her away as Aubria had intended, he passed Viola's trembling form into Cerise's care as the dark-haired girl exchanged a nod with Aubria and began to lead everyone else away.

Lane stayed behind, picking up the skein of rope Viola had

dropped and staring through the prison bars.

"Is there anything I can do for you before tonight, Aubria? I'd hate...well, I can pass along any messages if you wish me to."

"I need you to bring me a heart of the gods. As soon as you can. If you have to smuggle it to me on the way to the...just make sure you get it to me," she told him as soon as Cerise and Nathan led Viola and the horse back away through the orchard. Lane took her bizarre request in stride and awaited further instruction, since he knew as well as she did that that wasn't the only thing she'd wanted to ask of him. Touched by his dedication to her as a friend when he didn't have to act so nobly, she continued.

"Terran's hurt, and I don't know where they're keeping him," Aubria begged Lane with her eyes. "I don't think they'd let anyone else see him, but...you were my betrothed, once upon a time. If you feign a desire for revenge against the man who stole me away from you, they might let you see him."

She'd expected Lane to protest, or gently let her down that what she asked was impossible, but he didn't hesitate to comply; his blue eyes were steely with determination as he spoke. "I will get to him wherever he is. What would you like me to tell him?"

Aubria bit her lip and turned away from the window long enough to quell a rising sob. "Tell him...I will do what I must. Tell him that I must choose this path, and that it wasn't possible for me to be free, not really. Tell him...I love him, and I will always do so no matter where I am. I love him enough to compel him to do what he must to live and accomplish what he needs to, but...there's more than us at stake. I have to try, at least. Try to save everyone."

A breeze fluffed Lane's hair; she saw the sandy strands moving with the wind as she looked out of her little window with tears blurring her vision. "I can't imagine that any of this is easy for you to hear, and I hate to ask it of you, Lane. But—"

"Don't," he interrupted, and if the bars hadn't separated them he might have taken her hand in friendship or leaned in to fondly kiss her cheek. "I'm happy with Viola, more than I thought I'd be. I don't resent you for following your heart. I'm only sorry that it has led you here, and that you refuse the help of your friends to free you."

"Someday you'll understand," she told him, praying he would. "But if you don't, please know that I never meant to hurt anyone, and that there isn't anything I wouldn't do to save my home."

"I know, Aubria. I know."

He left her alone to accomplish the errands she'd sent him on. Drained of everything but a numbing sense of desolation that felt like it belonged to a completely different person, Aubria settled onto the hard bench and tipped her head back against the wall for a moment of rest. Her hand, black around her palms from when she'd gripped the metal bars, strayed into her pocket once more to finger the seven pointed edges of the potion bottle Terran had given her.

Those who unstopper the bottle and drink of the contents without great need or true purpose will suffer a death beyond the pale of pain, he'd told her when he'd passed it to her. To her, the potion had never felt menacing or foreboding. Whatever power contained in its sphere vibrated against her skin almost like the feeling of being drunk enough to feel as light as air, and the curious feeling of weightless, worry-less light reminded her of the faerykind she'd sworn herself to under duress.

If she was to die this night, and let herself be unduly executed for crimes she hadn't committed, then the faerykind who held her word had an obligation to answer any questions she had left, Aubria reasoned. So, her head still tipped back against the wall and the rest of her bare of any protections like the charcoal star had given her in the past as long as she remained within its borders, she called with her magic and her mind to Noblynn, somehow knowing that he would hear her and answer the call.

It took a few moments for a solitary light, gold outlined in silver, to enter her cell through the exposed window and hover in front of her like a living candle. If any of the guards opened her door to look inside, they'd perhaps think they had proof of her conspiring with faerykind to destroy the orchard...but, just as she'd guessed that Noblynn would come to her when called as if he'd been watching over her shoulder for some time, she knew that no one would disturb them unless he willed it.

"Why, Noblynn? I understand the other pieces...the lightning field makes sense as a binding on your power, and the first fruits from the orchard symbolize your link to this land. But you are beloved of the gods, so we've always been told. Is it their fickle nature to demand a mortal pay the price for your binding?" Aubria turned the potion bottle over and over in both of her hands in the hope that its innate warmth would spread to her chilled bones.

Noblynn hovered in place, and though he was but a being of light she sensed a feeling of remorse from him...but that was impossible, it had to be. She'd expected hostility and arrogance from him this time as he'd been when they'd met, but whatever had changed in herself that she was considering freeing faerykind from their binding to the land and the drain on their power must also have changed in him.

"Why must you sacrifice yourself for our kind, you ask? Why is it you that must pay the price for our way home?" His light dimmed in luminescence, softening to silver as he approached her. If he'd possessed human form, he might've sat beside her and taken her hand to pat as a grandfather or uncle would have; she didn't know what to make of his sudden change in behavior. "We are beloved of the gods, yes, but only our own. Your gods do not care for us, since our existence defies their nature...I digress. When we arrived in your lands we played with you transient creatures for amusement, though in many cases our rewards were as rich as our punishments were cruel. In our arrogance we sought to create a place here in this world where we could live and rule forever...and that kind of magic takes blood and sacrifice that we saw no need to undertake ourselves."

Aubria was beginning to understand, and unbidden tears that didn't belong just to her slid down her dusty cheeks like a cleansing river.

"We killed you, many of you, to craft this orchard. No fruit or root would wither, the myriad of magical and mundane harvests would be bountiful and slow to rot thanks to the river we blessed with our power, and any faerykind who partook of said bounty would feel refreshed and sustained for a significant length of time. Our gods would have gloried in this creation, and we hoped that the new gods we sensed in this land would favor us as well. But your court of deities preferred you, you mortals who live for a blink of an eye before you perish, to our radiance...and so they used the very thing we had poured our magic into to curse and bind us. To strip us of the forms we used to mingle among you and to leech our power more and more until we have faded to a fraction of our former glory." Noblynn's voice sung his story to her ears, though he spoke without any sign of music. Aubria waited for him to continue for several seconds until she realized that he'd said all he'd meant to. His light hurt her eyes, not because it was too bright in the choking darkness of her cell, but because of the knowledge she'd gained.

"Why should I help you, then?" she asked after several minutes of silence. "You care nothing for my kind. You stole our lives and security to make this orchard and...beautiful though it is, though *you* are, you are treacherous and I have no guarantee that you wouldn't treat all of us the same again. Why should I give my life to save you, to save an orchard that—though I love it with all of my being—you brought into being stained with human lives? Threats will not sway me...for my life is forfeit, and it will not persuade me to help you though we be thrice bound as I have been to others before."

Aubria had never thought she'd be this person, or a girl in a situation where she knew stories others did not and maybe never would. She was nineteen on the cusp of twenty, and tonight in the gray field she would burn when the lightning struck her regardless of whether or not she took action to save faerykind and her orchard home. Terran, though she loved him, couldn't save her...and here in this cell, she couldn't save him either. He would watch her die, the prince would make certain of that, and live enslaved to the crown until the prince tired of his defiance and ended his life as well.

"We did not understand, before. No, that is not true...many of us *chose* to not understand what it meant to be mortal. We had power of our own, and beauty, more than your people would ever possess even in the flower of your youth…but you have souls that transcend this plane of existence beyond our scope of understanding and our definition of life. We envied you that…we *do* envy you that," Noblynn told her, his voice a light in her despair like sunrise cresting the slope of a hill. "Those like Veritas served our primordial god, the king in the ether, and begged us not to toy with the mortals for sport and our own gain. They were punished alongside us…and though I cannot see your purpose in this world, Aubria Haight, beyond the purpose all mortals must serve, it is for them as well as myself that I ask you to break our binding to this land with your death. With your sacrifice."

"Why me?" she asked again. "If my gods love mortalkind so deeply…why force one of us to pay for your sins, and out of the goodness of our hearts besides?"

Noblynn didn't answer for a long time, as long as she'd taken to ask him to give her a reason to help the faerykind. When he spoke next, she heard both wonder and sorrow in his voice that she'd never expected to hear from one who had been so cold and cruel in the past.

"A final punishment. The mortals we so disdained would be the ones to free us, if they chose. They would have to find the pieces that would break our binding themselves, and they would have to choose whether or not we were worthy when the time came. I have bound you, Aubria Haight, to ensure your cooperation…but binding or not, I and mine could never cast against you should you choose not to help us. I can do no more than what I have to bring freedom to our kind. Indeed, we were ordered to treat you as we treated mortals in the past to show our true nature, so that we couldn't trick you into helping us by feigning benevolence."

Aubria leaned back and brought her knees up to her chest on the bench she sat on so she could rest her forearms and chin on them. Noblynn hovered in front of her, a beacon in her prison, and for the first time she deliberately stared into his heart as she hadn't dared before. The allure of him had pulled strong as a tide when she'd negotiated with him in the charcoal protection star endless years in the past…but now she felt like he was looking back, as any ordinary, honest creature would have. The light didn't blind her, though she couldn't see well at all, and with her mortal eyes she could discern nothing of what a heart of the faerykind really looked like.

But she knew, somehow, that every word he'd told her in this cell had been the sincere truth, and that hurt worse than when he'd seized her with lashes of flame and coerced her into a binding she hadn't wanted.

"The first fruits of the orchard aren't really fruit, are they?" she asked at long last, as Noblynn's light waxed and waned like a personal moon before her. "It's people. The first people born in the orchard you created, and their descendants. That was why you were so intent on learning my name...to make sure I had the proper ancestors. That's why the presence of the faerykind has haunted me all of my life, why I've seen so many signs of your presence when others didn't."

"We have watched your bloodline for many years, unsure if it was the right one. We could not learn your name through normal means, since it was forbidden to us until the proper time," he told her. The irrelevant regret for sending Lane on a wild goose for a special fruit chase gave Aubria a pang, but she tried to dismiss the feeling in favor of the larger issues in front of her.

"The proper time? Why wait until now? Why not convince me when I was a child, and didn't know any better?"

"We had to wait until you were fully grown and mature before we even thought about initiating an encounter with you...you had to experience some of the fullness of life before you could choose to throw it away," Noblynn answered her questions with more patience than she would've wagered he possessed.

The fullness of life...oh. Aubria realized that, in a way, her very first ritual to summon Veritas had started everything the orchard had been through in the past seasons of the year. If part of the fullness of life had involved her losing her maidenhead and experiencing the joys of what lay between lovers, that is. She would've blushed, but for once it seemed like she was beyond such things.

"What would've happened if my family line had died? What would you do to free yourselves then?" she asked more derisively than she meant to. "And if I'm of the first fruits of the orchard as well as the sacrifice…doesn't that only make two parts of the binding when we need three?"

"Fate has her ways of working in the lives of everything that dwells within this earth…even the faerykind. We had to hope, and have something to hope for. Nothing is crueler than a hope dashed again and again as the years stretch longer into the twilight of an age." Noblynn paused, as if his poetic phrasing had pained him. "The ritual itself is a product of mortals, but the three pieces will be in place if you wish them to. The field is merely the setting of where we slaughtered the host of mortalkind; the pieces would be the first fruit as a sacrifice, the lightning as the catalyst, and our repentance as the final portion."

"Your repentance…" Aubria trailed off, overwhelmed by the paradox of a faerykind who regretted the torment they'd inflicted on humans in the past. "Do you repent of what you've done, Noblynn? *Can* you repent? Do you even understand the nature of regret, being what you are?"

"We are immortal, child of earth," he told her in a calm voice that belied in its own way the eldritch nature of its existence; Noblynn's presence of light began to dim as he faded into the darkness. Beyond the locked door of her cell she heard the heavy tread of several people coming to fetch her for her execution.

"Regret is to us as dying is to you."

Noblynn's words echoed in her cell, and Aubria listened to them over and over as she stood and straightened her spine to greet those who would escort her to her death.

"One last thing," she requested of the fading light, utilizing her sudden boldness. "Why Merek? Why kill him and leave his death at my door?"

"The boy with the black heart entered one of our rings and found one of our maids in its heart. He attempted to do her harm, and though he could not as a man of flesh and blood, we do not suffer such evil to trespass in our realm. He was dealt with as we deal with all who forget due reverence."

Aubria watched his light fade from her perception as the guard jangled the keys at the door of her cell.

*A*bove, the skies were clear of clouds and twinkled with early stars and the sliver of a moon peeping out of the dusk a little too early for true nightfall. Beyond, ahead of the procession led by Prince Mardin, the Guide of Rites, and his henchmen, the skies over the field roiled with seething gray thunderheads threatening a lightning storm the likes of which the orchard hadn't seen or heard in decades.

Perhaps it bodes well, Aubria reasoned, though fear made her rope-tied wrists chafe all the more under their restraints. *Perhaps it will be quick, if I can delay the inevitable long enough to complete the ritual itself.*

She wasn't alone with the prince and his henchmen in the procession. A sizeable crowd from Loracre had followed in a march of torch bearing villagers grim-faced and intent on seeing justice done. The guards had allowed her the luxury of looking around, so she was able to witness the prince's attendants and pet wizards ushering Terran forward like a beast on a leash of enchanted rope alongside her own forceful escort. She had been relieved to see that they hadn't hurt him further, but his reprieve couldn't last much longer after her execution. She strained at the bonds of her magic, cursing her inexperience as she tried to send him some relief without alerting anyone to her magical abilities. One or two of the cuts sliced into his face under the whorls of the birthmark over his eye healed sluggishly, which would have pleased her a little had he not shaken his head at her and allowed the cuts to reopen.

Let it be, he seemed to say, and Aubria wished more than ever that she hadn't broken her bond to Veritas. He would protect Terran over her, she knew…but it would have been a gift to bid farewell to both of them.

When she could watch Terran no longer for the pain in her heart, she looked elsewhere and saw Mary Erdenwed walking alongside her father, half-supporting him though he was obviously stronger than she. She couldn't look at that for long without losing the fortitude she'd constructed so carefully around herself like the wall protecting Oseren from invaders, so she watched the others who called themselves her allies. Cerise's strength had diminished enough for her to lean on Nathan in public, and with bittersweet fondness Aubria wished them the joy of a happy life spent side by side.

Lane and Viola walked with their heads held high, Viola for once unafraid to show her tears, which would have moved even the great to share her distress. He caught Aubria's notice with a narrowed glare full of venom that would have made her sick with shame had she not guessed that it was an act. He approached the guards escorting her, and they grinned as if waiting for Lane to berate her in public as her cast off lover right before her execution. They let him draw near without comment, angling for something to gossip about in the tavern later that evening, but Lane surprised them when he spoke, his expression changing to one of soft concern.

"Darragh tried to take your place. He insisted that the debt of guilt would be paid with his death, since one Haight is much the same as any other. Prince Mardin denied him," he told Aubria with sorrow aging his face into what she imagined he'd look like after a decade or so passed him by. "I found this as well, and I hope it gives you comfort."

Shocked by his kindness and both dismayed by her father's offer and relieved that the prince had refused it, the guards watched mutely along with everyone else who had paused the procession to watch the conversation. They didn't think to stop him as he pulled a bulbous heart of the gods fruit from his pocket and set it in Aubria's hands, cupped even though the rope bound her; thankfully they'd bound her hands in front of her instead of behind.

Aubria swallowed, the weight of the fruit in her hands a reminder of why she had to be the one to walk into the field. She tried to smile up at Lane, but his lips only twitched as her eyes stung with emotion.

"Thank you, Lane. But I don't need it any longer."

Recovering their senses and their stern sense of justice, the guards grunted a protest, and one of them shoved Lane to the side after he'd taken the fruit back from Aubria. He gazed at her as if he would say more, as if it had occurred to him to offer his life for hers instead, but she shook her head and walked forward towards the field of her own accord to silence any more protests or interventions.

The potion was warm in her pocket, unduly so, as if it knew she'd decided to take her chances and drink it right before her demise. She'd planned to use the crown Terran had conjured for her on the night of his duel with the prince for protection against the lightning, before she'd known that it must strike her for the faerykind binding to break, but perhaps the potion without a name or definite purpose could prevent any pain and ease the passing she feared more than she'd imagined she would.

Aubria had other ideas, too, ideas that had occurred to her on the path to the field. She had to give herself freely to the storm for the ritual to work, to give the faerykind a reason to repent from their crimes against the gods and mortalkind, and mourn her passing…but no one had said anything about not bargaining with them once she returned their power.

If she returned their power. Aubria still had no idea whether or not any of this would work, despite what Noblynn had said to her in the confines of her cell. A pang of regret sang through her like a note on a harp as she realized that, if everything went according to plan, she'd never know for sure whether or not she'd saved the orchard and everyone she cared about.

She'd be dead.

The silence deafened Aubria—tempered as it was from the

crackling of the Guide sanctioned torches and the creak of the guards' leather armor—as she waited for the Guide to declare her sentence in his smug voice and thus seal her doom with the approval and support of the royal heir. She heard him talking, but most of her was already gone, already on the field waiting for the lighting to strike and remove her from this earth. Aubria had taken her last looks at her father and her friends and family, and she grieved the pain they would feel in mourning her, they who couldn't know all of the reasons why she had to do this.

Feeling his attention on her, Aubria at last made herself look at Terran. She wanted his face to be the last she saw, bleeding and hurt though he was. He held her gaze, his eyes blazing in his stark white face with the concentration of an apprentice trying to pass a difficult test knowing that failure awaited him. She sent a little more of her power to him on the wind, taking a memory of a kiss from her mind to his in the caress of an evening summer breeze.

I love you, but I have to go. Please understand, Terran, she told him the only way she could. Terran's eyes widened from their glare, and she realized with a surge of pleasure—the sensation reminiscent of a student experiencing success with a difficult concept—that he'd heard her.

Something poked at Aubria's back: a spear, wielded by one of the younger guards too eager for approval from the prince. She startled awake from her memories of that last time she'd seen Terran—hurt and trapped as no one with his power should have been—and looked around towards the Guide and Prince Mardin. They wanted her to say something, she realized, her last words that even heretics and witches were granted upon their hideous deaths.

Aubria wouldn't give them the satisfaction. With one last look at her father and Terran respectively, she turned her back on everyone and strode onto the field alone. Above, the assembled storm clouds roiled with terribly fury; lightning threaded through the black like veins of silver glittering on the surface of stone.

The gray soil, resembling quenched embers and old ashes more than wholesome orchard dirt, crunched under her boots as she put one foot in front of the other to carry her deeper into the desolation. If she was craven, she could run back to the group a few yards away now and fall upon the swords or spears of the soldiers who were in charge of ensuring her proper execution by lightning. But her fear faded into resignation as she stood still long enough to cut the ropes binding her hands with her insignificant magic and pull the potion from her pocket. Her back was to the crowd, but she heard several of them exclaim—Terran included, through the magical gag holding him silent so they could deny him even his farewell—as she tore off the wax sealing the ancient bottle and removed the stopper with shaking hands.

"What's she got there? More witchcraft?" someone hollered, but as she'd hoped no one, not even the valiant prince and his allies, not even the wizards with their powers, dared trespass on the field that was to be her grave.

Noblynn! Come to me, and bring all of the faerykind with you! she called in her mind as she took a deep breath and downed the potion fate had led Terran to bestow on her. It burned like potent alcohol on the way down, filling her mouth with fire and making her cough. The gorgeous bottle tipped from her nerveless fingers as she coughed and choked for dear life, stumbling further into the field only because in some distant part of her mind she knew she had to.

"Come, Noblynn," she spoke in her own voice around coughs, knowing as she did so that the call wasn't yet strong enough. "Come, and remember me when you regain your power. Protect those I could not."

A call from someone else stopped her as she gasped for air around the viscous potion clogging her throat, and she turned with dread slowing her movements as she faced those she'd left behind.

"Last chance," Prince Mardin called to her, his hand on the hilt of his sword as she walked with her head held high deeper into the field. "Tell me the secret of the Potioner's power and I will spare you. If you do not…"

"I can't tell you what I don't know," Aubria delayed, though she stood out of his reach and well within the confines of the perilous field. "But even if I knew of this power that doesn't exist, there is nothing you could do to me that would persuade me to give it to *you.*"

Mardin studied her face as he would a peacock that had snapped its beak at him before a chilling smile graced his features with icy glee. He withdrew and bowed to her one last time, though he looked as if he would rather beat her silly until she shared what she knew. This had been his plan all along, she realized: scare her into thinking he'd let her die on the field, and then dangle salvation and reward before her eyes like a farmer dangling a carrot in front of an ornery mule.

"I think you misunderstood me, fair maid. When I said that was your last chance, I meant it. I can no longer suffer either your disrespect or the treason of a Potioner I cannot trust. I will not let this upstart deny me what is mine by right. I will find another path to my rightful power."

Nodding at the wizard who held Terran's speech in his power, Prince Mardin waited for his man to unwind the spell so Terran could speak. Guessing what was about to happen, Aubria started back towards the safety of the orchard with her hands clutched about her burning throat. She croaked out a warning, wishing she was faster, but it was too late.

"Aubria, don't do this, I swear—" Terran called to her, his own voice almost as hoarse as her own as he strained forward to follow her onto the field.

Still smiling his sick grin of triumph, the prince drew his enchanted, anti-magic sword in one fluid movement and stabbed Terran through the heart.

The Potioner's voice had been weak, but the startled breath that whooshed out of him when the sword slid between his ribs like water through a sieve reached Aubria even at the distance she watched from in the deadly field. She'd thought nothing could be louder than the pounding of her fearful heart, than the roar of the lightning storm approaching from on high to destroy her and free the faerykind at the same time, but she'd never heard anything as loud as Terran's dying gasp as he crumpled to the ground with the prince's sword still in his body.

At the same time, the potion she'd guzzled down to the last drop acted all at once. Agony assaulted her body in waves as the heart and soul that she'd given freely to Terran began to wither away.

Aubria screamed as she never had before, her voice resonating with ancient power that didn't belong to her. The potion made of light and liquid gold had burned her throat like molten metal going down, down her throat to consume her organs from within, but she screamed for the faerykind to come to her as she stared at Terran's body and felt her heart melting within her breast. It was his name she should have been screaming, mourning him as a true love would, but she could not. The ritual she'd set into motion must be completed even if it cost her this along with everything else.

"Noblynn! Come to me and take back what was denied you!"

Aubria's voice echoed across the plain, louder than the storm as no mortal's should have been. The pain in her bones and blood vessels and behind her eyes thrummed with untold power and threatened to consume her at any moment. She repeated the call again, and again, as the villagers who'd come to watch her die looked all around nervously and began to flee the edge of the field lest the furious lightning strike them even there.

"I am Aubria Haight, first of the fruit of the orchard! I offer myself freely to save what is also mine! Return to your power, faerykind children!"

She'd turned her back on Terran to face the oncoming storm, the mass of black clouds churning above the field and her orchard heavy with the sky fire they carried in their endless folds. Her upraised hands invited the lightning to strike her where she stood, and she awaited its searing embrace with the will of someone who had lost the only thing they'd meant to live for.

She turned, so that the last thing she saw would be Terran's face. His eyes would be open in death, she knew, and as green as the grass he'd fallen on. *I'm coming, my love. Soon.*

Right when the lightning struck her, Terran's glassy eyes changed to the brightest yellow she'd ever seen.

27

The bolt struck her through her shoulder and rooted her to the ground like a spear plunged through her body. Aubria felt no pain, surprisingly, and found that though she could not breathe, she could still see the world from eyes that hadn't melted from nature's deadliest weapon. She hadn't been burned up instantly in a halo of fire from the sky.

Nothing else moved other than the lightning. It struck the ground in brilliant arcs of white light as the howling storm sparked closer and closer, like a hunting hound intent on a fox darting through the greenwood. Aubria listened to its shrieking power with eardrums that threatened to burst from the pressure and the noise, but she stared at Terran's body and the sword buried in his chest as if there was nothing else in the world.

Because that body was moving, and yellow light shone through the skin like a candle behind a paper screen. Veritas met her gaze through Terran's body, but he didn't resemble the truth spirit she knew, the one who had admitted to caring for her and admiring humanity. Now she saw into his heart as she had looked into Noblynn's, and understood why so many mortals feared the faerykind and the world they had come from.

Veritas's thoughts were a chaos when they reached her, and from the expressions of everyone who had dared remain to witness her execution—the prince and most of his guards, the Guide, her father, and her friends—she guessed that she wasn't the only one who heard the screaming howl of rage shrieking through her head like the lightning poised above the killing field. Wounds made by the priceless enchanted sword couldn't be healed by magic, so not even Veritas could repair what the prince had destroyed with one smooth blow from the golden blade.

Aubria heard the approach of something massive, or rather, *felt* the approach of the creatures she had called in the howling of the wind that stirred the dust on the field into swirling eddies and prickled the delicate hairs on her arms into watchfulness. Yet she had eyes only for Terran, and Veritas through Terran who was rising to his feet and pulling the blood slick sword from his chest with his eyes fixed on the prince.

Prince Mardin, who had turned his back on the fallen body as if it hadn't mattered to him to begin with, didn't notice Terran standing up with another spirit controlling his form. The prince had attention only for Aubria, though his interest was bland at best: he'd condemned her to death, punished the Potioner for his wrongdoing, and all he had to do now was watch the lightning burn her to a crisp.

Yet it hadn't burned her. Aubria watched in mute horror, her body frozen from the lightning that had slowed her perception and the world at large to the inching crawl of a caterpillar as Veritas pulled the sword free from his chest and cast it aside; it clanged against the ground like a death omen. The dull collar around his neck disintegrated into dust, unable to hold Veritas's power. The guards and the wizards whose presence was supposed to ensure the prince's safety fled in the face what appeared to be such dark magic, their vows to the crown and their courage forgotten. Arrogant though they were, in numbers though they were, even they must have guessed that the righteous rage within the creature they'd endeavored to coerce and capture would overcome their arts and defenses at once.

As the faerykind Aubria had called with what she thought were her dying breaths swarmed over the fields wrapped in cloaks of lightning threaded thunder, Veritas staggered towards Prince Mardin and whirled him around to face him. She didn't understand why at first, but when she saw him smile at the prince with his most wicked, otherworldly look of glee, it made sense. The skies above boomed with the swirling storm as Terran's hands reached out and gripped the prince's neck, the knuckles white with strain as they squeezed hard and then snapped his neck to the side in one violent arc. The prince dropped with a choked cry, his head turned backwards towards the field so Aubria could see the terrified light in his blue eyes fade, with his handsome mouth open in a silent scream.

The light keeping Terran's body alive flickered like a candle at the end of its wick. With no heir to pass his consciousness to, Aubria realized that Veritas had nowhere to go, bound to the bloodline though he was. Was he dying too, as Terran had died when the sword had pierced his heart?

Terran's eyes faded from yellow to a glassy green as he slumped to the ground and didn't rise again. His chest had bled at first—*so much blood,* she'd thought as she stared at the drenched ground where he'd first fallen—but the wound released the last trickle of blood. His skin looked thin and white like milk.

The hope Aubria hadn't known she'd been holding onto evaporated into the charged air of the field, and she fell to her knees and clutched her hands to her heart to hold it together. That is, if there'd been anything left to hold: either the potion she'd taken or the effects of serving as a sacrifice were taking their toll on her mortal body. Sandpaper skin rasped over her bones, her eyes were dry from the eddies of dust dancing over the field, and her throat tightened with thirst beyond belief.

With nothing else to look at, Aubria finally looked up at the faerykind she'd worked so hard to free from their punishment and waited for the end. The syrup slow flow of time sped up all at once as the lightning struck the ground in zigzag arcs from the foreboding clouds…each one of them striking her, each one of them sparing her from both pain and a scorching demise.

Is it the potion? Is that what saved me? She wondered without particularly caring; indeed, she felt irrationally annoyed that now when she least wanted her life the gods had seen fit to spare it.

But it wasn't the gods who had saved her. The lights in the clouds changed from brilliant arcs of lightning into the spheres she recognized as the faerykind…hundreds of them, thousands. They shone brighter now, each one of them an individual sun that hurt her dry eyes to look upon. Even with her eyes closed she couldn't see anything but the light, and the howling, shrieking sound of the storm deafened her into total helplessness.

We heard you call for us, first of the orchard, Noblynn's voice sounded in her head, not alone as she'd heard it in her prison cell, but multilayered and sonorous with the echo of his kindred singing behind his words in her mind. *We accept your sacrifice with humility…and though we are not of your kind, though we are merciless, you will find that our generosity waxes as boundless as our vengeance.*

Aubria could barely understand him: she felt like someone was pulling her apart at the seams and patching her back together with a total lack of skill. Fueled by the instincts for survival that she hadn't guessed would hold power over her after watching Terran and Veritas both die, she crawled away from the center of the field where the clouds churned. If she had to die, if she had been spared for a few more moments, she wanted to reach Terran's body…

With one last shock of sound, the screeching wind crashed down upon her in a vortex that held her in its eye as she would've held a jewel in her palm. Covering her ears with both her hands, Aubria lifted her gaze upwards and opened her eyes into slits so she could witness what was about to happen. The faerykind had swarmed in the clouds to regain their power from the lightning the gods had used as a tool to keep it from them, and with only a few more strikes the transfer would be complete.

But how was she not dead? How could her sacrifice, and all of her work putting the pieces together, not have led to her death?

The potion came to you by the will of the gods, child, Noblynn entered her head again as his commanding sphere began to descend from the heavens in the eye of the vortex that swirled around her.

Protected her.

"I still don't understand!" she shouted at him from vocal cords that wouldn't obey; her hair whipped about her head from the wind, and the dust caught in her lungs threatened to choke her for good.

The gods spared you from their wrath using the potion meant to find your hands, Aubria Haight, Noblynn told her. Aubria shook her head to order her thoughts, her whole worldview shifting sideways. *Why should a mortal have to die for the crimes of faerykind?*

*The important thing was that you believed it was necessary, so the sacrifice would be genuine...*Aubria answered back, this time in her head, but she trailed off as the lights in the sky danced all around her as they had when she'd summoned the faerykind before Litha. Yet they were spheres of ephemeral light no longer: within them, within the hearts no mortal was supposed to see, she saw their true forms taking shape and growing out from the center like a green bud bursting from its seed. She closed her eyes again against the brightness that blazed against her vision...

...and when she opened them again, the world had changed.

The vortex had diminished into a balmy breeze ripe with the scent of summer flowers, and the storm overhead had been replaced by a star-studded night sky hung like a tapestry with the bright slivered moon at its heart. The torches, blown out in the storm that had encompassed more than the accursed field itself, would have been of little use here. Faerykind who hadn't been able to take true physical form in centuries stood all around her in bodies as strange as they were wondrously crafted.

Noblynn stood in front of her, the most beautiful from the whole. Aubria had been right to assume that he had gray hair, but it flowed down his tall back like a curtain and belied no great age; his face bore no lines whatsoever, no signs of mortal aging, and aside from the stark

465

beauty and the pointed ears and the eyes that were still cold with ancient secrets, she wouldn't have guessed who stood in front of her now.

The rest of the faerykind—all in somewhat mortal likeness—shared the paralyzing beauty, pointed ears, and flowing hair that had been attributed to their kind in ages past, but the similarities ended there. As varying as the fruit that grew in the orchard, so too were the faerykind Aubria had always pictured: some bearing the traits of animals like butterfly wings or fox tails, some sporting webbed hands and green skin that looked dry already from standing in the open air, and some who barely resembled humanity at all.

Finally, she returned her attention to Noblynn. Her throat still hurt terribly—along with the rest of her body—and the grief she'd have to endure pounded at the door of her mind demanding attention and justice, but the wonder of what she saw now couldn't be denied.

"You protected me. From the lightning…"

"Yes. And no," Noblynn explained; his voice, masculine and clear, sounded like music, though it didn't echo with the voices of his diverse kindred any longer. "The potion meant to preserve and slow time— one we didn't know you had, I might add, though I glimpsed the bottle in your cell—saved you long enough for us to intervene. We spared you as much as we could from the lightning that was our salvation…but I think you will find that you are not the same as before, nor will you ever be again."

No, she thought to herself, not trying to stretch her consciousness out from her own skull, *I won't ever be the same again.*

The image of Terran falling to the ground with the prince's sword battered her mind, pushing her to the ground to show its mastery over her along with the physical pain she doubted would ever leave her alone. Aubria crumpled as she had before, digging her fingers into the dust in a struggle to stay conscious.

The faerykind who had come to the field and her aid were gathering, assembling in a circle of joined hands—or paws, or claws— and chanting words she as a mortal would never understand. Aubria knew they were working a spell, because their magic thrummed through her veins as if she were one of them, but the nature of their casting didn't reach her until she saw the shimmering veil of magic spreading out from under their feet to swell over the whole field. The gray soil sprouted fresh grass for the first time in centuries, and trees began to grow at rapid speed from sprouts to seedlings to mighty, fruit-bearing monarchs regal in their fresh robes of leaves, blossoms, and fruit.

Caught off guard by the wonder of such a change, Aubria laughed, a startled cry that reminded her of her own young life as tears streaked down her dirty face in awe.

Slowly, those who hadn't fled this part of the orchard reemerged from the trees to look with awe upon the fruitful field. The magic restored to the faerykind was still completing its work: the shimmering veil passed over the ground and into it in the distance, encouraging new trees to grow and bear fruit a hundred times quicker than nature intended. Aubria, her bones buzzing with power she was sure would finish killing her eventually, wrapped her arms around herself to hold her bones together as she watched her father and her friends come out from under the nearest trees. Darragh had a frightful burn on his face and right arm, she saw belatedly: a glancing rather than a direct hit from the supernatural lightning, one she realized he must have suffered when he'd taken advantage of the prince's distraction and the absence of any guards to try to save her from the storm's wrath.

He reached her in the span of a few moments, running to join her on the ground and weeping openly as he gathered her into his arms like she was a small child. Aubria hugged him back, hanging on for dear life as she choked on sobs that would have shamed her in front of Noblynn and the rest. Over her father's shoulder she saw the rest of her friends charging her direction, Viola on the warpath to reach her first after Darragh. A little behind them, Nathan reached up and plucked a pure white fruit shaped like a heart from a dangling bough; it glowed, faintly, as all of the faerykind glowed with their own luminescence.

Aubria couldn't stand it, neither her grief that Terran wasn't here to see what she was seeing nor the stress of everything that had happened to her this night. As her friends collapsed on her in one big heap, everyone silent and content to just *be* rather than chatter away the wonder of the moment, she released her death grip on her own consciousness and welcomed the coming black.

Thank you, child of the orchard, Noblynn's voice whispered in her head, as intimate as a lifelong friend; she would not see him after this, she realized. The faerykind would finish their healing song, and depart to the lands they'd left behind at the dawn of the mortal world. *We do not offer thanks often…but we offer it to you. You will know the proof of this in time.*

He was laughing at her, laughing as a solemn being like him probably hadn't laughed in decades. It would have made her angry, had she possessed the energy to feel anything but the desperation of sealing her own agony off so it wouldn't kill her, but she felt Darragh's arms tighten around her as he looked behind her. She didn't want to turn around, for fear of what she might see or what she *hoped* she'd see above her own life…but she could only resist for so long, and as she turned she held her breath for fear of disappointment.

Terran lay on the ground where he'd fallen, his green eyes still open to the night full of stars and the glow of magic. Then he blinked, color returning to his cheeks, and the sound of him taking his first real breath reached her from a distance as the sweetest sound she'd ever heard, sweeter than the singing of all the faerykind in the world.

"A-Aubria," he began hoarsely, sitting up and hacking out a gob of blood roughly the size of a thornbell.

But Aubria had already surrendered her consciousness to the beyond, and she passed out in her father's arms with the memory of those dead green eyes blooming with life the last thing she knew.

28

*A*ubria jerked awake from a nightmare both hideous and bizarre, bolting upright from the soft bed someone had laid her in. Her wrists were still chafed from the rope the guards had tied too tightly around her wrists, and the burns itched awfully when she ran her hands through her hair in a panic. Strangely, the first thing she noticed as she stumbled free from the world of her dreams was that her dreadfully tangled hair had been washed and combed while she'd slept, as if someone cared about how she'd feel when she awoke.

What's happened? She thought, bleary and confused as she swung her legs over the side of the bed—noting that someone had changed her into a clean nightgown bedecked with far too much lace than was good for it—and tried to stand. It took her a moment plagued with dizziness, but when her feet touched the cool wooden floor she felt like the earth below was giving her strength to rise and observe her surroundings.

The room wasn't Cerise's, nor was it her own: she recognized it as Viola's as soon as the name came back to her.

That explains the lace on this nightgown, she thought.

"Viola insisted that we bring you here when you collapsed on the field, shouting over your father that you needed 'a woman's care.' You were injured, though not enough to sleep as long as you have…but I didn't want to use magic on you, not when I wasn't sure how much you'd been exposed to in the first place," Terran's voice startled her, and she looked up and rubbed her eyes when she saw him standing healthy and well in her doorway. Aubria couldn't find a scratch on him, and her searching eyes spotted no blood marring his Potioner's uniform, but something felt off. As soon as she realized what had changed, she gasped.

"Your birthmark," she said, sounding slow and stupid to her own ears; dizzy again, she sank back onto the bed and waited for the weakness to pass. "It's gone!"

Terran closed the door behind him as he entered the room and sat on the chair near the door; she wanted him to come closer, so she could ascertain that he was truly well—the image of the golden sword piercing his heart haunted her—but she didn't have the courage to ask. He looked so different without the birthmark, she noted: the mark had given him an aura of foreboding mystery, and without it she could better appreciate the open, generous features of his face that she'd come to love.

"So is Veritas. When you freed the faerykind from the land and returned their power to him it broke our connection. Well, that and my death, however temporary that was," he told her. "Noblynn saved me as a gift to you, I believe."

Aubria struggled over what to say, which words to speak as the grief of losing the truth spirit she'd befriended slammed into her like a waterfall. *Oh, Veritas…*

"He's gone?" she asked, not wanting to believe it; she had more to ask, more she desperately wanted to know, and she rambled as her brain tried to get a better grasp on what had taken place like a soldier adjusting his grip on his sword. "He…he killed the prince, before he died, or whatever it is that spirits do…how long have I been asleep?"

"Four days, three hours, and twelve minutes. Far longer than you should have been, given your lack of concrete injuries, but understandable given…" Terran trailed off, waiting for her to pay attention to him again. Aubria noted the fuzzy feeling in her mouth and the thirst that hadn't been quenched in the specified amount of time, and as soon as she thought of it something deep within her gut *pulled* on her latent power and prickled over her tongue and teeth like sparks. The fuzzy feeling disappeared, replaced with the sensation of clean teeth and the faint taste of fresh mint.

"That didn't take you long," Terran teased, leaning forward to rest his elbows on his knees as he studied her with a teacher's interest. "I wondered how long before you'd notice."

"Notice what?" Aubria wanted to hear the answer spoken aloud; her head still ached, but another tug of the magic that felt like a limitless, untapped pool within her body quelled the pain.

"More happened that night on the field than the faerykind earning back their power. The potion you took spared you from the lightning long enough for them to arrive and prevent your sacrifice, since the terms of the bargain had been met with your willingness. We're going to argue about that later, by the way. I'm still furious with you." Terran wasn't looking at her like someone boiling with rage, and his taciturn mood had yet to return. "It's my opinion that the potion didn't just spare you from the lightning, it helped you…absorb it. And since the lightning was pure, untapped power—"

"I have some of their power?"Aubria asked, in awe and a little afraid; the faerykind didn't like to share, and if they knew she had some of what was rightfully theirs…"How do you know this?"

"Noblynn told me before he left, while we waited for you to wake up. That's why I'm not a disaster on your behalf, you see. I was promised that you'd wake up, even if it took a little more time than I was comfortable with," Terran smiled, oddly secretive, and Aubria almost smiled back before her pile of questions got the better of her. She couldn't decide which one to ask first, and the least relevant question jumped forward as it always did when she couldn't contain her curiosity.

"The field…have you tested the fruit that grows there now?"

"That's what you wanted to ask?" he chuckled, his eyes crinkling at the corners again. "I have. No one's named the trees or the fruit, but the juice runs like liquid gold and the fruit is sweeter than any of your honeypomme varieties. We'll need to conduct further tests to see what the benefits of the fruit actually are, but from what I can tell, the person who eats it gains a little bit of magic, enough to strengthen the spirit for a few minutes."

He was waiting for something, Aubria realized as he stared at her. There was something he wanted her to ask, a subject he was waiting patiently for her to circle around to so they could discuss it in the open. Her heart thumped in her chest all the louder as she gazed into his eyes and then looked away because she couldn't bear the weight of her own hopes.

Testing a theory, she reached out with her mind to Terran's and let the overflow of questions spill into him like the sea into a tide pool. *Do you still have your magic, or did you lose it along with Veritas? Did any of the faerykind stay behind? What of the prince? Is the king going to punish you or Loracre as a whole for his son's murder?*

She held one question back: *do you still love me now you're free of Veritas?*

Terran winced as her onslaught of questions hit him, leaning back in his chair as if that would stem the flow; his brow puckered with concentration for a moment, reminding her of his darker moods, but then his expression cleared and he sighed as he shook his head indulgently.

"Yes, I have my magic, which is relatively unchanged given the fact that Veritas and I are no longer bound. Whatever the faerykind did, they somehow made sure that I lost not even a shred of my usual power when they summoned me back from the brink of true death. I believe you now have magic to match or challenge me, which I'm sure will be the source of many headaches to come. Many of the faerykind chose to stay in our lands, in the orchard itself, though I doubt we'll see much of them for some time. You glow, too, like one of them, when you use your power…it's fascinating."

Aubria looked down at her hands in her lap, overwhelmed with information and the realization that she was now Terran's equal in all the ways she'd railed against in the past. The angry rope burns around her wrists snagged her attention, and she squinted as she pulled up her magic from the well deep within her spirit to heal the marks. Sure enough, her skin glowed as Terran's had whenever Veritas's presence had shone through.

Veritas...was he really gone? Had his death been the key to break the binding between truth spirit and Potioner? *I will mourn him all my life. Terran is here, and I will be eternally grateful for that no matter what happens...but oh, Veritas, I didn't want you to go.*

The other questions she'd asked were important. In fact, they were crucial to the task she'd almost died for. But she no longer wished to speak of them, not with the miraculous glow dissipating back into her skin and with Terran looking at her like she was as astonishing to him as he had been to her when they'd first met.

"I know what I want," she said aloud, too softly; clearing her throat and smoothing her dry palms over the cool cotton of her lace edged nightgown, she paused a moment before trying again. "I would've known it regardless of whether or not you came to Eldacre to sell your potions, though it would have taken me much longer to figure it out. I want to be able to go where my feet carry me, even if that means crossing the world over, but I also want to have a place to come home to...even if the people in that place almost got me killed. I wanted to be more than someone's wife, to have more of a purpose for my time on this earth, and you helped me find one. I can help people with the potions I can make now and the magic I discovered. But above all else...I want *you*, Terran Caird. I'm not sure if you—"

Instead of answering or waiting for her to finish, Terran held up a hand to stop her, smiling the truest smile she'd ever seen. Butterflies fluttered in her stomach at the sight of his handsome face crinkling about the eyes with joy.

"I have something for you. I should wait to hand it over...but I've waited long enough." He struggled to pull something out of his pocket. When Aubria saw what it was, an incredulous laugh bubbled in her throat. He'd brought her the wood beaded necklace he'd won from her in one of their first bargains, though it looked quite different from the last time she'd worn it. All of the beads had been painted: a third black like the bottles he kept poisons in, a third green for healing, and the last third blue to symbolize magic. In the center of the necklace, the part that hung below her heart, one red bead etched with the symbol Aubria had come to associate with all potion craft stood out from its fellows.

Terran approached her with the long necklace twined about his hands and knelt on one knee in front of her by her bedside, looking up into her face with his whole heart in his eyes as she'd never seen it before. "When I took this, I only wanted to annoy you."

"You did," she assured him, breathless. He fought back another smile as he continued.

"You seem concerned that I might argue with you regarding our feelings, or try to put you off. I'm a free man now, Aubria. You've given me everything I wanted, even if you had to drag me along with you. It would be an honor to share my days with you and to help you find everything you seek." He spoke confidently, but his hands trembled as he offered her the necklace a woman typically gave her betrothed to paint red before returning it to her on their wedding day.

Did he really doubt her answer? Aubria gave in to her impulses and leaned in to kiss Terran, knowing this time that there was nothing in the world that could keep the two of them apart. He kissed her back, reaching up from where he still knelt on the floor to cup her face in his hands with the beads still wrapped around them, like the most precious thing he'd held was her.

Except...

"But—Terran, this is all wonderful, but what about the prince? He's *dead,* and the king won't let that stand! Surely you've had word—" Her hands fluttered about his chest like nervous birds searching for a safe perch; after setting the necklace on her night table, he caught hers in his own and sat next to her on the bed she'd woken so recently from.

"Someone wants to see you. I had to fight them to have my turn first...but shall I call them now to see that you're awake and well?"

"Terran—" she spluttered, not wishing to be put off of such dire matters, but he ignored her protests.

"Would you enter, Your Highness?"

The door opened as Terran called, Aubria still locked in his arms, and she wrinkled her brow in confusion at the strange happiness in her new betrothed's voice. Then she jumped up in a fright, leaping to the corner of the room as Prince Mardin strolled into the room with a thunderous expression marring his charming face.

"Terran—" Aubria began her exclamation of alarm, fumbling for the new, coltish upheaval of magic she'd earned through her almost death...but her panic cut off in helpless laughter as she truly *looked* at the prince, whose eyes had turned wholly yellow instead of their customary blue.

"I've missed you, Aubria Haight," Veritas told her as he bowed with a jaunty flourish, mischief dancing in the eyes he'd stolen from the most important person in Lyrassan.

Mabon

"Stop! You'll mess up what little I've been able to accomplish so far!" Aubria snapped at her father as she smacked his hand away with a wooden spoon. The spoon really had no place being in her bedroom, given that she was preparing for the Mabon festival rather than baking any pies, but she'd been using the end of it to arrange the painstaking mass of curls she'd coaxed into her hair through magic. The freeing feeling of using the magic she'd been born with along with the measure she'd been gifted by the faerykind themselves in plain sight of anyone who cared to look hadn't yet worn off, and even now she smiled as the tickle of it zipped through her veins like friendly fire.

"Would you rather look like a hedgehog than a goddess of autumn? No? Then let me help," Darragh commanded; he swatted her hands away in turn and continued to grumble to himself as he picked up the pins from her night table and strategically tucked them into the braided rosette on the back of her head.

"If Mary was here she'd insist you leave off," Aubria grumbled back, though her words held no bite, and she was actually comforted by the familiar motions of her father arranging her hair and fussing over her dress.

After all she'd been through, Cerise and Viola and Mary had insisted that Aubria should be dressed more splendidly than anyone else at the Mabon festival. They'd delivered, fussing a little over Aubria's thinness from her ordeal, and tonight when she wed the Potioner she wouldn't be ashamed in her cream colored, lace enhanced dress and the golden shawl she'd purchased from Oseren so long ago. She'd added a few changes at her own discretion too, as discreetly as she could: the golden crown Terran had conjured for her lay atop her crown of curls, but she had transformed the gold into the same hues as the autumn season she was so fond of.

Instead of the star anise and citrus garlands everyone else wore, she wore the wood bead necklace Terran had altered for her. Often her fingers searched for the comfort of the smooth beads as she counted them over and over whenever her nerves got the best of her. It had been a nerve-wracking set of days after she'd awoken to find her heart's desires coming true, and by the time of the first autumn holiday Loracre and Eldacre both were still stirred up by the strife wrought by Prince Mardin and the Guide of Rites.

The prince had lived, seemingly, though only a select few knew that the royal heir had been replaced in all but body with the same truth spirit that had dwelled within the king's Potioner. Fortunately for everyone except the Guide—who had retreated into his home and hadn't been seen in the village since after the debacle of his biased judgment—the "prince" had had a change of heart and pardoned both his Potioner and the unconscious Aubria. He'd declared the miracles of his own health and Terran's resurrection "acts of the gods," and said that his business in the village was done now that the truth of the destruction wreaked upon the orchard had come forth.

Veritas hadn't lied, of course, as one whose nature demanded only truth…truth that had led him to vengefully claim Prince Mardin's life as soon as the binding released him by immediately entering another one with the royal bloodline, which the prince had invited by killing Terran as a last effort to gain the power he sought.

"I wanted to kill the prince, and then let myself perish as a creature still bound but not to a living host…but where the gods close a door, they smash through a window," Veritas had laughed as he, Terran, and

Aubria had rested in Viola's bedroom and consulted on everything that had taken place. "The power from the lightning…changed me. It changed the binding, and it changed you, Aubria. I tend to think that's for the good."

Veritas had wanted to visit for Mabon, to see Terran and Aubria joined in an early handfasting ceremony. But the prince had no reason to be in Loracre again, especially so soon, and for now his hands would be full curbing the wizards who had kept a surprisingly tight leash on their prince and ending all of the border disputes and petty wars Mardin had set into motion to gain authority over whatever parts of the world he could subdue. He'd also claimed that he'd legalize magic use again throughout the entire realm…but that might be too ambitious a goal for one royal.

Later, he'd told them, he wanted to join his own kind in the orchard as soon as he was sure he could dispose of the prince so a proper heir with a good heart and spirit could rein…but that was a dream, he'd said. Aubria had sternly promised him that no matter who held the reins of the binding he'd locked himself into she'd find a way to get him out. So they were bound again by her word, but this time she wouldn't change a thing. She was curious, too, now that Veritas could craft a body of his own what he'd look like…but that was something she'd have to wait a few years to see.

Back in the present, Aubria paused in the middle of a grove of fragrant cinnamon trees after several minutes of walking. Not long from now, she'd be enjoying the nocino liquor crafted for the fall rites at the altar—officiated not by the Guide, but by her own father and his new betrothed, Mary Erdenwed—with Terran, who she couldn't quite believe belonged to her.

Mabon had arrived in all its glory, and it was odd to her now that she'd once wondered if she'd ever see another. As Aubria walked through the trees that were well into transforming the vibrant green of their leaves into fiery oranges and russets and golds, she marveled at the beauty all around her. It *was* different this turn of the wheel, she knew for certain: the air smelled sweeter, the autumn harvest grew large and bountiful without any sign of blight, and the crops that had been destroyed by the spiteful faerykind were mostly underway to a complete recovery.

"The natural world reacts to the presence of faerykind. Growing things bloom, the soil sprouts life, and water flows sweeter," Terran said, speaking to her as he appeared from around a tree as if he'd chanced meeting her there instead of planning on it. Aubria hadn't imagined she'd meet him here, in this part of the orchard that shouldn't have been covered in new blooms the color of rich gold, but she smiled at the sight of him in his orchard clothes, colored deep green in preparation for their handfasting.

"You're not supposed to see me yet," she told him, her tone conspiratorial as she approached him; they met in the middle, under the boughs of two branches twined together from two different trees. He took in the sight of her with her matrimonial finery, with her autumn crown that he'd helped make and the dress that hugged her waist and breasts to advantage, and lost his speech for a moment.

"I know. I only wanted to tell you that I'm leaving in the morning to...how did you put it before, when you asked me to wed you...see the world," he said, then grinned as she swatted at him with mock outrage.

"*You* asked *me*, Terran Caird! I—"

He didn't let her finish, laughing her into silence as he swept her into his arms and kissed her as a reminder that it didn't matter who'd asked who. When they parted, Aubria was blushing like a maid, and so was he. Neither one of them had forgotten that, after the ceremony and the celebration that came with Mabon, they would be alone together to consummate their love in the physical ways they'd denied themselves in preparation for this night.

They even had a cottage, a true home deep in the orchard where the lightning field had once been. After selling the house near Eldacre when she'd met Sir Bor an age ago, she and Terran had set out one day with anyone who wanted to help carry building tools and wood from the sanctioned area of non-producing trees meant for orchard housing.

With joined hands, the two of them united those materials together and conjured a house that was as magnificent as it was modest. Aubria had never wanted anything more than her own cottage as far as size was concerned…with the exception of a potion workroom and a spare room for guests. Terran had already been heartily sick of the grand opulence of the Potioner's tower in Oseren, so he didn't gainsay her changes. They did have a stable, though, to house Cloud and Clearwater, since Terran had tracked down the horse she'd used for their journey to Oseren and purchased the mare for Aubria.

"Will we return, do you think?" Terran asked Aubria, leaving the option up to her; she sighed, relaxing happily in his arms. She glanced sideways at him, surprised by the question.

"Of course we will! I don't know when, or how long we'll be away…but our home is here, Terran. We'll always have a home here." The words resonated with her as if they'd been a spell, and she knew them to be true in the way that Veritas had always told her the truth.

Beyond, just under the trees, she spotted a few mirage-like spheres of light dancing within the circle of a faerykind ring. She'd seen such things all her life, and the appearance of one so near to her didn't worry her any longer. Aubria smiled, mostly to herself, and moved closer to the ring to pluck one of the toadstools from the earth for a good luck charm.

That should do it, she thought to herself, pleased with her find as she followed Terran out of the grove.

Acknowledgements

I can't say that it was anything but a joy to write *A Turn of the Wheel*. I've always enjoyed writing, of course, and I love every single one of my stories. But this one, Aubria's tale, caught me completely off guard. She knocked on my door and demanded that I tell the world about her adventures with the Potioner, and who was I to resist? I hope you've enjoyed reading about them almost as much as I savored creating them.

Writing books takes work, and there are a few people I have to thank.

Daniel, thank you once again for your support and the lovely author photo and book design you arranged for me. You will always have my love.

Salome, thanks again for the gorgeous book cover. You're one of the best in the business, I think, and your incredible art has never let me down.

Caroline, thanks for critiquing my book! Your comments were amazing and helpful, and you know just what to say to help me make my books better.

And, of course, thanks to you for reading. An author doesn't get anywhere without readers and people willing to take the time to review, and so far I've relished the time I've spent learning to connect with the people who read my books.

May you always have another good book on the shelf.

Catherine Labadie

Catherine Labadie

lives in the mountains of the picturesque Carolinas with her husband and her dogs Fannie, Heidi, and Zoey. *A Turn of the Wheel* is her third novel, and she has many more stories waiting in the wings.

Follow Catherine on:

http://authorcatlabadie.wixsite.com/catherinelabadie

Don't miss Catherine's riveting novel

LONG GROWS THE DARK

Available now!

BEFORE, Glenna served the princess who held her heart's desire
and fought an ancient corruption.
NOW, Gwendoline must ask for the help of friends old and new as
they battle the same corruption and discover if free will is truly within
their grasp.

CPSIA information can be obtained
at www.ICGtesting.com
Printed in the USA
LVHW031126141019
634125LV00001B/29/P